# ASTROLABE REBIRTH

# ASTROLABE REBIRTH

星盤重啟

**WRITTEN BY**
非天夜翔
**FEI TIAN YE XIANG**
(ARISE ZHANG)

**ILLUSTRATED BY**
**YU YU**

**TRANSLATED BY**
**MOON**

Seven Seas

Seven Seas Entertainment

ASTROLABE REBIRTH (NOVEL)

Published originally under the title of 《星盤重啟》 by 非天夜翔 Fei Tian Ye Xiang
Author© 2017 非天夜翔 (Fei Tian Ye Xiang)
This edition arranged with JS Agency
English Translation copyright ©2025 by Seven Seas Entertainment, Inc.
All rights reserved.

Illustrations by Yu Yu

No portion of this book may be reproduced or transmitted in any form without written permission from the copyright holders. This is a work of fiction. Names, characters, places, and incidents are the products of the author's imagination or are used fictitiously.
Any resemblance to actual events, locales, or persons, living or dead, is entirely coincidental.
Any information or opinions expressed by the creators of this book belong to those individual creators and do not necessarily reflect the views of Seven Seas Entertainment or its employees.

Seven Seas press and purchase enquiries can be sent to
Marketing Manager Lauren Hill at press@gomanga.com.
Information regarding the distribution and purchase of
digital editions is available from Digital Operations Manager CK Russell
at digital@gomanga.com.

Seven Seas and the Seven Seas logo are trademarks of
Seven Seas Entertainment. All rights reserved.

Follow Seven Seas Entertainment online at
sevenseasentertainment.com.

TRANSLATION: moon
ADAPTATION: Neon Yang
LOGO DESIGN: Mariel Dágá
COVER & INTERIOR DESIGN: M. A. Lewife
COPY EDITOR: Jack Hamm
PROOFREADER: Amanda Eyer, Pengie
EDITOR: Nikita Greene
PREPRESS TECHNICIAN: Salvador Chan Jr., April Malig, Jules Valera
PRODUCTION MANAGER: Clay Gardner
MANAGING EDITOR: Alyssa Scavetta
EDITOR-IN-CHIEF: Julie Davis
PUBLISHER: Lianne Sentar
VICE PRESIDENT: Adam Arnold
PRESIDENT: Jason DeAngelis

ISBN: 979-8-89373-800-1
Printed in Canada
First Printing: July 2025
10 9 8 7 6 5 4 3 2 1

# TABLE OF CONTENTS

| # | Chapter | Page |
|---|---|---|
| 1 | The Youth from the Black Sea | 9 |
| 2 | The Revolution of the Clones | 27 |
| 3 | The Fall of the Patriarchy | 43 |
| 4 | The Fight to Escape | 65 |
| 5 | The Spine of the World | 83 |
| 6 | The Primeval Heart | 107 |
| 7 | Phoenix City | 123 |
| 8 | The Black Plains | 145 |
| 9 | The Children of the Astrolabe | 165 |
| 10 | The Termination Command | 185 |
| 11 | The Pontiff of Dragonmaw | 209 |
| 12 | The Tides of Space-Time | 233 |
| 13 | The Night of Divine Grace | 255 |
| 14 | Going Against the Flow | 275 |
| 15 | The God of Creation | 295 |
| 16 | A Promise for the Next Life | 319 |
| 17 | The Eve of the Final Battle | 339 |
| 18 | Astrolabe Rebirth | 351 |
| 19 | Epilogue | 369 |
| ✦ | Character and Name Guide | 381 |

# THE YOUTH FROM THE BLACK SEA

In the beginning, the Creator pinned the compass of creation's fulcrum on humans and sent the other point out into the vast, chaotic, and unknown universe.

With the passage of time, civilizations rose to the peak of their grandeur before disappearing without a sound. Those who knew of the possibilities yet to come foretold the limitless future by reading the space between the stars, but their prophecies did not come to pass as expected, and those blueprints that existed within their collective imagination turned out to be nothing more than fantasy.

This was a terrible era. At the nucleus of the galaxy, only three landmasses were still inhabited by people. Mankind had undergone three different eras of explosive growth followed by sudden nuclear war, which had shrunk the population to less than five hundred million. The resources of the nucleus were completely exhausted, and huge pipelines ran through the core of the earth, harnessing the raw energy produced there. The surface was barren, and the Country of Machines occupied the greatest amount of land—the region known in ancient times as the Third Mainland.

The Central Computer was created to become the world's new ruling machine, replacing governments, parliamentary bodies, and all other systems of law. On the day it awakened, robots conquered the world. The humans living there were either exterminated, forced to flee, or subjugated.

In the aftermath, steel life-forms colonized the surface. Sulfur pollution from constant years of industrial production filled the sky, blanketing the City of Steel with yellow clouds, and though the surface was covered with forests of skyscrapers, they housed nothing more than icy steel factories.

Humanity instead lived deep under the surface. They became slaves to the metallic life-forms, and their daily lives were simple and regimented: They took shifts to sleep, and when the time came, they would get up and start working, as if they were animals kept in cages.

Our main character, A-Ka, lived in the city's underbelly. He was one of the human residents of the area known as the Ant Nest.

A-Ka was sixteen and held the role of maintenance technician in a production line. His daily tasks consisted of receiving various mechanical life-forms, helping them adjust and change their parts, and testing out the new techniques and parts that Central Technical sent him. Many odd robots passed into his care with all sorts of requests—logical or not.

"Replace my infrared vision scope. Desired model number: RM47," one android commanded.

"Sorry, the warehouse has run out of those," A-Ka answered. "You'll have to wait until next month."

"Replace my infrared vision scope. Desired model number: RM47," the android repeated.

"There aren't any more. The warehouse is empty."

"Rule Three of the Human Control Regulations," the android announced in its dead, robotic voice. "Humans are not allowed to reject any requests from intelligent life-forms, or they will be exterminated immediately."

A-Ka tried to think of a different way to phrase the issue. This rule was the exact reason the last maintenance technician had had his head blown off! A-Ka stared down at his client's laser opening, which was already starting to heat up. He only had ten seconds left to live.

"Counting down," the android warned. "Ten, nine—"

"Please wait a moment!"

Opening a drawer, A-Ka quickly pulled out a lens that had already been polished to perfection. He swapped the android's scope out with the "new" one, though it was actually a trash piece he'd taken off another robot earlier.

"The model doesn't match. The infrared lens will malfunction."

"That's an issue with the workmanship. It just needs some troubleshooting. Please return to the queue once more. Oh, and please rate my service before you go."

The android began to capture A-Ka's body profile. A-Ka watched it with trepidation; he knew that he would get a complaint for this, but that was still better than losing his head.

Eventually, the android left, and A-Ka let out a sigh of relief.

"Help me change out my power source."

Another being lay down at A-Ka's workstation. In his mind, A-Ka thanked the heavens. *This* one was a clone.

The residents of the City of Steel were split into three strata: at the top were the steel life-forms, in the middle were the clones, and at the bottom were A-Ka and the other original humans. Clones were quite different from the chilly, mechanical androids, and they were the beings closest to humans.

"Do you require a battery or a nuclear core?" A-Ka asked.

"Battery," the clone answered, before shooting a glance at the android that had just left. "I thought you might be shot point-blank by the laser and sliced to ribbons. It would have been a pain if you had. My pathfinding system has been glitching quite a bit, and if I don't get it replaced here, I won't know how to get back."

With that, the clone turned around, and A-Ka opened a small box built into his back. "Oh, your GPS has been affected by moisture."

After turning on a light, A-Ka replaced the faulty part with a spare. The clone simply sat there without making a sound, and A-Ka couldn't help staring at his side profile. All the clones were male and had identical features, so humans could only differentiate them by their outfits or their serial numbers. This issue had confounded A-Ka for a long while.

Compared to the steel life-forms like androids, A-Ka was more willing to provide services to the clones, if only because they could also feel emotions like joy, rage, grief, and contentment. Unlike the robots, they would occasionally be affected by their hormones as well. By contrast, if a human carried out the wrong command in front of an android, they would be exterminated, no questions asked.

"You're new," the clone remarked.

"How'd you know?" A-Ka took a look at the records on the computer screen, which indicated that this clone had not appeared at his workstation, at least not in the past three years.

"Because you're very curious and have spent so long watching me. Most of the humans fresh from the Ant Nest are like this at first."

A-Ka didn't dare to reply to that. According to the advice his predecessors had given him, it was best not to provoke the clones either. The effects of emotions like happiness and pain were stronger for clones, and as soon as the hormones in their bodies became imbalanced, they would kill any humans in front of them, just like an android.

"Losing focus while working," the clone said, "makes it easy to slip up, and your customers' reviews will drop as a result."

A-Ka hurriedly nodded. "Thank you for your reminder."

The rating system A-Ka was subjected to allotted him a total of five points. Every time he received a "D" he was docked a point, while receiving an "A" granted him a point. If he ever lost all five points, the enforcement system would mark him as necessary for disposal. Humans so marked were deemed no longer able to contribute to society. They would be brought to the Rebirth Processing Factory, where they would undergo protein dissolution—in other words, death. Their bodies would be broken down into their elements before being returned to the biological energy system, where they would be reassembled into new clones or turned into raw materials for nutrient production.

A-Ka replaced the battery for the clone's positioning system, then switched out his old navigation chip for a new one as well, so that the pathfinding would work even better than before.

"Done," A-Ka said.

"You are very technically skilled," the clone said easily.

"Thanks."

When the clone left, he casually scored A-Ka a "D."

Though A-Ka's heart filled with rage, he didn't dare utter a sound. Stealing a fleeting glance at the screen of his computer, he saw that there were still thirty seconds before he was off work.

The seconds squeaked by slowly. When the electronic chime finally sounded, A-Ka rapidly put the tools back into order and tidied his own belongings, then turned and headed toward the passageway behind him.

"Please leave the maintenance stand within ten seconds," an electronic female voice reminded him.

A-Ka entered the circular tunnel. The sound of footsteps was concentrated but orderly as the shifts changed for the maintenance area. Humans flooded into the central hall from every direction and passed through the metal detector that beeped incessantly.

Beyond the main door, the platform suddenly descended as it began its journey below the surface of the earth. Human workers of all ages wearing the same uniform as A-Ka converged on the platform from many other tunnels. They piled into the elevator as it went, the riders either aiming to go up or down. Their faces were harried as they pressed up against each other in that cramped, narrow space. None of them spoke a single word.

The first time the elevator came to a stop, two patrolling robots entered. The swarm of people hurriedly backed up to create space for them.

With a ding the red light lit up, and an electronic female voice warned, "Awaiting the passage of another elevator."

It was extremely stifling inside the elevator, and everyone was sweating, but they didn't dare to shift unnecessarily or say anything. That was when a person standing by A-Ka nudged at him with his wrist.

A-Ka turned his head. It was only then that he realized the two robots had their cameras turned toward him. The elevator's surveillance camera flickered to life, and a circle of light unfocused and then refocused as it locked onto the pocket on his chest. A-Ka felt like his heart would leap out of his chest from how hard it was beating.

"What did you do?" the person next to him asked quietly. "They seem to be watching you."

In that instant, A-Ka's entire body trembled. While he'd been working, he *had* secretly hidden away a chip.

The electronic voice of one patrolling robot sounded. "Warning. Your body temperature is elevated."

Everyone in the elevator grew alarmed. The patrolling robots each carried their own infrared sensors to monitor all humans within the Ant Nest. A-Ka instantly imagined what that would look like: Within the infrared sensing system of the patrollers, the outline of his overheated body would burn bright as a fire.

"There's n-nothing out of the ordinary, right?" A-Ka asked in a tremulous voice. "I-I haven't violated any laws."

The whole crowd was watching A-Ka now.

With another *ding*, the green light of the elevator came on again, and it continued to travel downward, rumbling loudly as it went.

"You must undergo an inspection," the patrolling robot said. "Warning. Beginning four kinds of inspection."

*I'm done for,* A-Ka thought. As soon as the patrolling robot found the chip he'd stolen, he would immediately be gunned down. Sweat dripped down his back as his mind went completely blank.

Just then, a middle-aged mechanic standing behind A-Ka spasmed, his face white as a sheet, perspiration pouring down his forehead like rain. Suddenly, he convulsed violently, almost hitting A-Ka. The man then grabbed A-Ka's shoulder, prompting him to turn around. He didn't understand what was going on.

"Save me... Save me!" That middle-aged mechanic seemed to be clutching at his last ray of hope as he seized A-Ka's hand.

At that second, everyone realized one thing: This man was about to be terminated.

"Arriving at the Ant Nest," the robotic woman's voice announced.

The elevator door opened, and the middle-aged man shoved A-Ka aside as he dashed away.

"Warning. Stop immediately!" Rushing out, the patrolling robots followed in hot pursuit. The people in the elevator swarmed out after them, only to see the man continue to sprint through the hallway.

"Get down!" someone shouted.

Noise exploded in the crowded hallway. The surveillance camera installed on the ceiling shot a small, thin, metallic nail. Revealing its wings, the nail began to dart wildly back and forth through the air like a dragonfly.

A loud crack rang out above the clamor as the fleeing middle-aged man took the flying nail straight through the skull. His limp limbs flew akimbo as it pinned him sharply against the wall.

The bystanders burst into agitated discussion. A-Ka remained covered in cold sweat. According to the conversations around him, that mechanic had garnered three "D" ratings today, so after he finished his last supper, he would have been escorted away to be disposed of.

While the patrolling robots cleaned up the cruel scene, A-Ka took the opportunity to hold his breath and leave the hallway. He walked faster and faster until he reached the end of it, where he couldn't help but run into the bathroom to shower. Turning on the cold water, he washed his body, trying to cool himself down even as his anxiety heated him back up. At the same time, he attempted to calm the frantic, violent beating of his own heart.

A-Ka's entire body was soaked and dripping with water when the horror of what he'd seen enveloped him. He knew what the final fate of that mechanic would be. The corpse would be taken away and put in a factory to freeze, then it would be dismembered and tossed in batches into decomposition solution to corrode, disintegrating into basic nutrients that would be used to create new clones or turned into animal fodder.

A wave of rage and pain flooded his heart. He wanted to scream, but he couldn't summon his voice for it. He wanted to vent, but nowhere was safe; there were surveillance cameras everywhere. He didn't even dare let out a wordless roar.

With his back to the surveillance camera, he pulled out the stolen navigation chip that he had stashed in his shirt pocket and examined it. The chip burned like a heated coal in his hand, terrifying him with its mere existence.

He needed to get rid of it quickly. The more he thought about it, the more it scared him. Walking out of the shower room, he dried himself off before starting toward his living quarters.

The humans of the Ant Nest came and went around him, each carrying out their own duties.

When he returned to his own section, A-Ka finally let loose a breath. He was absolutely exhausted, and this had only been his first day on the job.

He looked at his watch—he had just ten hours to rest. As he entered the living quarters, someone nodded at him. A-Ka returned the courtesy with a stiff smile.

"A-Ka-gege's[1] back from work!" a child called. "What was the surface like?"

A teenager also walked over and patted him on the shoulder. "How do you feel about your first day of work?"

"It...was all right," A-Ka said with a nod.

Among those who lived here, a large portion were younger than A-Ka. The Ant Nest was divided into fourteen thousand sections, and the workers from each section were their area's human representatives. The behavior of these human representatives on the surface directly affected the quality of life for the entire section,

---

1   Older brother or an older male friend.

while the rest of the humans were left to undergo training from the robots, to reproduce in relative privacy, or to learn skills.

People who went through many rounds of tests but never mastered any kind of skill were also deemed to be noncontributors, and the only thing that awaited them was disposal.

The "D" A-Ka had gotten today weighed heavily on his mind, as well as the fact that he was going to be sued soon. The legal system would analyze the video recordings of his work. If he was lucky, maybe he would only be given a "B," which wouldn't add or dock points. But if he was scored another "D," the pressure on him would become enormous.

The young ones were sitting in the lounge, reading. A-Ka sat to the side and was quietly eating his allotted meal when he noticed a very small child slumped by the table, watching him.

"Can I eat your fruit?" the child asked.

"Of course."

A-Ka handed the fruit to him, and as soon as the child got it, he ran off to share the special gift he'd been given with the rest of his playmates.

In no time, the electronic voice broadcast a notice: It was the hour for sleep, and humans who needed rest were to return to their sleeping chambers. Subsequently, A-Ka tossed the plates that he had polished off into the trash bin, and with an anxiety-ridden heart, did as he was told.

Every human had their own sleeping chamber that served as their only personal space within the Ant Nest. A-Ka set the noise for his chamber to the slumbering frequency before climbing in. The space was wide, enough to fit two humans side by side, and there was even a small green potted plant in the chamber. Soon after he entered it, the hallway outside darkened, and the hatch to the sleeping chamber closed.

A-Ka turned on the reading lamp and pulled out the aged navigation chip that he had stolen. This chip would be very useful to him. Still, he should rest a little bit before using it. He didn't want to go outside, at least not today. Besides, only the void of sleep would let him temporarily forget about the troubles of getting that "D."

After the slumbering frequency began to play, he lay there for a while, his frustration mounting as he tossed and turned. He forced himself to close his eyes, but he just couldn't fall asleep. Instead, his mind returned again and again to the machine that he had hidden away down below, as well as the navigation chip that he had stolen.

Sleep remained elusive.

After half an hour, A-Ka got up, opened his chamber, and slipped out.

Within the sleeping hall, row upon row of other chambers glowed with blue light. A-Ka left the hall rapidly, pressing down on the sensor to verify his fingerprint as he returned to the living quarters. Many humans were still in this area, which was fairly normal. A-Ka, however, ducked into a safety tunnel and descended the stairs to the bottom, hiding in a corner just before a bend.

Abruptly, he heard a quiet noise from behind him, as if the door had been opened by someone else. The blood froze in A-Ka's veins. Who was there? Aching to turn his head, he nevertheless forced himself to suppress the desire.

*You can't look,* he admonished himself. There were no robotic noises, so it wasn't a guard. It was probably a human coming this way for who knew what purpose. Unless...

Had someone else discovered this tunnel?

He heard the sound of the door closing and let out a relieved breath. Only then did he dare to turn his head back and look. No one was there. Regardless, he still felt uneasy, and when the surveillance cameras turned away, he stayed still for three seconds before darting out like an arrow and rapidly clambering into the garbage chute.

Sliding down the long chute, A-Ka traveled all the way to the waste container far outside the living quarters. The trash inside the container was incinerated once every six hours, and the area was filled with a pungent scent of smoke that had not yet dissipated.

He climbed out from a hole in the garbage chute and made his way down a rusty ladder. Now that he was outside, the sea breeze blew into his face, and the roar of the tides weighted the air around him, as if the sea itself was drowning him.

The garbage chute led directly to the harbor, where the sky, the land, and everything in between were dark. Lightning cracked, connecting the sky and the sea in brief flashes, and the crashing waves and roiling thunderclouds seemed to warn him to turn back as soon as he could.

With this kind of absurd weather, A-Ka began to regret coming here today. He was still drowning in the anxiety of recent events. Had someone discovered this tunnel? But how could that happen? The waste container had been unmonitored for a long time now, and there hadn't been any new footprints recently. Either way, this was not a good day to set out.

Compared with the vastness of the sky and the ocean, A-Ka was no more than a little black speck carefully crawling across an exposed reef as he picked his way toward a hidden cave by the shore. Inside the cave, he had stashed a machine of his own making.

While he made his way over, he prayed for it to still be there—that it hadn't been taken.

If the legal system became aware of what he had done, A-Ka knew that the only thing that awaited him was disposal. But since he'd been ten, when he had unwittingly discovered the passageway in the garbage chute that led to the outside world, he couldn't help wishing to breathe the air outside. Though that air was filled with the constant, pungent scent of sulfur and the surface of the ocean was stained with black crude oil, none of it could stop A-Ka's heart from yearning for freedom.

In the past six years, he had gathered survival necessities from the Ant Nest and some scrap steel from the garbage chute, and he had moved them here a little at a time.

At first, he'd only wanted to build a small boat and leave the City of Steel in search of a place where he could live. He had heard that on the other side of the ocean, there were still places for humans. There, no Central Computer called Father controlled everything, and there were no robots that could cruelly slaughter humans at any time. It was a nation where humans were truly independent.

A-Ka wanted to reach that place, so he began to use his knowledge to gather the necessary parts to make a vehicle that could carry him. However, the materials he collected were random bits and pieces of all kinds, and in the end, he had cobbled together a strange mechanical apparatus that sort of resembled the mechas the androids used.

He'd left enough space inside the robot for a place to sit so that it could be driven, and he'd given it a name, K. Compared to the intricate, complex workmanship of the City of Steel, which used nuclear reactors to power steel life-forms, this thing called K was more like a hunk of junk.

But A-Ka was very proud of his creation. At least K wouldn't take commands from Father or the legal system, and it wouldn't ever point a laser at a person. It would do whatever A-Ka told it to do instead. This power to control a robot, to make it follow human orders, gave A-Ka a massive sense of accomplishment.

He couldn't help but treat K as his only friend. After all, K was a secret that A-Ka had kept with great difficulty. He didn't dare tell anyone about it, but he hoped that one day he would be able to drive K away from here. Before then, he needed to install a setup on K that would extract tritium from seawater to supply power to its fusion reactor.

The interior of the cave where K rested was dark and damp, and the thunder and crash of the waves outside seemed earth-shatteringly loud. When A-Ka entered the cave, he turned on the light before pulling off the oilcloth draped over K.

The steel shell stared back at A-Ka. It currently had no intelligence, but A-Ka planned that, one day, he would help it achieve a simple sort.

Prying open the front cover of K's chest plate, he installed the navigation chip that he had stolen and tested it out by connecting it to the power source and waiting for the navigation system to initialize.

Outside, every peal of thunder was louder than the last, and the waves pounded wildly, as if something was slamming with all its might against the side of the cave. Afraid that water would get into the rocky cave, A-Ka couldn't wait around for K to start up, so he ran for the outside.

Just as he was leaving, some large object was caught up in a violent wave and swept toward the entrance of the cave.

"Ah—"

A-Ka's voice was drowned out by a huge bang.

In that instant, he saw something glowing in the seawater, and that something struck several rocks as it floated its way toward the entrance of the cave. Four or five metallic cracks echoed as it hit some rocks that were about thirty feet off the ground and then fell.

A-Ka had been drenched from head to foot by the surge of seawater, but he forgot all that in his shock. Sprawled in front of the entrance, he looked down and saw some shiny object being swept away by the black waves. It seemed to be something big, and maybe it would be of some use. Still, he didn't dare to head down rashly, or the tidal wave would immediately sweep him away.

First, he turned off K's power source to prevent any short circuits, then he peeked anxiously out from his position near the entrance. The waves gradually abated, allowing him to see the foreign object more clearly: a metal chest, aimlessly bobbing in the water, pushed now and then toward the shore by the waves before being sucked back into the ocean by the tide.

A-Ka prayed for the heavens to leave that chest behind. What could be inside? Maybe it contained the fusion reactor that he so desperately desired, or its material could be made into a new body for K.

The waves gradually quieted down as the sea recovered its tranquility; the tempest had passed.

With great difficulty, A-Ka navigated down to the beach, where black petroleum covered the entire surface of the ocean. He left a trail of footprints as he walked.

That was when a wave pushed the chest to the shore, and he saw it clearly!

Following the coastline, A-Ka sprinted toward the steel chest. When he had gazed upon it from the reefs above, it hadn't seemed real. As he drew closer, he realized that it really wasn't a chest—it was a sleeping chamber.

A-Ka stared at it suspiciously, but just as the waves were about to sweep it away again, he rushed into the sea and exerted a tremendous amount of strength to push it back to shore.

As he examined the sleeping chamber, A-Ka saw a faint symbol on it in the shape of a lion. "The Lion...Republic."

Though the exterior was mottled with rust and draped with seaweed, the object seemed very durable; it must have floated in the ocean for a very, very long time. But not all of it was intact. There was a hole in the top of the chamber, and through it A-Ka could see that it was half filled with crude oil, within which lay a corpse.

A-Ka sighed. Having drifted on the ocean for so long, it must have rotted by now. Was there anything valuable left?

Pulling out a wrench, he tried to pry open the sleeping chamber, but it didn't budge an inch. He panted loudly as he scrabbled at it for a long while before his eyes caught on a line of words on the lower section of the sleeping chamber.

"Year 7210, 4th month. Heishi."

*Year 7210?!*

A-Ka was shocked. They were in the year 10073, so this chamber was from almost three thousand years ago!

He stared at it for a long time before he realized that he couldn't keep dragging things out like this. He searched for the switch for the sleeping chamber with some difficulty, as this ancient machine's layout was completely different from all of the technologies that he knew.

Finding something this old was like acquiring a priceless gem, and he held his breath, imagining that he had discovered a new world. Thoughts of forgotten tech flooded his brain: Perhaps the

ancients had left behind some sort of energy source or a weapon. On a much smaller scale, even if it was just a few slabs of circuit boards, it would be useful.

A-Ka didn't know what he touched to cause it, but the entire sleeping chamber unexpectedly lit up. Shocked, he jolted and quickly backed away, his limbs flailing.

*At least there shouldn't be anyone still alive inside the sleeping chamber,* he thought. *It has been almost three thousand years.*

Slowly, the chamber opened, and A-Ka scrambled over to discover a second layer of the chamber nested within. The space between the two chambers was filled with crude oil and seawater, which spilled out in that instant, and wave after wave of heavy fog slowly rolled out. The inner layer was clear, and on it flashed a low energy warning.

The lid of the chamber opened. The fog within seeped out and dissipated.

Inside lay a man without a shred of clothing. His hair was very short and black, his hands and feet were even in length, and he was perhaps six feet tall. A-Ka stared at him unblinkingly, then reached out to touch his body.

That man was still alive.

# THE REVOLUTION OF THE CLONES

From afar came the electronic sounds of a robot patrol among the waves.

"Damn," A-Ka muttered.

Using the strength of all his limbs, he pulled the man out of the sleeping chamber, then hauled him onto his back as he ran toward higher ground. Four hundred yards away, two coast guard ships parted the waters as they rushed toward the shore.

His heart thundering in his chest, A-Ka clutched the man tight as he clambered up the rocks while the sound of sirens screamed in the distance. He pulled out a remote from his shirt pocket, then a huge boom came from inside the cave.

K staggered forward and crashed about, leaving a trail of smoke behind it as it charged outside. With one arm, A-Ka hugged the man, and with the other, he grabbed K's metal arm. K slammed against the rocks a few times and lost a few stray pieces, which rolled away and fell with a series of clanks into the sea below. Darkness swam across A-Ka's vision, and realizing he had no better options, he clasped the man to his chest and rushed behind K back into the cave.

After several minutes, A-Ka finally recovered. He patted that man's face to no avail; he was still unconscious. K took several large steps back to its original position and once again sank into silence.

Climbing out of the cave, A-Ka peeked down, only to see the patrol robots taking the sleeping chamber away. Now there was nothing left of it, only a man whom he had picked up and brought with him.

A *human*.

A-Ka looked at that man's soundly sleeping face and suddenly felt at a loss. What use was a human? If the chamber had been empty, he could have at least sourced some materials from it, but throwing this man back into the sea, even if he was useless, was not something that A-Ka could bring himself to do.

Well, things were how they were.

A-Ka stood and walked to K's side, then returned to adjusting its navigation system. The chip that he had stolen off the clone's body must indeed have been broken, because when A-Ka turned on the sound system, he heard nothing but static.

Until, without warning, a sound came from K's voice box. "System failure."

"Ah!" A-Ka jumped in surprise. He'd never expected K to speak. What was going on? He hadn't installed artificial intelligence software on the mecha!

K once again fell silent, its two icy eyes staring fixedly at A-Ka, filling him with suspicion. He opened up the circuit board on K's abdomen and swapped the voice controls.

K spoke again. "The patricide campaign must be…"

A-Ka was startled once more, but this time he found the reason: The navigation chip was producing the noise. Some strange messages had been inserted into the navigation data. A-Ka wired up the rest of the circuitry and began to broadcast the navigation system's narration again—only to hear a series of words that nearly sent his soul flying out of his body.

"Attention all members of the rebellion! The turning point of the revolution is soon to be upon us, and the password is 'The patricide campaign will mark the last day of our oppression, and a new era will arrive.' On November 27, at twelve o'clock in the morning, when the time for humans to switch shifts comes, we will break through their defenses and exterminate any robots that try to suppress us with force. When every district loses power, all members of the rebellion are to sneak into the Central Reactor Chamber. The vanguard will then force a failure in the defensive system. Our goal is to destroy the Central Energy Storage with explosions and thereby annihilate Father. I wish everyone success."

A-Ka was so stunned that he couldn't speak. All he could do was stand there and stare at K.

November 27, and today was November 25... Was this a joke? A-Ka couldn't believe it, but the navigation chip had been taken from the clone's own body. He didn't know that A-Ka had stolen it, so he couldn't have planted this clip of narration beforehand.

In other words, in forty-eight hours at most, the clones would ally with the humans and start a riot with the goal of taking down the Central Computer. A-Ka couldn't help but think about the impossibility of everything that had happened today.

He was so lost in his thoughts that he didn't notice that the man he had rescued from the beach was awake. When A-Ka turned suddenly, he rammed right into that man's chest. He let out a loud cry as he took a fist to the face and landed heavily on the floor.

The man's eyes were filled with killing intent as he stared coldly at A-Ka. Under the glow of K's light, they watched each other in silence for almost half a minute. A-Ka's brain filled with a buzzing noise, and he felt as if it was ticking down to an explosion. As the silence dragged on between them, A-Ka struggled to break free of the sensation.

"What are you trying to do?" the man asked icily.

A-Ka's eyes filled with tears of rage, and he sputtered and coughed as he gulped down air. "I saved you!" he shouted. "Is this how you treat the person who saved your life?!"

"Oh." The man looked A-Ka up and down, assessing him.

A-Ka looked back—and suddenly felt a little bewildered. The man in front of him was about twenty years of age, with bronzed skin and a well-built physique. His hair was short and even, as if it had just grown out. The line of his lips was as clear and sharp as the edge of a knife. He had a high nose bridge, eyes bright with spirit, and eyebrows dark as ink. His limbs were long and lithe, the lines of muscles on his torso were clear and powerful, and his pectorals were sleek and well-formed. Droplets of black oil clung to his chest, smeared there when A-Ka had carried him, but they didn't detract from his perfect body. In fact, the black oil glistened with the colors of the rainbow, adding a layer of rough glamour. He reminded A-Ka of a heroic sculpture from ancient times with the kind of beauty that came from an abundance of manliness.

"What, um, what's your name?" A-Ka asked.

"Name." The man furrowed his eyebrows slightly, as if he was thinking hard.

A-Ka was about to stand up when the man moved again, startling A-Ka into backing away. He harbored many and varied suspicions toward this man, and he had a lot of questions, too. Where had he come from? Why was the sleeping chamber that had held him built that way? Had he really slept at the bottom of the ocean for three thousand years?

A-Ka knew that if the sleeping cycle lasted for more than a month, a person's memories would slowly become sealed away due to the shutdown of the brain, so he was not surprised that this man showed signs of amnesia.

"How did you save me?" the man asked, his voice still cold.

"Well, you just woke up after being pulled out of the ocean…"

A-Ka described what had happened, but the man watched A-Ka with doubt in his eyes as he listened to his explanations. As A-Ka spoke, he thought to himself, *This person has indeed lost his memories.*

"Three thousand years," the man finally said.

"Yes," A-Ka answered, while at the same time realizing a terrible issue. If he really had slept for that long, based on what A-Ka knew, his memories might never return to him.

The man was deep in thought as he racked his brain, trying to recall anything.

A little gleefully, A-Ka said, "But the technology of the sleeping chamber you were in is pretty good, because when you woke up, you still had the ability to speak and think!"

The man didn't say anything.

"What are you called? At least think of a name." When the man didn't reply, A-Ka continued, "How about I temporarily give you a name? The chamber you were in had 'Heishi' written on it. You're probably called Heishi, right?"

"Heishi…" the man mumbled. He didn't reject it, and his silence suggested that he had accepted this name.

A-Ka covered K with the oilcloth again before producing a piece of fabric, indicating that Heishi should put it on. Some pins turned it into a simple, full-body robe. As Heishi quietly sat on a rock, that one-piece sackcloth robe made him look like he was a statue.

Having taken care of Heishi for the time being, A-Ka opened K's navigation system, once again listening to that string of words.

Undoubtedly, the revolutionary broadcast of the clones was much more important than Heishi at this moment, though he almost didn't dare consider what would happen if the words were true.

Would there be a riot? A-Ka could imagine it in his head: The clones rushing toward the Central District, taking over the City of Steel, and blowing up the energy storage. As soon as war broke out, he would easily be able to pick up a power source, escape to the bay, install it in K, and leave this place behind.

A-Ka was both overjoyed and nervous; thinking about the message sent adrenaline rushing through him. He decided to return home and see what would happen, but his mind was still filled with the imagery of robots malfunctioning.

"I'm leaving," A-Ka said as he passed in front of Heishi.

Heishi looked up, confused. In his eyes was a mixture of alarm and a little bit of helplessness. A-Ka's head once again began to hurt. What was he supposed to do with this amnesiac whom he had picked up like a piece of scrap? Take him along? He seemed to have some strength, and he could be useful, but he definitely couldn't be brought back to the living area. The consequences of being discovered by the robotic guards were unthinkable.

"Where are you going?" Heishi asked.

"It has nothing to do with you, stranger," A-Ka replied, disgruntled. "I saved your life, and you didn't even spare me a word of thanks."

Heishi didn't answer. Instead, he asked, "Do you have food?"

A-Ka was ready to explode from rage. "Don't you know how to find some yourself? It's not like I owe you anything!"

Heishi rose to his feet, and A-Ka immediately backed away. He pulled out an electronic wrench and brandished it at him. "Don't come at me, otherwise I'll fry you into ash!"

Frowning, Heishi looked around at his surroundings.

*I've had it,* A-Ka thought. *Saving this person has brought me nothing but trouble.*

He backed out of the cave. Still, for reasons he didn't understand, worry nagged at him, so he soon turned around and went back in. "Food and drinkable water are here." A-Ka opened the foodstuffs storage that he had squirreled away in the corner and pointed it out to Heishi.

Heishi reached a hand out and grabbed a water bottle, taking a gulp before tilting his head back and chugging down the whole contents of the large bottle. It was only then that A-Ka realized he was very thirsty.

"Hungry?" A-Ka asked as he opened a can and handed it over. Heishi hesitated for a moment before digging out a chunk of chicken meat with his fingers and pushing it into his mouth to chew.

"Okay, I'm really going. You take care of yourself, all right? Find somewhere to go."

The watch on his wrist began to beep, and A-Ka knew that he could drag it out no longer. He had already been gone for too long today. Running out of the cave, he returned via the path he'd taken to get here.

Worries weighed heavily on A-Ka's heart, and he kept thinking of the announcement in the navigation system. What if this was all only a joke? Could it be a joke?

The trip back took a whole half hour, and when A-Ka arrived at the waste container, he happened to turn his head and instantly went bug-eyed.

Heishi had followed him the whole way, zigzagging across the crude-oil-covered beach.

"Don't come over here!" A-Ka shouted anxiously.

Heishi stood still, and A-Ka took a few running steps toward him. "Don't go looking for trouble!"

The expression on Heishi's face remained cold and calm, and A-Ka's watch once again beeped in warning. There was no more time.

"Leave this place! Go anywhere else! *Don't* follow me!" A-Ka said.

With that, A-Ka scrambled headfirst into the garbage chute, and with his hands and legs moving in tandem, he started to climb up.

He followed the path he had taken to get back to the living quarters. As he went, he shot a look down at the ground underneath the garbage chute. This time, he saw footprints—two lines of messy ones! That meant they were the footprints of a human. After he'd first exited the garbage chute, someone had come by and entered it. Also, after doing that, they hadn't left again.

How could this have happened? A-Ka almost couldn't believe it. He wanted to go back and check for clues, but he had no time left, so he could only leave quickly with his heart in his throat. Now that he knew a human had found this exit, he could no longer use it as often.

As he climbed up the ladder to the safety tunnel, A-Ka was nearly caught on camera. Getting on the next ladder, he thought, *That was too close. I could have died right then.*

The laser-equipped surveillance camera turned to an empty spot, and A-Ka slowly went up, his back pressed against the wall as he peered out.

Inside the living area, nothing was out of the ordinary. Several clones stood in the hallway chatting. A-Ka passed by them, returned to the sleeping hall, climbed into his sleeping chamber, and closed his eyes.

His mind was still filled with overwhelming excitement for the coming riot, but his body had no more energy to fight off his exhaustion, and he eventually fell asleep.

Suddenly, a huge roar echoed from the Central Reactor Chamber, and the resulting explosion was like a blazing sun that dispersed its light over the entirety of the City of Steel. All the constructs, humans, clones, androids, were turned into ash in the high heat and bright light…

"The sleeping period has ended," an electronic voice announced. "Concluding sleep mode."

The hatch to the chamber automatically opened, and A-Ka startled out of his dreams, forehead covered with sweat.

"Are you all right, A-Ka?" one of the humans asked.

A-Ka barely managed to nod, and his head spun as he used the wall of the chamber to prop himself up. His feet caught as he tried to stand, and he almost fell over before several people came over to lift him up.

"Did you have a nightmare?" someone asked in concern.

A-Ka responded, "Yeah. Yeah, I did."

He almost couldn't tell what had been dream and what had been reality. He now felt that everything that had happened over the past six hours was only a fantasy. People came and went, and A-Ka stood outside the sleeping area for a long while as he mulled his dream over again and again. Then the bell rang, reminding him that he had two hours to get ready. When those two hours were up, he would have to go to work.

A-Ka went to the cafeteria to eat. A different group of people were present from the last time he'd eaten here. Just as he sat down with a myriad of things on his mind, a robot rolled over and said to him, "Designation 470023A, your guest is currently in the waiting room. Please arrive there within the next five minutes."

A guest? A-Ka randomly shoveled a few bites of breakfast into his mouth.

When he went into the hallway, he saw two clones standing outside the door to the waiting room. All clones had the same face and the same physique, and they each wore the requisite uniform their duties required, but as soon as A-Ka saw this one, his heart began to hammer in his chest.

"You stole my navigation chip." The clone strode toward him. "If you return it to me immediately, I'll forget about your past mistakes."

"Wh-what chip?" A-Ka subconsciously reached a hand into his shirt pocket, but his hand closed around empty air, and he remembered that he had installed the chip in K's body and forgotten to bring it back.

Another clone came over, snarling quietly at him. "Don't play dumb. You have no reason to keep that thing around. You'll only end up burdening all of the humans here with disposal."

"You don't have the authority to do this!" A-Ka responded angrily. In just a few seconds, he had cleared his mind, and he realized that this clone didn't dare to raise his voice—which meant the chip with the treacherous secret was real and not a dream. "I-I didn't take your chip," he insisted, though he was so nervous he almost couldn't breathe.

"You switched it out!" That clone gritted his teeth and his hand spasmed, then he grabbed A-Ka around the neck. "Where is it? Give it back!"

A-Ka's face flushed bright red, and he saw the surveillance cameras in the hallway turn toward their direction, but the clone's emotions were already out of control. His fingers squeezed A-Ka's throat until the cartilage of his airway made crunching sounds. Little by little, his vision went black.

"Stop!"

The clone's companion just barely stopped him from choking A-Ka to death. When the clone loosened his grip, A-Ka fell to his knees and gasped for air.

Through coughs, he said again, "I didn't take the chip!"

"The guards are coming!" another clone warned. "They've already spotted us. You can't keep talking with him any longer. Think of another way to get him away."

"Just you wait," the clone said, his expression dark.

The two clones left. A-Ka knew there was no getting out of it this time. He knelt in the hallway as he thought about his next move. It was too late now to go out and retrieve the chip, and even if he handed it over, it would be useless. Could he switch it for a new chip and hand that over? Maybe.

A-Ka leaned against the wall for support, his mouth filled with the taste of blood. He then went to find water so he could gulp some down and wet his hair. Right as he started in that direction, the bell sounded a signal to gather. When it rang, all humans were to report to the conference hall as fast as possible.

Damn, things were moving too fast and too suddenly! A-Ka knew that the clones had definitely alerted the robotic guards in this area, who then sent the signal to gather up all the humans. Perhaps they had given some false pretense to the guards to select some of the humans so that they could forcefully take him away.

But he couldn't refuse to go.

A-Ka entered the conference hall, which was packed with people. From all four sides came the roar of a crowd before the myriad of steel doors fell shut, trapping tens of thousands of people in this great room.

A strong light turned on, so bright that the humans couldn't keep their eyes fully open. That burning white light shining out from the darkness struck fear into their hearts. Two robotic guards escorted a human to the center of the stage, and a clone appeared right afterward.

A-Ka froze. The person on that stage was wearing a sackcloth robe, and he stood there with his feet bare and his hands bound by a pair of magnetic handcuffs. It was none other than Heishi, whom he had rescued from the ocean just a few hours earlier!

"The police found him in front of the access stair that leads to the waste container," the clone announced to the gathered people. "This human of unknown origin does not have a designation number, nor a section that he belongs to. He knows nothing. In the process of resisting arrest, he killed two enforcers. According to the first law of the Human Control Regulations, he should be put to death."

A-Ka held his breath.

"But he told us that he came here with the goal of finding a human, and this human is among you right now," the clone said, evenly and placidly. "If you are here, please step forward and explain the origins of this person."

The crowd of people began to whisper, and A-Ka's heart nearly leaped out of his throat. He could hardly think. Didn't he tell Heishi not to follow him? What exactly was going on?

A robotic guard's arm rotated around, revealing a magnetic slicer, which hovered near Heishi's head.

Heishi lifted his eyes to watch the buzzing blue magnetic slicer in front of his face. The hexagonal high-voltage beams sizzled and popped. All that was needed was one wave of an arm, and Heishi's head would be cut into six pieces.

"I'll give all of you ten more seconds," the clone said. "If the person he's colluding with doesn't step up, then this human will be disposed of, and we will begin to investigate the entire Ant Nest."

"Warning. Commencing with disposal procedure in ten, nine, eight..."

Heishi ignored that robotic guard, turning his gaze instead to stare at the group of people below the stage. His expression was standoffish, but his eyes were searching. The crowd began to quietly gasp in shock. This innocent man on the stage clearly didn't know that his headless corpse was about to fall to the ground.

"Six, five, four..."

"Wait." A-Ka took a step forward. "It was..."

He didn't even have a chance to lay claim to this stranger when Heishi whipped around. With one kick, he sent the guard flying before leaping toward A-Ka. The entirety of the hall exploded in chaos. A-Ka hadn't yet recovered his wits before Heishi landed in front of him.

"...An unexpected incident," A-Ka finished.

Streaks of light flew toward them, and A-Ka shouted, "Get down!"

A-Ka pushed Heishi toward the ground as the interior of the hall darkened. A moment later, Heishi righted himself and lifted A-Ka by his collar.

"Come with me," Heishi said.

"We'll die!" A-Ka protested. "Don't attack them head-on!"

Two flying guards came at them from the left and the right, and Heishi turned again on the spot, executing a beautiful roundhouse kick. The flying guards were swept aside, smashing into the wall with booming explosions.

A-Ka was struck dumb. He had only seen this kind of skill once in his study materials. It was a kind of ancient martial art!

"H-Heishi!" A-Ka was just about to tell him to surrender when the doors to the right opened. Robotic guards swarmed in, but

Heishi charged forward instead of backing up, rushing into the tunnel that the mechanical guards had come from.

The sirens wailed loudly, and A-Ka thought, *It's over, we're done for.* Everything had happened so fast that he hadn't been able to react in time.

"What is this place?" Heishi asked.

A-Ka came to a quick decision. "Run toward the end of the tunnel!" Grabbing A-Ka, Heishi rushed where he was told, and A-Ka shouted again, "Turn left!"

The two of them turned at a breakneck speed, slamming into the person around the corner. By now, the entire Ant Nest had been alerted by the sirens that were blaring from the main hall, and all of the doors had been shut. A-Ka still held onto a thread of hope, however, that when they arrived at the living area, they could rush toward the garbage chute and escape that way. With how things had turned out, this was his only option.

When Heishi stopped in his tracks, A-Ka felt a tug of worry. At the end of the tunnel, in front of the sole exit to the Ant Nest from the garbage chute, there was a clone—and behind the clone, there were two Exterminators.

"D-don't attack. I mean it. No matter what, you must not attack..."

The humanoid Exterminators were a type of android specially made to take down humans, and they had been outfitted with infrared tracking shotguns. If they pulled them out in the narrowness of this tunnel, Heishi and A-Ka's corpses would be on the ground in seconds.

Heishi also instinctively sensed the danger, and he took a step back. But even more robotic guards had blocked the path behind them. Up front were the clone and the two Exterminators, and behind was a whole troop of robotic guards carrying magnetic handcuffs.

"Seems like you've caused quite a problem, brat."

A-Ka couldn't help taking a step back too as he recognized that the clone was the one who had demanded the navigation chip from him. Unfortunately, his back pressed up against the muzzle of a robotic guard's gun.

"What exactly is going on?" another clone asked.

A-Ka immediately turned around and said, "Wait, it's me! The person this stranger wants to find is me!"

Four robotic guards came over, pinning A-Ka between them, before putting magnetic handcuffs on him and locking a laser headgear around his neck. A-Ka used his gaze to signal to Heishi that he shouldn't resist.

Heishi didn't say a word.

# 3

# THE FALL OF THE PATRIARCHY

AFTER A-KA was thrown in a prison cell, he stared without moving for quite some time. He didn't understand why he had stepped forward to confess that Heishi was looking for him. He hugged his knees and sat in the corner, his mind stuck on one thought in particular. What would his own end be like?

Humans were intelligent animals. For the sake of preserving his own life, he had long since memorized the many articles of the law. As A-Ka thought it over again and again, he felt that the problem at the moment was not necessarily that he would be disposed of, because the law did not mention the punishment for humans who attempted to escape unsuccessfully to the outside world. The only crime that they could link to him was the crime of leaving the borders of the Ant Nest, but A-Ka had been very careful not to reveal any of his movements in front of the surveillance cameras. As long as the law-enforcing robots couldn't determine if he had secretly left the Ant Nest, his guilt would be absolved.

The question of Heishi was even easier to resolve. Since he didn't have an identity and he was not an escapee from the other sections, it was possible that he and A-Ka would both be deemed innocent—assuming Heishi didn't reveal to these robots that A-Ka had sneaked out.

But as soon as that clone brought up the lawsuit, A-Ka would be arrested for the crime of theft and disposed of.

A-Ka was pleased that he had made a correct decision subconsciously. On the surface, it looked like he had saved Heishi, but in reality, he had saved himself.

At this point, A-Ka glanced at Heishi sitting across from him, considering how he would communicate his thoughts to him when it was likely they were being surveilled and their every movement recorded down. He found that Heishi was also staring at him. They were two cells apart, and the bars of the prison cells were made out of crisscrossing horizontal and vertical laser beams.

"Heishi," A-Ka said. Heishi wordlessly looked back at him. "What exactly did you come here to do?"

"It has nothing to do with you."

"You…!"

A-Ka was at his wits' end with Heishi, who looked around at his surroundings, eyes filled with suspicion. Just as he was about to reach out his hand to touch the laser bars, A-Ka yelped, "Don't touch it, don't touch anything!"

"Shut up," Heishi said coldly.

"Then go ahead, touch it. Don't blame me if you die."

Heishi was silent for a long time. Finally, he decided not to test it out and put his body in danger.

"Don't say anything." In the end, that was the only thing A-Ka could tell him.

Heishi stood there quietly, watching A-Ka.

Mulling it over again and again, A-Ka wondered how he was supposed to explain this entire situation to Heishi. This grown man whom he had picked up and brought back seemed to be an indescribable lunatic. He didn't know *anything*. When he was being interrogated, he probably wouldn't lie either. The deadliest thing was, he knew absolutely nothing about the current situation: the City of Steel, the status of humans in society, or their relations with the robots. Between the two of them, A-Ka was the only one who understood their situation was quite thorny.

When A-Ka lifted his head, he found that Heishi was still watching him.

"Listen, Heishi," A-Ka said. He realized that there might be a need to demonstrate the fact that everything around them was dangerous, so he pulled out a thin screwdriver from his shirt pocket and tossed it toward the laser cage where, with a sizzling sound, the plastic tool was cut cleanly into two pieces that then clattered to the ground.

Heishi stared at the remains of the screwdriver.

"Don't say anything," A-Ka warned. "No matter what you're asked, don't say anything, or else you'll die. First, tell me honestly, why did you come here?"

"No real reason. I need to find a way out. You can stay here and keep waiting."

A-Ka gritted his teeth. "I saved you twice, Heishi! Is this how you treat the person who saved your life?"

A noise came from outside, and the two of them grew wary, each sitting back down in their cells, but A-Ka couldn't stop sizing up Heishi. A-Ka thoughts moved between the man and the clones' revolution. He closed his eyes, when suddenly he heard a muffled boom in the distance, and the walls shook slightly. Soon after, the entire prison region went dark, and the laser bars flickered. From afar came the sound of shots being fired.

A-Ka jumped to his feet. Someone was trying to cut the power source! What was going on? According to the information that he had received from the chip, wasn't the revolution of the clones supposed to happen tomorrow?

The lasers hummed as they lit up the faces of the pair. The situation was getting stranger and stranger. After a few more seconds, the lasers went out and all remaining light vanished.

A-Ka ran out of the cage, but with one tumble, he slammed into someone's embrace. A powerful arm held him, making his heart jump.

"Let me go!" A-Ka yelled.

The person—Heishi, of course—grunted without emotion and pushed him aside.

*I've really had enough of him,* A-Ka thought.

As soon as the cells opened, all the prisoners tried to find a way to escape. In the pitch black there was little chance of finding the way out, so A-Ka could only do his best to remember the path.

"This way, Heishi! Come with me!"

He ran toward the exit on the left, but near the exit he heard the sound of robotic treads moving, as if there were many patrolling guards coming their way. Turning on his heel without thinking, he ran back into the depths of the prison.

"There's danger. Turn around!"

A-Ka raced into the depths of the tunnel, where there were rows upon rows of prison cells. As soon as the lasers had disappeared, all the humans inside had grown agitated, and the prison was filled with chaotic shouts as they pushed and shoved at each other. A-Ka staggered when someone shoved him, and he steadied himself on another person.

"Heishi, Heishi!" A-Ka shouted, but there was no response; he had probably run off, but A-Ka couldn't spare any more time to find him in the darkness. A jumble of voices were shouting:

"We're free!"

"Get out quick!"

"Something's gone wrong with the energy system!"

"Everyone be careful! Get down!"

In that moment, A-Ka felt someone with a robust physique throw themself onto him, and they rolled about on the ground as lasers scattered like fireworks overhead. The robotic guards opened the main door to the hallway, and the light beams zipped through the air as pained cries and fresh blood spilled all around. A-Ka's heartbeat seemed to stop in that instant; he felt some slippery fluid on his skin, and his head swam.

"Heishi, is this your blood?"

"Here." Heishi's voice was as flat as usual—so much so that it seemed unreal.

Still unable to see, A-Ka felt someone lift him before they leaped into the air. Heishi tugged him into some enclosed place, and then that sensation was followed by a period of tumbling about.

The main entrance shut tightly, and A-Ka realized that they had entered the tunnel outside the prison complex. He couldn't see anything, but he managed to feel his way around until he bumped into an overturned manhole cover, which he knocked on a few times.

"Heishi, are you still there?"

There was no sound, and his surroundings were intensely quiet—until a deafening boom rang out and the cover in front of him was shattered. A-Ka sat back in surprise, then he remembered the blue-toned light he had stolen from a clone once, found it in his pocket, and turned it on—only to see Heishi there with his hand covered with blood. If it weren't for the blood, A-Ka would have wondered if Heishi was a robot.

"You're really strong," A-Ka said, a little bit of fear lingering in his heart. Nevertheless, he inspected Heishi's hand. The skin on the back of his hand had been sliced open. "Doesn't it hurt?"

Heishi didn't respond to that. Instead, he said, "I'm leaving. You should be careful."

Heishi left. In his absence, A-Ka realized his anger was completely gone. He could only hold his cold blue light up as he moved forward.

In the blink of an eye, Heishi disappeared to who-knew-where. A-Ka used his light to illuminate the path in front of him and cautiously began to search for tunnels to travel down. He was deathly afraid of running into any robots.

After circling around for a while, he found that there was a person in front of him. Once again, it was Heishi.

"Let's go together," A-Ka said. "You're not familiar with the passageways here."

Heishi didn't respond, but neither did he fall into step with A-Ka. Instead, he continued to walk into the depths of the tunnel. Then he stopped in his tracks and looked back to study A-Ka before glancing away again. One of his hands seemed to grasp something that didn't exist, as if he was holding his own blue light. A-Ka realized something: Heishi was learning.

He guessed that Heishi was imitating him to understand his own movements. In other words, other than language, a section of Heishi's memories on movements and thoughts was completely blank, like that of a small child. However, he didn't have the luxury of interrogating Heishi right now to confirm that; the most important thing at this point was to protect his own life.

As he caught up with Heishi, he pondered how to explain his thoughts to him.

"This place is called the Ant Nest. It's where the humans live, and you are a member of the human race."

Heishi's frigid expression still said, *I won't pay attention if I don't want to.*

"We need to think of a way to escape this place." Heishi did not react to that. A-Ka continued, "This light helps us see the road clearly. It's usually reserved for clones, which aren't robots. Robots have infrared sensors installed on them, so even if it's pitch-black, they can still see people. So…"

"You talk too much," Heishi said.

A-Ka paused for a moment, then finally exploded with an angry roar. "Getting to know you was truly the worst luck of my life!"

"*What* did you say?"

Heishi glared back at A-Ka with a ferocity that made him take a step back and not dare to shout again. Nor did he dare to answer Heishi's question. Thankfully, Heishi didn't resort to violence, only faced ahead and kept walking forward.

"Outside, there are other people rebelling," A-Ka said as he followed behind Heishi, realizing that right now was not the time to argue. "We can take the opportunity this chaos provides to leave this place."

Heishi grunted and tilted his head, as if he was distinguishing the noises within the darkness. A-Ka was certain that Heishi had fully understood, so he followed him forward.

A-Ka's blue light shone upon the tunnel, revealing the sections of the path ahead of them: a large hall, a tunnel, another large hall, and one more tunnel. Most of their dividing steel doors were open. Once in a while, they would see a steel door that was only halfway shut—probably stuck due to the problems with the energy source. A-Ka passed the light over the walls several times, trying to find a map of the tunnels, but he slowly realized that it was futile. Only the Ant Nest's living quarters had a guidance map. After leaving the Ant Nest, the robots and the clones both had navigation systems installed in them, so they didn't need maps.

Since the two of them had been blindfolded when they were brought in, they didn't know where they had been brought to. A-Ka could only blindly follow Heishi as they walked forward.

Thinking about it, it occurred to A-Ka that his luck had actually been pretty good since Heishi had appeared. No, more than that: It was as if Heishi had brought A-Ka the goddess of fortune and the winds of change. Without Heishi, the clones would likely have taken A-Ka away and disposed of him. As for whether the clones had been warned early by the loss of that navigation chip, subsequently kickstarting their battle, that was also wholly outside of what A-Ka could imagine.

After walking for an unknown amount of time, A-Ka's body began to sag from exhaustion. "Wait for me a bit. I need to rest."

Heishi stared at A-Ka with silent impatience before saying, "I'm leaving."

"Where are you going?"

"It has nothing to do with you."

A-Ka was at a complete loss for what to say to Heishi. He seemed to be holding a grudge over the words they had first exchanged by the shore.

That conversation had been an unhappy one, but A-Ka didn't know the root of it all was the hostility in his face when Heishi first met him.

"Wait for me. You won't survive on your own here," A-Ka said.

As Heishi walked away, his footsteps slowly faded into the distance.

Soon enough, A-Ka was alone.

Cocking his head, he placed his ear against the wall, but he didn't hear a thing. In front of him was a long tunnel used to transport supplies for basic living needs. There were many of these throughout the Ant Nest, crossing over each other and shuttling back and forth in the space under the earth, transporting goods. Finding the tracks meant that they had basically gained access to that network of thoroughfares.

A-Ka rested for a while until he once again slowly began to follow the rails. He didn't expect to run into Heishi, but there he was, tilting his head up to study something that looked not like an exit but an electrical box.

"Here, pull down the switch on the outside," A-Ka said. "This one is magnetically controlled, so it won't be affected if you cut off the electricity."

Heishi obeyed, and there was a rumble of steel scraping as it opened a door embedded in the ground.

"Well done," A-Ka said. "If you went on your own, you wouldn't have been able to find the exit."

Heishi didn't respond, so A-Ka walked forward into the tunnel so deep that he couldn't see the end. Heishi was right behind him.

They heard the faint sound of an explosion in the distance. A-Ka had no way of knowing if the clones' plan had been put into motion, and he was starting to get anxious. If he didn't escape in time and the clones as a whole lost, what could he do then?

As they walked along, Heishi suddenly pulled A-Ka to a stop—the two of them had almost walked headfirst into a minecart. The road was blocked.

"What now?" A-Ka asked.

Heishi went forward and pushed the minecart with both hands.

That minecart must have weighed at least a ton, and Heishi's body arched with effort as he threw his entire strength behind it and pushed forcefully. A-Ka was just about to stop him when he saw that the minecart had slowly begun to move. Bending downward, A-Ka joined Heishi in pushing that barricade-like mine cart into movement. He panted heavily as they moved it, inch by inch, along the tracks.

After some amount of time, they finally reached a turn in the tunnel. The rails that extended forward like thin strands of spider silk lay within a large hall, the walls of which were riddled with cavern entrances. Heishi listened for a while longer and then chose a path.

A-Ka stood at the entrance of one of the caverns, hearing moans coming from inside. Could that be the exit?

Their surroundings gradually chilled. The climate control system had been temporarily halted due to the lack of power.

"What's wrong?" Heishi asked.

"It's cold."

Heishi callously walked away, obviously not understanding the meaning of "cold."

*Why did you even ask?* A-Ka thought, buzzing with misery and irritation. As he shivered, his attention fell on the sackcloth clothes that he had given to Heishi, which he hadn't stopped wearing. Though his body was strong, A-Ka figured he should still find Heishi some other clothes to put on. It would be even more of a pain if he got sick.

As they continued along the rails in that tunnel, the space was so dark A-Ka couldn't see his fingers with his hand outstretched in front of him, and he tripped over something.

The bodies of several clones lay on the tracks, and A-Ka heard someone moan, "Save me... Save me..."

A-Ka took a deep breath as his heart began to race.

That surviving clone turned his head and saw A-Ka and Heishi. "Which squad...are you from?" His head had been destroyed, one eye protruding from its ruined socket, and his abdomen had been shot clean through by a bullet. Seeing that A-Ka was not a clone, he said, "No. Humans."

His trembling hand lifted as if he wanted to grab A-Ka, but Heishi pulled A-Ka a short distance away.

"What happened?" A-Ka was also desperate to know whether they had won or lost this battle.

"Human," the clone said weakly, "you should go."

His eyes closed.

A-Ka lifted his blue light and shone it over their surroundings. It looked like this place had experienced a harsh battle; in front of them were many destroyed robot guards, and the circuits fizzled and sparked now and then in their destroyed shells.

Peeling the clothes from the corpse of the clone who had spoken to them, A-Ka gave them to Heishi to wear. Heishi untied his sackcloth before extending his arms into the vest. When he put it on, he eyed the clone, and A-Ka knew he had questions.

As expected, in the next moment, Heishi opened his mouth. "Why do all these people look the same?" he asked, clearly suspicious and confused by the scene he saw before him.

"They're clones, built by the robots to be their servants and messengers."

"How about you?"

"I'm a human. Within the City of Steel, my class is below the clones."

"Class?" A word that Heishi was unfamiliar with.

A-Ka had Heishi put on his clothes properly, and as they walked, A-Ka haphazardly explained the concept of classes within the city, as well as the organization of human society into various constituents. He also described how the clones carried out the commands of the robots and helped them to control the humans, and how the clones completed certain tasks that the steel life-forms were unable to perform on their own.

The clones were controlled by a unified operation. They were not afraid of being hurt or falling ill, and as soon as their organs were damaged, they could easily obtain replacements. Their blood types were all the same, and their organs could be swapped out at will, so the clones' existence was a much easier one to manage than that of the humans. They were just like living robots.

"How did clones come about?" Heishi asked.

"They were created by humans. During the Golden Age, we conquered the sky and the land. There was nothing we couldn't do. The army of robots, with Father at their head, and the clones—they were both made by humans, to serve us. But the clones betrayed mankind first, and Father after that. Eventually, when the robots captured the clones' production lines, they brought the clones under their control."

"What about humans? Humans like me."

"Some of them stayed here and were forced to become slaves," A-Ka said. "I'm one of those. As for the rest, well, some escaped, and I hear they created a new country on the other side of the Great Ocean."

Heishi nodded, and A-Ka's heart leaped as he recalled the moment Heishi washed ashore. Could he have come from that distant continent? The humans in the Ant Nest had all kinds of rumors about the mythical land on the other side of the Great Ocean.

Some people said that place was a realm of magic, where nature itself was at their command, and the humans there could use their mental abilities to change the world. Others said that the escapees had all died, and the so-called mythical land was merely a misty and unrealistic legend.

There were people who believed that the armies of the mythical land would one day arrive at the City of Steel, destroy Father—this great demon that they themselves had created many years ago—and free the humans here. Instead, it was the clones within the city that had first incited this bout of revolution.

After he listened to A-Ka's explanation, Heishi's expression grew chillier.

"Did you come from the mythical land?" A-Ka suddenly asked.

During their escape, A-Ka had wondered many times about Heishi's origins. Maybe he was a lucky survivor who floated away from a ship that perished, or perhaps he came to the Third Mainland three thousand years ago with some specific orders to fulfill. Either way, Heishi had completely forgotten everything, and all A-Ka could do was hope that someday in the future he would remember again.

Aside from asking questions, Heishi spent most of his time deep in silence, observing the outside world. A-Ka didn't want to disturb him, so he let his question drop and tossed Heishi a pair of boots to wear.

The air grew colder and colder, and the breaths that A-Ka puffed out turned into white fog. It was a good thing the two of them were wrapped in thick layers of clothing. When they passed through the aftermath of a large battle, the ground was covered with the corpses of clones and the destroyed wreckage of robots as far as the eye could see. Clearly, this place had experienced a soul-shakingly huge conflict.

The further in they went, the more corpses they saw, until they came upon a dense pile of bodies outside a door. At the end of this otherwise ordinary hallway, there stood a door with no markings. A-Ka realized that this must be a very important place, but he wasn't sure why. Almost a hundred clone corpses and robotic shells were strewn around, as if they had been protecting something vital, but there was just the blank door at the end of hallway.

"Why would they have died here?" A-Ka said aloud. When he looked back, he saw that there was no path of retreat, so they could only stubbornly push ahead.

*Could the Central Control Chamber that holds Father be inside?* he wondered abruptly. However, he immediately dismissed that hypothesis. This was only a track interchange area for the goods transportation system. There was no way that Father would be sealed away in this remote underground space.

Heishi moved the scattered flesh and metal bodies aside, revealing the entirety of the door. He used his shoulder to push at it, but it didn't budge.

After a moment of contemplation, A-Ka said, "Let me try."

He opened the control panel next to the door, inside of which were dozens of password locks. This would be an extremely tricky problem to solve. Glancing around, he found that the clone lying closest to the door was holding a card tightly in his hand. He then understood that the rebels were only half a step away from entering this door.

What exactly could be behind the door? A-Ka's curiosity almost made his hands shake. Using the security card, he opened the door. It slid open, since it had its own power source, but he was greeted with nothing but darkness. Then, a cold light flickered on inside the large hall and illuminated A-Ka's and Heishi's faces. They saw emptied nourishment chambers all around the room. In the middle of it all sat a human obviously on the brink of death.

A very old man.

"You're finally here," the old man said.

The sudden sound of his voice startled A-Ka badly. "Y-you! Who are you?" A-Ka hurried forward and inspected the old man's condition. Many multicolored tubes were stuck in him like pins in a cushion—all of them serving as life support.

The old man lifted up his murky eyes as he looked toward A-Ka. "Where is General Liber?"

"G-General Liber? I don't know... Many clones died out there. Are you all right?"

"The revolution failed..." The old man's voice faltered. "How did you come to this place?"

A-Ka gave him the short version of how they had escaped, and the old man managed to hold himself together to hear it to the end before he said weakly, "So, at the end of it all, it's a human who stands in front of me... My own mother's kind..."

"What does that mean?" A-Ka was puzzled, but he tried to lift that old man. "Are you able to move?"

"I am about to die," the old man said. "Child, help me... Take these things away..."

Heishi took the blue light from A-Ka and lifted it up, shining it on the old man's face. A-Ka observed his wrinkled features, feeling a sense of familiarity, like he was someone A-Ka knew. Especially that pair of indigo-blue eyes; it felt like he had seen them somewhere before.

"Do we know each other?" A feeling of déjà vu washed over A-Ka again, and he felt as if he was standing in the middle of a great puzzle.

The old man didn't respond. He merely reached out a trembling hand to grab A-Ka's own, and A-Ka hurried to meet it. The old man pressed A-Ka's finger against the handle of his wheelchair, and there was a sudden, light click as A-Ka felt something prick through his fingertip.

It hurt so much he yowled. He shuffled back a few steps, but when Heishi went up and grabbed at that old man's collar to toss him out, A-Ka shouted, "Wait!"

The old man's body was connected to dozens of tubes, and Heishi had lifted the old man off his wheelchair with a hand around his throat. He could hardly lift a finger to resist. Heishi's actions hastened the old man's oncoming death, but even as his eyes rolled back, a complicated, strange, and faint smile appeared on his face.

"Don't be so rough. Put him down," A-Ka said hurriedly.

Doing as he was told, Heishi set the old man back into the wheelchair.

A-Ka lowered his head to look at his own ring finger, where a drop of blood was beading on the tip. His head spun as he heard the sounds of mechanical beings coming from somewhere.

*Damn it!*

"Take this...and give it to General Liber..." the old man croaked out. He handed a chip to A-Ka before closing his eyes.

"H-hey! Wake up!" A-Ka said, but there was no point. The old man's head drooped.

He was dead.

The mechanical sounds drew ever closer. A-Ka speedily hid the chip and turned to Heishi. "Go."

Heishi dashed toward the tunnel just as lasers shot in from the outside.

"Be careful!" A-Ka called.

Within seconds, Heishi returned. "Quick, move back! There are enemies!"

A-Ka slid the security card, and the main door slammed shut. Explosions resounded in twos and threes from the other side. They were trapped in this room.

"We have to find an exit."

A-Ka and Heishi split up to find a way out. As A-Ka searched through all of the possible places in the room they might escape from, he couldn't help thinking of the indigo eyes of that old man, as well as his familiar face. He knew he had seen this old man somewhere, and often at that...

While he was musing, he saw Heishi come to a halt in the large hall and stare at the old man's body with misgiving.

"What's wrong?" A-Ka asked as he straightened up.

"I know him."

A-Ka jolted. "Really? What's his name?"

Heishi shook his head and said nothing. A-Ka wanted to dig more into the old man's origins, but Heishi didn't have an answer for any of his questions—he had forgotten everything.

A-Ka had no other options. "Fine, let's just search for the exit."

"No need to search anymore. This place is a prison."

In an instant, A-Ka snapped out of his fog. From the moment they'd first stepped inside, every sign indicated that the old man was a prisoner. Aside from the entrance, there were no other ways they could get out of here. Heishi's conclusion must have been correct.

What should they do?

Just then, another series of loud bangs came from the outside, so forceful that they began to deform the door. A-Ka knew he needed a place to hide, but the door had already started to warp under the pressure from the outside and sparks were flying. On instinct alone, A-Ka turned and ran toward Heishi, while Heishi shot in a clean line like a bullet across the room. The two of them collided in midair and clung to each other tightly.

At the same time, the door blew open with a boom, sending shrapnel flying everywhere. Heishi hugged A-Ka as they landed on the ground and rolled into a corner.

"Quick! Take him away!"

"Heavens, he's already dead!"

"Humans?"

"There are two humans here!"

"Don't attack!"

"What's going on?!"

The inside of the room devolved into pandemonium as many clones rushed in. A-Ka's head throbbed with pain while he stood up, protected behind Heishi. A bright light swept back and forth.

"We escaped here," A-Ka explained.

"When did you come in?" a clone asked him anxiously. "When you two came in, was Doctor Callan still alive?"

Heishi was about to open his mouth and answer, but A-Ka pinched his palm and answered instead. "He was still alive. He asked me to pass a message to General Liber."

The tunnel outside suddenly rattled with more explosions, and this time, the sounds were as clear as crystal, as if the entire world was going to be overturned from the percussive force of those blasts. The earth trembled, and several clones swayed, almost falling over.

"There's no time to explain more! Take them away!" said the clone squad's leader.

Under the protection of the clone squad, A-Ka and Heishi raced back into the tunnel. Robotic guards soon surrounded them on all four sides, their numbers growing by the minute.

Occasionally, A-Ka could hear someone shout, "Hold them there! They're counterattacking!" and similar phrases.

A-Ka didn't know why, but he was woozy and nauseous as he staggered along, dizziness threatening to drown him. He scrabbled desperately at the air a few times before he caught Heishi's hand, but Heishi pushed him aside. Without support, he could no longer stand and plummeted headfirst to the ground.

Heishi came back and frowned. "Why are you so weak?"

"Don't bother with me, then!" A-Ka snapped. He couldn't stop panting, and his vision had blurred, as if a bad fever had overtaken his body.

Without another word, Heishi lifted A-Ka into his arms and continued running alongside the clones. Behind them, members of the rebellion followed, carrying the old man's body as well as his wheelchair.

They bumped their way through the passageway. A-Ka drifted in and out of consciousness for an unknown period until a sudden burst of bright light sent him reeling.

They had emerged to blazing sunlight. A-Ka shielded his eyes with his hand. Everything around them turned a brilliant white, like they had been enveloped in a burst of solar wind that came from a star. A-Ka had never breathed the fresh air of the surface so vividly before now, and he felt that the scorching sun was a pillar of fire radiating heat so strong it scorched his soul.

"I'm going to die..." A-Ka said, not knowing why he felt so weak.

"Hang in there!" Heishi said into his ear.

All this time, Heishi had been hugging A-Ka to his chest, and as they moved forward, A-Ka could feel Heishi start sprinting.

Next to A-Ka's head, he realized clones were talking.

"He's only feeling a temporary burst of faintness..."

"I can't see a reason for it..."

"Humans, come with us! We're almost about to start!"

"Let him soak up the sun. Don't move him now..."

The voices washed over A-Ka like waves lapping against the shore, and in an instant, he grew calm. This was the most mysterious moment he had experienced in his life. The movements of his surroundings seemed infinitely distant from him, but he also saw them with extreme clarity, as if a magnetic field extended from his mind across the vast expanse of the earth and sky and he was keenly aware of every single minute movement within that field.

Slowly, it retreated, and its final focal point only encompassed the outline of one person by his side: Heishi.

His outline grew clear again, and he said something to A-Ka, whose five senses at last returned to him.

Heishi's brows tightened into a pretty knot. "Are you all right?"

"I'm... I'm okay."

A-Ka came back to himself, his body soaked with sweat, and lifted a hand without thinking. Seeing that Heishi was watching him with worry, he grabbed Heishi's hand and interlocked their fingers, putting Heishi slightly more at ease. With new clarity, A-Ka recalled his period of weakness and connected it to the needle that the old man had pricked him with. What exactly had been injected into him?

A clone came over. "Humans, hurry and get on the ship. You can't stay here any longer."

Heishi once again lifted A-Ka in an embrace, but A-Ka said, "I can walk on my own."

He shuffled along behind the clone onto a small airship. The instant he walked into the lift, what he saw left him tongue-tied.

On the platform that spanned almost four hundred square miles, millions of war airships turned and launched, soaring into the sky, while the protective magnetic layers surrounding the launch platform shot down the mechanical aircraft that attempted to ambush them. The sky was filled with balls of fire, and in a deafening burst of brightness, an airship exploded, trailing a plume of smoke as it plummeted into the ocean.

Like a wasp nest that had been prodded until it erupted, tens of thousands of airships left the earth behind as they ascended into the sky, releasing row upon row of laser-guided bombs, which flew toward the heart of the city.

# 4

## THE FIGHT TO ESCAPE

A-KA HAD BEEN BROUGHT into a small fighter airship that only had a single clone as the pilot.

"Find a spot, sit down, and fasten your seatbelts! I'm in charge of taking you guys over to the mother ship!" the pilot shouted above the din.

The old man had tasked A-Ka with handing something over to the clones' General Liber, so he quickly sat down. Through the cabin windows, he could see that the skies were filled with glowing flames, while mechanical troops swarmed like a hive of killer bees, obstructing the sky from view.

Suddenly, the aircraft's motion shook them to their bones.

Heishi tightly gripped the grab handle above him as the pilot called, "Watch your heads!"

Flipping in midair, the fighter craft turned to one side and narrowly slipped through the gap between the metal tentacles of two giant, jellyfish-like craft.

"Are you guys going to win?" A-Ka asked.

"Can't say for sure. I don't know which bastard leaked the news, but the rebellion plans were pushed forward!"

A-Ka's heart twanged with fear.

"We're going to the central region of the Country of Machines," the pilot continued. "You guys be careful."

"Don't go there! You'll die!"

"That's where the main forces are. General Liber is on the front lines. No turning back!"

A flash in the distance illuminated the entire world, and a ring of fire blossomed outward as some unidentified thing whistled toward them. The blinding light blotted out the entirety of the battlefield.

In that instant, all sound grew distant, and their surroundings became incredibly peaceful. Heishi seemed to have seen something, and he slowly rose and walked toward the cockpit. A-Ka grabbed him, trying to get him to sit back down. It was far too dangerous for him to be standing, but the words that A-Ka shouted were drowned out by this void of silence. He realized that the sound of the explosion had been so loud it had rendered everyone temporarily deaf.

Just as he grabbed Heishi's hand, interlocking their fingers, he felt that the light carried a wave of energy that was faintly calling to them.

*What is that?*

For a moment, A-Ka forgot that he was trapped in a dangerous situation, and his eyes fixed on the thing inside the white glow.

It was then that the small fighter craft broke out of the circle of light. As sound returned to the world, A-Ka saw his surroundings clearly.

It was a truly breathtaking view: The clones' mother ship was as large as a city. Floating in the air, it spewed millions of fighter crafts that rushed toward the Central Computer like a giant wave.

But the Central Computer, Father, stood firm against the onslaught, radiating with light as it directed dense masses of flying robots to block the forward motion of the mother ship. In the sky, black clouds roiled as they gathered into a vortex, the magnetic field splitting the world into countless little broken pieces.

This was a battle of gods. In front of such might, A-Ka couldn't help but shudder.

Right then, Father's defenses once again released flash bombs, one of which pierced through the mother ship's flank. The steel body exploded apart, sending shrapnel shooting in all directions.

"Be careful!" Heishi pushed A-Ka to the ground.

A piece of high-speed shrapnel flew toward their cabin and pierced the pilot's forehead. In the background, a sonic boom echoed. Blood spurted everywhere inside the cabin, and the fighter craft rocked wildly, spiraling toward the earth below. A-Ka slid to the tail end of the craft.

"Don't worry about me! Go take the pilot's seat!" A-Ka cried.

Heishi was of the same mind, and he scrambled over the chairs in a fierce headlong charge, pulling aside the pilot's body before grabbing the joystick.

A-Ka directed him. "Keep it steady. Pull toward you!"

Heishi fiercely yanked at the joystick, and A-Ka fell forward, landing near the cockpit. He speedily took the copilot's seat and began tapping away rapidly with his thumb, manning the antiaircraft gun. The laser turrets on the craft activated, pulverizing the meteors of debris flying at them.

"Now what?" Heishi asked.

"Do you know how to fly a ship?! Go toward that large one!"

"I *don't* know!"

"Just move the joystick! Quick, we're going to die!"

"Shut up! We can't rush into the center of things and take bomb blasts head-on!"

The mission had trumped everything else in A-Ka's mind, to the point where he had forgotten that they needed to survive this as well. He wanted to rethink things, but reality forced him to stay resolute.

"Hurry. Just go," A-Ka said.

Suddenly, another piercing boom disrupted the world around them, and the small fighter airship was sent rocketing toward the Central Computer. A fiery glow bloomed outside the cockpit, and the ensuing shock wave slammed A-Ka headfirst into the bridge. His head felt like it had been split in two, and the explosions lingered like a haunting in his ears.

Through his vertigo, he felt Heishi patting his face.

"Wake up!"

A-Ka hazily lifted his head, which now bore a dripping wound, only to be struck dumb by what he saw.

The two of them were stuck at the edge of the cockpit. Beneath them was nothing but air, as they were some thousands of miles off the ground. Not too far from them, the huge mother ship was being bombarded incessantly, the defensive layer shuddering violently under the onslaught of each new blast. Any time now, it would throw them and the rest of the fighters off. The small fighter ship was tilted almost 70 degrees in its position on the turret, and it could fall at any point.

A-Ka gathered his wits about him and flipped the switch on the nearby emergency button, turning on the backup lights, which began to flash the word "Damaged." The power was low.

"Do we leave the ship behind?" Heishi called above the ear-piercing siren.

"No way!" A-Ka said, just as loud. "There are over six hundred floors in the Central Tower. If we ran all the way down, we would die without a doubt!"

Heishi let out a frustrated, helpless sigh. "What should we do?"

"There's no more power. We need to find a way to recharge the ship's energy supply."

How could they do that? A-Ka looked at the 12 percent left of the power supply bar, his face filled with consternation and his head ringing.

Heishi slowly calmed down and asked A-Ka, "Are there any transportation devices nearby?"

"That won't work..." A-Ka lifted his gaze toward the heavens, where the fight between the mother ship and the Central Computer was entering its most chaotic stage.

In a flash, multiple thoughts passed through his head: First, abandoning the ship and running for their lives was too dangerous. Between here and the ground they would be caught in the middle of the crossfire, and if they escaped on foot, they could not run quickly—a bomb could blast them into smithereens at any point. Second, finding a new mode of transport was not possible. In the Country of Machines, Father controlled almost all of the flying ships.

"Here, there is only Father," A-Ka explained. "We cannot break the control that it has over the flying robots."

Heishi also lifted his head to the sky, where he saw countless humanoid mechas shuttling back and forth.

"What about those?" he asked.

"Those are the clones' mecha suits. We have no way to use them."

"Maybe there are broken suits?"

"There's no time to fix them right now. We'll have to rely on blind luck. Let's find a way to recharge the power."

Heishi could only nod. A-Ka's mind was clouded with worry, but after a moment, he looked up into the depths of the tall computer tower. A daring thought had struck him: They could use Father's energy source. There should be ports for the robots to charge themselves.

Now, A-Ka had a plan.

"Hold onto me," he said.

Heishi grabbed A-Ka's hand, allowing A-Ka to climb out of the ship. As he looked down, he instantly felt the metal he was braced against spin underneath his feet.

"Be careful!" Heishi warned.

*Doing acrobatics on an airship that's almost sideways is a sign of how insane I've become,* A-Ka thought. Before, he would never have imagined that such a thing might happen. Clearly, humans could do anything when standing at the gates of life and death.

Activating the charging port on one side of the ship, he pulled out the power cable and wrapped it around his waist before looking for the closest opening.

It was only thirty feet above them. But the entire Central Computer tower was shaking, and its exterior was as smooth as a marble. There was nothing for him to grab. How would he climb up there?

Heishi saw what A-Ka was trying to do and shouted, "Come back in. I'll figure out a way."

"Okay, but *how*? Every wall is made of incredibly strong metal."

Not answering, Heishi pulled A-Ka back into the cabin and took the cable. "How does this connect?"

"Clip the latch on and that's it," A-Ka said.

Heishi looked around his surroundings, then found a rubber plunger used to clean out the inner pipes of the generator. "Use this."

It was... It was really a toilet plunger.

"I-it won't work," A-Ka protested. "That's way too dangerous."

Heishi didn't respond. Instead, he dashed forward and leaped up toward the platform high above, toilet plunger in hand. With a sucking noise, it stuck against the side of the tall Central Computer tower. Watching this, A-Ka was dumbfounded. Below Heishi's feet was a mile drop, and his body was shaking with the force of the explosions. The power cable was still wrapped around his waist.

A-Ka didn't dare to breathe. He could only watch as Heishi steadily progressed upward, seeing him press one hand against the outer wall and use the friction of his palm to steady his body while with his other hand he pulled the toilet plunger off and hurried to stick it in a higher spot.

*That works?!*

A-Ka stared with his mouth open as Heishi used the toilet plunger to climb higher and higher up Father's body. He was simultaneously absolutely terrified and greatly amused.

Heishi approached that opening and set up the connection. The power instantly came back to the cabin, and all of the lights came on.

"It worked!" A-Ka shouted loudly. "Heishi, come back, quick!"

But Heishi didn't move an inch. He remained where he was, and though A-Ka's anxious voice called to Heishi, the continuous explosions drowned him out.

*Shit!*

A-Ka turned and saw that the mother ship that spanned the sky was on the verge of falling. A blue light shot out of Father's tall tower, piercing the mother ship's abdomen. That explosion released a burst of energy, but Heishi merely held one hand against the connection point as he stared fixedly at the power cable connector.

There was a blue glow where the cable plugged in, and a voice faintly reverberated in Heishi's mind—a man's voice, but too indistinct to comprehend.

The airship was already fully charged, and A-Ka was shouting for him, but Heishi was still sunk into a trance. A-Ka was almost ready to fall into despair.

Far above their heads, explosions resounded in twos and threes on the mother ship, and debris began to fall from on high. A-Ka's breathing quickened.

Just as a fireball was about to engulf Heishi, a shabby, tattered robot rushed out from the glow of the fire. A-Ka's eyes widened; he couldn't believe it. The shabby robot in front of him was K! How was K here? That was *his* robot!

K dashed through the flames, slamming into Father's outer wall, then reached out to grab Heishi. Immediately, Heishi came back to himself, his face filled with astonishment as K lifted him with one arm. Together, K and Heishi flew toward the small fighter.

In the next instant, before A-Ka could process all of the irrational things that had happened in this short span of time, K tossed Heishi into the cabin.

"Leave quickly!" K said.

That robot turned and stepped onto the roof of the small ship, which wobbled gently. A-Ka felt a shiver go up his spine. He could not just accept this reality where K stood in front of him, alive.

"You... K, how are you...?"

"Hurry and go!" The voice that came out of K's body was worried, and with another solid kick, K helped the ship detach from where it had been stuck. The robot then turned and flew toward the mother ship.

Just as the airship was about to fall, A-Ka pulled up on the joystick. There was another sky-shattering detonation, and the mother ship broke through the Central Computer's defensive layer, smashing into Father's tall computer tower. Piercing blue light spewed out like an energy tsunami, overturning all the flying robots in the air.

That wave of energy radiated outward, starting a chain reaction. It first sent the battered mother ship flying before it cracked open the ground of the entire City of Steel. As more explosions sang in a chorus, the cracks widened.

A-Ka had not realized that he was witnessing history being made right before his eyes—the first time in three thousand years that the tides had turned against the might of the robots. His only thought was that they had already come this far, so they had to stay alive no matter what.

All of the navigational systems were useless in this firefight, and he couldn't tell which way was up. He could only rely on his own instincts and place his trust in Heishi's steering.

The huge energy wave washed over the ship, turning it into a grain of sand caught by the tide as it was swept far away. Finally, all of the blue light disappeared, and in front of them was the ground, spiraling up to meet them.

The airship trailed smoke behind it as it fell toward a desolate plain. Before it could crash, it skimmed a mountain, toppled over a cliff, and sank into a large river with a series of violent shudders.

A huge boom sounded as water wildly rushed in through any available crack. A-Ka unsteadily made it to his feet, grabbed Heishi's hand, and flipped the escape pod switch—but the escape hatch was stuck.

"Heishi," A-Ka shouted, but he remained unconscious.

"Damn it!" A-Ka kicked at the hatch a few more times, but the water flow grew heavier and heavier. He pulled Heishi onto his back, searching for an exit, but Heishi was heavy and dense as a piece of steel. The two of them were trapped in the fighter as the water level rose higher and higher.

As the water lapped at Heishi, his eyes popped open. He grabbed A-Ka's waist and then kicked forward with his foot. With a leap and a dull thud, an entire section of the metal sheet flew loose under the water.

The two of them were swept like foam on the ocean, this way and that, as they rushed to the surface. Though they completely lost their sense of direction, they managed to crawl onto the shore with great difficulty.

Bedraggled, A-Ka coughed out a few mouthfuls of water before meeting Heishi's gaze. Then, the two of them began to laugh and laugh.

"Ha ha ha!" A-Ka didn't know why, but he kept laughing until he was completely out of breath.

Even Heishi couldn't resist a smile, after which he wiped the water off his face and sat down on a rock.

The area they had crashed into was a barren one, but A-Ka and Heishi were still within the borders of the Country of Machines. A-Ka checked the direction of the sun and confirmed their position. The two of them climbed to a higher spot and saw the main road in the distance.

To the eastern side of the plains, plumes of thick smoke rose from where Father and the clones' mother ship had fought their final confrontation. That blast had twisted time and space for an instant, sending them some 250 miles away from the City of Steel. It had also brought along quite a few robot weapons that had burst through like meteorites, each embedding itself in the rocky earth.

A-Ka picked through the debris of the robots to find a few useful scraps, and after melting them with a nuclear furnace, he turned them into a new small wrench. Holding the tool in his hand suddenly reminded him of his robot, K, and he found himself with so many questions that his brain almost exploded.

Why was K in the mother ship? There had been a person inside K! A-Ka recalled the few sentences it had said—there was definitely a person steering it. But how did this person know them? Or was it because of the battle? Had someone unknowingly stumbled across K in that cave before climbing inside it and directing it into battle, unknowingly saving A-Ka and Heishi?

No matter how A-Ka thought about it, he couldn't figure it out, so he had to put the matter aside for now. Before, the only desire in his mind had been to find a fusion engine for K, but now, when there were fusion engines scattered about everywhere, he no longer had a need for one.

"I'm leaving," Heishi announced.

"Where are you going?" A-Ka asked.

Heishi's reply came exactly as A-Ka predicted it would: "It has nothing to do with you."

One of these days, Heishi was going to make A-Ka burst like a furious firecracker. He never should have saved him in the first place.

"I rescued you from the ocean!" A-Ka said. "*And* I saved your life again in the living quarters. Can't you be a little nicer to me?!"

"I've also saved you quite a few times. Now we're even," Heishi said.

"Excuse me, when did you do that? If I hadn't brought you out of the Ant Nest..."

Heishi and A-Ka stood there, the tension thick in the air, before A-Ka realized that there was no point in arguing. Truthfully, he would never have survived the journey here if Heishi hadn't been there. Likewise, without him, Heishi wouldn't have been able to find the path to the surface.

"Whatever, let's not talk about this any longer," A-Ka said helplessly. "Where are you going?"

"I have a mission."

A-Ka was taken aback by that. "What mission? You've remembered your identity?"

Heishi stared off into the distance before finally shaking his head slightly.

"Okay, then what did you remember?" A-Ka asked.

"Nothing. I only know that I have a mission."

"Well, fine. You also don't know what the mission is, so where are you going?"

Heishi seemed annoyed by the question, and when A-Ka went over and reached for Heishi's shoulder, he turned away to avoid it.

A-Ka was too tired to continue talking with this maniac. Hopping off the rocks, he returned to picking through the fallen scraps of robots on the plains. After a while, he saw that Heishi had also come down and was wandering around without a purpose.

"You're not even remotely familiar with this world," A-Ka shouted, "and you don't have a destination in mind, so don't just mill around! If you get lost, you'll have no way back!"

Heishi picked up a rock, hefted it high with his hand, then hurled it into the distance as he let out an enraged roar.

A-Ka understood a little of what Heishi was feeling. He was someone without a past, without a future, who didn't even know his own name. That kind of confusion and frustration, locked in the depths of the mind like a demon, would leave anyone feeling bitter.

A-Ka walked over. "Hey, man, don't take it to heart."

The muscles of Heishi's body were all tense, but at A-Ka's voice, they slowly relaxed. Despite that, he shot A-Ka a cold glare.

"Where are *you* planning on going?" Heishi asked.

"I don't know." A-Ka smiled. "At least we've escaped, haven't we? The world is so big, there will always be somewhere to go. Plus, I've saved your life twice now, so why don't we travel together?"

"I don't owe my life to anyone."

A-Ka persevered. "But I saved you two times."

What he didn't expect was for Heishi to snap his hand out and cup A-Ka's head with his palm. Confused, A-Ka didn't move.

Heishi said mildly, "One time." He pulled his hand away, then brought it back again. "Twice. Now I've saved you twice."

With that, he walked away.

"What does that even mean?!" A-Ka called after him.

From a distance, Heishi turned back. "I could have killed you just now!"

A-Ka threw up his hands.

Three hours later, A-Ka had managed to finally disassemble one of the mecha. Heishi was still nearby, drifting aimless as a cloud. He didn't come to assist, but neither did he wander too far.

"Can't you come over and help me out?" A-Ka yelled.

"Say 'please.'"

"Ugh! *Please.*"

Lifting a hand, Heishi casually tugged off the entire arm of the mecha and threw it on the ground.

A-Ka sized up Heishi. *This guy has so much strength. But he's not a clone, and he isn't a robot either...*

The blood of the clones was not red, and robots didn't even bleed.

This time, Heishi didn't keep going. Instead, he stood to one side and watched A-Ka pick through the scraps, not asking anything else or even speaking. However, he did react when A-Ka put together a laser gun and handed it to him.

"Keep this on you for protection," A-Ka said.

Heishi looked at that laser gun for a while before taking it and mimicking the clones as he clipped it to his waist.

"After we leave this place, we need to pass through the region around the City of Steel as we head west," A-Ka said to Heishi. "Getting to another mainland is how we'll survive."

"When will we leave?" Heishi asked a little impatiently.

"We need to make the proper preparations, or we'll die on the journey."

"You'll die, but I won't."

"Fine! In that case, why don't you just go on your own?"

Heishi sniffed haughtily through his nose before he suddenly asked, "Did they die?"

"Who?"

Then, A-Ka realized the current condition the City of Steel was in. Father's fate was not one he could easily determine, but from the knowledge he had amassed over the years, that being was all-powerful. The Central Computer that rose from the ground was only one portion of Father, and its even more colossal mechanical body lay buried under the earth. A-Ka really couldn't say for sure, so he could only explain what he knew in vague terms to Heishi.

A-Ka also remembered the chip that that old professor had given him, and he pulled it out and studied it carefully for a while. Of course, neither of them could see anything special about it, and Heishi had absolutely no interest in this chip, so A-Ka just stowed it away again.

Night fell, and in the shelter of the robotic debris, they turned on the nuclear stove, huddling by it to stay warm. Heishi returned to the riverbank and used the laser gun to shoot a few odd-shaped fish. Due to spending their lives in wastewater, the bodies of the fish contained a large amount of heavy metals. A-Ka only ate a little, and he didn't let Heishi eat too much either, to prevent either of them from being poisoned. Afterward, they ducked inside of a broken robotic shell to sleep.

In the middle of the night, a heavy snow began to fall on the plains. The north wind gusted over the desolate landscape. A-Ka was so cold that he couldn't stop shivering. He didn't know where Heishi had gone. Shrinking into the robotic shell a little more, A-Ka tried his best to hide in a spot sheltered from the wind. He was so cold he couldn't bear it, feeling like he was almost nothing but a piece of ice.

Just as he had frozen almost to the point of hallucinating, a warm body pressed against his spine.

"Where did you go...?" A-Ka asked, voice garbled by his stiff tongue.

"It has nothing to do with you," Heishi responded curtly.

A-Ka was so cold that his teeth chattered, and he had no way to deal with it otherwise, so he turned around and pressed into Heishi's embrace. Heishi's chest felt as hot as a nuclear furnace, and after a long time, A-Ka grew warm enough to fall asleep.

The next day, A-Ka was woken by the cold, alone. When the sun hung directly overhead in the sky, Heishi came back. Climbing out of the pile of robotic debris, A-Ka shivered as he found Heishi dragging a clone corpse by the leg back to camp.

He tossed it in front of A-Ka. "Eat."

"Don't joke around! How can we eat people?"

"He's not the same kind as you."

A-Ka knew that, compared to humans, clones were basically just a collection of proteins, and a dead clone even more so. Nonetheless, as he stared at that clone's face, frozen to a greenish purple, he found there was no way he could eat a living creature whose shape and features resembled a human's.

"I... I won't eat that," he said.

"Then I'll eat it myself," Heishi said.

Hysterically, A-Ka cried out, "If you eat this clone, don't talk to me ever again!"

Heishi rolled his eyes. "Why do you have to be so troublesome?"

A-Ka huffed. "Either way, you aren't allowed to eat clones." He simply could not accept the sight of Heishi standing in front of him, sawing off a humanlike leg before roasting and eating it.

Heishi hesitated for a moment, but finally he let go of that clone's body and went in search of other food.

They were not the only beings that had ended up on the plains, but all the clones inside the scattered mechas had died. At one point, Heishi pulled an arm off a mecha and swung it around experimentally, like it was a sword. Unfortunately, it was a little too bulky to use as a weapon.

"Don't take too many things with you," A-Ka said. "But... What, do you like heavy weapons?"

Heishi didn't speak.

A-Ka was torn between embarrassment and laughter, but he helped Heishi peel off a long strip of metal from a mecha and weld on a handle. Heishi tested it, and when he swung it, the wind whistled around it. Afterward, he slung it on his back like a broadsword.

"Let's go."

A-Ka organized his own hastily gathered satchel. Inside it was a compass, a box of healing supplies that the clones used, a few stimulant injections, a portable energy stove, a wrench, an assortment of screwdrivers, other tools for fixing broken electromagnetic equipment, and a set of magnetic field generators.

Heishi glanced at him indifferently. "What did you bring all this for? You can't even carry them."

Sure, A-Ka had brought so many things that carrying the pack was a little taxing, but he persisted. "The repair tools of a technician are like a soldier's gun. They'll be of use in the future."

On the flat plains, the large flakes of snow that fell were so white they hurt the eyes. Heishi put on a pair of sunglasses that he had gotten off the clone's body, then he and A-Ka stepped out into a new, unknown world.

# THE SPINE OF THE WORLD

A-KA AND HEISHI had spent six days walking in the snow. Their surroundings were devoid of human habitation. They passed through a small grove of trees before coming out of it and entering a huge mountain range.

A-Ka's satchel was now being carried by Heishi, but even with his help, A-Ka was still a little short of breath, and their daily travels wore him down. When they came to a fissure in the mountain range, he was almost tempted to lie upon Heishi's back and have Heishi carry him as they clambered over the mountains.

"This is the ridgeline of the Astrolabe," A-Ka said. "Jingchuan."

As usual, Heishi listened with a chilly expression. As they sat before the fire, A-Ka finished eating the wild fox that they had caught. The meat was foul and smelly, and there was no salt, so he had to fight to keep it down.

"The Astrolabe is our world," A-Ka explained to Heishi. "It's a huge instrument, with seventeen smaller astrolabes revolving around it. Every landmass is its own separate island. They're like gears in a machine, all nestled together."

Heishi grunted absentmindedly, before asking, "Are you done resting?"

"No," A-Ka said, sounding a little helpless. "I know I've slowed you down. Very sorry for that."

This sentiment of A-Ka's was sincere. Heishi was almost too sturdy: He didn't dread the cold, his strength was extraordinary, and he could walk a whole day without resting. Of course, to make up for that, he also ate a lot. After all, he was a human from three thousand years ago, and back then human genetics had been at its peak; hence, it was known as the Golden Age. He was unlike A-Ka and the rest of the humans of the Black Iron Age, struggling under the control of the machines with their fragile constitutions.

During their time together, A-Ka had been observing Heishi, trying to figure out exactly what he was. Finally, one direct piece of evidence convinced A-Ka that Heishi was indeed human: excretion. Heishi sweated and sometimes wanted to bathe. The way he bathed was to take off his clothes, stand naked in the snow, and use it to cleanse his body.

Besides that, any human would need to eat, and they would produce excreta then. He'd been convinced Heishi must do that too, although he avoided A-Ka when doing so for a while. That kind of shame seemed to be innate.

Eventually, A-Ka got his proof. He'd been watching Heishi from afar. Heishi had just finished wiping down his body, and after his bath, he knelt in the snow, unmoving. Under the shining sunlight, his bronzed skin made him look like a perfect statue of an ancient male god. A-Ka had only seen people squatting or sitting to urinate; this was the first time he had seen someone kneel to do the deed.

After he left, A-Ka went over to go take a look, but Heishi caught A-Ka by the collar and tossed him into the snow. Even A-Ka realized he was being a pervert at that point, so he had to admit defeat and flee.

*Aside from Heishi's not-so-great temper and his frequent tendency toward violence, he's a good companion overall,* A-Ka thought.

"Have you seen humans from the Bronze Age?" A-Ka asked.

Heishi raised an eyebrow. A-Ka realized that he might have made Heishi mad, so he stuttered out an explanation. "I-I didn't want to pry about your past. I was just curious."

"No," Heishi responded. "I don't know what that is."

"The Golden, Silver, Bronze, and Iron Ages. I'm a human from the fourth one. It was said that before the Golden Age, there was an even more ancient, original mankind."

Heishi listened silently. Over these past few days, A-Ka would tell him about some things every now and then, and though Heishi had looked as if he wasn't paying attention, A-Ka knew that he had probably taken it all in.

"The original humans created everything on this mainland," A-Ka said, "including the cloning techniques, computers, and artificial intelligence. Over fourteen thousand years, their bodies evolved to become stronger and stronger."

"And the generations afterward called them the Golden Age of humankind?" Heishi asked.

A-Ka nodded. "That was the most splendid age of man. I don't know if there are any more humans from the Golden Age like you. Maybe there are more in the mythical land or the Curran People's Confederation."

"If there are, so what?"

"Don't you think they could figure out something about your mission?" He picked up a tree branch and drew a map on the ground. "After we pass through Jingchuan, we'll cross the mountain range from this patch of highland here and arrive at the Aijia Strait. From there, we might be able to wait for a ship that's going toward Curran."

"Or we might be captured by the robots and shot full of as many holes as a wasp nest. This is the sixth time you've told me about your plans."

A-Ka shrugged, defeated.

Suddenly, Heishi's expression changed a fraction, as if he had heard something. "Stay here," Heishi commanded before he picked up his makeshift greatsword and slid down the slope, sending up a flurry of snow in his wake.

The sounds grew clearer, until even A-Ka could hear them. That was the roar of airship engines and the sound of machine guns firing, along with the shrill screams of women and the lower, confused cries of men.

The robots had chased them down! A-Ka fell into a panic. He followed the small path until, within the snow-covered valley, he saw a group of humans sprinting for their lives and trying to hide as two robotic patrols hovering in midair pursued them, bullets flying as they chased their quarry.

Up on the cliffs, a human figure leaped from ridge to ridge. It was Heishi. He spread his arms, his oversized sword in one hand, before he jumped down headfirst from on high.

"Be careful!" A-Ka roared.

Heishi didn't say a single word in response as he landed on one of the robotic patrols. The hovering killing machine turned, and the bullet hail changed targets. A-Ka decisively flipped his bag over, dumping out its contents with a thump, and even while he lifted his head, his hands never stopped moving as he assembled the magnetic field generator.

The fleeing humans rushed up the slope of the mountain. Heishi pressed down on one of the robotic patrollers, as if he was controlling a particularly wild bird of prey, and the machine collided with the mountain. The second robotic patroller turned and flew toward Heishi, opening its gunports, taking aim at him, and preparing to fire.

With a click, A-Ka put the last screw of the magnetic field generator's external cover in place. After knotting a rope around it, he quickly picked up the other end of the rope and began to spin it in rapid circles—then let it fly up and away.

With a whoosh, the electronic box flashing with the gray-gold of metal flew up high before it detected a metallic object nearby and was pulled toward the other robotic patroller. Clinking quietly, it stuck to the body of the robot. A humming sound started as the blue light of the magnetic field shone. Heishi turned and pushed off the patroller, hopping toward the steep slope, as the second robotic patroller's antigravity engine was neutralized and it slammed into the cliff with an earth-shaking boom. One part of the mountain range collapsed—the impact had caused an avalanche.

"Run, quick!" A-Ka shouted.

Collapsing snow swept Heishi down the mountain. The humans rushed toward the high ground, and the two robotic patrollers sizzled with electricity before exploding, which started another chain reaction. Under the snow that covered the ground, the mountains stood tall, reflecting the bright sunlight.

Eventually, the sky-splitting booms faded away, and the world regained its stillness.

"Ack, ack, bleh!"

A-Ka struggled halfway out of the snow with great difficulty. Heishi hurried over to him, used one hand to lift him the rest of his way by the shirt, and dragged him out of the snow field.

One by one, the other humans clambered out of the snow. They had barely survived, and each of them was still in a state of shock.

A-Ka nodded at them. He counted seven of them: two women, four men, and one small girl. Everyone sat under the sunlight in the snow field, all of them exhausted beyond belief.

"When did you guys escape?" a woman asked A-Ka.

"Seven days ago," A-Ka said. "I'm called A-Ka. He's Heishi."

"Thank you," one man said. "Those two chased us the entire way here."

Heishi replied coldly, "I was only protecting myself."

A-Ka smiled awkwardly at Heishi's behavior. "Don't put it like that. Everyone here is human, and since we're all humans, we should help each other out."

The gathered people began to smile as well, but Heishi walked away. In the distance, a few more men were digging in the snow.

"Friend! Come help us!" one of them shouted. "There's still a guy here. Let's get him out!"

A-Ka went over and bent to look, but after helping them pull the person out, he froze—it was a clone, his face covered with chips of ice. As he staggered to his feet, the human standing next to him punched him square in the face.

"You lied to us!" that man said angrily.

"Hey, wait. If you have something to say, say it nicely!" A-Ka was startled to see the clone fall back to the ground.

The men surrounded them. One person holding a gun pressed it to the clone's head. "Why did you send a signal to the robotic soldiers?"

"I didn't!"

"You were contacting the soldiers," the leader of the men accused. "You wanted them to capture us!"

"I only wanted to listen to the news from headquarters," the clone protested.

A-Ka jumped in. "Wait, please. Let him speak first."

"This has nothing to do with you, bro." The leader blocked A-Ka with his arm, trying to push him away.

Shuffling slowly, A-Ka backed up. Heishi had been standing off to one side, studying the small girl who was traveling with the group, but he suddenly and keenly felt the tension in the air. Turning, he walked toward A-Ka and the others.

"What's going on?" Heishi asked icily.

Everyone looked at him before their gazes traveled down to the broadsword in his hand. No one dared to speak.

Finally, the leader introduced himself. "I'm Tapp."

Heishi nodded. A-Ka gestured for them to release the clone, and Heishi asked the assembled group, "What crime did he commit?"

"On our way here, we kindly took him in, but he dared to send a secret signal to that robotic patrol squad as he traveled with our group," Tapp explained.

"I didn't!" the clone said. "I helped them escape from the City of Steel and only had good intentions. I just wanted to listen to the news from headquarters along the way. Even if we ignore that they destroyed my transceiver, they were the ones who forgot their debt to me and tried to kill me! You ungrateful humans…"

In that moment of heightened emotions, that clone clearly wanted to fight Tapp, but the group of men stopped him.

"What did he use to contact the patrol squad?" A-Ka asked Tapp.

Tapp turned and made a gesture, and another person brought out an electric signal transceiver.

A-Ka took a look. "Hmm. This device can only receive signals. It can't transmit messages. He didn't lie to you."

"But he still drew the robotic patrollers to us," one of the men insisted stubbornly. "He was receiving a message when his signal was tracked."

"It can't send messages, which means that the robotic patrollers can't figure out where the signal came from, so he couldn't have been the one to draw the patrollers down on you," A-Ka reiterated.

The clone glared at them, and everyone else shifted uncomfortably.

After a short silence, Tapp said, "Bringing him along is too dangerous. Let's kill him."

"*You!*" The clone could hardly believe it.

"Wait!" A-Ka interjected. "Why do you need to kill him?!"

"The clones aren't on the same side as us. Who knows what tricks they're up to?"

"You can't just *kill* him!" A-Ka looked toward Heishi, but Heishi was ignoring them. Still, Tapp and his group seemed to be a little fearful of him and Heishi. A-Ka pressed on. "Hand him over to me. I have questions to ask him."

A-Ka held out a hand, and the clone grabbed it, using it to pull himself to his feet. With the clone in tow and Heishi alongside him, A-Ka walked away.

"Wait!" Tapp shouted from behind them.

A-Ka turned back. "What else do you have to say?"

Tapp sized up the three of them, almost as if he were estimating Heishi and A-Ka's fighting capabilities. Finally, he gave up on whatever he was imagining and just said, "You'd best be careful of that guy."

"Thank you for the reminder," A-Ka responded.

Night fell, and A-Ka, Heishi, and the clone sat in a cave, where they had started a fire. The rest of the humans had chosen to stay within the valley to rest, lying down in an area sheltered from the wind.

"General Liber has died," the clone said. "The revolution failed, and Father is currently rebuilding the City of Steel. It has also sent out robotic patrollers to track down the humans and my clone brothers that escaped."

This piece of news was about as bad as it could get.

"What other word is there from headquarters?" A-Ka asked.

"You seem to be well-informed on our movements," the clone said. "There were no more than ten humans involved in the Patricide Plan, so how did you learn about it?"

"Um, we got mixed up in it by chance. So, have they all been defeated?"

"Not yet." The clone shot a glance at Heishi. "Headquarters had the rest of the wounded troops escape past the Aijia Strait to Andoria to form an alliance with the humans of Curran before we think of a counterattack plan."

A-Ka thought about that for a moment before nodding.

"Have all the people in the City of Steel died?" Heishi asked.

The clone sighed. "Well, our loss can't be counted as a total defeat. For now, Father will need at least ten years to repair itself. Our main body of troops bought us quite a bit of time in the end."

"And what is Andoria?"

"The country of clones. Our clone ancestors, those who gave us our forms, lived there. We clones trace our heritage back to our four progenitors, but one of them was involved in a scheme many years ago. After the plan failed, he was captured by Father. It was he who stayed in the City of Steel, fomented rebellion in the hearts of all of the clones there, and started this war."

A-Ka sucked in a breath. The clone's words had revealed a very important piece of information: They were still in danger, at least for now.

The clone repeatedly toyed with a small mechanical device. "I can't connect with headquarters. Those idiotic humans broke the transceiver." After saying this, he realized that A-Ka and Heishi were also humans. "Sorry, I didn't mean you."

A-Ka nodded. "By the way, why don't you have a serial number?"

"As soon as the revolution began, all clones stopped acknowledging the serial numbers that the robotic government gave us. We gave ourselves unique names," the clone said. "Mine is Feiluo."

"I'm A-Ka."

"Heishi."

Now that Feiluo had joined them, A-Ka didn't have to deal with the slab of rock that was Heishi on his own every day. When they set off the next morning, the other group of humans came over to check in with them, asking if A-Ka would join them. Thus, A-Ka's small three-man group was absorbed into this camp of human refugees. Crossing mountains and fording rivers together, they headed to the Aijia Strait, hoping to travel across the ocean to a new mainland.

Of all the clones that A-Ka had interacted with, Feiluo was one of the better-tempered ones. He was extremely polite to Heishi, and Heishi didn't treat him like he treated A-Ka.

"Thank you for saving me," Feiluo said without warning one day while they were on the road.

"You're welcome." A-Ka still held a certain amount of goodwill toward clones as a whole. After all, when he and Heishi escaped from their confinement, it was the clones who had saved them. If they hadn't allied with them then, they would definitely have died within the City of Steel.

"In the end, I've found we must still depend on humans to change this world."

A-Ka half mumbled, "Humans, huh?"

The revolution of the clones had actually begun because of a human. A-Ka had not expected this, but after thinking about it carefully, it seemed within reason.

Humans had a wealth of emotions and complex ideas, which was something that the steel beings were unable to achieve. But due to their emotions and their ideas holding each other in check, they hindered one another, oppressing the rest of their own kind. When the Creator gave humans their brilliance, many flaws were also mercilessly bestowed upon them. The entire world had changed because of humans, for the Creator had pinned the compass of creation's fulcrum on humans and sent the other point out into the vast, chaotic, and unknown universe.

Humans differed from each other in a thousand tiny ways, and each person that walked this world was a unique being. At the heart of it, even the clones were chasing after this individual identity. Take Feiluo, for example: He had given himself a name, turned his jacket inside out, and stuck a piece of straw on his hat to indicate his difference from other clones.

"I once heard an older clone brother say that this is the awakening of my 'self,'" Feiluo said to A-Ka. "Every one of you humans has their own concept of self, but we don't. We must first awaken our own sense of self before the revolution can truly begin."

"So, right now, what is your understanding of yourself?" A-Ka asked him curiously.

Feiluo shook his head. "It's hard to say, but at least there is one thing that is clear—I am not the same as I once was."

Instinctively, A-Ka felt that this topic was deep and hard to comprehend. Every person had their own identity. They were all individuals, from the oldest adult to the youngest child… He looked toward the train of humans and saw that inquisitive young girl following Heishi, asking him a bunch of questions. Every now and then, Heishi would nod or shake his head, but most of the time he remained silent, simply observing this small child.

"Children are very mysterious living creatures," Feiluo continued. "For clones, as soon as we are born, we are already equipped with an adult's form. We do not experience any sort of childhood. The childhood of a human's life must be very happy."

"Honestly, I can't remember my own childhood well, and the feelings I *can* recall weren't very happy," A-Ka said.

Heishi carried the small girl piggyback as he walked. Staying by Heishi's side, A-Ka gently kidded with her.

"And what's your name, little one?" he asked.

"Ann," she responded timidly.

A-Ka smiled. "Ann, keep your chin up. We will find hope."

She nodded.

The sun rose and set.

This was an almost endless stretch of road, as traveling through the snowy mountains was very difficult. They couldn't find food, which caused everyone despair and frustration. Only A-Ka persisted, using his magnetic field generator to set down a magnetic trap. Sometimes he caught one or two birds that fell into the trap, and even a roe deer once. He always handed the food to the girl and the women to eat.

At first, Heishi found this bizarre, but he gradually got used to A-Ka's ways.

Just when everyone was on the brink of collapse, Feiluo led them out of the snowy region into an expansive plain. If they kept going forward, they would reach the shoreline of the inland sea on the western side of the continent.

They had spent almost half a year on this journey. Now, as everyone exhausted the last of their energy, they finally saw the first light of day. The whole group's clothes were in tatters, especially Heishi's; on the journey here, he had been in the lead every time they broke a path through the brambles. Now, Heishi simply went around with his torso bare, tying his shirt, which was just a few strips of cloth, around his waist.

At one point, in order to save Ann, Feiluo had been bitten by a venomous snake. Fortunately, because he was a clone, he wasn't affected by venom.

A-Ka was also completely bedraggled, his clothes torn beyond repair. The cloth straps of his satchel had also broken. He'd had no choice but to borrow two strips of cloth from Heishi and tie them together around his body.

Two people had died of sickness on the journey. A-Ka couldn't save them; all he could do was bring the survivors here. The most troubling thing was that one of the people who had died from hardship had been Ann's mother. Ann joined A-Ka's little squad after that. Throughout the rest of their journey, Ann kept asking where her mother had gone, and Feiluo answered that her mother had gone ahead to scout out the road. Despite her mother's absence, Ann didn't cry or make a fuss.

This was a very spacious area, and the oldest place on the Astrolabe. It lay at the Astrolabe's very center, bridging the distance between the snowy mountains and the primordial forests below, separating the Country of Machines from the western shore. This region was called the Primeval Heart. Historically, this place had been called the

Creator's laboratory because many different kinds of species lived on these plains. In the prehistoric era, T. rexes had run rampant in the area. Even the mechanical troops couldn't survive here.

Establishing supply lines would take too long and be too difficult an undertaking. So, when the humans escaped from the City of Steel after the revolution many years ago and arrived at the edge of the western shoreline, they could only cobble together this base of operations for the Rebel Alliance.

However, everything here was temporary. Everyone knew that sooner or later Father's patrols would arrive and occupy the entire western shoreline. Only by leaving the landmass and drifting across the seas toward the countries on the far side would they survive.

The humans living near the Primeval Heart were constantly wary of ambushes from both the wild animals living on the plains as well as the mechanical troops from the even more distant Eastern Continent. Every day here was gut-wrenching, spent in a state of constant, unending anxiety.

In the Ant Nest, A-Ka had heard legends surrounding this place. Back then, he had thought it would be nice if he could make his way here one day. After all he'd been through, he realized how laughable his original idea of driving K across the great ocean to seek out the famous mythical land had been.

"After crossing the border here, we'll see Martha Town," Feiluo said.

Their ragtag group, covered in the dust of the road, stood on a slope on the plains and looked downward. No one spoke for a long time.

From border to border, on the open plains that spanned hundreds of miles as far as the eye could see, every inch of space was packed with humans. These people sat or lay down or congregated in front of the wire netted fence, waiting for Martha Town to let them in. The wire fence stood like a border between countries, at the edge of their last hope, mercilessly refusing anyone's approach.

A-Ka had never expected that there would be this many people. At a glance, there had to be tens of thousands gathered here.

Quite a few humans must have escaped from the prison that was the City of Steel since the revolution. They each took their own paths, spreading out across all corners of the mainland. A-Ka had thought that his group, which had directly crossed the high-altitude plains, was near the front of the pack. He'd certainly never expected that there would be this many ahead of them who had no lodgings and no place to rest.

The humans crowded in front of the wire netting, shouting loudly. "Let us in!"

Behind them was a uniformed group of resistance fighters in battle gear, holding weapons as they watched over the refugee groups on the plain.

A-Ka stood at a distance, his face filled with confusion. "What should we do?"

Heishi shrugged, looking wholly unconcerned as his gaze swept over that plain.

"Don't worry," Feiluo said. "I'll try to negotiate."

The sun would set soon. The winter days were short, the nights were long, and the winds were bitingly cold. Feiluo led Ann, A-Ka, and the rest through the crowd to the front of the wire fence.

Behind it, a rebel soldier immediately pointed his gun at them, asking warily, "Who are you?"

A bright light shone overhead, landing on the faces of those present. Feiluo swept aside his dirty bangs with a finger, revealing his forehead and his indigo-blue eyes. "One of your own," he said, "from the 7th Troop."

"The 7th Troop was dissolved!" the other said. "The brothers in the City of Steel all died!"

Feiluo fell silent. From every direction, quite a few armed troopers came over, lifted up their helmets, and revealed their own indigo-blue eyes. They were all clones.

"Are there humans here?" A-Ka asked. "I have a few things I want to say. We *all* escaped from the city."

"Everyone here is a refugee from the City of Steel," one of the clone soldiers answered. "You're not special. Go wait outside." He then pointed at Feiluo with the mouth of his gun. "You, you're one of us. You can come in."

"Wait for me here, just for a bit," Feiluo said to A-Ka and Heishi. "Ann, let's go. We're up first."

The small door in the wire fence opened a crack, and Feiluo had Ann go first. Ann was a little afraid, turning her head back to look at them.

Heishi, in a rare departure from his usual stone-cold demeanor, spoke words of comfort. "Go. You will be safe."

This series of events roused the displeasure of many around them, and the crowd began to shout. Feiluo squeezed through to the other side of the wire fence and nodded to A-Ka, indicating for him to remain calm, before he took Ann with him as they disappeared into the darkness of the night. The people behind A-Ka crowded him until he could hardly breathe, and he turned in hopes of finding an empty space to sit down in, but he couldn't even take a step forward. Finally, Heishi grabbed his collar and dragged him out of the crowd.

The rest of the group found an empty spot and watched the xenon lamps high above the wire fence turn the night into daytime with their light. Tapp and the rest were still nearby.

"That clone definitely won't let us in," Tapp said disdainfully.

"I trust that he will."

In his heart, A-Ka had another thought, but he didn't say it. He felt that Feiluo would save him and Heishi, but he might not save these temporary human companions. After all, Tapp and the rest of his group had tried to kill Feiluo.

The calls of animals echoed in the distance. Under the cover of darkness, the depths of the plains seemed to hide countless dangers that were unknown to the humans.

The long night deepened, and the sky shone with a brilliant starry river as the plains sank into a heavy sleep.

Startling awake from his dreams, A-Ka looked around. It was still nighttime.

"Come with me," a clone said in a low voice. "Don't disturb the others."

"Where's Heishi?" A-Ka asked.

"Who?"

"Heishi?" A-Ka saw that Heishi wasn't by his side. This was the first time that Heishi had left him since they left the City of Steel behind them, and A-Ka grew anxious as he shouted again, "Heishi!"

"Shh!" The clone shoved a hand over A-Ka's mouth. "Don't disturb the others. Come with me."

"But my friend..."

"We have orders from Lieutenant Colonel Feiluo himself! If you have anything to say, then wait until you see Feiluo to tell him."

A-Ka stopped struggling. Still dazed, he was brought in front of the wire fence. A crack opened within the fence to let him pass, and the clone nodded toward the guard. "That's him."

The clone brought A-Ka to a warehouse, and A-Ka couldn't help feeling wary. The clone then said, "Soon enough, Feiluo will be waiting outside for you. Go in."

A-Ka gritted his teeth and went into the warehouse, only to find that it had been remodeled into a bathroom. At this point, his head cleared, and he understood that they were letting him wash up. After his long journey, his body was itchy to the point of extreme discomfort and caked in mud. He could finally take a good shower.

A-Ka turned on the hot water, and with its rush, the inside of the bathroom filled with steam. As the hot water rained over his skin, A-Ka felt a sense of relief from head to toe.

In the foggy bathroom, he suddenly saw a silhouette. His voice rose hopefully. "Heishi?"

Heishi stood to one side, untied his own clothes, and began to wash up as well. Turning his head, he stared at A-Ka. His gaze made A-Ka feel extremely awkward, so he shifted to one side to let Heishi pass. A-Ka had seen Heishi's body many times by now, so it was no longer strange to him, but this was the first time his own body was undergoing Heishi's scrutiny.

A-Ka's hair was drenched, and water dripped down his face as he smiled at Heishi. "It's great to see you. Here I thought you might be gone…"

Heishi faced A-Ka, looking at him without saying anything, until he finally opened his mouth. "Thank you for looking after me on this journey."

When A-Ka heard this, he felt it was a little out of the blue, but his smile grew. "It was you who protected me, you know."

Then, Heishi reached out a hand and pulled A-Ka into his embrace.

A-Ka's heart began to pound violently. In the foggy vapor of the bathroom, he pressed against Heishi's naked, muscular chest, feeling the powerful beat of his heart inside his fiery hot abdomen.

A-Ka felt a sense of foreboding. "You…?"

Heishi only hugged him for a short period before letting him go and cupping A-Ka's jaw with one hand. He peered into his eyes.

"Thank you." Heishi's eyes were set deep in his face, like black obsidian that had been hidden underneath the surface of the earth for millennia, shining with a mesmerizing brilliance. "Take care of yourself in the future."

"Heishi?"

Heishi wiped away the water on his face, turned away to dry himself, put on his clothes, and left.

"Heishi!" A-Ka threw on his clothes to chase after him, but Heishi had already put on the clones' uniform and walked away. In that instant, A-Ka sensed the worsening rumblings of something wrong.

"Wait!" He raced after Heishi, heading toward a crowded area where Feiluo stood.

"Quick! The ship is boarding!" Feiluo was waiting at the other end of the pier. At its front, many people were lining up. The surroundings were silent and peaceful, but blinding white lights shone on the dock. Many people turned their heads to look at Heishi and Feiluo. In the silence of the night, their discussion was very obvious to those around them.

"You've finished saying your goodbyes to A-Ka?" Feiluo asked.

Heishi nodded, and the tacit agreement between the two of them immediately confirmed many of A-Ka's guesses.

"You're staying?" A-Ka asked Heishi.

"He still has things to do, so he's having me send you off first," Feiluo said. "Just come here and be quiet, okay?"

"But what is he even going to do?" A-Ka said in disbelief.

Feiluo wore a complex expression but didn't respond. Instead, he led A-Ka through the crowd.

A-Ka tried, "Because there's only space for one of us, he willingly chose...?"

"No! It's not like that!" Feiluo hurried to respond. "A-Ka, don't ask any more. Just trust me, Heishi is only—"

"I saved him from the sea. How can I leave him behind now? I'll go together with him or I won't go!" No matter what Feiluo said, A-Ka couldn't stop worrying.

As they were talking, Heishi finally couldn't stay quiet. "Why do you care about me so much?"

A-Ka sighed before his temper spiked. He'd been a little moved by the look on Heishi's face, but as soon as he heard these words, his desire to care evaporated.

"Hmph! None of your business," A-Ka sneered. "Whatever. Up to you. If you want to stay, then stay."

Feiluo smiled in the background as Heishi said to A-Ka, "I have a few things I need to handle. If fate wills it, we will meet again."

A-Ka's heart once again rose in his throat as he looked at Heishi, trying to figure out from his expression if he was lying. From afar, the ferry let out a whistle, breaking through the awkward silence hovering between the three of them.

"It's time to get on the ship," Feiluo said. "Come, Percy!"

Feiluo led a small boy over. In the darkness of the night, A-Ka couldn't see the child's face clearly; A-Ka could only tell that the boy was a little smaller than him.

"This is Percy. Percy, this is A-Ka." Feiluo introduced them to each other first, then continued, "A-Ka, I'm leaving Percy in your care. After you reach Phoenix City, please bring him to the human orphanage."

A-Ka felt this was a strange turn of events, but since Feiluo had entrusted Percy to him, he took the boy's hand in his own.

"Quickly," Feiluo said.

They boarded the ship from a small side passage. Looking out from the side, A-Ka saw that Heishi was still standing alone under the pier's spotlights.

"Will we never see each other again?" A-Ka asked suddenly.

Heishi lifted his head, gave A-Ka a look, then turned and left.

*This guy...*

A-Ka's heart was filled with all kinds of emotions, but he didn't know what he should say. After a short silence, he pulled a chip from his shirt pocket. That was the chip that the old doctor imprisoned underground had given A-Ka when they escaped from the City of Steel. He had demanded that A-Ka bring this chip to the rebel camp and hand it to General Liber.

But the revolution had failed, and right now A-Ka had no idea who to hand this chip over to. Maybe the chip itself could serve as a reminder for Heishi, or perhaps he could decode the contents of the chip and deliver them to the right person.

"Help me pass this to Heishi," A-Ka said. "As a memento."

Feiluo took it and stored it securely before saying to A-Ka, "Take care of yourself."

A-Ka tugged on Percy's hand as they were brought to the lower levels of the ship. Inside, many humans who had escaped were all crammed together.

After Feiluo showed them a space behind a pile of boxes, he had them sit down, and with one knee on the ground, he said to Percy, "Percy, Dad is leaving."

A-Ka's eyes went wide with shock, and he didn't dare to speak. Was he actually sending his own child to an orphanage?!

Percy reached out a hand and hugged Feiluo's neck, clearly already missing him. After a long time, Feiluo let out a sigh and shifted Percy's hands aside before telling him, "Listen to A-Ka-gege. When things are finished here, Dad will come to Phoenix City to find you."

After A-Ka heard this, he relaxed. "Heishi will also come then, right?"

"He will," Feiluo assured him. "May the winds be in your favor."

Feiluo left the hold of the ship, his footsteps gradually receding into the distance.

Loaded with its cargo of human immigrants, the large ship set off, leaving the Central Mainland behind as it headed toward unknown islands over the seas.

The moon shone down on them. A-Ka was still worried about Heishi. Since the day he had appeared, he had seemed as if he was carrying some secret that was unknown to anyone.

The only sound outside the ship was the sound of waves lapping against it, and the quiet, peaceful moonlight scattered across the endless waves, shining over A-Ka and the lonely Percy. Everyone around them was already deep in slumber, and it was then that Percy gently wrapped his hand around A-Ka's and tugged at it.

"Is Heishi your good friend?" Percy asked quietly.

"A comrade in arms. We fought guarding each other's backs, and we escaped from the City of Steel together."

Percy nodded. His hands reached into his own bag slung at his side.

"Let me do it," A-Ka offered. "What are you looking for?"

A-Ka helped Percy dig through his messenger bag, pulling out a small dagger, a piece of chocolate, a portable water filtration device, and a transmitter, inside of which was a picture of Percy and Feiluo: the two of them standing shoulder to shoulder under the sunlight, against the backdrop of a desolate landscape.

# THE PRIMEVAL HEART

PERCY PICKED OUT A PIECE of chocolate before feeling around for A-Ka's hand and placing the chocolate in the center of his palm.

"This is for you," Percy said to A-Ka. "Feiluo gave it to me. It's very tasty."

It was with this that A-Ka finally realized something: Percy was blind.

"Are you Feiluo's son?" A-Ka asked.

"Adopted child. My birth father and mother both died, so Feiluo adopted me."

"Have you been with him for very long?" A-Ka asked.

"Two years," Percy said. "Thank you for saving my dad. When I heard headquarters announce that the revolution failed, I thought that he'd died. I never expected that he would still be alive. When he came back, I was so happy I couldn't speak. I don't know how I could repay you. Thank you, A-Ka. I..." He paused. "When I first boarded the boat, I wanted to say something, but I thought, since you and your friend separated, you wouldn't be in a good mood..."

A-Ka could never have imagined that his own careless actions had given this orphan boy, living among the clone army, a ray of sunshine and hope in his dark existence. "You're welcome." He began to smile as he pulled Percy into his arms. In that moment, he could almost sense the limitless hope and joy overflowing from Percy's heart, and this intense surge of warm emotion influenced his own mood, leading him out of his inner turmoil.

The moonlight turned peaceful and serene, and the two youths in the cabin snuggled up against each other. Tired, A-Ka closed his eyes and fell asleep.

On January 15, a typhoon swept over Martha Town. The seawater swirled toward the land, and all the humans waiting for aid on the plains scattered toward the mountains. When the typhoon passed, no one knew how many refugees had died from lack of food, drinking water, and medical aid.

Within the darkness of the storm, a group of people were walking single file along a muddy mountain path. Heishi wore a hooded windbreaker as he stood at the head of the squad. He was on the summit of the mountain. Off in the distance, the sea was vast, with no far shore in sight, and only lightning strikes slashed across the sky, building fragile bridges between the heavens and the earth.

"Heishi!" Feiluo shouted.

Heishi leaped down, rejoining Feiluo and his line of people as they moved forward one step at a time. Feiluo said into his ear, "There won't be any problems."

Heishi shook his head. His lips moved a little, but the wind and the thunder drowned out all their voices. Feiluo sidled a little closer to repeat himself. "I said, they'll definitely arrive safely!"

"I'm not worried about the ship," Heishi replied. "I'm worried about what happens after those two arrive in the new mainland. That they won't be able to make a living."

"They'll be able to do it." Feiluo smiled. "My friends will take care of them. A-Ka and Percy will live a comfortable life."

Heishi nodded. In front, another clone officer turned back and said unhappily, "Lieutenant Colonel Feiluo! Are you sure this is the right place?"

Feiluo called loudly, "We'll be there soon. Hold out a little longer!"

The wild wind was so strong it seemed like it was trying to blow the squad off the cliff. Before them was the end of the path. Feiluo took a few steps back, roaring, "Open up your hang gliders!"

With this strong tempest, they would certainly be blown into the cliffside by the wind as soon as they opened their hang gliders, shattering all the bones in their bodies. But Feiluo led the way and leaped off, opening his glider with a whoosh. In that short instant, Heishi hesitated, until he also ducked down and dove into the darkness. The violent wind gusting by his ear paused for a beat, and the glider shook open. In the quiet night, he flew toward the distant other edge of the cliff.

They were in a dead wind zone.

Heishi opened his eyes, only to see that Feiluo had lit a fluorescent lamp on the other side of the gorge. A cavern was situated high up on the cliffside.

Five special forces troops protected Heishi as they flew toward the cavern. It wasn't until they landed solidly on the ground that Heishi breathed out. He folded up the hang glider.

This mountain cave led deep into the darkness. It seemed to have been left unused for many years, yet two guards were stationed outside. When they saw Feiluo, they saluted.

"We're here. This is the place," Feiluo told Heishi.

"The Primeval Heart." Heishi stood in front of a set of doors, lifting his head to look at the strange symbols over the doorway. The center of the doors contained a large chunk of a glowing gem.

"According to the investigations the rebel alliance carried out here," Feiluo said, "this is a historical relic from almost fifty thousand years ago. No ancient sites predate this one in the entirety of the Astrolabe mainland. Just three thousand years ago, this relic was activated for a short period of time. Our people tried to use explosives to open it, but the door's material..."

When he got to this point, everything grew quiet. Everyone saw what was strange—there was a small hole in the door that was no more than an inch in diameter. It glowed with light.

"Last time I came, this hole wasn't there, commander," a clone said.

"I... I don't know how it got there," one of the guards said. "When we were stationed here, the hole was already in the door."

Heishi asked, "When were you guys stationed here?"

"Three months ago."

"This isn't right," Feiluo murmured. "Who would punch through the main doors here? What is the purpose of making such a small opening?" Feiluo shot Heishi a look of disbelief.

"It was the mechanical life-forms." Heishi had guessed what Feiluo was thinking. "Before we arrived, robots must have already made it here."

"But that's impossible! With the troops standing guard, who could have used a laser to pierce through?" Feiluo said.

Heishi shook his head very slowly, signaling for Feiluo to stop talking. Taking a look at the guards standing to the sides, Feiluo understood what Heishi was getting at.

Heishi pressed his hand against the gem. The doors let out a loud rumble before they slowly began to open.

Feiluo stared.

All of the clone troops seemed to sense something in that instant, and they grew alert, pulling out their weapons as they stood to either side.

As the doors opened, a brilliant, eye-catching ray of light shot out. Floating in midair behind the doors was a humongous astrolabe, glowing with a gentle light.

"What is this place?" Feiluo mumbled.

"The Primeval Heart, the laboratory of the Creator." Heishi's voice echoed within the large hall. "There's no danger here. You can come in."

The guards walked into the great hall. Heishi and Feiluo craned their necks up to look: The depiction of the Astrolabe's mainland in the center looked like a huge model of an islet floating in the air.

"Why is this laboratory so big?" Feiluo asked.

"Because of the Creator's physique," Heishi said. "His kind were giants who came from the Void."

Feiluo glanced at Heishi, his gaze filled with both suspicion and shock. He then turned to his subordinates and commanded, "Please, for Heishi's sake, keep this a secret."

The guards nodded and took their positions to stand watch within the great hall.

Heishi climbed the gargantuan staircase onto the tall platform, where he found a huge control stone. In here, all of the fixtures were ten times larger than what humans usually used. Feiluo followed Heishi.

"How do you know about this place?" Feiluo asked.

"Father told me," Heishi answered. When this sentence caused Feiluo to grow guarded, he added, "Calm down. It didn't seem to like me very much."

Feiluo furrowed his brow but didn't speak; there were too many unknowns about Heishi. This man had been mysterious and circumspect since he'd appeared. Most of the time, he never spoke a word. Even A-Ka couldn't see through him.

Heishi observed the control sphere before he placed a hand on it. The model of the Astrolabe mainland instantly lit up, and light rays crisscrossed over it, projecting silhouettes of living beings.

"The Creator fashioned the Astrolabe fifty thousand years ago," Heishi explained to Feiluo. "Within the laboratory he left behind are the models of the life-forms that he once invented."

Countless kinds of living creatures, from cellular organisms to insects to mammals, appeared one by one in that glow. Feiluo quietly watched; what was happening before his eyes far exceeded all of what he understood of the world.

"The living creatures on the Astrolabe," Feiluo said, "as I recall it, were nurtured by nature."

"Within the limits of your knowledge, that is correct," Heishi said. "In reality, that's not the case. Records from humans of ancient times show that humans created clones...but see here."

Heishi lifted his head, flicking an eyebrow up, and within the stereographically projected hologram appeared a diagram of a human cell.

"Heavens," Feiluo mumbled. "This is..."

"The first clone body. It's one of the techniques that the Creator tested out—using cloning to incubate even more life. However, for reasons unknown, he gave up on this method. And then there's this..."

Within the hologram appeared countless sets of matrices. Feiluo knit his brow. "What are these?"

Heishi gave Feiluo a look. Feiluo thought of something, and his entire body began to tremble. "These are the mechanical life-forms'..."

"Right. Their soul matrices. If they were coded according to this method, then the mechanical life-forms would be able to have their own souls."

Feiluo instantly turned around, grabbing Heishi's shirt as he stared at him. "How do you know all this? Tell me!"

Heishi pushed Feiluo aside. "Don't get excited. There's more to come."

The images appeared in quick succession as Heishi controlled the light sphere. "I got these from Father's database, and they differ from what you all know. After the Creator made humans, he sealed this laboratory away. Three thousand years ago, several human explorers discovered it, stealing away the soul matrix technique and the method of creating clones.

"After that, the clone civilization flourished. As for how the cold robots also gained the ability to think and have emotions, one of the explorers in the group ignored the warnings of his peers and programmed soul matrices into them. After that came..."

Feiluo's voice shook as he whispered, "The revolution of the machines."

"Your world changed from that point onward," Heishi said. "But one of the explorers, a member of the 'Thunderbolt' squad who became known as one of the new gods, discovered an emergency mechanism the Creator left behind. Now, what I want to find is that emergency mechanism."

"Will it let the Rebel Alliance be victorious in the end? If so, then we'll use all of our resources to help you in this effort."

"But Father has taken away a key piece of information. I don't know how it found this place within your kind's territory." Heishi paused, then asked, "Who do you think is most likely to be colluding with Father?"

Feiluo shook his head. "I don't know. We have too much information, and it's all poorly organized. Only a few of the higher-ups in the army know of this place. There are no more than seven, including myself."

"Then it must be one of the seven. Has anyone else come here recently?"

Feiluo glanced at his subordinates, and one of them responded, "General Macksie came here before. At that time, the guards who were in this place were two different brothers."

Feiluo's forehead furrowed. "Heishi, let's set aside the issue of who stole the information for now. How will it help you if we can find the information that was stolen?"

Heishi shook his head. "This is the destiny I was born for, and it's of vital importance. There's a section of code that can completely stop Father's operations."

"But Father's central processing unit is connected to the Nucleus of the entire Astrolabe," Feiluo said with a frown.

"Correct." Heishi nodded. "To restart Father means that the entirety of the Astrolabe will be rebooted."

Heishi's words shocked everyone present.

"What will happen after the entire Astrolabe is rebooted?" Feiluo asked in disbelief.

"Many changes will happen in the world, but... I forget. I've forgotten so much information. Too much time has passed, and I've slept for too long..."

Heishi narrowed his eyes and turned his head back and forth, as if he was trying to shake that section of memories from his own mind and capture that fleeting thought. The clones watched the holograms that the light and shadows created, staring at the magnificent light that emitted from the Astrolabe. But no matter how hard Heishi tried, he couldn't recall that segment of memory that had been wiped clean.

"I really can't remember..." His forehead was covered in a cold sweat.

Feiluo knew that this matter was one of great importance. "Don't rush yourself, Heishi. Think carefully. Is there anything that is connected to all of this?"

"My first memory was seeing A-Ka," Heishi said, narrowing his eyes. "That time on the beach, A-Ka saved me..."

It wasn't until this moment that Feiluo learned of the connection between Heishi and A-Ka.

"Would he know anything about your background?" Feiluo asked, concerned.

"The probability is very low," Heishi said. "The only clue is that I slept in the ocean for three thousand years."

At this moment in time, A-Ka was currently resting in the ship's cabin. The sound of the waves caused him to once again remember the day that he rescued Heishi and the words that Heishi had spoken to him many months later in the bathing chamber.

"What are you thinking about, A-Ka?" Percy asked gently. "Is it your friend?"

"Mhm," A-Ka replied. "When I met him, it was also on the sea. Are you awake now? Do you want to drink some water?"

"Thank you, but I can do it on my own." He felt his way along until he opened his water bottle and drank a mouthful.

Percy was only twelve years old, and his blindness was congenital. According to him, one day a robotic squadron had wanted to capture and kill all of the people in his village. The villagers fought back in self-defense, but they were still ruthlessly slaughtered. As they were fighting, the division that Feiluo led had rushed onto the scene. Feiluo had discovered him in the wreckage and taken him with them.

Percy was very mature. He didn't cry or throw tantrums, and he would often try to guess at other people's intentions. Such a traveling companion was a blessing.

The ship's journey was long and slow. Twice a day, the clones would come down and hand out food and water, and during set hours, the passengers were allowed up onto the deck in shifts to breathe in the fresh air. The rest of the time, they had to remain crammed together in the lower levels of the ship. Two months passed like this.

After chatting with their compatriots in the cabin, A-Ka learned that the people around them all possessed special skills. Some of them were masters of design, some were familiar with production, some knew how to cook, and others were even artists. Life within the cabin was comparatively pleasant. Sometimes, a bard would play the harp for the children. According to him, long before the revolution in the City of Steel broke out, there had been quite a few people wandering around on the mainland.

The experiences of A-Ka's comrades opened new doors in his understanding. He gradually learned that the Country of Machines really was not the entirety of the world, and that all this time, humans and clones had been thinking of ways to destroy this country of metal demons that controlled the Astrolabe and forced the residents of the mainland to live in abject poverty.

"Father's power is on the verge of collapse," one man said to the crowd. "For history to flourish, this path is inevitable. The robots that have no ability to create will never be considered intelligent life-forms…"

This was the first time A-Ka had heard such a sentiment. It made him curious; he sat and listened with a great deal of interest, but the other listeners expressed boredom.

One small child sighed. "I've heard this revolutionary manifesto a hundred times now."

"I've heard it two hundred times now," another child said. "I want to hear Uncle Moran tell history stories instead."

Moran, the wandering bard traveling with them, had curly brown hair and a pair of azure eyes. Though he was not young anymore, he was kind, amiable, and the favorite of the little children on the boat. When he heard them say his name, he began to smile and plucked the strings of his lyre twice, making it ring crisply. The kids all clapped, and the bard began to sing a lilting historical ballad.

"In the depths of those faraway stars, the Creator activated his Astrolabe..."

The song detailed the tens of thousands of years of change that had happened in their world. A-Ka combined his existing knowledge with the story that this bard was telling. Gradually, he began to understand more—the legendary Creator had abandoned his compass of destiny in the depths of the universe. Past legends had dubbed it the Astrolabe, which was also the world that the Creator had used to test and grow countless living beings.

That god had left behind a place within the depths of the Astrolabe, the Room of the Stars, where he had once observed the trajectory of the development and movements of this world. The room was constructed from countless combinations of gears, both large and small, whose teeth ground together beneath the layer of land covered by the ocean, causing the mainland to slowly revolve. The entire world moved like the internal mechanisms of a massive pendulum clock. All the lands and islands were inlaid on its bedrock, and this chunk of bedrock was the Astrolabe.

In the prehistoric era, the Astrolabe flourished with abundance. There was no war or carnage, and humans and other species lived in harmony.

Ultimately, the Creator, for reasons unknown, left behind the world he had crafted with his own hands, abandoning this country of God. When the robots rose to power, not only did they seize control of the Third Mainland, the Astrolabe's largest territory, they also raised Father to the role of man-made god. The other lands, both large and small, began to pray to the Creator, eagerly awaiting his return.

But this was only one set of beliefs. Moran also taught A-Ka about other faiths. A-Ka really liked the stories that Moran told, and he was equally fond of A-Ka and Percy.

"Though you cannot see the world," Moran said earnestly, using his fingers to gently stroke Percy's closed eyes, "you have a pair of eyes in your heart, and they seek the light in every moment."

Percy began to smile. "Thank you."

"Uncle Moran, if you believe that the Creator is only an artifact of a faith, then what *is* faith?" A-Ka asked.

"Faith is born of humans. It is the power that propels someone forward. Under the light of faith, the shadows brought about by death and horror dissipate..."

"Teacher Moran," a young person said in amusement, "I don't think that simply believing in the God of the Stars will bring about salvation. Haven't you seen how many people have risked their lives despite being atheists?"

A-Ka didn't understand his point, and he shot the youth a look. He knew that there were many young people around his age on the boat, and all of them were spoiling for a fight, preparing for when they arrived at the Second Mainland to build their new lives from the ground up with nothing more than their hands.

The bard smiled. "Faith is not the same as worshipping a deity. The people that you have mentioned are those who have faith in themselves, but there are others who believe in the existence of a god. At the root of it, they adopt these beliefs so that they can believe the moral compass they have in their own heart. Young ones, when you grow up, you will slowly begin to understand."

The youths in the cabin didn't continue that debate with Moran, but it was obvious that they didn't wholly agree with him. A-Ka could only keep these words within his own heart.

He really liked this environment. Though they spent every day waiting and didn't know exactly when they would reach the shore, the entire ship was like a huge classroom. Everyone had knowledge of their own, and A-Ka learned a lot because of that.

One night, a storm hit the boat. Lightning raged across the sky above the sea, and the large ship bobbed like a single leaf on the vast ocean. Seawater sloshed in from the windows, and the people inside closed them in a rush as their terror grew and grew. The violent jolting of the ship caused many of the passengers to throw up, become dizzy, or fall into despair.

As the boat fell into the grip of horror, the bard Moran knelt in the middle of the cabin, praying in a low voice.

"The God of the Stars who created everything, your light guides the destiny of this land... May you look favorably down upon us and lead us to the bank filled with light."

His voice traveled through the cabin. Slowly, those within it began to calm, and more and more of them knelt on the ground, joining Moran in prayer. The thunder grew softer, and though the lightning still lashed out, it no longer seemed like it wanted to destroy everything.

As A-Ka observed this, he realized that Moran's prayers seemed to carry the power to soothe human hearts. In the face of his words, the wind and rain gradually lessened, and everyone slowly sank into sleep, no longer fearing the struggles out at sea.

Nevertheless, lightning burst across the sky, and in his dream A-Ka seemed to sense something—a kind of change in his soul. As thunder rumbled, he felt that he could clearly see the essence of the world. Illuminated by lightning flashes, the seawater split into protons, neutrons, and electrons. Countless gas molecules collided before separating again within the darkness. He seemed to view this through a pair of eyes created from nothing but spirit, and as he looked at his surroundings, he studied the segments of the ship, the creases on the sails, and even the dowels holding the wooden buckets together. Percy remained sleeping soundly by his side. When A-Ka looked at that water purifier with a complicated structure in Percy's shoulder bag, he understood the countless precisely oriented parts that came together to form it.

He saw the principles that were the foundation of the world.

Another bolt of electricity shot downward, and A-Ka suddenly jolted awake. His surroundings returned to normal. Within the dark cabin, a lantern glowing with white light swayed gently.

Moran hadn't yet slept, and he lifted his head, looking askance at A-Ka. Seeing that A-Ka's face was covered in cold sweat, Moran shook his head. He walked over and placed one hand on A-Ka's forehead.

"What did you see?" Moran asked.

"I..." A-Ka mumbled. "I had a dream."

Moran smiled slightly. "Dreams are the eyes of humans, through which they see the world and themselves. Sleep, child."

A-Ka's breathing evened out, and he once again fell into a deep sleep.

The next day, excited shouts rang out across the deck, and the refugees within the ship cabin all rushed outside. A-Ka went along with the crowd and saw land in the distance. Their journey had finally reached its end. Every person started cheering loudly and crying.

The chimes of a bell tower rang in the distance. A-Ka began to smile. In the sunlight, a lively port city appeared on the horizon.

"That's Kurlovich," Moran said, "a port city of the Second Mainland. It's still a good distance from there to Phoenix City."

A-Ka brought Percy to the prow of the ship and described the scene to him. "There are many seagulls," he said. "All the houses are white under the sunlight. It's beautiful, very beautiful…"

Percy closed his eyes, feeling the slight breeze that blew from the west, and he nodded. "Yup!"

# PHOENIX CITY

THE BOAT DOCKED. The clone troops of this place were not defensive and wary like the ones on the Eastern Mainland, and the friends that they'd made along this journey said their goodbyes as they disembarked.

It was a completely new world. Even just within the port city, A-Ka became turned around many times and lost all sense of direction. Thankfully, he could tightly clutch Percy's hand the whole time to prevent them from losing each other. This place presented many surprises, and most of the rumors that he'd heard turned out to be incorrect. The rumors A-Ka had heard said that the Second Mainland was the home of the clones, but that actually wasn't the case. There were more humans here than clones, and they were scattered along the streets in stalls, selling cakes, robotically produced parts, and even ingredients for alchemy.

A-Ka and Percy traveled down the road alongside the harbor. By the afternoon, they'd crossed less than half of Kurlovich. In ancient times, this port was where a large portion of the gold trade had taken place, so the mainlanders called it the Port of Gold. Humans lived in peace and ran their businesses, their lives fulfilling and happy.

"Shoo, outsiders!" the owner of a fruit stall called coarsely.

A-Ka flinched a little from being shouted at. Curiosity about everything filled him, but he was also afraid of breaking the rules here.

Percy couldn't see, so he anxiously asked A-Ka, "Gege, what's wrong?"

"Nothing." A-Ka had wanted to ask the stall owner if he could get some fruit for Percy to eat, but without any money, it seemed like eking out a living in this land would be very difficult. They needed money. Once they earned some, they could survive here.

Though doing that would be difficult, A-Ka was still filled with confidence. He asked a passerby for directions to Phoenix City, planning to first fulfill Feiluo's request before figuring out a way to make a living.

But they had no traveling funds, and as the sky slowly began to darken, A-Ka felt a little at a loss for what to do next. Would it be better to find a job here and earn some money to travel before taking Percy on the road? He stopped outside a watch store for a while, but just as he was about to go up to the counter and ask something, he suddenly saw a familiar silhouette: The bard Moran emerged from one of the structures along the street with many people following behind him.

"What's wrong?" Percy asked.

"I just saw the bard from the ship," A-Ka said. "He seemed..."

"Uncle Moran!" Percy called out.

A-Ka hurried to press his index finger to Percy's lips, hushing him, but Moran had already heard. He turned his head and saw them.

"Why, if it isn't Percy." Moran smiled. "What are you two doing here?"

"Gege's looking for a job," Percy said, "so that he can use his skills to get us something to eat. How about you?"

A-Ka saw that Moran had many people following him, some of them even clones, and was surprised. A-Ka wasn't ignorant to the ways of the world like Percy, so he had guessed that Moran came from an extraordinary background. After all, they had chatted a lot while they were on the boat; A-Ka had gotten a sense for him. Still, he hadn't expected Moran to have this much influence.

After recalling that these two were going to Phoenix City and guessing that they did not have the funds to travel, Moran turned and said a few words to one of the people beside him.

"Yes, Your Excellency." The man immediately pulled a stack of thin golden cards from the pocket of his shirt. That was the money used on this mainland. Earlier, A-Ka had seen the residents exchanging bronze and silver cards for goods. Moran handed the cards to A-Ka.

Understanding Moran's intent, A-Ka shook his head. "This... No, I can't accept these."

Moran smiled. "I'm lending these to you two. It's a pity that I have to travel to Dragonmaw City, otherwise I would take you two along with me."

"In the future, could we seek you out in Dragonmaw City?" A-Ka asked. "I'll repay you this money then."

Moran smiled. "Of course." He thought for a moment more, until he flipped open his travel journal and handed a bookmark to A-Ka. "If you have the chance, you can find me in the Palace of the Stars when you visit Dragonmaw City."

"Your Excellency, it's getting late," one of his attendants reminded him.

Moran nodded and bade A-Ka and Percy goodbye. Before turning and leaving, he kissed Percy's forehead.

Now that A-Ka had obtained some money, he heaved a sigh of relief and secured them passage on a steam coach heading toward Phoenix City. Since he was curious about everything, he didn't mind describing the sights to Percy.

A teenager leading a kid half as old as he was, like two little know-nothings, drew the attention of many kindhearted people along the way, and they finally managed to stumble their way to Phoenix City.

When they walked out of the Phoenix City steam-coach station, A-Ka finally felt that he had come home. This was despite the city being nothing like the haven for humans their traveling companions on the boat had described.

The real Phoenix City was a huge industrial metropolis that was actually very dirty. Robotic cars came and went on the streets, while the houses were stained a dark yellow by the pollution from the city's factories. Steam and black smoke billowed into the sky, and noise seemed to envelop the entire world around them. Yet everything appeared to move with great vitality, and humans bustled about as if they were welcoming their arrival.

"Don't block the road!" someone shouted at A-Ka and Percy.

"Why are you being so nasty?" the station attendant raged. "Can't you see that kid's blind?"

"Sorry, sorry," A-Ka hurried to apologize.

Throughout their journey, people kept discovering that Percy was blind. Regardless of whether their intentions were good or ill, A-Ka always felt a little sad and guilty every time strangers asked about it; he was afraid that Percy would be hurt.

But Percy always remained very positive and smiled. "Sorry, we're newcomers."

A-Ka held Percy's hand as they climbed down. Immediately, A-Ka was lost and could only follow the crowd. It was in moments like this that he missed Heishi and would always think, *If only Heishi were here, then everything would be all right.*

Facing this unknown world, A-Ka was filled with confusion and a touch of insecurity—he was even afraid that he might not be able to protect Percy. If Heishi were by his side, he would at least be less worried.

"Gege, where are we going now?" Percy asked.

A-Ka thought of Feiluo's request: After arriving in Phoenix City, he was to send Percy to the human orphanage, but A-Ka wasn't willing to part with Percy so quickly.

"Let's go to the orphanage to take a look," A-Ka said.

The travel money that Moran had given them had dwindled to almost nothing. On their journey, A-Ka kept buying Percy treats. The two had experienced so much hardship beforehand that they wanted to eat everything, sparing no thought for their future. When A-Ka realized how depleted their funds were, he was afraid that the only way he would survive was to check himself into the orphanage as well.

It was nearing evening in Phoenix City, and the sunlight pierced through the dark clouds, scattering a thin layer of glowing light across the city. The sound of the machinery that enveloped the entire city gradually quietened. A-Ka bought a map and began to study it closely. That was how he learned that the city was split into human and clone districts, dividing it into eastern and western regions. Guided by the map, they arrived at the human residents' community center. However, the community center had already closed for the day, and the great doors were shut. One worker emerged and gave A-Ka directions after hearing his plight.

"The orphanage lies within the inner ring of the city. Since it's evening, you guys can go in to rest first and come back tomorrow to fill out the paperwork."

"Will we need to pay for it?" A-Ka asked.

The worker shook their head. "No, you don't need to pay. It's straight down the main street, but you may need to get a ride. Otherwise, you won't be able to get there before it gets dark."

"Thank you," Percy said.

A-Ka nodded, and he left clutching Percy's hand in his. They traveled along a river flowing with polluted water, and perhaps it was because a farewell was imminent that A-Ka's spirits sank low. He fell silent.

Percy suddenly asked, "Gege, what's around here?"

A-Ka had a look around, only to see that the ground was covered with wastewater and garbage from the industrial processes around them. He thought for a bit before saying to Percy, "Mm, this is a very good city. As for the specifics…"

A-Ka portrayed their new home as a beautiful place, but in his heart, he sighed.

He brought Percy with him as they entered the inner ring of the city to find the orphanage. It wasn't until the sky grew dark that they arrived outside a waste processing factory. On the door hung a tarnished plaque that read "Human Orphanage." The entire place was fenced off with a layer of wire netting.

After the guard listened to A-Ka's story, they opened the door in the wire fence. "Why don't you come in?"

At the same time, a truck loaded with a large amount of coal drove into the refinery next to the shelter. This orphanage gave off the impression of a prison to A-Ka, but he didn't say that to Percy. He simply told him, "We'll stay here for the night."

Percy nodded, and the two of them were given numbers. They weren't subjected to any more questioning before they settled down. In the hall, the children were getting dinner.

"You're over sixteen. You can't live here," a woman said to A-Ka.

"I know," A-Ka said. "I'll leave first thing tomorrow morning."

The woman brought A-Ka and Percy to a room. "After nine o'clock, we lock the doors."

A-Ka inspected his surroundings. The room was devoid of people, with only a single light overhead and two sets of bunk beds. The other set seemed to have occupants who were not there at the moment.

Percy sat down quietly on the lower bunk. The kids who slept in the other bunks came back; they were both a bit older than ten, and one of them was even a little taller than A-Ka despite his young age. They gave the two of them a glance.

"Where'd you come from?" the older boy asked.

"We're from the City of Steel," A-Ka said with a smile. "This is my little brother." Percy also said hello.

The larger youth understood and nodded. "Refugees from the east." After saying this, he passed no more judgments, climbing onto his bed and lying down.

It was obvious that the smaller kid was afraid of this larger one. The two of them didn't chat, and the other kid didn't dare to strike up conversation with A-Ka. A-Ka's emotions grew heavy again. He went out to get food for Percy, and as he swept his gaze over the fare, he saw that the orphanage-provided dinner was a kind of gray mixed-grain gruel. He sniffed it and could tell that there were oats, wheat, and several other kinds of coarse grains in it, so he didn't get any for Percy, instead letting him eat the snacks that they had bought.

At exactly nine, all of the lights throughout the orphanage were extinguished. Outside the window, a soft rain began to fall, and bright white lights shone down on the street below. Once in a while a large truck would rumble by. The other two kids lay quietly in their beds.

A-Ka stared out of the window for a while as a sense of confused unease began to rise from the depths of his heart. The winter night was very, very cold, but compared to the icy chill, the loneliness inside A-Ka was harder to bear. He slid under the thin blankets, hugging Percy, hoping that he would be a little warmer. Until now, he had yet to completely accept that this was the human society that he had longed for—after all, it was so different from the new life that he had imagined.

Percy pulled out a small mechanical device and started tapping nonstop against the keys. A-Ka knew this was a transmitter, so he asked quietly, "Who are you contacting?"

"Daddy," Percy answered. "I'm telling him that we've settled in. The transmitter uses a code to send our words to every transfer center in the rebellion troops' headquarters in every city, and they send it along to him."

A-Ka was a little surprised; Percy being able to remember that complicated a sequence meant that he was very smart. In another moment, the green light flashed, and a series of messages came back. Percy began to smile.

"I've gotten in contact," Percy said.

"Could you ask if Heishi is still there?" A-Ka didn't hold out much hope, but to him, Heishi was his only friend, or perhaps even the person he cared about the most.

Percy sent out the message, and when the reply came, he said, "He's still there. Heishi's with my daddy."

This was an unexpected piece of good news. "What did Heishi say?"

"He told us to take care of ourselves. He heard that Phoenix City isn't as hospitable as he expected, but at least we are still free."

As the transmitter clicked along, Heishi's sentence seemed to flip some switch in A-Ka's mind, pulling his thoughts far away from this rainy night as he came to a decision.

Percy closed the transmitter, whispering to A-Ka, "They're going to save the rebel hostages. I hope there won't be danger."

A-Ka nodded, trying to comfort him. "Sleep. If there's anything else, you can talk about it tomorrow."

Far away on the other mainland, Feiluo shut the transmitter and sat silently with Heishi in the armory. Heishi turned a grenade casing over and over in his hands like a toy puzzle as he disassembled and reassembled it.

"You shouldn't have told them," Heishi said darkly.

"I'm used to telling Percy everything," Feiluo said. "Since he was small, he's had a kind of…special power, you know?" Feiluo lifted his eyes to look at Heishi, smiling warmly. "Though he's lost the sight in his eyes, he can see something different from those who still have it."

Heishi furrowed his brow. "What can he see?"

"He can predict danger," Feiluo explained. "I don't know if all you humans have this strange ability. Once, a robotic patroller was approaching us when we were all sound asleep, and he happened to be there. We were in a rush to leave the Central District and head toward the rainforest in the south, and in the middle of the night he woke me up, saying, 'Daddy, I dreamed that those big cold fellows are coming.'

"Thankfully, our troop discovered them early, and only three people were lost. We managed to retreat successfully from the swamp," Feiluo said. "That's why, whenever I make an important decision, I always ask for his opinion through the transmitter."

Heishi smiled a little, but his expression seemed skeptical.

Feiluo didn't explain any further. "I know you don't believe me. Forget it."

"If Percy's dreams really do have the power of prediction, then you could let him try perceiving who stole the important information stored in the Primeval Heart."

Feiluo smiled ruefully. "I don't think that's possible. The only things that appear in his dreams are things that involve him and me. Things that are personally relevant."

Heishi had taken apart and reassembled that grenade casing three times, yet they were still in the warehouse waiting for night to fall. Once it did, Heishi would join Feiluo's troops and set out to save a few hostages that had been detained by the Iron and Steel Corps. One among this group of hostages was the soldier who had been standing guard over the Primeval Heart three months before Heishi arrived.

Heishi looked up at Feiluo. "If your guess is right, and General Macksie has been plotting with the Iron and Steel Corps, what will happen then?"

"It's difficult to say." Feiluo shook his head slightly. "Brigadier General Macksie's position is very important. He's one of the three founders of the revolution. If this comes to light, it'll definitely cause some shifts in the highest levels of the army."

Heishi was gradually starting to understand the structure of the clone army. The three decision-makers within the clones' forces were Liber, who had lost his life leading the failed revolution; Commander Angus, who to this day still remained in Phoenix City; and Macksie. All were the same rank. For one of the top-level executives to have actually been a spy sent by Father, who managed to sneak his way into the rebel forces... If this came to light, then the results would be unimaginably catastrophic.

At this moment, Feiluo felt as if he had collided head-on with a huge problem. Ever since Heishi had walked into the Primeval Heart, one enigma had followed another. This truth was not one that could be revealed yet.

"Where is General Macksie right now?" Heishi asked.

"In Phoenix City. He's meeting with Angus. Because Liber perished while carrying out his duty, they have to settle on a new battle strategy to prevent the Iron and Steel Corps from fighting back. He'll probably return here in about a month. If we want to make a move, we'll have to do it quickly. If we wait until he returns, he'll soon learn that you and I entered the Primeval Heart."

Heishi nodded before getting up and looking out of the window, where the sky was already growing dark. Feiluo picked up the firearms that his subordinates had prepared as he pushed open the door and walked into the dark mountain range.

The night passed, and thousands of rays of sunlight shone down on the far end of the continent where Phoenix City sat. In the early morning, A-Ka brought Percy to the orphanage office, explaining their situation to the supervisor.

"I'll go find a job," A-Ka said to the supervisor. He sat there with one knee propped over the other. "As long as we can make enough to support ourselves, then my little brother won't need to enter the orphanage."

"All right," the man agreed without much concern. "Go. I pray for your success."

A-Ka held Percy's hand as they walked out of the orphanage. After the rain from last night, the clouds hanging over the horizon had dissipated and sunlight now streamed through the clouds. As Percy stood in the sunlight, tears suddenly began to flow down his face.

A-Ka was shocked. "What's wrong?"

Percy smiled as he wiped at his face, shaking his head. "I-it's nothing."

"Well, let's find a place to stay." A-Ka adjusted the messenger bag on his back, switching it to his other shoulder, and they walked into the bustling, busy world of Phoenix City.

"We're not accepting technicians." The person in charge of the maintenance shop looked A-Ka up and down with an odd stare.

A-Ka grasped Percy's hand, saying, "No worries. I'll go ask at some other places and try my luck there."

A-Ka led Percy out. This was the fifth shop that he had tried; none of the factories were accepting technicians, and they had virtually none of the money that Moran had left them. He used the last of it to buy two hot dogs, and he squatted with Percy by the side of the road as they ate.

"Is finding a job very difficult?" Percy asked him anxiously.

"Don't worry, I'll find one."

A-Ka's requirements were that they just had to include room and board, and that they would also take in Percy. But a large portion of the workshops didn't believe that A-Ka could even repair things, no matter how he explained his past experience again and again. He even tried calling at a few of the clone-run repair shops, but they would ask about Percy's origins as soon as they saw him. A-Ka would answer that this was Feiluo's adopted child, and Feiluo was a clone. At one particular shop, the people who heard this began to laugh loudly.

"Adopted child?" the clone boss said, before calling, "Hey! Come over and take a look! This little brat's a clone's son. We've gotta keep him here."

"Which one?" someone asked.

"What serial number?"

Everyone surrounded them, making A-Ka feel threatened, but Percy tugged at his hand and said quietly, "Don't be afraid, A-Ka."

Percy pulled out an army insignia and handed it over. On it was Feiluo's military rank, his troop, and designation. The gathered group did believe him after that—but what came with that belief was a period of long silence.

"Your father owes me a lot of money. A very, very large amount," one clone said after a long while. He leaned forward.

"What are you trying to do?!" A-Ka pulled Percy behind him, shielding him from the clones' intimidation. Percy was confused and didn't know how to respond. "Listen, these matters are between you and Feiluo. Go find him when he returns and settle them then."

"You guys will be taken away," the clone said, smiling, "and your organs will be removed to be sold."

"Don't scare him!" A-Ka snapped. Unwilling to engage further with them, he took Percy and left.

After asking around at a few more places, he realized that Feiluo's reputation was terrible, to the point that A-Ka stopped daring to bring him up. Instead, they returned to the region where humans gathered so that A-Ka could try to find a repair factory.

Percy asked, "Should I ask Feiluo?"

"No. No need to worry him."

A-Ka remembered Heishi's words clearly: At least they were free. Despite walking from dawn to dusk with Percy in tow, he had nothing to complain about.

Once again, it began to rain.

"Let's spend the night near here," Percy said.

A-Ka saw a waste processing factory across the street. This was the westernmost district of Phoenix City. They stopped, and he hid with Percy in a huge concrete pipe for the night.

In the heap of junk across from them, a beggar was starting a fire, and he lifted his head to glance at them. A-Ka was afraid that he would come over to take their things or to frighten Percy, so he kept staring at him. A short while later, a man wearing a windbreaker and holding a black umbrella walked through the sulfurous rain and paused to exchange a few words with the beggar. A-Ka suddenly felt that there was something not quite right.

"What's wrong?" Percy whispered.

"Nothing," A-Ka said. "Go to sleep." He hugged Percy, letting him place his head in his lap, no longer looking at the beggar in the distance. Percy closed his eyes.

The man in the distance chatting with the beggar seemed like he wasn't leaving. A-Ka couldn't hear what they were saying, and he had no motivation to pay them any further attention. But, slowly, Percy began to shift and sweat until he finally jolted awake.

"Percy?" A-Ka asked. "Are you sick?" He felt Percy's forehead.

Percy opened his eyes. "I had a dream," he said in a small voice, his breath a little heavy. "Is there someone near us?"

"You heard footsteps?"

"They've noticed us."

A-Ka jumped and glanced up into the distance, where he saw the man who had been hanging around, talking with the beggar for almost half an hour. A-Ka didn't think he had time to ask Percy why he said it like that, so he just said, "Get up. Let's go."

It was already deep into the night, and the streets were devoid of people. A-Ka didn't know exactly where they should go, nor if he and Percy would be met with danger in this unfamiliar city.

"I think we should wait here for a little bit," Percy replied, surprising him.

"Why?"

Percy didn't respond, but when the man in the distance finished, he turned and strode toward them. A-Ka's mind raced as he thought of what that clone shopkeeper had told them—this city was extremely dangerous and disorderly. If that man was a threat…

"Go with him," Percy said into A-Ka's ear.

"Who are you guys?" The man wore a black windbreaker, and he inspected A-Ka from head to toe.

A-Ka pushed Percy behind him. "What does it have to do with you?"

Percy tugged A-Ka's sleeve, a wordless reminder.

"If you don't want to die, don't stay here. Come with me," the stranger said in a quiet, deep voice.

A-Ka hesitated for a split second, but the man didn't give him long to make a decision as he immediately started to leave. A-Ka looked at Percy before turning back to the man. Finally, he grabbed their things, took Percy's hand, and rose to leave the waste treatment area.

The man wearing the black windbreaker pulled something from his pocket in a habitual manner. A-Ka thought it was a gun, but right as his anxiety spiked, he heard a light click and a small flame burst from the object. The man had a cigarette dangling from his lips, and the end of it burned with the slight glow of fire.

"Who *are* you?" A-Ka asked.

"Shahuang," he answered.

A-Ka lifted his head to look at Shahuang. He had rough skin, and the hood of his black windbreaker shadowed half of his face. His nose was aquiline, and he wore earrings, while an inch-long scar sliced down the side of his face. His black windbreaker had an insignia pinned to it, on which was written "The Iron Blood Fighters."

"What are the Iron Blood Fighters?" A-Ka asked.

Shahuang stiffly lifted up his collar, using his arm to block the insignia. "A name," he said coldly.

A-Ka furrowed his brow. "I'm A-Ka, and this is—"

"I know he's Percy," Shahuang said.

"I've heard your voice before," Percy said. "In the energy supply store."

A-Ka remembered that morning, when he'd taken Percy job hunting. At the clone-run store where they'd menaced A-Ka and Percy about being taken away for organ harvesting, this man had been present. He hadn't been wearing a windbreaker then.

"Your eyes can't see, but your heart's very clear." Shahuang tossed the cigarette stub away. "You're really that bastard Feiluo's son?"

Percy stopped walking. With a frown, he said, "If you say bad things about my dad, then I won't go with you."

Shahuang grinned crookedly and peered out from under his cap at Percy. "Though you're small, your temper's fierce. Ah, well. Let's pretend I didn't say that."

With that, A-Ka and Percy followed Shahuang forward. In a small alley darkened by the night, the eaves of the houses sagged with dripping water, but one light shone out in welcome over a door there.

"On Feiluo's behalf, I'll take you guys in." Shahuang pushed open the door under the light and went in.

"I don't need someone to take me in! I can work," A-Ka said.

Shahuang hit the lights, and the dim yellow bulbs flickered on, revealing the interior of the room. To his pleasant surprise, A-Ka found that they were inside a weaponry repair shop. This was a good opportunity!

"Let me work for you!" A-Ka offered with enthusiasm. "You just need to cover our food and housing."

"You can handle that? Don't break my things while you're fixing them." Shahuang took off his cap as he considered A-Ka. He shrugged out of his windbreaker, before asking, "Do you know how to fix firearms?"

A-Ka had Percy sit down before he went to the counter to look at the weapons that Shahuang had. He pulled out a firearm, which let out mechanical clicks as he tugged at various parts, his fingers moving nimbly and professionally. Shahuang watched A-Ka, then nodded.

"They're all older models, though," A-Ka noted.

"A small medieval knife can kill people just as well," Shahuang said easily. "The ability to take lives has nothing to do with the time period they're from."

A-Ka could tell that the person in front of him was either a killer or someone who used a gun very often; his wrists had traces of bullet scars.

"You can sleep behind the counter, and this little one can go sleep under the stairs," Shahuang said. "Starting tomorrow, help me watch the store."

A-Ka had found a place to stay at last, and though it wasn't quite what he'd imagined, just having a place to settle down with Percy was the best outcome he could hope for. Shahuang tossed them two sets of bedding. The blankets had the smell of damp and mildew, but A-Ka still spread them out on the floor and prepared to sleep.

He smiled at Percy, who was tucked nearby under the stairs. "Good night, Percy."

"Mm. Good night, A-Ka."

A-Ka turned off the light, and the room sank into darkness. The only sound was Shahuang's snoring upstairs.

During the dark of the night, in their quiet little corner, Percy's transmitter suddenly buzzed to life with a series of beeping noises.

A-Ka immediately pulled the transmitter from Percy's bag, and after he plugged in a data cable, a line of words appeared on the screen. This was a decoder that A-Ka had made out of some spare parts, and though the frequency band was not stable, it could still manage to receive a portion of the messages.

*Percy, this is Heishi. I'm looking for A-Ka.*

A-Ka ducked his head to enter a message.

*This is A-Ka. Heishi, what's up?*

No response from the other side. A-Ka then entered another line of words.

*Heishi, are you able to send and receive sound on your end? I'll see if we can use the radio frequency of the transmitter so we can talk.*

Heishi's message came back.

*No need.*

A-Ka didn't understand. What was wrong? He found the talkback module, connected it to the miniature transmitter, and began to adjust the frequencies—but the earpiece was dead silent.

"Heishi?" A-Ka murmured. "Where are you? Can you hear me? Maybe there's a problem with the earpiece? Heishi... Hm?"

"I hear you," Heishi said on the other end.

A-Ka began to smile as he squirreled deeper into his blankets. "Where are you?"

"Still on the Eastern Mainland."

"When will you come here?"

Heishi sat in the darkness on a distant shore, watching the rolling tides. A gentle breeze blew past, bringing with it a slight hint of salt. He didn't answer A-Ka's question.

"Do you remember the day that you found me?" he asked instead.

"What about it?" The question was out of the blue, and A-Ka didn't know why Heishi wanted to contact him in the middle of the night to ask it.

"It's nothing," Heishi said quietly. "I suddenly had a strange feeling, so I wanted to chat with you."

A-Ka's smile grew gentle. He lay in his blankets, the side of his head on his pillow, as he asked, "What feeling?"

"I can't describe it clearly," Heishi answered. He looked off into the distance.

A-Ka mumbled, "Why did you have this kind of feeling?"

"My father," Heishi answered.

"'Father'?" A-Ka furrowed his brow.

"Not Father, but rather…the person who made me," Heishi said. "My father."

A-Ka's drew in a sharp breath. "You remembered your past?" Heishi didn't respond, so A-Ka followed up with another question. "Who created you?"

"Why did you save me?" Heishi said, not answering.

A-Ka thought of the day he had discovered Heishi. "Well, for… for no reason at all. I saw that you were on the beach, so I just… Speaking of which, your temper seems to have improved a lot. Did something happen?"

"Was my temper that bad?" Heishi asked.

A-Ka smiled. "I still remember the first day we met. You almost choked me to death, and you were very annoyed with me."

"Hormones," Heishi said quietly. "My scrambled memories, my logical side telling me to accept a master, and my inner aggression were in conflict."

"What does that mean?" A-Ka asked.

Heishi dodged right by that question too. "That day, when the robotic guards were about to kill me, why did you stand up?"

"I'd found you, so I couldn't let you die just like that. My conscience wouldn't let it go. What about it?"

"It's nothing," Heishi said.

"Have you found a clue related to your father? Who is he?"

"He has no name. He's already left this place." The communicator went silent before Heishi added, "My master is already long gone."

Suddenly, A-Ka understood how Heishi was feeling. He had matters weighing on his mind but couldn't tell anyone, or perhaps he was trying to think things through. After experiencing so much confusion, he had no way to keep it all to himself and needed to find someone to talk to.

"The feeling in your heart is called loneliness," A-Ka told him.

"Is it?" Heishi said, though he didn't sound like he cared. "It's very strange. I just want to find someone and sit with them."

"Where's Feiluo?"

"Not here."

"And when will you come back?"

"As soon as I can."

"Will you come and live with us?"

"Live?" Heishi repeated.

"We've already found a place to stay. We're currently in the shop of a person called Shahuang."

"Shahuang..." He paused, thinking. "Do you recognize the leader of the Mercenary Association, Huixiong?"

"Who's that? Your friend?"

"Feiluo helped me get in contact with him. Tell me about your current situation."

A-Ka, nestling further beneath his blanket, quietly shared his experiences with Heishi. On the other end, Heishi didn't speak for a long time, listening intently to the story until A-Ka had spoken for almost ten minutes, getting up to the point where they had arrived at Shahuang's shop.

He was almost nodding off, when he murmured, "Heishi?"

"I'm listening," Heishi said. A-Ka hummed, and Heishi heard his tiredness. "I'll come to you very soon. Before that, do your best to stay put."

"All right, Heishi, be careful. Don't do anything dangerous."

Heishi broke off the communication, and A-Ka gradually fell asleep to the static of the radio waves.

## 8

# THE BLACK PLAINS

THE NEXT MORNING, A-Ka began working his temporary job. Shahuang's store provided repair services to the mercenaries in the old city district. He also resold guns on the side, a large portion of which were illegal firearms from unknown sources. A-Ka's job was to retrofit them and make some adjustments before putting them out for sale. Utilizing his skills from the City of Steel, A-Ka modified a selection of the electromagnetic weapons, which made Shahuang very pleased.

When the three of them sat down together to eat breakfast, Shahuang was wearing a dirty white collared shirt with the sleeves rolled up, and he had made three portions of tomato soup. He also set down a large basket of bread. Percy and A-Ka, who were absolutely starved, began to wolf down the food.

"Based on your appearance, I didn't expect you to be able to repair firearms," Shahuang said.

"I learned a little of those skills in Father's nation," A-Ka said, "but unless it was necessary, I rarely touched them."

"You didn't steal one away from the City of Steel for self-defense?"

A-Ka shook his head. The weapons from that city had left a strong impression on him. The mechanical life-forms used the weapons that humans had created to massacre them, which had always made him feel a natural aversion toward firearms. But he had to do this work to stay in Shahuang's store. Plus, this was nothing more than a job, and he had to do his job well, otherwise he and Percy would have no food to eat.

After that night on the boat, A-Ka found, to his surprise, that his ability to sense the outside world had undergone an evolution. Before, when he was working single-mindedly, his focus had been concentrated solely on the mechanical parts in his hand. Now, as soon as he entered that state of flow where he lost sight of everything else, his sensing capabilities seemed to expand outward.

It was a difficult feeling to describe. The machine gun in his hands would disassemble itself in an orderly fashion in his mind: The sight, the grip, the chamber, and other spare parts laid themselves out clearly. This was just like how those lightning strikes had laid bare the principles of the world to him that night on the dark sea. Every basic building block making up a more complicated structure revealed itself to him.

In a daze, A-Ka reassembled the gun and put it on the counter.

"That's it?" that mercenary said. "This Desert Eagle is something that even the precision instruments store couldn't fix!"

A-Ka nodded. "It's fixed. There was a problem with the positioning mechanism on the trigger…"

"Did you check the blueprints?" the mercenary asked.

"I didn't," A-Ka said, getting impatient. "Didn't you want your gun fixed? It's done. What more do you want?"

The mercenary tested it out and found that it really was good as new. All it lacked were bullets. He turned to Shahuang and said, astonished, "Hey, bro, this little brat…"

"A Desert Eagle?" Shahuang, who was sitting to one side, rose and came over. He took the gun and inspected it. "Huh, the manufacturer closed down, right? How did you fix it?"

"I..." A-Ka hesitated, feeling nervous, and he kept his eyes on Shahuang as he said, "It was the internal structure. As long as you can find the problem, it's easy to fix."

"This young one's very smart." Shahuang began to smile as he handed the gun back to the mercenary, patting A-Ka's shoulder a few times.

The mercenary couldn't believe it. This gun had lain disused for many years. Since there was no way to either fix it or return it to the factory, he had originally intended to treat it as scrap. He'd been hoping to turn it in for some money and possibly sneak it by Shahuang's new repair apprentice for a better deal. He hadn't expected that said apprentice would be able to fix it in just a few tries.

"Twenty-five gold pieces," A-Ka said.

The mercenary hurriedly pulled out the money and paid up.

A-Ka glanced over at Shahuang sitting in the corner, but he only smiled to himself.

Had Shahuang noticed A-Ka's potential? Whether he had or not, A-Ka felt that he shouldn't explain his methods in depth. There was also Percy's dream to worry about—A-Ka had tried to talk about it with Percy several times, but Percy never gave him a clear answer, so he could only let it be for now.

Time went on, and A-Ka and Percy had worked in Shahuang's store for almost a week. In the beginning, the customers who entered the shop were all mercenaries with lean faces and grim expressions, and when they saw A-Ka and Percy they seemed a little surprised. Their attitudes toward A-Ka were rotten, but they were extremely polite to Percy, and before they left, they would often give Percy a tip.

A-Ka kept the money, and Shahuang would give A-Ka some additional pay each day, depending on business volume. Then, A-Ka handed it all to Percy to take care of.

The two of them had basically nowhere to spend this money. While repairing firearms for Shahuang, A-Ka couldn't help thinking of his original treasure, his lost robot, K. Back then, he had worked so hard to save a few scrap parts, but in the end, he'd lost them all at once.

This reminded A-Ka of the day he and Heishi were escaping from the City of Steel, when K had shockingly appeared in front of them. Who had been controlling it? A-Ka mused over it while he worked on the machine gun in his hands. A few fixes later, he found himself thinking about Heishi, the other person who had escaped with them. How was Heishi now? Was he in any danger?

That night, he resolved to ask Percy to contact Feiluo so he could question him about Heishi.

The next day was frigid, and a thick layer of snow blocked the door to Shahuang's shop. The polluted snow in Phoenix City was gray and stank of the acrid scent of sulfur, and it piled up in front of the doorways in the alley. To combat this, A-Ka outfitted a small robot with automated snow-clearing capabilities and put it to work.

In Phoenix City, privately tinkering with robots was forbidden, but the regulations against doing so were lax, and the daily lives of the humans and clones were heavily dependent on mechanical devices. The rebel patrol squads largely turned a blind eye to such automated machines.

A-Ka had nothing else to occupy his time, so he used the scraps in Shahuang's store to start casually putting something together. If possible, he wanted to make another robot like K. This time, it wouldn't be for escape, nor would it be for him to fight in. It was simply his innate interest in metal and machines that compelled him; building a robot felt like playing with blocks. He could make tens of thousands of changes, each filled with its own joy. There was a special sense of delight that came with being a creator, like the moment that the device he built himself began to move.

Just as he was thinking about this, the bell over the main entrance dinged.

"We're closed for the night," A-Ka said. "You should come back tomorrow."

The door swung inward, and a tall, sturdy man walked in. Like a mountain, he towered over A-Ka, and on his head, he wore a military cap with the emblem of the Rebellion. He looked down his nose at A-Ka.

"Where's Shahuang?" The entire store shook with the boom of his voice. Percy, who was peeling potatoes in the kitchen, jumped in surprise, and the plates and bowls clattered.

"He's…" A-Ka apprehensively watched the man, feeling that he was talking with a huge gray bear. He pointed toward the back of the shop. "He's inside."

"Hey, Huixiong." Shahuang, who had a cigarette dangling from his lips, lifted a mug of whiskey toward Huixiong as he leaned against the doorway. "Welcome. And here I thought that you'd died in the City of Steel."

A-Ka's brow creased. This was the first time in a long time that he'd heard that name, and he couldn't help glancing again at Huixiong.

"This blasted winter drags on and on," Huixiong growled. "I've really had enough!"

Huixiong took off his military greatcoat, tossing it casually under the stairs, where it landed on Percy's bunk. This action revealed a sturdy, muscular body that seemed as though it might burst out of his shirt. This was the first time that A-Ka had seen such a powerful, well-built man. Huixiong's physical bulk was easily that of two average adult men. On top of that, he was definitely over six feet tall. Even the sturdy Heishi would be overshadowed if he stood next to him.

Huixiong took a large gulp of whiskey, then spluttered a little, his face turning bright red. "A person outside the Party has joined the secret operation team, and oh man, it's insane what they ended up finding in the Primeval Heart! Though the revolution failed, Father's system is about to be destroyed thanks to the intel that man provided! This guy... They call him the Savior of the World, because he was left behind by the ancient gods as the key to ending Father. In the Primeval Heart, he..."

Craning his neck a little, A-Ka eavesdropped eagerly on Huixiong and Shahuang's conversation. Suddenly, the door to the room opened, and Shahuang took a look outside—directly meeting A-Ka's eyes.

"Shahuang, can I use your magnetic welding coil?" A-Ka asked, shifting awkwardly.

"Sure, why not?" Shahuang said. "But don't test out your new weapon in my store. If you want to use it, take it to the river behind the little alleyway out back."

A-Ka nodded and began to collect the mechanical arm he'd built. Just as he was thinking of eavesdropping some more, Shahuang came to the door and closed it, cutting A-Ka off from their conversation.

The next morning, the weather was clear, but something in the air had changed. Shahuang did not go out, and the number of patrols on the streets had greatly increased.

A mercenary walked up to A-Ka. "Oi, young one, is the kid in Alley Sixteen your little brother? He got stopped by the patrol."

A-Ka put down the work in his hands and rushed outside, only to find that there were far more sentry posts than usual along the street. Percy held an electronic cane used by the blind in one hand and a bag of bread in the other. He looked up in confusion.

"He's my little brother!" A-Ka said.

"Don't wander outside," the clone patrolman said, looking him over before returning the bread to Percy. He was still holding an epaulet in his hand. "Who gave you this?"

"My dad," Percy answered.

The piece of Feiluo's pauldron that he had given to Percy had remained in his pocket all this time. The clone patrolman smiled. "Interesting. You're a clone's son?"

"Let's go." A-Ka watched the patrolman warily, taking Percy's hand as they turned to leave.

"General Macksie's coming back in a few days for an inspection," the clone said. "If you don't want any trouble, then you all should stay obediently in your houses. Don't go out."

"What's happening outside?" A-Ka asked Shahuang the moment he got back.

Shahuang was slumped in a chair, his two booted feet resting on the round table and his cap covering his face. From under the brim, he said, "Macksie's coming, so he wants to take a tour around, give some speeches, and mobilize the troops in preparation for war…"

"He's the person in charge around here?" A-Ka asked.

"One of the three," Shahuang drawled. "The clone regime wants to counterattack by mobilizing all its troops so that they can wage war on the City of Steel."

"They've only failed once."

"In the meantime, the inhabitants of Phoenix City are on tenterhooks," Shahuang replied. "They all need to find something to do to occupy themselves."

A-Ka didn't say any more.

That night, Shahuang hummed the song of the Rebellion, "The Black Plains." It was one that A-Ka had heard Feiluo sing multiple times. The lights had been extinguished very early on since the city was under curfew, so the room was dark as midnight.

After A-Ka fell asleep, he awoke to a knock on the door. Blearily, he climbed out of bed, but Percy had fumbled around and gotten to the door first.

"Who's there?" A-Ka asked.

Shahuang, on the other hand, seemed like he had been waiting patiently. "Come in," he said.

In the darkness, that person placed something on the counter before entering Shahuang's parlor. The door closed behind them. A-Ka turned on a light, only to see that the object on the counter was a long-range rifle. He began to adjust it for the customer, thinking that he was probably another one of Shahuang's so-called friends. As he worked, he peered in that direction curiously, trying to hear if the visitor had brought any news from the mainland. But Shahuang had shut the door tightly, so A-Ka couldn't make out even a whisper.

The rest of the night, A-Ka didn't sleep well. It was the second night in a row that he'd felt restless, since the night before Huixiong had come by and disturbed them. But a noisy hubbub outside woke him early the next morning. People flooded out into the streets, their cheers thundering forth—all of this because the leader of the rebel forces was coming.

A-Ka pushed open the window and looked outside, only to see that every street, no matter how big or small, was packed with citizens streaming toward the central square. Some had brought fresh flowers, others carried food, but they all tried to push their way to the front as they headed forward, waiting for that legendary figure to arrive in Phoenix City.

Never had so many people gathered in one spot in the city like this before. It was as if they were celebrating a grand festival. The sounds of the celebrations thundered in A-Ka's ears, and he closed the window. The next thing he did was check on the visitor who had arrived last night, but they weren't there, and Shahuang was still sleeping soundly.

Percy noticed what he was doing. "Are you looking for that guy from yesterday? He brought us something to eat." On the table was a box of fresh fruit, which still had water droplets clinging to it. "He got up earlier this morning, and after washing the fruit and telling us to eat it, he went onto the rooftop."

A-Ka clambered up the stairs to find him, only to discover that the door to the roof was locked from the outside. A-Ka knocked on the door. "Excuse me, are you out there?"

That man in a windbreaker propped the rifle up on a railing and wiped the lens. Turning his head back, he glanced at the securely locked door to the roof but didn't respond.

"Thank you for the fruit," A-Ka tried. "Why don't you come down and eat breakfast?"

The man on the rooftop stayed silent. A-Ka waited a little longer, but when he didn't get a reply, he comforted himself with the thought that everyone who came by Shahuang's place was a little odd, so he didn't pay him any more mind.

A-Ka and Percy were eating the fruit for breakfast when they heard people singing outside, their voices turning into a chorus.

"Oh wayward souls, we have finally returned to our homeland…"

"Our destined hero leads us forward…"

"The future is at our feet…"

The city had been lit by the fires of passion, and although A-Ka was not interested in the Rebellion and their affairs, he couldn't escape being affected by the emotions in the air.

"Can I go outside and look?" Percy asked.

"No," A-Ka responded, without even thinking about it.

An instant later, someone else knocked on the door. Before either of them could open it, it slammed open, and Huixiong appeared in the doorway.

"Macksie's here!" Huixiong said. "Don't you guys want to go out and look?"

"Eh, nah," Shahuang said. "There's two little ones in the house, though. You can take them with you."

Huixiong grinned. "Are you going?"

Percy looked at A-Ka. A-Ka didn't really want to go; his mechanical arm hadn't been fully outfitted yet.

"Percy, you can go with Huixiong," Shahuang said. "He'll make sure you're safe."

A-Ka glanced at Huixiong in consideration. In the end, he said, "That's fine. Just make sure to come back soon."

Huixiong took Percy's hand and led him out the door.

"You know," Shahuang said once they were gone, "Huixiong once destroyed a graveyard with his bare fists alone, so there's no need to worry about your little brother."

"Instead of worrying if he can protect Percy," A-Ka replied, "I'm more afraid that he might *do* something to Percy."

Shahuang began to smile. "He doesn't like little kids like that. You don't need to worry there. Now that your bodyguard has come, no one really needs to be afraid anymore."

"What?" A-Ka asked, confused.

Shahuang finished his breakfast. Without answering A-Ka's question, he went back to his room and sat down, slumped in his chair as usual, using his cap to cover his face. He turned on the radio, which was broadcasting nothing but the news of General Macksie's tour.

A-Ka returned to his spot behind the counter, adjusting his mechanical limb. He had used the scrap parts in Shahuang's store to put together this arm and hand. Now, he held it up to inspect it. It creaked as he added a light slingshot to it.

What was the visitor upstairs doing? He had gone onto the rooftop in the morning, and he hadn't come down since.

A-Ka pushed open the window and peered outside only to see the square that was swarming with people. The crowd seemed endless; A-Ka had never seen so many people before, and they kept rushing in from all sides, as if they all wanted to bear witness to such an important moment in history. In the center of the square was the steam coach station that led to the south. The railroad tracks stopped at this point, as if they could not extend even an inch further into the hitherto unknown, uninhabited part of the world.

The hands of the large clock pointed at 9:50 as a steam coach pulled into the Shakespeare District of Phoenix City. When the doors of the car opened, the crowd went wild.

"Macksie—"

"Macksie, you've come!"

Countless people shouted Macksie's name, and several Rebellion officers left the carriage, followed by a squat middle-aged man.

A-Ka couldn't help wanting to take a look outside, so he climbed up the outer ladder. Not far away was the rooftop, where he saw the long black windbreaker of the man who had arrived last night. His two hands were pushed deep in his pockets as he stood still in the corner, looking into the distance.

"Hey!" A-Ka shouted to him.

That man was about as tall as Heishi and wearing a pair of earmuffs. A-Ka bet that he heard; he just didn't turn his head.

A-Ka stood on his tiptoes, staring toward the square. He knew that many people in Phoenix City had been anticipating Macksie's arrival, since his actions in the Rebellion had become the stuff of legend. The news on the radio said that he had participated in the battle at the City of Steel and had single-handedly destroyed two large-scale Exterminators. Carrying orders from the deceased General Liber, he had come to assemble the Rebellion troops in the north and lead them in establishing their front lines, but for now he had returned to Phoenix City. Right here, humanity was going to raise the banner of revolution and march to regain their stolen homeland.

The sound of "The Black Plains" song was so loud it echoed in A-Ka's ears, but it slowly died down, and Macksie began to speak.

"Today is a momentous day in history," Macksie said. His voice was rich and vigorous, and he took off his cap as he continued, "We've fallen victim to the cruelest blows in all of history, and at the cost of the lives of countless soldiers, we've whittled away at Father's menacing power, but this is nowhere near enough! We will gather…"

Every structure in Phoenix City shone with a stark white light that was thin as a surgeon's needle. On the rooftop of the repair shop, Heishi clenched his teeth around a bullet, set the rifle in place, loaded it, and pointed it at the center of the square—right at the platform where Macksie stood.

Positioning a laser sight in front of one eye, Heishi observed Macksie from over four hundred yards away. The general gesticulated as he spoke, waving around a marshal's military cap, rousing the enthusiasm of the crowd.

A few seconds later, the killer pulled the trigger.

*Bam!*

As if a giant had swung a hammer into the ground, the entire world seemed to shake.

In that instant, time seemed to slow down drastically as Macksie's grand forehead burst open, a blossom of blood flowering on it. In the sunlight, his brain matter glittered and reflected like a crystal.

The entire square of people was rendered speechless with surprise. This shock was far too much for them to comprehend. For almost five whole seconds, no one could speak as they watched Macksie's headless body topple over onto the platform and roll off.

This city-rattling gunshot caused the death of one person and the awakening of another.

At the repair shop, the sound of the gun's recoil brought the dozing Shahuang swiftly to his feet.

Outside, the sound sent a spike of panic through A-Ka. He hopped down and rushed into the shop—only to run right into the arms of Shahuang, who was exiting.

Gripping A-Ka's collar, Shahuang bellowed, "What did that bastard do?!"

"I don't know!" A-Ka pushed Shahuang aside. "I just heard the gunshot!"

"Shit!" Shahuang rushed up onto the rooftop, kicking the door furiously. "Open the door, you fucker! What did you *do*?!"

Regardless of Shahuang's efforts, the metal door stayed firmly shut. Grabbing Shahuang, A-Ka shoved him to one side before resting the mechanical limb on his shoulder and sending a blast at the door.

With a huge boom, that attack sent the door to the entire rooftop flying. Shahuang and A-Ka hurried through, only to see the corner of that windbreaker fluttering away as the shadow of the sniper vaulted over the railings and leaped into the alleyway below. The man lifted a hand, his index and middle finger pressed together, as he saluted slightly at A-Ka.

The blood in A-Ka's body congealed with horror.

A second later, he pounced to the front of the railings, shouting, "Heishi!"

Heishi bounded toward the small alleyway behind the repair shop. When he landed, he lifted his head and stared at A-Ka one more time—until he turned his back and sprinted away, disappearing in the darkness at the other end of the alley.

A-Ka also vaulted over the railings, but he fell onto an oil can before landing on the ground and rolling over it, his head spinning.

"Wait!"

Struggling to his feet, he chased after Heishi.

Macksie's death caused absolute panic. As nearly a hundred thousand people in the square regained their senses, they simultaneously let out shouts and cries without clear meaning. Rage and grief, even despair, mingled together in the tumult. Many people wanted to rush onto the platform to see his corpse, but the clone guard squadron leveled their guns in warning. In response, the crowd of humans rioted, an enormous swell of them trampling over each other as they overturned the speaker's platform.

A-Ka had never imagined that something like this would happen. Racing out of the small alleyway, A-Ka chased after Heishi until he finally caught sight of his silhouette—but they were surrounded by chaos, and Heishi really ran too fast for A-Ka. The sky bristled with patrol aircraft, and when A-Ka saw Heishi again, the clone police had already begun to circle around him.

From his shirt pocket, A-Ka pulled out a monocular positioning device that he placed over his left eye. Dragging the mechanical arm he'd built behind him, he sprinted through the main street. The place was crawling with soldiers who were trying to capture Heishi and disperse the residents. Phoenix City had exploded into chaos that the rebellion troops were only beginning to suppress.

What was *happening*? Wherever A-Ka went, he saw that quite a few people were starting gunfights with the rebel troops, and most of them were actually mercenaries he recognized!

This desire for destruction swept through the crowd, and people began to pick up rocks and smash windows, destroying the buildings surrounding them. In a short half hour, A-Ka personally witnessed how history would, in vital moments, complete its cycle—how destiny could change the courses of hundreds of thousands, millions, or even tens of millions of lives at once.

With a loud roar, two security mechas controlled by clones pursued Heishi, and the defensive equipment revolving through the air began to blare a warning.

"Disperse quickly. In ten seconds, the sixth block will enter lockdown... Ten, nine..."

Heishi raced ahead on the path. Sensing danger, he whipped to the side as two mechas blocked his way forward with a clatter of metal. He tossed the rifle in his hand to one side, and in an instant, it disassembled itself before clicking back together in a new shape: a magnetic cannon that sent a blast toward the mechas.

The burst of light caused the mechas to lose their ability to move. As they halted momentarily, A-Ka dashed up from behind. Just then, the clone soldiers' encirclement of the street was complete, and thousands of them drew their firearms as they rushed toward Heishi.

Turning his head, Heishi swept his gaze around the circle. The defensive satellite in the sky had finished its countdown, and a laser beam shot toward him. In a flash, A-Ka rushed to the intersection of the two roads, bent one knee to the ground, and lifted the mechanical arm with his left hand. With his other hand, he reached to pull out a rocket he kept in the heel of his boot. Stuffing it into the arm, he jumped from the ground and rushed forward. Like lightning, A-Ka flew toward Heishi, activating all the firepower of the mechanical limb at once and clearing them a path.

Heishi reached out for A-Ka.

They grabbed each other's arms as Heishi leaped up from the ground and executed an elegant flip through the air. He pulled A-Ka to his chest in an embrace before the two of them smashed into a skyscraper like a cannonball.

A cacophony of cracking noises echoed as A-Ka and Heishi clutched each other. A-Ka used the mechanical arm to protect their heads as they shattered the glass of the tall skyscraper. He didn't know how much they wrecked before they rushed out from the other side. His head spun as he tried to make out where they were. Heishi, much more composed, lifted A-Ka into his arms and hurried into an underground structure.

"Hey, I can walk on my own," A-Ka protested.

Heishi set A-Ka down but took his hand in his own, and the two of them sprinted through the underground parking lot until they found a passageway and scrambled in.

Half an hour later, they had managed to shake off all of their pursuers. A-Ka lay down in the sewer, gasping for air. He had taken a bullet, which had embedded itself in his side, and knew that he needed to get it out as soon as possible. When he reached to touch his side, his hand came back covered in blood. But since Heishi didn't know he had been hurt, A-Ka just pulled his jacket on and covered up the wound.

Heishi rose to his feet and stood at the intersection of the sewers, his brow furrowed deeply. "How much longer do you need a break?" He sounded like he was in a hurry.

A-Ka bristled in anger. "Can't you have a little sympathy?" When Heishi just stared at A-Ka, he asked, "What? Am I acting strange?"

"Why did you chase after me?"

"Because I'm afraid for you! Why didn't you say anything when you came back? Were you the one who brought the fruits that Percy and I ate yesterday? I was wondering who had given us something so good to eat."

Heishi grunted in agreement, but his expression seemed a little anxious. A-Ka turned over and got up with great difficulty, leaning against the sewer wall, before taking tentative step after tentative step.

This just made Heishi wary. "Hey. Where are you going?"

"You should go ahead on your own." A-Ka held back his anger and heartache. "You don't need to worry about me anymore."

Heishi hurried after him. "It's dangerous outside!"

Fury exploded from A-Ka's chest. He turned around and pressed the mechanical arm against Heishi's chest. "Why did you stay? And why did you come back?! You won't tell me anything! I treated you like a friend and ran out to save you without a thought for myself, but you don't care! What do you take me for?!"

Heishi froze. A-Ka glared like an angry rooster as he panted.

"So, that's what's going on?" Heishi seemed to find this somehow amusing. "You're angry?"

"Stop acting like you don't understand human emotions. Seriously, get lost!"

"Wait." Heishi walked behind A-Ka in silence. After thinking for a while, he finally said, "I just don't want to drag you into all this."

"And I don't want to hear it. Go away!"

ASTROLABE
REBIRTH

# 9

# THE CHILDREN OF THE ASTROLABE

**A**-KA WALKED TO THE VENT and stood there, catching his breath. Then he exerted some effort to pry aside the grille blocking it off. Instead of letting A-Ka finish, Heishi had him move to one side. There was a huge bang as he sent a punch against the grille.

"Come with me." Heishi pried the grille the rest of the way off, grabbed A-Ka's hand, and climbed up.

They entered an expansive underground space, the junction point of several sewers in Phoenix City. A-Ka limped ahead, clutching his abdomen, his feet staggering through blood and his eyes spinning with vertigo.

When Heishi discovered the wound A-Ka had been hiding, his expression instantly changed. "What happened? Were you hit? Why didn't you say anything?"

A-Ka shoved Heishi aside, but Heishi came back, holding him tightly. "Don't move! Let me take a look!"

A-Ka had lost so much blood that his head spun. Heishi hurried to help him flat on his back, taking off his own jacket and spreading it out on the ground before letting A-Ka lie down. He then unbuttoned A-Ka's collared shirt. The bullet hole wasn't large, and upon seeing it Heishi flicked his weapon. With a sound, it shrank as if it had a mind of its own, turning into a pair of sharp tweezers.

"What...is that?" A-Ka asked.

Heishi didn't respond. He merely lowered his head and began to pull out the bullet. The pain that shot through A-Ka was so great that he screamed.

"Don't move!" Heishi hissed nervously.

Despite Heishi's words, A-Ka twitched and shuddered through the procedure until Heishi finally extracted the bullet and tossed it to the ground, where it landed with a clink. Taking off his own shirt, Heishi pressed it against A-Ka's abdomen.

"We don't have any disinfectant, so we've got to get out of here quickly." Heishi was a little at a loss for what to do next.

A-Ka found it strangely funny to see him so anxious now. "No worries, I won't die."

Heishi suddenly hugged A-Ka with a strength so immense that it hurt. At first, the force of the gesture worried A-Ka, but he then sensed that Heishi was trembling.

"Sorry... Sorry..." Heishi mumbled.

"What did you say?" Was he joking? A-Ka couldn't believe the words coming out of Heishi's mouth.

As if Heishi also noticed that he was being too emotional, he let out a long sigh and stopped. "I'll carry you on my back. We need to get out as quickly as possible and find some medicine to prevent your wound from getting infected."

Heishi forestalled any argument on A-Ka's part by picking him up. A-Ka's entire body felt boneless, so he slumped against Heishi's back like a dead dog.

"You made that weapon yourself?" Heishi asked as he walked.

"Mhm," A-Ka said from his position on Heishi's back. The firmness of Heishi's stride gave him comfort. He turned his head, watching the walls of the dark, deep sewer as they passed him by. It was as if they had returned to the day when he and Heishi escaped from the City of Steel. "What about yours? Where did your weapon come from?"

"I found it in the Creator's ruins," Heishi answered. "It's an ancient weapon that can be controlled via thought."

A-Ka was very interested in this, but he really was not in a position to study it further; he decided that he would borrow it from Heishi after they got back. "What're the Creator's ruins?"

"The place where everything came into existence. During the Golden Age, it was the center of the world. It was then that the Creator made this realm."

"You've remembered your past?"

"Only a portion. Your world is called the Astrolabe, and it's controlled by a preset program. The CPU that controls the Astrolabe is buried under the ground, where no one can find it. It's called the Nucleus."

"I...don't get it. That's not what the history books say."

"You can think of the world as a huge ecological spaceship. On a certain day in the distant past, it came from the depths of the galaxy and stopped here. The goal of this experiment was to study the origins of life, and through that, to discover some of the laws governing the microcosms within the universe."

A-Ka was stunned.

Heishi continued, "So, this ecological spaceship underwent the passage of time for tens of thousands of years before finally turning into what you see today. The programs that had been coded in, through the energy provided from the underground of the Astrolabe, adjusted and controlled the laws of the entire world. Like, earthquakes, volcanic eruptions, tsunamis, tornadoes...

"The Creator did some experiments, and after establishing the ecological petri dish of the Astrolabe, left this place. Humans were free to evolve and flourish. Then, about five thousand years ago, some adventurers discovered the laboratory in the Primeval Heart. Within it they discovered several technologies, including ones to create the clones and computers. In the depths of the Eastern Mainland, they built another laboratory, where they created Father."

A-Ka dimly sensed that Heishi might be the key to unraveling all of this. He held his breath, not daring to disrupt Heishi's story. After a long silence, Heishi continued.

"Originally, Father's earliest purpose was to be a computer monitoring system that the Creator set up to oversee this world. It reported every result of the experiments back to the Creator, and it was also in charge of terminating any experiments that extended beyond their expected limit.

"Later, the Creator felt that Father's determination criteria were too rigid, and it was difficult to maintain the numbers that he wanted anyway, so he didn't use it on our world. But the adventurers didn't know about this past decision, so they created a new Father with its consciousness that we know. After it awoke, it continually expanded its own capabilities, linking up with the Nucleus of the Astrolabe. At the same time, it acted to remove the parts of this petri dish that had gone out of control according to its calculations.

"Thus, both Father and the clones rebelled, creating the City of Steel that you know now. Right now, Father is preparing to perform the final linkage between it and the Nucleus, to end this experiment that has gone on for tens of thousands of years. It will clear all experimental results so that it can begin anew."

"Then, what about the Creator?" A-Ka asked.

"He has already vanished," Heishi said. "He left our communication range, so Father has no way to make contact with him. According to Father's own protocols, it will end the entire experiment, stopping all of the movements of the Astrolabe, before turning itself off to conserve power."

"And that's to say..." In that instant, A-Ka felt a flash of terror.

"In the not-too-distant future," Heishi said, "after annihilating all of the sentient organisms this world created, the Astrolabe will terminate its power-producing functions. The surface will become a desolate land of sand and stone—a dead world that waits for the return of the Creator."

"When will that happen?" A-Ka asked, his voice shaking.

"Very soon. Feiluo has gone to investigate this countdown, but it'll be within a year," Heishi said. "But, before the Creator left this world, he made an emergency system. This emergency system is equipped with the power to determine whether or not to terminate the experiment, but it does not rank higher than Father's commands. When it issues its command to the Nucleus of the Astrolabe, I'm not sure whether the Nucleus will obey the command of the emergency system or those of Father."

"Where is the key to the emergency system?" A-Ka asked.

Heishi turned his head and gave A-Ka a look. A-Ka dug through his thoughts for a long time before he said, "What are the conditions that need to be met for the emergency system to kick in?"

"Someone needs to get close to the Nucleus of the Astrolabe and send a command to it. The Nucleus in and of itself does not have any consciousness. It only stores energy and the terminal that is used to execute the command. The only passageway is under Father's tower, but it's already been connected to the Central Computer by lead wires."

"So, we can try, but this emergency system..." A-Ka suddenly remembered something and stopped breathing for a second. He asked, "Is it that chip? Who else knows about this?"

"That chip only recorded the explorations of the adventurers. It doesn't have the voice command needed to enter the Nucleus," Heishi said. "The old man that you found underneath the City of Steel was one of the adventurers who entered the Primeval Heart back then."

A-Ka remembered the assassination that Heishi had carried out. "Then, why...?"

"There were only four people who knew about this matter," Heishi said. "You, me, the dead Liber, and General Macksie. Father discovered their plans and sent robots to kill Macksie, before creating a copy of him, who would then sneak into Phoenix City to gather the armies and start a war. He intended to send the battle strength of millions of clones into the City of Steel, where a trap would be laid beforehand. That way, everyone would die at once.

"But General Liber, through some method or another, discovered that something was wrong. Unfortunately, it was too late. He knew very few things about the secrets of the Nucleus, and in the end he was sacrificed. Now, I've killed the spy pretending to be Macksie. After this, they'll take back control of the upper ranks of Phoenix City. If this succeeds and we find the emergency system, there's a 50 percent chance that Father will shut down and reboot the Astrolabe."

"When the Astrolabe is rebooted, what will happen?" A-Ka asked.

"It'll return to the environment of the Golden Age," Heishi said. "The reboot will release the power of ions and expedite the growth of all plants, cleansing the pollution that you guys have wreaked upon this earth over these past few centuries. It will turn the environment and atmosphere into one more suitable for plants to grow. Do you think this is necessary?"

A-Ka had once read in a book that, during the Golden Age, the lands were green and flourishing. "I like the sound of that world," A-Ka said. "It's just like a terrarium."

"But after thousands of years, or even tens of thousands of years," Heishi said, "humans will still destroy it, as they always do."

"I won't," A-Ka said quietly. "But I can only speak for myself."

"You really want it that way?"

"Of course," A-Ka responded in a small voice. "Wouldn't you want a world where the wind blows and the sun shines and all kinds of organisms thrive?" Heishi seemed to be mulling something over, but he said nothing more. "Well, thank you for trusting in me."

"I only wish for you not to be entangled in such a complex problem," Heishi said in a deep voice.

"But I'm willing—I'm willing to help you."

"I'm not planning to go through with this."

A-Ka smiled. "If you weren't, then you wouldn't have come to Phoenix City." When Heishi didn't reply, A-Ka added, "I get it, but it went all right when I helped, didn't it? You should have told me some of what was happening."

"Don't tell anyone else about this," Heishi reminded him in a quiet voice.

A-Ka knew that the urgency of what was going to happen would fill everyone with horror, especially since they hadn't yet found the emergency system.

"No matter what," A-Ka murmured, "there will always be hope."

As Heishi finally reached the exit to the sewers, he pushed open the steel door to let in the golden afterglow of the sunset. A-Ka stared down at the scene below in shocked silence. The entire city seemed to have been bombed, with smoke rising from all directions. Many places had already turned into rubble.

In this brutal battle, clones and the humans engaged in a life-and-death struggle for Phoenix City. A-Ka hadn't realized it, but while he was unaware of what was happening outside, strife had spread shockingly fast. Heishi, still carrying A-Ka on his back, walked toward the Western Quarter, where the mercenaries were screening any human residents who wanted to enter.

"What's going on?" someone shouted.

"Are we separating?" another mercenary roared angrily. "I've tolerated those clones for far too long! I'll go beat them to death this instant!"

The human migrants on the other side of the wire netting responded with a hundred cries of agreement, and A-Ka began to realize how deep the conflict between the clones and the humans ran. The entire population of humankind in the Western Quarter shouted in favor of reclaiming their resources and usurping the last power-holder of the clones, Commander Angus. With emotions running high like this, there was no way to eliminate the schism between the species.

The mercenaries guarding the sentry post at the entrance of the Western Quarter interrogated Heishi when he walked up. "Who's there?"

Heishi, still carrying A-Ka on his back, said: "My chest pocket."

From Heishi's pocket, A-Ka pulled out a card. After the mercenary checked it, he immediately said, "Hurry up and get in. This place is too unsafe!"

Heishi brought A-Ka into the streets of the Western Quarter. Half of Phoenix City had already been taken over by the humans.

The Mercenary Association occupied the tallest building, fifty-two floors high, and had its doors open wide; many people poured in and out. Heishi took A-Ka inside.

It was the first time that A-Ka had entered this place since coming to Phoenix City. Heishi put A-Ka down and let him sit while he went to fetch some medicine. Others immediately noticed A-Ka's presence, and some mercenaries came over, asking him about the specifics of the situation outside. When Heishi returned, he gave A-Ka a shot of antibiotics to prevent infection, fed him a rapid-healing capsule, and moved to hoist him up again.

"I can walk on my own!" A-Ka protested.

"Come with me, then." Heishi pulled A-Ka into the elevator. They traveled up to the third floor and entered an expansive conference room. "You can rest here."

With this, A-Ka finally lay down, exhausted. His abdomen throbbed, itching a little; he could feel the wound slowly healing.

Not long after, footsteps woke A-Ka.

"Who is our little friend?" a deep voice asked. "Your companion?"

"A comrade in arms," Heishi said. "One of us."

A-Ka opened his eyes and saw that quite a few people had arrived in the conference room: Heishi, of course, along with a red-haired man A-Ka was not familiar with, Huixiong, Shahuang, and a man wearing a hat, as well as a woman in a wheelchair.

"Your little brother is safe, no need to worry," Shahuang drawled.

When A-Ka heard Percy was all right, he let out a sigh of relief.

"Let me introduce our group," Huixiong spoke. "You're looking at the leaders of the Phoenix City Mercenary Association."

A-Ka's eyes bugged in his head.

Shahuang propped his feet, clad in polished black riding boots, on the conference table. "I think we've frightened this little friend of ours out of his wits."

"You... Weren't you running a repair store?!" A-Ka asked with a yelp.

"Selling firearms is just his side job." The woman smiled warmly as she spoke. "Shahuang is our trump card, in charge of passing on intelligence and news about the clone regime from within his store. I'm the bookkeeper, Lilith."

The hat-wearing man took off his accoutrement, revealing a bald head covered with scars. He said very civilly, "I'm the leader of the Mercenary Association's troops, Rang Marx."

The red-haired man wearing a jacket held a silver gun in his hand, and he twirled it once before placing it on the conference room table. "I'm the leader of the gunslingers, Gerb," he said with a smile.

On the road to Phoenix City, A-Ka had heard quite a few rumors about how the humans and the clones coexisted in this city. On the surface, the clones held all the power, but the humans were working in secret and acting in the dark. They were much more cunning than the clones and understood the need to keep themselves hidden. In truth, there were not many humans left after the bloody battles with the Iron and Steel Corps. But because of this, the ones who had survived were the cream of the crop. They lived in different corners of the city, appearing fine with the current state of affairs, but they were actually turning every citizen into a soldier. As soon as they picked up arms, they would be ready to fight.

"The Mercenary Association is the hidden strength of the humans," Huixiong said with a rumble. "As long as there are humans living within Phoenix City, they'll accept our orders."

"I know you," Heishi said calmly. "When Feiluo sent me here, the first point of contact he introduced me to was Shahuang. You used the mercenary system to get involved in the battle between the clones and Father."

"Yes," Huixiong said. "But that clone commander is not so familiar to us, and I think this is a good opportunity for our two sides to understand each other. Since you're a human, we will stand behind you as staunch supporters no matter the situation."

Lilith opened a notebook. "Feiluo told me that you are the savior of the humans, that you brought a secret back with you, and that you were seeking our help. Before meeting us, he could not disclose what the secret was, which is why Shahuang got in contact with you—but you then sniped the leader of the Rebellion, the clone general Macksie. I hope you can give us an appropriate explanation for your actions."

"There is no longer any way to control the rioting," Huixiong continued. "The clone troops have surrounded the area, so you must prove that you really have the ability to save us all, Savior, or we'll have no way to deal with this turbulent situation."

"I will prove it," Heishi said coldly, "but not right now. Have you found Macksie's chip yet?"

"It was snatched away by a clone in the chaos," Gerb said, smiling. "Without the chip, we have no way to prove that he was being controlled by Father, which means that you are the murderer who plotted and carried out General Macksie's assassination."

"That was another one of my comrades in arms who took it," Heishi said. "He's called Feiluo. Send someone out to find him."

"But you lied to us!" Shahuang protested. "I thought that you would use some clever method to expose Macksie's identity, but it was just this?"

"A bullet was the best method," Heishi said quietly.

Shahuang jumped to his feet and yanked Heishi toward him with one fist. "You stuck your little whoreson mistress in my store just to do *this*?!"

"Who're you calling a mistress?" A-Ka would not take this lying down, and he pressed the mechanical limb against the back of Shahuang's head. "I didn't know that Heishi would come back at all!"

Coolly, Heishi said, "Sit back down. Your wound hasn't healed yet."

A-Ka pulled back his weapon, and Shahuang chuckled. "You're not stupid, brat. That thing you pressed so boldly against my head was made from parts from my shop. Do you really want to open fire, just like Heishi?"

"Let go of him," A-Ka demanded.

Though Shahuang was furious, he had no choice but to let go of Heishi's collar.

"Thousands of people died because of that single shot of yours," Lilith said, with a hint of menace in her voice. "There's no longer any way to control the situation."

"What should come will always come," Gerb said. "Vice-President, this is something that no one had the power to predict. Not bringing up the conflict between the humans and the clones doesn't mean that it doesn't exist."

"All right, let's not argue anymore," Huixiong said in a low voice. As soon as he opened his mouth, the conference room quieted.

"Are you the president?" A-Ka asked.

Huixiong glanced at A-Ka. "Yes, but that isn't important. Son of God, I want to hear your opinions."

Huixiong used a strange term of address for Heishi, one that A-Ka had never heard before. He narrowed his eyes at Heishi but didn't speak.

Thinking Huixiong's request over, Heishi was quiet for a second before saying, "Have Angus come over to negotiate."

"And then what?" Shahuang asked. "You think he'll come?"

"Find Feiluo. He has the chip that Macksie dropped," Heishi said. "Have Angus deal with it on his own."

"The situation has changed, and we cannot confirm whether or not Angus is also being controlled by Father," Huixiong warned. "If he does turn out to be a spy, or one of Macksie's subordinates is with him..."

"Then you're done for. Might as well prepare for your funeral ahead of time, President," Heishi said, unconcerned. He stood, picked up his coat, and reached out a hand to A-Ka, leading him out of the conference room.

In one of the resting areas in the offices of the Mercenary Association, Heishi and A-Ka sat shoulder to shoulder on the bed. Picking up the chip that he had given to Heishi, A-Ka turned it over and over in his hands, and Heishi toyed with a small knife, not making a sound. Little by little, A-Ka had begun to understand something: why Heishi wanted Angus to come in person. It was so they could avoid any hint of the secret being leaked.

Today, A-Ka seemed to have met an unfamiliar Heishi. After all, ever since A-Ka rescued Heishi from the City of Steel, he had been as cold as a glacier and just as quiet. He'd certainly never shared his past with A-Ka. Now that Heishi was slowly remembering it, he had also become more human, with a more vivid air. He was able to think, speak on his own, and plan ahead like a human would.

What exactly was he? Was he a human? Or was he a man-made organism from the ancient past that had been given consciousness?

Heishi noticed that A-Ka was studying him. "What are you looking at?" he asked curiously.

Their shoulders touched, and A-Ka turned his head to watch Heishi, while Heishi looked back at A-Ka. Their faces were very close, and in that instant, A-Ka felt that Heishi was a little uncomfortable.

"It's...nothing," A-Ka said.

Heishi glanced away. "Do you know how to make a decoder?"

A-Ka remembered that during their hasty escape, with no tools at their disposal, they hadn't been able to access the contents of the chip. Now, as long as they had the correct supplies, A-Ka could throw together something to read chips.

"I can," A-Ka said. "I'll go find the supplies."

Heishi went outside to find someone who could take A-Ka's list of supplies, and soon after they brought the materials. A-Ka slid on the metallic goggles that technicians wore, then began to put together the optical-printed circuit board and other complicated mechanisms. First, he hooked up the magnetic coils to the chip, cracking the encoding it used.

Suddenly, without lifting his head, A-Ka asked, "Heishi, are you a human?"

"Be more focused when you're working."

A-Ka pushed his goggles up and darted his eyes toward Heishi. Ever since they'd parted, he felt that Heishi's attitude toward him had grown much gentler.

"I can split my focus many ways," A-Ka said, smiling. "I've seen you bleed, and your blood is red, so I think you're a human."

"I guess I count as one," Heishi said.

"Why do you know about all of this stuff? About the Nucleus, that emergency system..."

"Because I'm the Eliminator left behind by the Creator."

A-Ka almost zapped his own fingers. "Wh-what?"

Heishi was still playing with the knife in his hand and not lifting his head. "I wasn't named 'Heishi.' Heishi is what the adventurers who ventured into the Primeval Heart called the other laboratory they created."

"Wait, you... You've remembered your own past?"

"No. This segment of memory isn't from my own brain, but it was something that the records in the Primeval Heart told me. After all, I have no way of knowing about things that happened outside my chamber while I slumbered."

"So, what's your real name?"

"I don't have one. You gave me the name Heishi, so you can call me that. My creators programmed me to eliminate all of the unexpected changes to the petri dish caused by unforeseen processes."

"Then...how long have you lived for?"

"For longer than you think. Every five thousand years, I awaken once to check if the Primeval Heart has been disturbed."

At this point, A-Ka had wholly forgotten about the chip; his eyes were locked only on Heishi. "So, your body is so well-built because you're not human."

"Not only that, I can understand pieces of knowledge that humans are unable to wrap their heads around. The only reason many of my memories were destroyed is because that group of human thieves sneaked into the Primeval Heart, smuggled me out, and cut the power source."

A-Ka let out a sigh, and Heishi continued, "So, I had to spend almost three months putting together the broken pieces of my memories. After the power was cut, I nearly died from exhaustion in the middle of the ocean."

"Do you remember what your Creator looked like?" A-Ka asked. "Why did he want to create the Astrolabe, a laboratory this large?"

"Focus on making your decoder," Heishi said.

A-Ka could only lower his head, consulting a decoding manual as he began to study the symbols from the chip on the display screen. With this explanation, he finally understood why Heishi was so powerful, and it seemed like his abilities were not limited to just the ones he had displayed so far.

"Really, all that's to say," A-Ka said, trying his best to make his words lighthearted, "you need to be the one to start up that emergency system."

Heishi didn't respond.

"Does this mission have any life-threatening danger?" A-Ka asked.

The small knife slipped and cut into Heishi's palm, and a little blood ran from the wound. A-Ka was startled, but before he could get up to examine the wound, it had already healed over. A-Ka picked up Heishi's hand, pressed their fingers together, and lifted his eyes to meet Heishi's gaze.

Heishi's brows drew together. "Is that very important to you?"

A-Ka sat back down, putting together his data chip decoder. If Heishi died while destroying Father, the humans and the clones would be given a beautiful homeland—but was he willing to let Heishi die? What if it was A-Ka in Heishi's shoes?

A-Ka pondered these questions as he began to decode the chip. He couldn't resist asking, "What's the actual start-up procedure?"

"I'm only in charge of surveillance, not activation," Heishi said. "You've guessed wrong. Starting up the emergency system has nothing to do with me."

With this, A-Ka let out the breath caught in his chest and nodded a little. Heishi seemed to notice, but he didn't say anything.

With a grin, A-Ka asked, "After Father is destroyed, will you keep sleeping? Or will you live on as a human?"

"The laboratory has already been destroyed, and you lost the sleeping chamber, so how can I keep sleeping?"

"Thank you," A-Ka said, beaming. He could tell Heishi didn't get it, so A-Ka said, "For helping us do all this. If you succeed at this mission, let's live together. You can sleep in my bed."

"But I haven't decided to help. I'm only planning on handing the chip to Angus."

"You will," A-Ka said. "You like humans, and you don't like the mechanical troops. I know that in your heart, you're willing to help us." He paused. "Say, when you go to start up the emergency system, can I come with you?"

Heishi didn't even think about it before rejecting him. "You cannot."

"But I can help you."

Heishi said coldly, "That place is beneath the ground where Father stands. I cannot bring you there. What could you even do?"

A-Ka persisted. "When the time comes, you'll know."

Heishi let out a muffled grunt and stopped replying.

At that moment, A-Ka let out a real sigh of relief. He had put together the decoder, and he found that he really had gained a new ability: seeing all the components that made up a mechanical device. The sense seemed to extend to anything that wasn't living and allowed him to disassemble something once, then gain the ability to assemble anything else that resembled it.

He stuck the chip in the card reader slot of the decoder, and the image of a person showed up on the holographic projector. It was an old man, the person whom they had met underground in his last breaths: Professor Callan.

His voice buzzed with static, and the image was blurry. As soon as Callan appeared, he opened his mouth. "Commanders of the clone regime, my descendants…"

A-Ka became nervous. Heishi got up and closed the door before standing with him in front of the table, staring at the projection.

"You haven't watched it either?" A-Ka asked quietly.

Heishi shook his head so slowly it was almost imperceptible.

Electronic static continued to issue forth. "…I am your paternal originator, Callan…"

"He was one of the original four adventurers who entered the Primeval Heart," Heishi said.

"I trust that you have already received my last communication and have sent out your troops to destroy the man-made god. My life is reaching its end, and I am unable to help you any further… No matter which commander is listening, please remember the words I am about to say next.

"When I was designing the blueprints for the first clones, I left behind a control mechanism. In your brains, there is a place where a disused implant chip is located. Father utilized this weakness by sending out radio waves to activate them. In the beginning, you might not be able to sense the existence of the chip, but with the influence of the radio waves, their control will strengthen and produce results…"

"Damn," A-Ka muttered.

Heishi made a gesture, telling him to remain quiet.

A series of anatomical charts appeared on the holographic projection, which provided analyses on the weak points of the clones. Professor Callan then said, "You all must be careful. Father has planted spies within the clones. Humans will forever be your allies because they are not under any influence of Father's. Now that you have received this message, you must ask them for aid.

"As for the location of the Astrolabe's Nucleus, it is right underneath Father. Through the flow of pure energy, the Nucleus influences the entire land, and in these past years, Father's communication pipelines have continually spread toward the Nucleus. In less than a hundred days, Father will complete the process of linking up with the Nucleus. At that time, it will forever gain control over this world of the Astrolabe.

"Go find the Son of God in the Heishi Laboratory. He has lived for ten thousand years, and he awakens once every five thousand. The predestined fate of the Son of God is to awaken once the world of the Astrolabe is on the verge of collapse. At that time, he will save the living inhabitants of the world."

## 10
## THE TERMINATION COMMAND

"**Is this talking about you?**" A-Ka asked Heishi. "Why does it sound like it isn't?"

Heishi's expression darkened.

Professor Callan continued, "The Son of God is the only one who can shut Father down. After finding him, you must listen to the truths he speaks and carry out his orders. My time is almost up. I've extracted the essence of my genes and put them into this vaccine vial.

"I hope that when you find it, the power of the Eye of Truth can be of use to you. The person who receives this injection will be able to analyze the internal structures of anything, aiding the Son of God in entering the Nucleus of the Astrolabe..."

A-Ka came to a startling realization. "That was the injection he gave me!"

"This is something they *stole* from the Primeval Heart," Heishi said. "A power that never belonged to him in the first place."

"But he's having me bring you into the Nucleus of the Astrolabe. This works out great! Now you can't leave me behind."

Heishi was shocked into silence for a moment. Gripping A-Ka's shirt collar, Heishi stared intensely, but A-Ka only smiled back. He wasn't sure why, but he had a sense that under Heishi's standoffish facade, he was a good person with a warm heart.

Suddenly, Huixiong's deep voice came through the door. "There's been a new development."

Heishi pulled the chip from the decoder and handed both items to A-Ka, who stashed them into his tool bag. Heishi was silent for a moment more, as if he was thinking about the current situation.

Once again, Huixiong knocked on the door. "Can you hear me? What happened? If you don't open the door, I'm going to break it down."

Heishi indicated that A-Ka should go open the door, so A-Ka let Huixiong in.

He really towered over everyone, even Heishi, and as he looked down at him from above, he said, "Your friend isn't willing to come."

"The reason?"

"He believes that you lied to him, because you only told him to retrieve a chip that would fall from Macksie's person in the chaos. However, you didn't say that you were planning on murdering General Macksie, which led him to shoulder the crime of betraying his people."

"I'm only using the fastest and most straightforward method to accomplish this mission," Heishi said.

"Then *you* have to persuade him."

"Fine. Connect me with him."

"We can't find him. After telling our mercenaries about this, he disappeared."

"I have a method," A-Ka interjected. "Where's Percy? I'll bring Percy along to find him."

Heishi gave A-Ka a look, hesitating a little.

"Why don't I go with you two?" Huixiong said.

Percy was sitting in a small room, entering something into his transmitter. As soon as A-Ka pushed the door open, Percy stopped—but only briefly. When he realized it was A-Ka, he once again began to tap in encoded messages.

"Are you able to contact your dad?" A-Ka asked.

"I can, yeah." Percy said. "A-Ka, did you get hurt?" When A-Ka replied affirmatively, Percy asked, "Where? Was it serious?"

A-Ka sat down by Percy's side and pressed down against his shoulder, then lifted Percy's hand, placing it against his own abdomen. The wound had already healed, leaving behind a bullet-shaped scar.

"Feiluo's very angry," Percy said. "He says he'll find a way to save me, but he thinks Heishi lied to him."

"Can you persuade him?"

Percy nodded. "I'll try."

"We need to find someplace to speak with him face-to-face," A-Ka said. "Let's first agree on a location to meet. It'll just be the two of us and the president of the Mercenary Association."

Percy sent that information over. This time, there was a long pause before the reply came.

A-Ka, Percy, and Huixiong left the Mercenary Association and headed toward the meeting location.

"You haven't told me yet," Percy piped up. "What exactly happened?"

A-Ka didn't dare tell him about Heishi's mission, so he only spoke of the part involving Macksie being controlled. Percy nodded and didn't pass any judgments.

Feiluo was standing in a pile of rubble when they arrived. When he saw A-Ka, his brows creased deeply. "Percy, come to me."

But Heishi appeared behind them, silent as a shadow. Seeing that, Feiluo immediately flew into a rage. He came forward, fully intending to fight Heishi. "Friend, is this how you repay me?!"

"He was already being controlled, so he needed to be eliminated as quickly as possible," Heishi replied. "I didn't know how many of your people had their chips activated by Father. To prevent the news from spreading, I couldn't tell you anything."

"You..." Feiluo walked over and pressed Heishi against the wall, raising his fist.

"Please, don't fight!" A-Ka hurried forward. He still really liked Feiluo as a friend, especially since they'd escaped the City of Steel and had fought to survive on that journey together.

Feiluo gave A-Ka a hard stare before looking at Heishi. He wanted to say something more, but he quashed his urge to do so.

"Give me the chip and you can have your son back," Heishi said.

Feiluo pulled out the chip that was still stained with blood, throwing it at Heishi's face. "You only came to help the humans," Feiluo said furiously. "You'll kill all of the clones. I should never have trusted you in the beginning!"

After saying this, Feiluo slammed one fist into Heishi's handsome face, and Heishi staggered backward.

"Feiluo!" A-Ka moved forward to stop him.

"See you again—never." Feiluo took Percy's hand and left.

Hurrying to Heishi's side, A-Ka tried to examine him, but he waved his hand, indicating that he was fine. When A-Ka looked at his expression, he seemed a little crestfallen.

"Feiluo's not a bad person..." A-Ka said, trying to intervene.

"There's nothing to say," Heishi said quietly. "Let's go."

Back within the conference room of the Mercenary Association, a silence hung over the group as they stared at the transceiver in the middle of the table. Heishi sat at the table's head, and A-Ka sat in a corner, intently studying Heishi's knife.

The transceiver suddenly sounded with a man's voice. "He's agreed to the negotiations! He's willing to come in person!"

The gathered people let out a collective sigh of relief. Huixiong's was the most exhausted. It was pretty clear that the pressure on him had been the greatest.

"Have him come alone," Heishi said.

The messenger on the other end of the transceiver left to pass the message, and a moment later, A-Ka heard them beginning to sing the marching song "The Black Plains" outside the Mercenary Association skyscraper.

He hurried in front of the window. Nightfall was approaching over Phoenix City, and the sky darkened as the fires of battle swelled around them. The streets had been blasted into a blackened mess. Still-burning embers were scattered everywhere. As they crowded along both side of the road, the mercenaries rushed to the end of the street, still singing "The Black Plains."

Someone was walking toward them over the blackened streets, and the mercenaries began to open a path for him unprompted. The person wore a military cap—General Angus was here.

Downstairs, someone passed on the message, and Huixiong went forth, opening the great doors to the conference room. A clone came in, plucking his military cap off his head before sweeping his gaze over the people gathered in the room.

"Please sit," Heishi said.

The atmosphere seemed to ice over. Angus replied, "You must first prove your identity."

"I want to show you a message before we discuss the matter of my identity," Heishi said.

A-Ka pulled out the decoder and the chip from his bag and turned it on. Professor Callan's form and voice appeared on the holographic projection.

"... Clone commanders, my descendants..."

The conference room was silent as a graveyard for a while, until the full contents of the chip finished broadcasting. Heishi then flicked his finger, and the small implant chip that could control a clone that had been retrieved from Macksie's head spun along the length of the table, slowly coming to a stop in front of Angus.

"I am the Eliminator, the child of the Creator," Heishi said calmly. "I am here to pass judgment upon you all."

That moment seemed superimposed over another in A-Ka's vision: Heishi taking on the form of a deity, his voice filled with menace and rage that made the listeners flinch at his intimidating aura.

Angus picked up the chip and glanced at it.

"Those sitting here include representatives of both the humans and the clones," Heishi said. "May the judgment begin."

Everyone held their breaths.

"In the past twenty thousand years, you, the life-forms that were nurtured on this Astrolabe, have changed this world. You've consumed the energy within the Nucleus of the Astrolabe and have killed each other. This is mutual slaughter between members of the same species—choices caused by warped emotions. As experiments, you are failures."

Heishi's voice held no emotion at all, as if he was just an observer stating the reality of things. "Likewise, you have destroyed the environment of the petri dish. You have also interfered with my Creator's intentions, smuggling the destroyer that he left behind out of the Primeval Heart and giving it life." His voice turned deep and hoarse. "The environment of the Astrolabe is no longer able to provide you with the resources you need for living, and according to the direction the experiment is developing in, it is already pointless…"

"This isn't fair…" Angus's voice trembled.

The higher-ups of the Mercenary Association finally reacted, too. "Not fair at all!" Huixiong agreed.

"No one can determine our fate!" In agitation, Angus jumped to his feet, pounding a fist on the table. "And the mistakes that our predecessors have committed shouldn't be our burden to bear!"

"Sit down," Heishi said. The conference room went silent, but no one moved. "I said, *sit down*."

Angus didn't dare defy Heishi's order, so he sat down timidly.

"This is unfair." Huixiong smiled, but it was a bitter expression. "No one can determine the fate of the humans and clones."

"There is someone who can," Heishi said. "The destroyer that you all let loose. It shall determine your futures."

"We aren't experimental results," Angus said as he straightened up, as if he wanted to prove the absurdity of Heishi's words. "We are living beings who have intelligence and consciousness. We are on the same level as the Creator!"

"This doesn't constitute a reason to maintain the experiment," Heishi said.

Angus seemed to have lost all reason as he bellowed again, "This isn't fair!"

Heishi swiftly splayed out his hand. The bracelet around his wrist shifted and assembled, becoming a six-foot magnetic sniper rifle, the muzzle of which was pointed at Angus.

"Three," Heishi said coldly.

The room was dead silent.

"Two."

"Heishi," A-Ka said, his voice quivering.

Angus backed up, and Heishi flicked the sniper rifle. With an ear-piercing screech of metal on metal, it disassembled itself, returning to its original form and wrapping itself around his wrist.

Another second more, and Angus would have exploded into ash. This commander of the clones had, in the nick of time, escaped with his life.

"So, we're all going to die?" Shahuang began to chuckle. "Here, let's drink to that. Either way, our final days aren't far away."

But Huixiong looked into Heishi's eyes, and he said carefully, "I imagine that you did not come here to tell us of an outcome that cannot be changed."

Heishi's fingers drummed on the tabletop. "I want the armies of the humans and the clones to mobilize at once in order to draw away Father's firepower. I'll need a group of people to protect us as we sneak into the City of Steel. I also require a portion of code that comprises the very core of Father. According to my previous investigations, this code is composed of two parts. One part was stored in Macksie's brain, which is this."

Heishi gestured to the chip in Angus's hand.

"And the chip with the other portion, if my predictions are right, should be somewhere under your protection, Commander Angus."

Angus looked at Macksie's chip, trembling uncontrollably.

"These chips control the two primary functions of the entry and execution of the program, and after they're assembled that piece of code can cause a temporary shutdown of Father's core. Though Father will still be able to attack afterward, the shutdown will terminate several major defensive measures in the Nucleus region. With that, we'll finally be able to successfully enter the passageway leading to the center of the Astrolabe.

"Now, give me the chip you're hiding. Aside from this, I'll need my technician to travel with me. Give me an answer after you consider your options."

Everyone in the conference room started.

"What are you planning?" Huixiong asked.

"I will link up with the Nucleus," Heishi responded, "to save you all."

"I don't believe you," Angus said coldly. "My clone brothers and I won't pin our hopes for our future on you, stranger!"

"Calm down, Commander!" Huixiong thundered. "Humans and clones must work together. This is our last chance."

"No, this person's a madman!" Angus snapped. "I won't accept his conditions!"

As Heishi was about to say "Up to you," his eyes slid to the side, where he saw A-Ka's pleading gaze. Changing his mind, he said, "You can't leave. Give me the execution chip. I know that you have the power to do so, Commander Angus."

"Absolute nonsense," Angus said.

He moved to go, but Huixiong stopped him. "Please wait, Commander."

Angus suddenly turned back, sweeping his furious gaze over the upper ranks of the Mercenary Association. There were armed soldiers guarding the doors. "Are you going to detain me here?!"

Shahuang gave Huixiong a look, and Huixiong said, "Let's begin the vote."

"Aye." Shahuang raised his hand lazily before placing a rifle with the mark of the Mercenary Association on the long table.

"Aye," Gerb echoed with a grin. Pulling out his own gun, he set it on the table.

"In favor," Lilith said. She handed over a rose brooch made of gold.

"In favor," Rang Marx agreed.

Huixiong sat at the end of the long table, silently watching Commander Angus. After a long time, he spoke. "General Angus, for the future of the clones and the humans, you cannot leave."

In the conference room, no one spoke.

Huixiong continued, "Give us the command to shut down the system. The clones can choose not to participate in this mission. We humans will shoulder the burden of carrying out the entire process."

Angus took a few steps forward, his voice filled with menace. "I shall not."

"Take him away," the woman in the wheelchair said. "Son of the Creator, please rest first. As soon as there is news, we'll notify you."

Heishi stood and nodded. He gave a look filled with meaning to everyone in the conference room before he and A-Ka turned and left.

To ensure they were not disturbed, the Mercenary Association had cleared out a small unit on the top floor for Heishi and A-Ka. There was even a small flower garden on the balcony. This was the suite the previous president of the Mercenary Association had lived in. At night, flying patrol units circled around, their yellow lights scanning the ground below, and in the distance buzzed the indistinct sounds of static over the radio waves.

During the middle of the night, A-Ka woke up for some reason. He took a look at Heishi sleeping beside him, then got to his feet and walked out of the apartment. Once outside, he inhaled a breath of fresh air and climbed onto the rooftop, sitting up high while hugging his knees. The entirety of Phoenix City spread out beneath him. On the horizon, the central tower controlled by the clones glowed with lamplight, reminding him of the day they escaped the City of Steel.

Soon enough, Heishi joined him outside. A-Ka turned his head toward Heishi and gestured for him to come up. The two of them sat shoulder to shoulder on the rooftop, staring far away. For a while, neither of them spoke.

"Couldn't sleep either?" A-Ka asked. Hearing only silence from Heishi, A-Ka murmured, "I wonder how Feiluo and Percy are doing."

He leaned on Heishi. In the distant darkness, flames dimly painted the night sky a bright red. There had been no news from the Mercenary Association, which indicated that they had so far been unsuccessful in forcing Angus to give up the termination command chip.

"You didn't need to treat Feiluo like that," A-Ka said.

"I just don't understand the emotions you humans and clones feel."

A-Ka recalled how Feiluo and Heishi had fought—and how Heishi actually hadn't returned Feiluo's blow. For some reason, this small detail was preserved like an amber-encased flower in A-Ka's heart, causing him to revisit it again and again.

A-Ka understood that Heishi's existence was more akin to a machine left behind by the Creator, but of course, this was a secret that only he knew. Technically, a messenger of God did not need to be equipped with many emotions, the way Father wasn't.

"I feel like..." A-Ka said tentatively.

"What?" Heishi asked.

A-Ka hesitated, then met Heishi's eyes. "Do you think you have the emotions of a human?"

A-Ka thought about how Heishi had changed from the first time they'd met to the moment they were separated and then reunited. On top of the raw emotional reactions that Heishi had when they were escaping, he possessed the emotional characteristics of a human. Plus, as they deepened their understanding of each other, these characteristics became more and more obvious to A-Ka. When he was injured in the sewers and Heishi revealed his concern for A-Ka, he was even more convinced of his conclusion. Though this feeling was immediately dampened by the accompanying truths that Heishi revealed, in hindsight, A-Ka was sure that Heishi had felt concern for him.

"No, I do not," Heishi said.

"You do," A-Ka insisted. "You really seem to. Besides, you were designed with humans as the model."

"When the Creator made me, you humans didn't exist and neither did the clones. You still think that's how it is?"

When Heishi put it like that, A-Ka saw the contradiction, but he still replied, "What you said is true, sure, but the Creator was also an intelligent being. How would you know that he wasn't like humans?"

"Because that's impossible." Heishi responded without needing to consider it. "Logic, communication, identification, and judgment are all part of reason. But joy, grief, sorrow, and contentment? Those are emotions."

"You also get angry and impatient."

A-Ka was trying to explain the essence of being a human to Heishi, but he didn't even look at A-Ka. Instead, Heishi's eyes were focused somewhere far away.

"Basic reasoning skills are observation and judgment, while high-level reasoning skills are perception and analysis," Heishi said. "By the same principle, basic emotional skills are reactions caused by external stimuli, encompassing all kinds of simple feelings. These are the basic skills for any living being. I am not equipped with high-level emotional skills."

"What are high-level emotional skills?" A-Ka asked.

"High-level emotional skills..." Heishi thought for a moment. "They're the ones that only you humans have. Understanding body language, instincts, grudges, and the thing that you call love."

"But when Feiluo attacked you, why didn't you dodge him or return the blow?" Heishi paused for a moment, and A-Ka observed his expression with a smile. "You're really the same as us humans. You have complicated emotions and even feel loneliness and unease."

Heishi was only pensive for a short while before his cold demeanor resumed. "No, it was because I knew that he was only venting his anger and not trying to kill me."

"And why did you accept his anger?"

This time, Heishi deeply thought that over. When he answered, it wasn't aloud—he just shook his head.

"After parting ways with Feiluo, did you feel that something was wrong in your heart?" A-Ka asked.

Heishi continued to maintain his silence, but A-Ka knew that he was searching the depths of his heart, thinking about some things that even he hadn't realized.

At this point, a muffled explosion sounded in the distance, and Heishi roused abruptly, squinting his eyes in the general direction it came from.

"Infrared telescope," Heishi muttered.

A-Ka went back to his room to find it, but at that moment, the transceiver in the bag began to beep with the chime of an incoming message. A-Ka turned on the transceiver, only to hear Percy's anxious voice on the other end.

"A-Ka, their army is moving out," Percy said. "I don't know why, but they're going to fight again. You need to leave that skyscraper right away."

"Is Feiluo there?"

"He's gone to persuade the army not to attack for now. Why is this happening? Wasn't there a ceasefire?"

"The people from the Mercenary Association have detained Commander Angus. Listen to me, Percy, keep yourself safe, and no matter what, don't go outside…"

"This is really unreasonable," Percy said. "Can't they send him back? Feiluo and the temporary leader were arguing loudly, it nearly scared me to death—"

"This brat's sending messages to the enemy!"

"Kill him!"

A frenzy of sounds issued from the transceiver, and A-Ka's eyes widened with shock. "Percy!"

As if Percy had been caught by someone, he let out a shrill cry. The transmission cut off. A-Ka knelt in front of the bed, breathing rapidly.

Heishi was standing behind A-Ka. He had heard the entire exchange.

"I'll go notify Huixiong."

Another battle broke out unexpectedly, and this time the fighting was fiercer than before. The fires of battle once again baptized Phoenix City in catastrophe over a long, sleepless night. Six magnetic aircraft swept toward the humans' district from the tall tower in the north, and the entire Western Quarter awoke within moments.

The tower of the Mercenary Association was filled with furor. Heishi ran down the stairs, asking, "Is Angus willing to hand over the code?"

"Not yet!" Huixiong said. "He won't agree no matter what we say. We must first fight off their attack. Mercenaries, pick up your weapons and prepare for battle!"

With a huge boom, the entire building shook as thousands of bullets made of light shot out of the aircraft, shattering the glass that made up the facade of the building. The clones were bombarding the skyscraper as they began their efforts to rescue the captured Commander Angus. In the disorder, Heishi shielded A-Ka as the two of them escaped the skyscraper.

The dark night continued, the fires of battle igniting all around. Huixiong's voice issued forth from speakers around the city: "My human brothers, please support us! We have found the machines' weakness, and we are counting down the days until our victory! We are in our darkest hour. Macksie had turned against us and the Rebel Alliance..."

The humans and the clones had long struggled over resources; when the humans heard that they'd been betrayed, they snarled in fury and raised the guns in their hands, throwing themselves into battle. But the humans' firepower was weaker than the clones', and they suppressed the human troops with just three rounds of sweeping bullets.

A-Ka equipped his mechanical arm, and Heishi's wristband turned into a heavy machine gun that accurately gunned down the aircraft coming right for them.

The ships of both humans and clones turned into fireballs as they spiraled in twos and threes to the earth below, where they erupted with loud explosions.

For a while, there was nowhere to hide. Just as A-Ka was about to flee somewhere with fewer people, someone rushed him from the side and covered his mouth, dragging him toward the skyscraper that was going to collapse.

Heishi's expression tensed, only to settle when he realized that it was Feiluo.

"What the hell is your side *doing*?!" Feiluo yelled.

Under the hazy sky, A-Ka explained what had happened. Feiluo let out an anxious breath as Heishi rushed to his side.

"Where's your son?" Heishi asked.

"He's been detained by the Rebellion soldiers because he was passing messages to you," Feiluo said. "Come with me. We have to go."

Even now, Feiluo's face was dark with anger as he brought Heishi and A-Ka around the defensive line, close to the base of the Rebellion. They came to a stop in front of a vent, and Feiluo spoke. "A-Ka, I know you can open this entrance to this pipe. If we crawl up along the vent, we'll be able to reach the command center."

A-Ka lifted his head, looking toward the tall building shrouded in the velvet of the night, where he saw the flash of lights from surveillance machines patrolling above. Without a word, he put on his pair of infrared mechanic's goggles and began extracting a few tools from his pack to unlock the security system. Heishi and Feiluo stood silently to one side.

Eventually, Heishi asked, "Why did you come back?"

"Because Percy got captured, of course! He's being held in the command center, so I have to go in to rescue him."

"The termination command is on a magnetic chip that can be wiped," Heishi said. "If nothing's gone wrong, there should be thirty megabytes of code in there."

Feiluo thought deeply for a moment before answering, "I'm not sure where Commander Angus put it. In theory, since Liber also received it, there should be at least one backup. I'll take the two of you into the building, where you can search through the deceased's belongings. Perhaps you'll find something there."

"Why would this chip be in the hands of the clones?" A-Ka asked.

"You think that launching an assault on the machines on all fronts is a joke?" Feiluo said. "If Heishi hadn't brought up the shutdown codes, then you humans wouldn't even know about this secret weapon."

A-Ka flashed back to when he had just discovered Heishi. Liber had made secretive but extremely thorough arrangements, mobilizing all of their forces in the City of Steel. Perhaps he had been relying on the shutdown codes he had.

"I get it," A-Ka said. "The headquarters of the Rebellion *must* have that backup. Thank you, Feiluo!"

"I'm not planning on helping Heishi," Feiluo said without warmth. "But, the way things are, the fighting will only stop if we retrieve the termination codes. Otherwise, we wouldn't have to wait for the Iron and Steel Corps to attack us—we would die at the hands of our own."

"This was your original sin," Heishi said.

When Feiluo heard these words, he immediately flew into a rage. Grabbing Heishi, he shouted, "Say that again!"

"Stop fighting!" A-Ka called as he squatted in front of the vent.

Feiluo let out a vicious snarl as he pushed Heishi aside.

"Liber still died in the end," Heishi said.

"We did not despair before this," Feiluo said, "because Angus knew that the chip that would execute Father's shutdown program was still in our hands."

"Foolish," Heishi replied. "Even if you had both chips, they could only be used once to temporarily turn off its nuclear core for three minutes. You would have nothing to protect against its external defenses and the Iron and Steel Corps' patrols. Didn't you find that strange?"

Feiluo forgot their conflict and stared into Heishi's eyes. "What?"

Something like electricity shot through A-Ka's body as he understood.

"The previous movements of the troops were just a trap that Father set in place via Macksie," Heishi said.

In that instant, Feiluo's blood froze.

Heishi, however, remained unchanged. "Macksie was a puppet of Father, and he obtained these two original chips from the Creator's laboratory. From this, he learned of the termination codes for the nuclear core and lied to Liber and Angus, telling them that this was the only opportunity to completely destroy Father."

Feiluo's voice trembled. "S-so…the strongest forces of the Rebellion, including General Liber, were sent to…the City of Steel."

"Yes. Everything was as that computer predicted. Liber, believing that he could use the termination command to save this world, initiated that attack. As expected, it failed."

With a click, the security system outside the exit of the vent unlocked.

A-Ka stood. "It's done."

"If General Macksie had all this time to lay the trap," Feiluo murmured, "then perhaps he has long since destroyed the chips."

"Not necessarily," Heishi said, his voice not carrying a hint of emotion. "Father hasn't yet exterminated you all. Perhaps it was planning to use the original chips to lay the same trap again. This time, Macksie was only halfway through carrying out his plans when I shot him.

"Pray for your futures," he concluded, then he hunched over and squeezed into the vent.

The three of them crawled through the vent carefully. Intermittently, they reached crosshatched fields of lasers. Each time they approached these areas, A-Ka pulled out a card that he had made himself and pressed it against the pressure-driven security system. After he did that, the lasers blocking the path ahead of them disappeared with a hum.

"When did you gain this power?" Feiluo asked.

"After we left the City of Steel," A-Ka said.

"No, he's always been like this," Heishi said from up ahead, where he was inching forward on his elbows. "Even in the city, he was able to develop his own humanoid mecha."

From afar came the sound of numerous explosions. They reached a fork in the path, and Feiluo lowered his head to study the fluorescent map in the pipes. "The place where they're keeping Percy is to the left. I need to save him, otherwise he'll be disposed of when the sun rises."

"Let's go together!" A-Ka said.

"You need to find the codes. The greater good is more important," Feiluo said.

The three of them fell silent for a moment before a rare smile grew on Feiluo's face. "I'll save Percy, don't worry."

In the darkness, Heishi reached out a hand, looking into Feiluo's eyes. Feiluo was still for a bit before he, too, reached out a hand. This brief gesture indicated that the two of them had reconciled once more. Feiluo then opened the cover of the pipe and sneaked into the hallway outside.

As Heishi and A-Ka continued to crawl forward, A-Ka began to smile.

"What're you happy about?" Heishi seemed to be able to sense all of A-Ka's movements, even in this pitch-black tunnel where they couldn't see their hands in front of their faces.

A-Ka grinned. "Feiluo's a pretty good friend."

"Oh, shut up."

Dawn approached, and A-Ka continued to worry about Percy as the sky slowly lightened outside. With one kick, Heishi removed the iron bars blocking the exit of the vent.

"Head down in a moment," Heishi warned.

The instant that Heishi leaped down, he spun in the air and flicked out an electric whip. With a sizzling crackle, the whip toppled the robotic guards like felled trees. A-Ka poked his head out of the vent, then stepped onto Heishi's shoulder before jumping down to an office desk.

"Hurry up," Heishi said. "The guards are going to come any minute now."

A-Ka began to crack the code for the table, but Heishi was impatient. He made A-Ka step away before he shot right at the table.

The recoil echoed loudly as A-Ka yelled above it, "You can't break it open with brute force, or the contents will be destroyed!"

In the meantime, the shot had alerted even more guards.

"It's too late!" Heishi said. "Find it quick! I'll hold off the guards!"

Footsteps came from the hall—clone troopers. Heishi ran out, and A-Ka trembled as he searched through the table's drawers, which were stuffed full of documents.

"Who's there?!" someone shouted from outside.

Right after that, several successive gunshots rang out, and a bullet tore through the door. Fresh blood came with it, and A-Ka's heart tightened with worry.

"Heishi!" he called.

"Finish your job!"

Heishi's voice sounded near at times and far at others—like he was jumping from place to place. A-Ka searched through the cabinet in front of him and didn't find anything, so he inserted his decoding chip into the second cabinet, undoing the password-protected lock.

Would something as important as the termination command be kept in a place like this? As A-Ka pondered this for a second, his thoughts shifted in another direction. Could the chip be kept where the others were? However, Angus's office was their only clue; otherwise, finding a miniscule chip in such a large building would be like searching for a needle in a haystack.

Outside, Heishi was panting for breath. "You have three minutes. The guards here aren't easy to defeat."

"Don't rush me."

Where exactly could it be? A-Ka's nervousness seemed to have reached a critical point as more and more guards arrived. If he didn't find this key item soon, both he and Heishi would die here.

All at once, A-Ka's blood rushed to his head, turning his limbs to ice, and the gunshots and explosions in the corridor grew distant. All sound disappeared. The structure of the building appeared as clear as day in his mind's eye, every steel wire and brick defined to the smallest of details. The desk was connected to the floor, where there was an activation switch. The circuitry led toward the wall, where it was linked to a safe embedded in the bricks. An incredibly complicated alarm system was set up in front of the safe.

With a whoosh, his perception of his surroundings returned to its normal state.

"You're still not done?!" Heishi yelled.

Grasping his decoding chip, A-Ka ran to the wall. There was a bookcase there, and after thinking for a second, recalling the route of the wires, he returned to the desk and turned the knob on the swiveling armchair. The bookcase swung open silently, revealing the safe hidden behind it.

"A-Ka!"

"Found it!" A-Ka shouted in response. "Seriously, don't rush me!"

His hands waved as he turned the knob of the combination lock on the safe. Heishi crashed into the office, pressed his shoulder against the door, and used his electromagnetic light gun to draw a circle that welded the steel door shut. Behind the door, the clone guards began to shout and shoot their lasers, and the door silently began to glow red and cave inward.

"Hurry up, there's too many of them!" Heishi said anxiously.

A-Ka held his breath, recalling the internal structure of the safe. Heishi turned his head, watching A-Ka. "You found it?"

A-Ka's head ached terribly. "Ugh, what was the location of the last gear?"

Heishi moved to try brute force once again, making A-Ka's face twist with fear. "Stop, there's a bomb inside!"

The last digit was currently set to 0. Anxious beyond belief, A-Ka turned it to 1 before turning it back to 0. He was unable to sink back into the silent ocean where he forgot everything else and could see the structures of everything around him. The steel door was about to be broken through.

In that moment, Heishi said, "Let's take a gamble, just this once."

A-Ka's back was covered in cold sweat. "No way... It's too dangerous. There are high explosives in the safe. If the numbers are wrong, then the chip will be destroyed, and so will we."

As the two of them stood there, the future of mankind was like a roulette wheel marked in red and black that slowly began to spin. The marbles of fate rolled full speed toward a final position too foggy to determine. The fate of everything would be decided in this brief second.

Without giving A-Ka any time to protest, Heishi grasped A-Ka's hand, rotated the knob to 1, and pressed the button.

"Capture them!" the clone guards cried.

## 11

# THE PONTIFF OF DRAGONMAW

Instinctively, A-Ka flinched and shut his eyes. In that instant, Heishi pulled him into his arms.

The passage of time slowed to a crawl, and the sounds of the cacophonous world around them fell away. With a light click, like a delightful note of music, the safe sprang open, revealing an aged chip inside.

A-Ka opened his eyes. The door of the safe had activated.

Extending his hand, Heishi snatched the chip. With one arm still around A-Ka, he shielded his forehead with the other, then turned and charged toward the floor-to-ceiling windows. In just two quick steps, he reached the glass and slammed into it shoulder-first.

A-Ka screamed. "Heishi, you're *insane*!"

Heishi's blow shattered the bulletproof glass, sending the tiny shards flying. They looked like a shower of gems as they scattered under the first rays of the early dawn sunlight. Guards rushed into the office, but Heishi and A-Ka had already tossed themselves out of the building some hundreds of yards off the ground.

Time, which had slowed before, seemed to come to a halt. The only thing that A-Ka could hear within that complete silence was the slow beating of his and Heishi's hearts.

In the next moment, the two of them plummeted downward like a kite with a broken string. A-Ka let out an involuntary cry, but then Heishi's armband split into countless metallic shards and formed, layer upon layer, into a pair of metallic wings. With a whoosh, they spread open, acting like a hang glider, and he and A-Ka soared into the distance.

"This is insane!" A-Ka shouted, but in exhilaration this time.

"Shut up," Heishi replied coldly. "You make too much noise."

But when A-Ka looked up, he found that the corners of Heishi's mouth were actually slightly upturned, leaving a faint trace of a smile on his face. The two of them flew into the light of the early dawn.

At noon that day, the battle finally concluded. The entire city resounded with the tune of "The Black Plains" as the defeated humans were escorted into the plaza like prisoners of war. From a nearby building, Heishi bent over and watched the scene.

"Did it work?" Heishi asked.

"Not yet." A-Ka's brow was furrowed deeply in thought. "This chip with the main program is very ancient, and if I've guessed correctly, it should have come directly from the ruins that the Creator left behind..."

He put the chip from Macksie's head together with the main program chip, but he found that there was still a third port that needed a connection. What was this port for? A-Ka had a dim, ominous premonition: Was there another piece they were missing?

"This was technology from tens of thousands of years ago," Heishi said. "All the computational techniques that you humans and clones are now using were stolen from within the Primeval Heart."

A-Ka was out of time to study the other port, so he connected the chip containing the main program to the data cable. With a somewhat defeated sigh, he said, "I don't really agree with calling it 'stolen,' but all right… Let's look at what's inside."

Right as he finished speaking, the decoder spat out a densely packed encoded volume with 256 faces that formed a huge, glowing ball.

"If you're sure that's it, then we must immediately head down to tell Huixiong," Heishi said.

A-Ka's pupils expanded slightly as he looked at that encoded ball. He held his breath.

"Is there a problem?" Heishi studied the strange shape.

With a finger, A-Ka moved the encoded ball, turning it in a different direction. The red, glowing ball was only two-thirds complete, and the last third was blank space that now faced Heishi.

"What?" Heishi murmured. "There's a *third* piece?!"

"I-I guess this is something else that Father prepared ahead of time," A-Ka said in an unsteady voice. "At its core, it's afraid of the termination codes being leaked, so it deleted this section."

"Impossible. How could General Liber not have found this blank space? If one part has been deleted, then the command code is useless, so why would he have gathered the armies to storm the City of Steel?"

"But this is the original chip. What General Liber had was just the backup. When he copied it, the entire shutdown encoding must have been complete. As for where that last chip went…only the heavens know…"

As Heishi glanced at A-Ka, the two seemed to come to a tacit understanding.

A-Ka frowned. "Wait—what if the last piece is in Angus's head?!"

"Quick!" Heishi said.

A-Ka stowed the chip away before the two of them sprinted down the stairs.

At twilight, the sun still shone dimly over the black plains that had been scorched by the fires of war. The captured mercenaries were forced to kneel on the ground in a line.

"Hand our people over," a clone officer called, pressing a gun to the back of one prisoner's head. "Otherwise, for every minute that passes, we'll kill one person."

The mercenaries were gathered behind the defensive line, but though the crowd's emotions were turbulent, none of them stepped forward.

A moment later, Shahuang pulled Angus forward and pressed a gun to his forehead. "And if you guys kill a hostage, I'll kill him."

The clone officer jeered. "Shoot all you want. The clones have never had a leader. Have you not yet understood? We are all one body. If you kill Angus, anyone else can take his place."

Heishi and A-Ka ran through the rubble toward the mercenary headquarters. As others spotted them, they began to mutter among themselves. When A-Ka looked ahead, he saw Feiluo kneeling on the ground, hugging Percy with one arm while using his body to shield him. Percy's eyes were closed, and he leaned against Feiluo's embrace.

"Feiluo! Percy!" A-Ka tried to rush over, but a mercenary grabbed the collar of his shirt and dragged him back.

The clone officer who was issuing orders said menacingly, "These are our traitors who were colluding with the humans. Since you seem to care about them so much, we'll kill them first." Upon saying this, that clone officer walked toward the father and son.

"No!" A-Ka shouted angrily.

"Wait!" Huixiong's voice suddenly rang out. There was a disturbance within the mercenary base camp. Huixiong exchanged a few words with Heishi, then said, "We accept your terms. Give us a few more minutes."

The clone officer put his gun away. "Ten minutes. If General Angus isn't handed over to us then, I will kill ten of you humans."

A-Ka shot him a vengeful glare before turning and running toward the humans' base camp. Within it, he saw that the high-level members of the Mercenary Association were gathered, with Angus standing as straight as a pen in the midst, his expression cold and set.

"Even if you guys kill me now, there's no use," Angus answered decisively, as if he already knew that he was going to die no matter what.

"Where's the part that was deleted?" Heishi asked calmly. "I have reason to believe you have a backup."

Angus fell silent. Shahuang put his gun away and walked up, grabbing Angus's collar, as if he was about to hit him.

"Hey, hey, don't be hasty!" Huixiong said. "No one is allowed to attack right now!"

"I suspect that the encoded bit is right here, in this bastard's head." Shahuang pressed his gun hard against Angus's head as he spoke. "How about we saw him open and take a look?"

"It's not in his head," Heishi said.

"I also suspect it's not there," that red-haired man called Gerb said. "Just hand it over, Angus."

"I don't have it," Angus said measuredly. "This world is fated to be destroyed. There is no hope left."

As soon as those words were spoken, everyone's hearts skipped a beat. A strange expression appeared on Huixiong's face, while A-Ka's heart beat extremely violently as he suddenly imagined the worst-case scenario.

"You guys can kill me now," Angus said. "But if you do, you'll never be able to find the third chip. Input, output, and execution—the three main sequences. We were each in charge of one part. That last part was inserted into Liber's brain."

The same thought flashed through everyone's mind: *Damn it.*

A-Ka could hardly think. Liber had already been lost during the battle to take the City of Steel, right? Where exactly were they supposed to find the chip now?

Heishi was silent for a moment, then murmured, "Better prepare for your funerals."

"No!" A-Ka said. "There's still hope! Let's think about it a little more…"

Everyone's faces were as gray as ash, and for a while no one said anything at all.

"There's still five minutes left," Huixiong said after glancing at his watch. "Should we give up?"

"There must be a way," A-Ka said. "Let's think about it again… Could Liber have survived?"

"He's dead," Angus said calmly. "Every time a clone brother dies, a signal is sent through the quorum-sensing system to Phoenix City. Halfway through the battle—the instant the mother ship crashed into Father—General Liber perished."

"I'm familiar with the City of Steel!" A-Ka said. "I'll go back to search. I may be able to find the chip."

The mercenaries maintained their silence. Finally, Huixiong sighed.

Despite his conviction, A-Ka knew that returning to the City of Steel to find a single chip would be almost impossible. That last explosion had been like an energy wave that'd pulverized even the mother ship, so in all likelihood the chip had already long since been destroyed. Even if it had survived the explosion, the city would have been flattened and rebuilt by now by the androids.

"Three minutes," Huixiong said.

"Let's surrender." Shahuang put his gun away as he let out a long sigh. Within it, there was an endless well of reluctance and hopelessness.

Their shadows stretched long under the light of the setting sun, falling over the blackened plaza.

"A-Ka and I will go back," Heishi said.

"You won't be able to find the chip," Angus said. "Don't lose yourselves in pointless hope, because what comes with that hope is everlasting despair."

Tears welled up in A-Ka's eyes as he yearned for a miracle. When he glanced toward Heishi, he thought that he might have some way to deal with this, but even Heishi seemed to be out of options.

"There are only forty seconds left," the clone officer reminded them from the plaza.

"Go, Angus," Shahuang said. "Your duty is done."

Angus walked toward the center of the plaza, but at that moment, a huge boom echoed in the distance—as if something had split open space-time and was now rushing silently toward Phoenix City.

"The Iron and Steel Corps!"

"The Iron and Steel Corps have invaded!"

"No, not the Iron and Steel Corps! Be careful!"

A huge shadow enveloped the entire plaza as a golden airship flew over them. The clones backed up swiftly; they had no time to kill the human hostages as they each pointed their guns toward the sky and fired bullets of light.

"Percy!" A-Ka rushed out despite the danger of being hit with a bullet. With his body hunched over, he activated the hidden rocket propellers in his boots, flying toward Percy and Feiluo.

"Watch out!" Feiluo cried.

In a flash, the golden airship emitted a beam of magnetic light into the hail of lasers, which dissipated with a hum across the field. All of the guns crackled with electricity before they turned into hunks of useless metal.

Heishi grabbed A-Ka with one powerful arm and, with the other, dragged Feiluo and Percy back into the humans' camp.

As a whole, the clones retreated some distance, and Angus took the opportunity to run back to his own camp. In the space between the two sides, the golden ship lowered until it came to a stop. The door to its cabin opened, and a middle-aged man emerged, observing his surroundings.

Then, that man said, "General Angus, you have violated the sixth commandment."

"This is a conflict that the humans started!" Angus retorted.

The human side was entirely silent, and A-Ka asked quietly, "Who is this person?"

"The Curia request that you all immediately stop fighting," the middle-aged man said solemnly. "If any commandment is violated again, we will evacuate all humans in Phoenix City to Dragonmaw City in batches."

Angus chuckled without warmth. "Pass this message along to the pontiff of the Curia for me: I'd be very glad if he did so."

"Angus, you should know who came up with the commandments in the peace treaty," the man said. "Your ancestor gave the clones a place to stay in Phoenix City. If you are making light of what it means to start such a war, you should be clear on what the consequences will be."

Huixiong, who had been silent all this time, finally spoke up. "We aren't starting a war. Father implanted a control chip in Macksie, turning him into a spy for the machines who was deeply entrenched in the Alliance camp. Before he could begin a second futile battle, our brother carried out an assassination to stop him."

"The pontiff already knows what happened," the man said. "He requests that General Angus and the President of the Mercenary Association, Huixiong, as well as all parties involved in this matter, gather in Dragonmaw City and undergo mediation. Everyone, please come with me."

Turning on his heel, the man boarded his ship. There was a minute of silence on both sides before Huixiong took the lead and stepped out. "Let's go."

Percy whispered to Feiluo, "Dad, let's go. They're not bad people."

On the ship en route to the Western Mainland, A-Ka had previously heard the bard Moran bring up that the Curia believed in the God of the Astrolabe, the extraterrestrial Creator that had made this very world. Since Heishi was with their group, there shouldn't be any danger—so when Heishi walked onto the ship, A-Ka followed him. Angus and Huixiong also boarded after they both ordered their troops to temporarily halt the battle.

The airship slowly ascended into the air, heading toward Dragonmaw City in the southern part of the Western Mainland. It flew at a low altitude, and from the portholes in the cabin they could see the devastated land below them, as well as Phoenix City, which was charred by the flames of war.

Heishi also stood there on the deck, watching the land below him through the transparent glass.

"A-Ka," Percy said in a small voice.

"Percy." This was the first chance A-Ka had to speak with Percy since they'd been reunited. He bent over to inspect the rope burns on Percy's wrists. "What happened? Are you okay?"

Percy smiled. "I sent Uncle Moran an electronic message, telling him about the things that happened here. He once said that if we ran into any future difficulties, we could go find him."

No wonder. With that, A-Ka let out a breath.

"You guys ran into an official of the Curia?" Feiluo asked as he gently wiped Percy's face. "Why didn't you say so?"

"I wasn't clear on his position," A-Ka said. "He told us that he was only a wandering bard."

Upon reflecting on it in detail, A-Ka realized that Moran was no ordinary bard; after all, he had left the Eastern Mainland aboard a boat right as the battle to kill Father occurred. For him to appear in the Rebel Alliance's headquarters at such a time and place, in order to board that boat, suggested that he and General Liber might have communicated before in some fashion.

As for what the Curia did, A-Ka wasn't sure. When he saw Heishi, Huixiong, Angus, and that middle-aged man sent by the Curia standing together and chatting, he went over to them.

"The last chip has already been destroyed," Huixiong said. "It was in General Liber's hands."

"The Curia have received the news of General Macksie's betrayal," the middle-aged man said as he bowed politely to Heishi. "The pontiff asked me to pass along his regards to you."

Heishi's expression remained placid. "Does he still have a backup copy?"

The man thought silently for a moment before shaking his head. "Hmm. Perhaps there's still a way. Do not give up hope."

Huixiong let out a long sigh and leaned back against the railings. "With the current situation, our only chance is to once again seek refuge with the Curia."

"Are you friends of Uncle Moran?" A-Ka asked.

That man turned around and said politely, "I am Archbishop Igor, my friend, and on behalf of the pontiff, I would like to express his regards. He greatly respects the bravery and effort each and every one of you have exhibited."

A-Ka waved a hand, indicating that he didn't need to be so formal.

"The precursor to the Curia was founded by one of those original four explorers from all those years ago," Heishi explained to A-Ka.

With this, A-Ka finally understood. Back then, after the four adventurers had entered the Primeval Heart and left the Creator's laboratory, they had gone their separate ways, each establishing their own forces. Among them, Doctor Callan had obtained the cloning techniques, and with himself as a genetic source, created the group now known as the clones, becoming their father. General Gallo took command of the humans. Using the Creator's techniques, he built Phoenix City to allow humans and clones to coexist peacefully, creating the first republican regime. Professor Ricard took the computational techniques and the chip that made up the core of the Creator's various programs and created a huge, primordial computer. After undergoing evolution from the changes written into it, that computer became Father.

The last explorer had arrived in Dragonmaw City, gathered many followers, and taught them to believe in the Creator.

A-Ka's heart suddenly soared. "Does the pontiff have a method to restore this chip?" In this bleak, dark situation, he thought he saw a single beam of light.

Archbishop Igor sighed. "It's very difficult. Aside from a few defense mechanisms and modes of transportation, the Curia don't use any computer-related technology in order to prevent Father from sneaking in. However, there are quite a few records preserved in the church. We may be able to find another way to deal with Father."

A-Ka held the chip out for Igor to examine. Igor was wholly ignorant about any of it and could only respond, "When you see the pontiff, you may discuss this matter with him in person. We are about to arrive."

The airship steadily approached Dragonmaw City. It was a land covered with fresh wildflowers, and along the road from Phoenix City to Dragonmaw City, the earth that was blackened and barren slowly turned green—into a true paradise.

In a quiet voice, Feiluo described the scenery below to Percy.

"Since Dragonmaw City's founding, we have never accepted any clones or humans who grew up in technology-based civilization as believers," Archbishop Igor explained to those gathered. "Welcome, everyone, to the Country of God."

A breath of fresh air washed over them, and the glass shield around the airship dissipated as they slowly entered the territory of Dragonmaw City, coming to a stop at an empty port on the outskirts. This was a world frozen in time, and many mechanisms and transportation devices that A-Ka could see were ones that he had only read about in books. The main road was paved with cobblestones, and of all the buildings in the city, not a single one was taller than six hundred feet. The most grandiose of them was the temple in the center of the city, which was topped with a huge bell.

The strange architectural style made A-Ka feel that everything was very new and exciting in this country they were entering. At the empty port, a horse-drawn carriage came to a stop to pick them up.

When they'd arrived here, Angus had gone extremely quiet. The whole city had an awe-inspiring tranquility and sanctity about it, enveloped as it was in the last weak light of the day that shone just before nightfall.

Igor led them along a path to the side of the central temple. The passing clergy bowed to them in greeting, though their gazes paused on Heishi's face.

"It grows late," Igor said. "Everyone, please get a good night's rest. Tomorrow, the pontiff will invite everyone to dine together for lunch. At that time, he will also discuss the situation at hand."

A-Ka was still a little worried, but Heishi gave him a look to say he shouldn't be too nervous. After all, so many days had already passed, and if the world was going to be destroyed, one night wouldn't make a difference. To that, A-Ka could only nod, his heart heavy. Igor showed them to their rooms, and after informing them that their dinners would be brought to them, he saluted Heishi.

"May the God of the Stars protect all of you," Igor said elegantly before turning and leaving.

A-Ka lay on the bed and released a long sigh before sitting up again. Setting aside the satchel he was wearing, he clambered onto the chair in front of the window and peered out. In the calm outside, night had already fallen, and the garden was filled with blooming calla lilies. Gentle music drifted out from somewhere unknown, echoing melodiously.

Thinking to himself that this was all far too cozy, A-Ka returned to the bed. When he saw Heishi sitting on the side of it, his mind distant as he stared at nothing, A-Ka poked Heishi's waist with his foot.

"What is it?" Heishi blinked at A-Ka.

"It would be very nice if we could live here for our entire lives," A-Ka told him. "The world that I hope for is just like this."

Heishi considered this for a moment. "The world you humans used to live in was exactly like this. There weren't any robots or computers back then, so why did you need to create them?"

A-Ka thought for a moment, then smiled. "This lifestyle has its perks, but it's also pretty inconvenient. There's no tap water, so they need to get water from the river, and there's nothing to do for fun. Industrialization has its own merits as well."

"If you like this sort of environment, I could tell the Curia and get them to let you stay within Dragonmaw City."

A-Ka scrutinized him. "Will you stay as well?" When Heishi didn't respond, A-Ka said, "Having a flower garden to tend to and making a few small things sounds pretty good."

"Maybe later," Heishi said easily.

The nights in Dragonmaw City were a little chilly, so A-Ka and Heishi wrapped blankets around themselves as they stretched out on the same bed. Through the window, A-Ka watched the starry sky outside.

"Heishi, do you have memories of your childhood?"

He thought that Heishi would say no; after all, after he had been made by the Creator, and he had always been kept in that laboratory. Unexpectedly, Heishi responded, "I remember a little."

A-Ka turned his head to look at Heishi. Of his own accord, Heishi stretched out his arm and let A-Ka pillow his head on it, and the two of them stayed there in this position without speaking.

"What was it like?" A-Ka asked.

Heishi didn't answer, replying with a question instead. "How about you?"

"I... Actually, since I was old enough to understand, things were the way you saw. We absorbed the training, studies, and nurturing that the robotic life-forms enforced, but there was only one thing that left me with a deep impression. It's related to Father."

"Related to what about Father?" Heishi's voice was even.

"On the day before we come of age, all humans have to sync up with Father to pledge our loyalty. It's an uncomfortable feeling," A-Ka recalled. "It was like a monster was forcing itself into my brain."

"This is one of the special functions that Father has. Ever since the petri dish was started, it was equipped with the power to investigate the thoughts of any living being. As long as it was able to sync with you in a mental link, it could read any of the thoughts in your mind."

"Yeah. To be honest, in the beginning, I never had the idea of opposing Father."

"I did find it a little strange. Technically, humans like you would definitely not be able to survive under Father's gaze. You would have been destroyed by it before you came of age."

A-Ka had to admit that Heishi was right. The lax regulations in the City of Steel itself didn't mean that Father was foolish. Allowing him, a human, to secretly sneak out was not an oversight on Father's part, but rather something that would never have happened under normal circumstances.

For the humans living within the city, their thoughts had once been, or were destined to be, exposed to Father's inspection. Such exposure would target for preemptive elimination any human with any iota of a desire for freedom that might grow into an escape attempt. This was also the reason why, in the end, the clones created the Alliance and recruited agents on the inside by having those from the outside interact with them.

"The clones also undergo a mental inspection by Father," A-Ka said. "It's just that their inspection isn't as frequent as for us humans."

"How frequent was it then, for humans?" Heishi asked.

"About once every ten years. Really, I see now that it might be called an inspection, but in reality it's to kill the humans that have the seed of escape planted in their hearts."

When A-Ka was small, he had heard that many people would disappear in the process of these regularly scheduled inspections, but he had never thought about it in this way. He was starting to understand the gist of things.

"The clones have no logic to speak of, so they act on their emotions alone," Heishi said. "Humans, on the other hand, cling desperately to living and are afraid of death, so they became Father's slaves. There's not too much difference there."

"It's not like that." A-Ka turned over and slightly shook Heishi, whose eyes were still closed.

But Heishi didn't open his eyes. "Continue. I'm listening."

A-Ka began to smile, then used his fingers to pry open Heishi's eyelids, looking at his dark, deep, gemlike pupils. Heishi started counting in a dark voice: "Three." Afraid of being on the receiving end of one of Heishi's beatings, A-Ka yanked his hands back.

He recalled the day he had undergone the mental inspection. A vast sea of blue light had been everywhere. "That kind of feeling is hard to describe," A-Ka murmured. "It was very uncomfortable, as if someone had dug through every nook and cranny of my soul..."

"I know," Heishi said. "A pair of godlike eyes take you in from head to toe, which is why Father is able to strike such terrible awe into your hearts. You humans have a saying: 'When you gaze for long into an abyss, the abyss gazes also into you.'"

"But this was not an exchange that I meant to start..."

"What did you see within Father's thoughts?"

A-Ka was taken aback. Heishi had actually guessed what A-Ka was going to say next. "How did you know?"

That day, within Father's mental sea, he had indeed sensed something out of the ordinary. That shaky uneasiness seemed to come from a deep foundation, but also from a secret place that A-Ka's own soul yearned for. Initially, his brain hurt like it was being scorched by some bright light, making him feel as if he might retch, but gradually, the discomfort disappeared.

In the depths of Father's thoughts, he'd found, hidden very far away, a soul. Its voice spoke in A-Ka's ear as if it was saying something to him, but A-Ka's expression filled with confusion, and he had no way to answer.

"What did it say?" Heishi asked.

"I don't know," A-Ka said, smiling a little bitterly. "It's not like I could understand it."

"What did *you* say?"

"Well, I... I said I was very lonely, and—I took it to be a Father that would be able to do anything, you know? In the City of Steel, the humans all said that Father was a god that could do anything. So, I told it my wish."

"And what was that?"

"I wished..." A-Ka thought for a moment before continuing, "that there was a gege who would protect me, because growing up, I had always been kicked around and picked on by the clones."

Heishi opened his eyes, looking at A-Ka. His gaze was bright and warm, and the corners of his lips turned upward as he slowly smiled.

A-Ka goggled at the sight. "You... You're smiling? Heishi, you're smiling!"

Heishi's smile vanished as quickly as it had come, and he said solemnly, "Go to sleep."

In that moment, A-Ka forgot himself a little because of how handsome Heishi's smile was, and his heart filled with adoration. In the span of a second, that look had brightened the entire evening. With the fragrance of the flowers and night music, it was as if countless things had crossed paths in A-Ka's soul before erupting within the depths of his heart. A-Ka stared at Heishi, but Heishi rolled over like it was nothing, showing his back to A-Ka.

Nevertheless, A-Ka said, "When you smile, you look really good, Heishi." Heishi grunted. A-Ka couldn't resist adding, "I feel like I've fallen a little bit in love with you, you know. Just that sort of thing."

At this, Heishi tensed awkwardly. "Don't say stupid things!"

A-Ka hadn't been lying down for long, but he hurriedly pushed himself upright. "I didn't mean that, or not like *that*! Like what the textbooks described, between people... Just like how I love Percy, Feiluo also loves Percy, and Percy says he loves Feiluo."

Heishi didn't know how to respond to that.

A-Ka felt that the longer he went on, the more he dug himself into this pit, so he just shut up and set himself back down quietly behind Heishi.

Then, in the darkness, Heishi spoke. "You can treat me like your gege."

"Thank you, Heishi," A-Ka said, comforted. From behind, he hugged Heishi's waist and turned his head, resting it against his sturdy, powerful back.

"I will protect you," Heishi said, "but only you."

A-Ka murmured in agreement, and he fell asleep in the fragrance of a sea of flowers.

It was the most comfortable night of sleep he'd had since they had left the City of Steel, and it wasn't until the sunlight came shining through the window that the sound of knocking woke him. He thought he'd only slept for a few short minutes, but Heishi had already gone off somewhere or other. A faint whiff of his scent still clung to the blankets.

"The pontiff requests your presence in the Hall of Faith to partake in the midday meal," a young archbishop said very politely. "Please bathe first, as there is some time left. Clean clothes have been placed here."

A-Ka nodded. "O-okay."

Inspecting his new clothes, A-Ka found that they consisted of a simple set of technician's pants and a jacket. With that, he undressed and padded through the room before pushing open an inner door to the bathing room, only to find that the large bathing pool had already been fully filled with water so hot there was steam rising off it.

A-Ka stepped into the bathing pool, only to tread on something soft, which led to him uttering a loud shout. "Aah!"

He was so startled that he jumped, only to fall back into the water and swallow a mouthful of it. Then, he felt someone grab his wrist and pull him into an embrace, startling him a second time—and it was Heishi?!

"What?" Heishi asked impatiently.

A-Ka was still jittery from shock. "Wh-why are you here?"

"I'm bathing," Heishi said, like it was obvious.

His hair had grown much longer since A-Ka first met him, and when it was wet, the strands stuck to his forehead. As he stood up, he hugged A-Ka in his powerful arms, and A-Ka could feel how sturdy his muscles really were. Their warm skin pressed together as Heishi placed A-Ka at the edge of the pool.

"You wash first…" A-Ka said, still a little out of it.

"Why don't you just come in?" Heishi asked.

A-Ka stared at Heishi as the latter rose from the water, walking to get the soap. Finally, A-Ka's brain put the pieces together: Before, Heishi had been lying in the water, but A-Ka hadn't seen him at all, and with his clumsy step he had trod on Heishi's thigh…well, the part at the top of his thigh.

"I can do it myself," A-Ka insisted.

Still, he couldn't resist sneaking glances at Heishi. His physique was beautifully complete, just like a human built with the Golden Ratio in mind. He had just the right amount of muscle in all the right places. His height was also exactly six feet, the epitome of the ideal human. His physique was more well-proportioned than a clone's, and compared to those mass-manufactured beings, Heishi had an air of warmth that was unique to humanity. It was clear from the male scent that clung to his skin and the feeling his heat imparted to those around him.

"Were you created according to the Golden Ratio model?" A-Ka asked.

"I don't know," Heishi said. "But I can confirm that my father's features and physique were different from mine."

"I feel that the Creator *must* have liked humans." A-Ka smiled. "Or it was even partial to them, which is why it made you in the shape of humans."

"Perhaps," Heishi replied. "But I cannot say whether or not my father's world also experienced this era of humans."

"It should have."

A-Ka had begun to feel that humans were an extraordinary species. The way they experienced their joy or rage, along with their intelligence, set them apart from other living beings. Perhaps it was precisely because the Creator was partial to humans that Heishi was friendly toward them. At the very least, his interactions with them were different from his interactions with the clones.

Sitting in the warm water with his legs up, A-Ka hugged his knees. He and Heishi each rested quietly at one end of the bathing pool. A-Ka had a strong urge to lean on him. He'd enjoyed the feeling of leaning against Heishi's body to sleep the night before. His back was just like a father's back: broad and dependable. Though A-Ka had never had a father, he got that sense from Heishi.

"Can I hug you?" A-Ka asked.

Heishi said nothing, and A-Ka realized it would be a little awkward. This sudden, strange desire made him smile. "Um, just joking. Don't take me seriously."

To A-Ka's surprise, Heishi said, "All right, come over."

He opened his arms, and A-Ka scooted his way. The two of them came into contact in the warm water. A-Ka shivered a little, and when his fingers touched Heishi's arm, he couldn't help pulling them away. But Heishi grabbed A-Ka's hand and tugged it back, letting A-Ka press that hand against his chest.

Where A-Ka's hand lay, he felt a heart that pounded rhythmically, its beats both powerful and firm. This was the first time A-Ka had touched someone else's body like this, and an unfamiliar feeling rose in his heart. His breathing quickened as he stroked Heishi's muscular arm in the water. His shoulders, arms, abdomen, and legs were being caressed by the slick sensation of flowing water, but his muscles remained firm and powerful.

A-Ka drew closer to Heishi, hugging his waist and leaning on his body. They pressed together, naked—and in that instant, A-Ka felt a sudden, unexpected feeling of safety, as if he had found some sort of a home to return to in his life.

"Father," A-Ka murmured.

Heishi didn't speak. This was the second time that A-Ka had sensed something like this. The last time was in the depths of Father's thoughts, when he had been facing that silhouette of light.

A-Ka's breathing almost stopped. "It's Father…"

Heishi responded quietly, "You've felt it." A-Ka raised his head in disbelief, but Heishi reached out a hand to pet his hair. "This was bestowed by the Father of All Things, and through my male hormones, my heartbeat, and the flow of blood, it has the effect of calling to humans."

"What is it used for?" A-Ka murmured while watching Heishi's eyes.

"It doesn't have any use," Heishi said. "It's just a scent that he left on my body. It has nothing to do with me."

"Will you let me hold onto you like this for a while?" A-Ka asked.

"I will."

A-Ka hugged him, and Heishi pulled his arms to the side and leaned slightly back. Placing his elbows against the side of the tub, he allowed A-Ka to lie in his embrace like a newborn infant. A moment later, Heishi dabbed a little flower balm from the nearby scent box onto his palm and spread it on A-Ka's skin. Wrapping one arm around A-Ka, Heishi next pressed his other hand against the back of A-Ka's neck.

At Heishi's touch, A-Ka's heart filled with peace. He didn't say anything, merely enjoyed Heishi's warm palm rubbing over his neck and back. Eventually, Heishi spread the flower balm all over A-Ka's body.

A moment later, Heishi sat up, his arms still around A-Ka, and shifted so that A-Ka was sitting with his back to Heishi's chest.

A-Ka's breathing quickened, and his skin grew bright red as he leaned, gasping with sudden harshness, against Heishi's body. Something seemed to be sprouting in his heart. Methodically, Heishi cleansed A-Ka's entire body. When he was finished, he ran his fingers through A-Ka's bangs.

"Thank you," A-Ka breathed. He felt a little woozy, so it was good when Heishi lifted him up out of the water.

"As blood rushes upward, it's easy to get dizzy," Heishi said.

With that, he carried A-Ka out of the bathing room, then tossed him some clothes, letting him put them on as he put on his own.

When they left the side room, traces of that warm feeling were still left in the depths of A-Ka's heart. He turned his head to look at Heishi and reached for his hand. Heishi let his fingers relax and accepted the gesture. When they came to the end of the hallway, Heishi curled his fingers slightly, squeezing A-Ka's hand as he pushed open the door.

Music began to sound. Within the large golden hall, Moran was administering some treatment to Percy's eyes, but when he heard the music, he lifted his head and smiled.

"We welcome you, Son of God."

## 12

# THE TIDES OF SPACE-TIME

**O**N ONE SIDE OF THE TEMPLE, bright, warm sunlight scattered down, coating the earth below, its rays giving the humans who soaked it up a sense of languid comfort. Upon seeing Uncle Moran, A-Ka remembered that stretch of time when they had first left the City of Steel and spent their days together, all of them in the same boat. In his surprise and delight, he let out an exclamation and rushed forward to hug Moran.

Angus and Huixiong were standing behind Moran on either side. They seemed to have been in a disagreement, which was interrupted by A-Ka's arrival. A-Ka, pressing his hands against his knees, bent over to look at Percy's eyes, then looked back to Moran.

"Can you cure him?" A-Ka asked.

"I will do my best," Moran answered after some thought. "Percy was born blind, so my plan is to initially help him recover a little bit of his sight. The first step to success would be restoring his ability to sense light and dark."

Percy closed his eyes and smiled gently. "Actually, I have no urgent desire to be able to see. As long as everyone is well, then it's all right."

Moran smiled back. "Yes, but if we don't treat your eyes, you're likely to have more trouble in the future... However, this is good enough for now."

A disciple carried a tray over, and A-Ka helped Moran tie bandages over Percy's eyes.

"Will this alone allow him to see?" A-Ka asked curiously.

"No," Moran said. "It's just a preliminary preparation. If I could treat his blindness with herbal salves alone, I wouldn't need to be the pontiff. I could just change professions and go cure people of their illnesses."

"You're the pontiff?!" A-Ka and Percy simultaneously shouted in surprise.

Moran shushed them.

"You are too humble, Your Excellency," Archbishop Igor said. "His medical skills are renowned through this entire mainland. I believe that curing this boy will not be difficult."

No matter what, A-Ka would never have imagined that the wandering bard he'd met on the ship was actually the pontiff of the entire continent. Moran took on a significant glow in A-Ka's eyes.

As he thought about it, the corners of his mouth twitched; this was the first time in his life that he had met such an important figure! Vertigo hit him all at once.

"Y-y-you... Uncle Moran, you're actually, really...?" A-Ka had yet to recover from shock.

"I'm just the caretaker of a small city," Moran said warmly. "How many people do you think still believe in the Star faith right now?"

Moran ruffled A-Ka's hair before leading him and Percy to a long table and indicating that they should sit down. When Heishi walked toward them, Moran pressed his hand to his left breast in salute, but Heishi only responded with a single nod.

"Everyone, please partake of the midday meal," Moran said. "No need to stand on ceremony, my honored guests."

The guests took their seats and began to enjoy a sumptuous meal.

To Angus and Huixiong, Heishi said, "You two keep talking. Don't mind me."

"I believe their rage has died down completely," Moran said.

Huixiong lowered his knife and fork, but just as he was about to speak, Angus said, "Your Excellency, Phoenix City is not as peaceful as you imagine it to be. The humans and our brothers have already reached..."

"I assure you that, after this matter is settled," Moran said patiently, "the conflict in Phoenix City will no longer cause problems for you all. If everything goes smoothly, the situation which is causing such despair for all of the inhabitants of the mainland will be changed for the better."

Huixiong broke in. "Place that hope on *their* shoulders. I, myself, am more than willing to do battle with Father."

A-Ka glanced up at him.

"You will get that chance," Moran said, sounding unruffled. "The humans and the clones must be united. After this long, difficult battle, that will be our only chance to bring about the final outcome."

"Uncle Moran—no, Your Excellency the Pontiff," A-Ka corrected, then continued, "I would like to ask about Father..."

With a glance, Moran indicated that A-Ka should not say any more. A-Ka put on an expression of intense focus, but Moran began to chuckle and said, "I would rather you still called me Uncle."

A-Ka smiled. "All right."

At this point, Feiluo came over and took his seat. He nodded at Moran. "Thank you for watching over them on the ship, Your Excellency the Pontiff. It was a temporary oversight on my part. I hope you do not mind."

"Hello," Moran replied politely. "I'm only a traveler who wanders the edges of the world. I was honored to offer my services to Percy, Lieutenant Colonel Feiluo."

A-Ka felt like there was some kind of tacit agreement between Moran and Feiluo, which he connected back to that day when they were first on the ship, drifting over the ocean toward the Western Mainland. What Moran had done in the ship's cabin indicated that they might have met before.

Heishi seemed to be able to guess A-Ka's suspicion. "What were you at the City of Steel to do, Moran?"

"Just taking a look," Moran replied as he took a piece of bread he'd been handed. "I happened to enter the city and witness your revolution."

A-Ka was surprised. "You've really been there?"

Moran nodded. "Originally, my goal was to rescue Professor Callan. Unfortunately, I was one step too late, and something else changed in my travel plans, which upended everything."

"No matter what, I should still thank you for saving Percy," Feiluo said.

"It was as simple as lifting my hand," Moran said. "Percy's power surprised me greatly. His dreams often foretell the future. Percy, have you been having that one dream lately?"

"Not anymore," Percy answered neutrally.

A-Ka gave an involuntary full-body shiver.

Even Heishi seemed taken aback. "You can see the future?"

Percy nodded, and Feiluo's gaze held a slight bit of accusation as he looked toward Moran.

A-Ka thought of the days when he and Percy had been traveling companions on their journey away from the Country of Machines. Indeed, Percy had told him many things about the future—unwittingly,

A-Ka had thought. Most clearly, he remembered the incident when they were sheltering for the night in the tunnel and Percy had known the identity of Shahuang, who had come to search for them.

"No need to worry while you are with the Curia," Moran said.

But Commander Angus interjected, "Feiluo, this adopted child of yours can actually see the future?"

"Only sometimes. It's not a boon," Moran said, his voice taking on an edge. "Commanders, everyone, I would rather Percy not need to say anything."

"In this war, is there a chance of us attaining the final victory?" Huixiong asked Percy.

Percy didn't speak, and Moran replied instead. "That's enough." He nodded politely, but he was clearly unwilling to let Huixiong ask any more questions. After he rose, he added, "I believe that once Percy's eyes are healed, he will no longer be visited by these kinds of prophetic dreams."

"This isn't fair!" Angus protested. "Why aren't you letting him tell us the final outcome? If he really can see, and his dreamscape can predict a destined future..."

A-Ka suddenly interjected. "If his prediction told you that you would lose, would you no longer fight?"

No one said anything, and after a long while, Huixiong began to smile. "Interesting," he said. "Then we'll act according to the previous plan."

"I need to gather the opinions of my troops," Angus said.

"I will give you three days to prepare," Moran said. "Archbishop Igor, please take them back to Phoenix City now."

Huixiong nodded, and under Igor's lead, he and Angus left the Hall of Faith. Moran was silent for a long time before he said, "Everyone, I wish to hear of a plan for the general offensive on the City of Steel."

A-Ka nodded. He knew that Moran likely had his own concerns, so A-Ka bade them farewell and left the table with Percy. At one point, as they walked outside, A-Ka paused. He had some questions he wanted to ask, like what exactly Percy's dreams looked like, or if he had hidden anything from them—things that he hadn't mentioned yet.

"Percy," A-Ka said. "Your shoelaces have come undone."

"Huh?" Percy turned around. Only the two of them were in the flower garden. He sat down on a bench, and A-Ka knelt to retie Percy's shoelaces.

"You've never mentioned your dreams to me before," A-Ka said.

"Uncle Moran told me not to. Ever since I was small, the villagers treated me like a demon. They were terrified of me witnessing their deaths."

"Did you?" A-Ka finished retying Percy's shoelaces and sat down next to him. Sunlight streamed down from the clear sky, turning the garden into a sea of golden splendor, and the flower waves swayed back and forth under the faint breeze. "How did you and Uncle Moran meet?"

"When Daddy went to join the war," Percy said, "he left me in the care of the human habitat in the army camp. I had a dream, and I dreamed that they lost the battle. There was a very large ship that slammed into a pointy tower. Daddy's ship crashed onto a barren plain and turned into a ball of fire. He helped a group of humans escape, and they all ran into a valley, but they were mowed down by an airship's machine guns."

A-Ka's breathing seemed to almost stop, and he felt that the blood in his veins was as cold as ice. "Then what?"

"Later, he appeared in a laboratory in the City of Steel," Percy said. "His body was opened up, and a chip was retrieved from his brain.

He died. But after the chip was removed, I dreamed again that he turned into a ball of fire."

A-Ka remembered the first time he had seen Feiluo. He and Heishi had been resting on the mountain when they happened to run into him leading a bunch of humans. He comforted Percy. "Well, your dream wasn't accurate, right? Feiluo didn't die."

"Mhm," Percy said, smiling. "Uncle Moran told me that too. He said that the future is undetermined, and the past is undetermined as well. The only thing that is determined is the present. That was a proverb of the ancient philosophers."

There was something not quite right with Percy's dream. Was it because he wasn't in it, or because Heishi wasn't? If A-Ka and Heishi hadn't met Feiluo that fateful day, it was possible that the outcome awaiting him would indeed have been him getting captured and taken back to the City of Steel.

"What else?" A-Ka asked.

Percy thought for a moment before replying, "When I was by your side, I also often dreamed of a young man who was fiddling with some strange mechanical devices... I don't know what that was about. One day, while we were crossing the great ocean on the ship, I also dreamed of the scene today—both of us, sitting in the hall, eating lunch with Uncle Moran."

"Were there any involving Heishi?" A-Ka's mind was on the mission that they were going to carry out, which was filled with changing variables.

"No," Percy said. "He never appeared in my dreams. But once, when I was awake, I thought I heard two voices. I thought that those were probably you and him..."

"What were we saying?"

"It seemed to be something about a large airship," Percy said. "A mother ship and Father and a person called Liber."

"General Liber?! Are you sure it was us?"

"I don't know. One voice seemed to sound like you, but it also wasn't *that* much like you. It was a little hoarse, and there was the sound of static."

Confused, A-Ka tried to absorb that.

Percy continued, "Most of the dreams I have are extremely fragmented, and there are many things that I can no longer recall about them. Actually, I'm most worried about Daddy."

"Hey, it'll be all right. He's already escaped that death, and he won't be in any more danger. Did you dream of him again after that?"

Percy thought for a bit before responding, "Not anymore."

A-Ka let out a sigh of relief. "Then that's good! How about me? Did you dream of me?"

"I constantly have this one dream," Percy said. "The dream is of a sea of glowing blue, and a person walks into that blue ocean."

"And after that?" A-Ka asked anxiously.

Percy leaned on A-Ka's shoulder. "Do you know what that blue light is?"

A-Ka held his breath. He knew that no one could be clearer on the answer than him. "That's Father's consciousness," he finally said. "Was there anything afterward? After that person went in, what happened to the blue light?"

Percy answered in a small voice, "After that, that person never came out again. There was a very tall, pointy tower that collapsed, and all of the clones collapsed, completely paralyzed. A great fire burned the city. It rained, and the rain extinguished the flames. Grass and trees grew from the ruins. And there were many humans. They came from underground, returning to the surface of the earth."

"That person... What did they look like?"

Percy lifted his head. His cloth-covered eyes turned toward A-Ka.

"Was it a man with black hair and black eyes, very tall...with a really good build...?" A-Ka asked.

"No," Percy answered. "I didn't know who he was because his silhouette was very blurry. The person you mean, is it Heishi?"

A-Ka's voice was shaking a little now. "Heishi wants to confront Father so he can end all of this. I'm afraid that he'll sacrifice himself... I don't know why, but I keep feeling that he's made his preparations to never come back."

"No, that person wasn't him." Percy smiled faintly. "A-Ka, don't worry. Though I haven't seen what Heishi looks like myself, I feel like that person isn't him. Because Heishi has never appeared in my dreams, you know? Even that night when the clones and the humans were battling, I had a dream, a dream of when Uncle Moran would come to save us..."

A-Ka smiled too. "So, it was that dream sequence that reminded you?"

"Yeah. After I woke up, I sent a message to Uncle Moran. I also dreamed that we all got on the airship, but of the people who climbed onto the ship, there was still no Heishi."

A-Ka was silent for a while until he suddenly realized that something wasn't right.

"The person who walked into the blue light, was it a stranger?" A-Ka asked. Percy didn't say anything, and A-Ka suddenly understood. "That person was me, right?"

The dressings covering Percy's eyes grew wet with his tears. He hugged A-Ka, and in that moment, A-Ka couldn't summon any words at all.

"If you could sacrifice yourself to let everyone survive," Percy asked, "A-Ka, would you still go?"

A-Ka was silent for a long, long time. He lifted a hand and patted Percy's head.

"Yes, I would," A-Ka eventually admitted.

For some reason he couldn't explain, his fear of death was no longer as intense as it had been in the beginning. After he and Heishi had struggled to escape annihilation, leaving the City of Steel and arriving in Dragonmaw City, everything that A-Ka had seen, without exception, showed him what little life force was left in this world. If it were his choice, he would not live in a world like this. Instead, he would rather leave behind a beautiful world like the one he had always wished for, so that everyone who continued to live would be a little happier and able to enjoy a good life.

"So would I." Percy smiled. "As long as Daddy is able to live well, I'd do it."

A-Ka thought of Heishi, and his heart throbbed once with pain. "But without you, he wouldn't live well. Thankfully, I don't think you'll need to shoulder that duty."

"Mm. Before Uncle Moran met me, I always felt like I brought misfortune to those around me. But, slowly, I began to realize that changing variables often appear in my dreams. Now, I think the future that my dreams foretold can change."

"Because your dreams didn't have Heishi in them! I believe the future can be changed, too."

"Hopefully," Percy said.

Suddenly, Feiluo hurried toward them. "What are you guys talking about?"

A-Ka stood up, and Percy said nothing else.

Spreading his arms out, Feiluo hugged Percy, then ruffled his hair. "Do your eyes feel uncomfortable?"

Percy beamed. "They feel cold. Uncle said he'll operate on me in a few days. After the surgery, he thinks I'll be able to see."

Feiluo nodded before saying to A-Ka, "His Excellency the Pontiff has something to tell you."

As A-Ka left the flower garden, he turned and looked back, only to see Feiluo with his arms around Percy. The two of them stayed on the bench, quietly talking to each other as they gazed at the sea of flowers.

If A-Ka continued along this path and perished alongside Father, it might be worth it if that let everyone live happily, like how Percy and Feiluo were in that moment.

When A-Ka walked into the pontiff's study, he saw that Moran was mixing a bottle of medicine as he spoke to Heishi. Heishi was standing to one side, his head raised to examine the books on the bookshelves.

"This path you're on is of great concern." Moran nodded to A-Ka before continuing to talk to Heishi. "I imagine that, no matter who goes, they will have no way to change a fate that has already been destined. This is something that is difficult to accept, so it will be an unhappy experience."

"What would happen if fate changes?" Heishi asked.

"As soon as fate changes, the moment you return, you will find that the butterfly effect will have triggered many subsequent outcomes," Moran said. "The next time you see Dragonmaw City, it may already be in ruins, or perhaps I will have died."

A-Ka stood there, completely lost, as he listened to the two of them talking. He felt a sliver of anxiety. Neither Moran nor Heishi said any more, and the study fell into a peaceful silence.

"What medicine are you preparing?" A-Ka asked curiously.

"Anesthetic," Moran answered. "For surgeries."

"What did you want to tell A-Ka?" Heishi asked. "Tell him."

"Please sit, A-Ka," Moran said. "Feel free to serve yourself some coffee. Do you remember your problem that I mentioned when you arrived here?"

Making his way over, A-Ka poured himself some coffee at the table. He was still thinking about the prophetic dream that Percy had told him about, but he didn't know how to express that to Heishi. If Percy's dream were to become reality, on the day that Father was annihilated, when Heishi rebooted the Astrolabe, A-Ka himself would return to nothingness alongside Father.

When he'd heard Percy say it, A-Ka had been very composed. He'd felt it was nothing special; dying this way would be much better than being slaughtered by the unfeeling mechanical guards in the City of Steel. However, when he saw Heishi, A-Ka felt a little sad for some reason, and that small unwillingness to part grew stronger inside him.

"What's wrong?" Heishi had noticed A-Ka's strange demeanor.

"Nothing much." A-Ka managed a smile as he shook his head. His eyes were aching at the edges, but he pushed past it and said to Moran, "We only found two portions of the code to enter the Central System, and there's still one section with General Liber, but Liber is already dead." When Moran nodded, A-Ka continued, "I was wondering. Is there a backup copy in Dragonmaw City?"

He watched Moran with anticipation, but Moran had known what A-Ka was going to ask. He smiled apologetically. "It's a great pity that I have to let you down. Though I knew from Percy's dreams that the total mobilization would end in failure, I did not obtain a backup copy from General Liber."

"Is that so?" A-Ka said dejectedly.

"Allow me to ask you two a question," Moran said. "If you were to be parted after this is all over, if everything that you've done so far is not for your own sakes, would you carry on regardless?"

Heishi looked at A-Ka with a question in his gaze. A-Ka was a little lost, and he said nothing.

Moran continued, "To restart the Astrolabe, perhaps... It's just a possibility, but it may cause you two to encounter hardship. Not only would it change the future, it may even affect the past."

"I'll do what A-Ka says. He begged me to give humans and clones a new world," Heishi said. "A-Ka?"

A-Ka's eyes watered, and upon hearing those words, he was no longer able to control his sorrow. "I..." Moving forward, A-Ka wrapped his arms around Heishi tightly and buried his head against Heishi's chest as tears began to roll down his cheeks.

Moran put down the medicine and went to A-Ka so he could stroke his back.

"It seems like you are not yet prepared," Moran said. "Rest for another day. We still have plenty of time."

"The general offensive is going to start in three days, right?" A-Ka asked, wiping away his tears. "I am willing. I can do it."

Moran studied A-Ka, as if he had long since known that he would respond in that way. "The world will remember the price you paid," Moran said solemnly, lowering himself to one knee. "Son of mankind, please allow me to express my greatest respects."

A-Ka hurried to lift Moran to his feet. "No need for politeness, Your Excellency. Is there any way to obtain that section of code that was General Liber's?"

Returning to his position in front of his desk, Moran explained, "As you know, after the materials from the Creator's laboratory went missing, one human created Father and the City of Steel, one human created the Country of Clones, and there was one more person who founded the Faith of the Stars."

"Yes," A-Ka said.

"Just like the others, the first pontiff of the Faith of the Stars brought back a portion of the Creator's heart. We call it the Wish of the Tides."

"What...what's that?" A-Ka asked, confused.

"Technically, in our universe, time does not always flow forward. Elementary particles can be found everywhere, and through their back-and-forth vibrations, they generate a kind of energy. This energy pushes all physical objects to brush through time, and from there they reach the other shore...I imagine. Perhaps I'll let you see this first. You'll have a better idea of it then. Please come with me, you two."

Moran opened a hidden door in his bookcase and guided them through a silent corridor as they descended to the lowest level. This path was very different from the rest of the splendid structures of Dragonmaw City's Curia, and the moving stairs they eventually reached led toward the depths of the earth.

Moran removed his pontiff's necklace, which displayed a five-pointed star that illuminated the ground before them. "This is the Curia's sacred ground," he explained. "Only by using the key that ignites the stars can we enter this place."

As they descended the first segment of rotating stairs, the stars of the sky began to shine in the darkness. This galaxy adorned the silent night like gems spread out on a goose down bed. Then, they began to flash in surges, sending thin threads of white light toward them.

A-Ka squinted. "Those are lethal lasers, aren't they?"

"Correct," Moran answered. "The first pontiff created this place, and he accompanies me by my side. Be as careful as possible in everything you do."

A-Ka watched the lasers intersect as they traveled toward their bodies. However, Moran's pendant seemed to possess a strange power that deflected the sea of lasers. It generated a warm, golden protective sphere that reflected all the light that approached it. Though, in A-Ka's eyes, while the lasers were densely packed and formed intricate patterns, it would not be impossible to pass through them.

Of his own accord, Heishi took A-Ka's hand. "There are gaps in this laser array."

"Only to you two," Moran said. "A-Ka's eyes can perceive the structure of everything in this world. That injection that Professor Callan gave him turned him into the offering that can enter the center of the planet. Anything and everything, he may deconstruct it at will."

A-Ka felt his heart jolt. *So, that's how this is going to go.*

"An offering," he murmured. "Then I am an offering for God?"

"An offering for the Son of God," Moran corrected. "The ties between you and Heishi are made up of unseen connections. It was because of you that he awoke, and likewise—"

Heishi interrupted Moran's words. "That's enough, Pontiff."

Moran smiled.

A-Ka, however, wanted to know what Moran was going to say next. "Let him finish!"

Heishi's hand that was wrapped around A-Ka's own tightened a little, and he felt Heishi's gaze grow reproachful. A-Ka could only remain silent.

"I'll tell you later, A-Ka," Moran said. "Right now, let us go take a look at the Wish of the Tides. I trust that you'll be able to figure out its intended purpose."

Suddenly, Moran stopped in his tracks. They had arrived at the center of the laser array, and as they crossed an unseen perimeter, all the stars in the sky instantly winked out, revealing the walls around them, which began to shine with a pure white light. The ceiling and floor also began to glow with a milky light. They illuminated a white room devoid of any decorations. The light surrounded them from every side, enveloping their bodies.

In the middle of the room was an advanced cryosleep chamber that looked brand-new.

"This is the same chamber that Heishi was in when he arrived on the beach!" A-Ka exclaimed.

"Yes," Moran said. "But if you take a closer look, is it exactly the same?"

A-Ka bent over to inspect the chamber, and he saw that on its outside was a shining plaque that held the words *Heishi Z9925*.

"I can confirm that it's exactly the same," A-Ka said, pressing his hand on the lid of the chamber. "Heishi. His name is right here."

"But I originally had no name," Heishi said. "It was A-Ka who gave me a name like humans have based on the writing on the chamber."

A-Ka focused his gaze on the interior of the chamber, and in an instant, the structure of the chamber appeared in front of him: the oxygen supply, the sleeping system, the internal circuitry. This cryosleep chamber was powered by a matter-and-antimatter energy supply that humans had no way to use, and it was enough to supply the chamber with the power needed to sustain life for a hundred thousand years. It was a pity, then, that its energy supply had already been drained, and there was no way to get it working again.

"The first pontiff left the Primeval Heart inside this chamber. It escaped from a lava passageway underneath the ground, passing through the deep sea and the seafloor of the Western and Eastern Mainlands before finally being brought to the shore."

Moran pressed the five-pointed star necklace on the outer lid of the chamber, and the chamber lid slowly opened, revealing the young boy sleeping soundly inside.

A-Ka shifted backward in surprise.

Heishi also sounded a little taken aback as he asked, "He's really the...?"

"Yes," Moran replied. "This is His Excellency, the first pontiff. He passed away many years ago."

The little boy's features were still as vivid as if he were alive, and clutched in his hand was a ring-shaped object. Moran first knelt down on one knee in front of the chamber, quietly saying a prayer, before plucking that ring from his hand and closing the chamber.

Moran handed the ring to A-Ka, who took it and held it up to the light to observe it. It had a complicated internal structure, and for the first time in his life, A-Ka felt dizzy and befuddled as he studied an object. The power circulating within the ring depended on the strange, flickering particle of light locked in the microcosmic world of the gem inset into the ring.

"It's like it's alive," A-Ka murmured.

"Indeed." Moran nodded approvingly. "Within it exists a city."

Heishi frowned, while A-Ka exclaimed, "No wonder! How can so many lives exist in this single gemstone?"

"They are a kind of life-form completely different from us humans," Moran said as he took off his five-pointed star necklace. "Or perhaps the Creator made the world within the gem and left it on this land. This gemstone contains many mysteries that we are unable to discern."

"In this gemstone," A-Ka said, "there is a kind of...a single..." He stared at the bright red gem. There seemed to be a crack in the middle. When he looked closely, however, he found that it was a strange structure.

"An emitter," A-Ka murmured. "A particle emitter."

Moran smiled and nodded.

A-Ka returned the ring to him. "A kind of helical particle emitter, which can cause particles to generate their own spin as they circle around the tower, allowing the user to jump through space."

Moran put the ring on as he brought them away from the underground chamber.

"But what use does the emitter have?" A-Ka asked, following him. "You need another one that matches it, a completely identical receiver, to communicate with the other and create the energy needed to jump. Is there another ring in this world that's exactly the same?"

"You're right. This ring produces energy that can only be received by an identical ring."

Moran escorted them out of the underground chamber and closed the secret door.

"But I can't figure out what this has to do with us obtaining that section of code that Liber has," A-Ka said.

"It's entirely the same thing, A-Ka," Moran replied. "Nothing in this world is exactly the same, especially microscopically. The only thing that is completely identical in structure to it is itself."

That's when A-Ka understood. "You mean the chip from the past!"

"Yes." Moran nodded. "Use its power to jump and you two can return to the past. Do you still remember the moment that we met on the boat?"

A-Ka recalled it right away. When he had first met Moran, he had been wearing this ring on his finger as well.

Moran explained, "Almost a year ago, the day I left Dragonmaw City and headed toward the Eastern Mainland, I was not comfortable leaving the sacred relic with the Curia, so I brought it with me. This ring has the power to fix its own position, so you can travel from the present to the past, find the Liber from back then, and get his section of the passcode."

A-Ka had no way to express the shock in his heart at the absurdity of these words. He stood there for a long time, not making a single sound.

"Now, I must converse with the life-forms in the gem to confirm that they are willing to send you back," Moran continued. "Why don't you and the Son of God take this day we have to rest?"

"When will we begin the mission?" Heishi asked.

Moran thought for a bit. "We still have time left. After all, interacting with the flow of the past will not be recorded in the current time. You two could leave in the small hours of the last day before the invasion, but I do not recommend that you wait that long. Still, you do not need to set off *today*. Tonight is the Festival of Spring's Dusk, a time to celebrate when all the beings of this world flourish and grow. I suggest that you two take a stroll around the city."

"Tomorrow, then," Heishi said.

Moran nodded, satisfied, before he made an imploring gesture.

A-Ka couldn't respond—his brain was as empty as a blank sheet of paper. Not in a million years would he have guessed that Moran could solve their problem this way.

Heishi trailed behind them. After A-Ka had walked for some time, he came to a stop in the long hallway and raised his eyes to look at Heishi. As usual, Heishi maintained that cold, calm expression; no matter whom he was facing or what he heard, he always bore this poker face.

"You don't want to go?" Heishi asked.

A-Ka fell silent, then he stepped forward and hugged Heishi, leaning on his body as if entirely unable to part with him. In that instant, the light in Heishi's eyes changed to something unfamiliar. Complicated emotions gathered there, and he lowered his head as if he wanted to say something but couldn't find the words.

Finally, he placed his hand on A-Ka's head, just like Feiluo did to Percy. "What happened?" he asked. "A little earlier, you seemed out of it."

A-Ka searched his thoughts for a long time until he mustered up a weak smile and said, "No, nothing happened."

"Are you afraid that it'll be dangerous when we return to the past?"

"Uncle Moran said that he was afraid we would meet with hardship."

The corner of Heishi's mouth curved a little, and he seemed to be trying to hide something as he said, "If you're afraid of hardships, then you shouldn't have agreed to go at all, don't you think?"

"Refusing isn't going to resolve the issue in any way, all right?!" All of A-Ka's grief at the thought of parting with Heishi evaporated.

"This isn't like you."

"This isn't *like* me?" A-Ka didn't know whether to laugh or cry. "What am I even like, Heishi?"

Moving to A-Ka's side, Heishi gave him a look. "Do you remember the day when you stepped out of the crowd of humans?"

A-Ka and Heishi stood face-to-face. Heishi's gaze was as familiar as always, no different than the expression that he'd worn that day when he stood on the platform, the guns of the mechanical guards pressed against his head.

A-Ka began to smile. "I remember."

Nonchalantly, Heishi pointed a thumb at himself, then poked at A-Ka's shoulder with his index finger. "Believe in me, and believe in yourself."

A-Ka's dark mood burned away like fog under a rising sun, and his smile blossomed. "All right, Heishi."

# THE NIGHT OF DIVINE GRACE

**T**HAT EVENING, A-Ka finished packing his things into a small bag. To Heishi, who was lying on the bed, he said, "The pontiff mentioned there was a festival today, so I want to see it. Want to go together?"

Heishi was silent for a moment before he nodded.

Together, they went to explore Dragonmaw City. There was one major difference between this place and Phoenix City: Dragonmaw was filled with humans as far as the eye could see.

Moran had given A-Ka some money, and he spent a little of it buying a few of his favorite foods, like the buttered crepes they made on this mainland. They felt too expensive in Phoenix City—though he often bought some for Percy, he was loath to eat them himself.

When A-Ka bought a crepe at the stall, he was salivating so much that drool almost spilled from his mouth. However, when he handed a crepe to Heishi, he only stared at A-Ka oddly. Regardless, A-Ka stood in front of the stall, wolfing down his food. They had even put fresh fruits in the crepe! The sunset stretched its rays down the long street, and he felt that if every future day of his unfolded like this, he would be very lucky indeed.

"You really like to spend time among other members of your species," Heishi noted.

"This is called liking a good crowd!" A-Ka explained as he grinned. "You know, I'd imagined that when you came back to Phoenix City, I could take you around and show you the sights. Phoenix City has its charms, though it isn't as good as Dragonmaw City."

Heishi was wearing a pair of sunglasses as he and A-Ka walked side by side through the market. There were quite a few hawkers selling their wares along the street, and A-Ka curiously stopped to check a few of them over before buying a little trinket for Percy.

"What about you? Do you like this kind of life?" A-Ka asked.

"It's all right," Heishi responded after a moment's thought. "You enjoy being around these people because you are the same as them, but I'm not." Unlike his typical reticence, Heishi seemed to have quite a lot to say today.

"If you think of yourself as a human as well," A-Ka suggested with a smile, "then you might not feel as lonely."

"Perhaps." Heishi had on a strange expression as he passed a girl selling flowers on the roadside, as if he couldn't figure out why she would harvest the genitals of plants living in the wild only to sell them to her own people at a higher price. At another stall, A-Ka bought a small voice changer and a signal transmitter. When he looked back up, he saw that Heishi was still judging the flower seller.

The girl's face turned slightly red under Heishi's attention, but she smiled. "Sir, would you like to buy a flower?"

"No," Heishi said flatly.

*He can be such a boring guy,* A-Ka thought.

As A-Ka was haggling over the price of his new tech with the stall owner, Heishi knelt down in front of a different stall—one that sold bracelets.

"Do you want one, sir?" The owner smiled. "It's just seven silver pieces!"

Heishi lifted one of the bracelets, framing it with the sunset as its backdrop.

Squeezing through the crowd, A-Ka asked, "Do you want it? I have money, so let me buy it for you."

Heishi waved his hand, pulling out a small box from the chest pocket of his jacket. When he opened it, there were multiple golden bullets of varying lengths inside. "I'll trade these for your goods," he said. "I only want one."

"This is a matching pair of bracelets, so they're a set," the owner said. "They're not sold separately!"

"I only want one," Heishi repeated.

Seeing that the owner had no way to get his point across to Heishi, A-Ka cut in. "Let's just get them both. Give me the one you don't want."

Heishi shot A-Ka a glance before flipping a golden bullet to the stall owner. He then picked up the two bracelets and tossed one of them at A-Ka.

How strange Heishi's personality was. A-Ka hoped that, if he were to keep interacting with humans in the future, those exchanges would teach him how to act, little by little.

Neither of them was familiar with the area, and since Heishi and A-Ka both didn't know where they should go, they meandered through the market, one following after the other. When the setting sun smeared a lavender glow across the distant mountain range, the market grew even busier. Colorful lights were strung in unruly lines above the streets of Dragonmaw City, and more and more people appeared, so A-Ka had to grab Heishi's hand to prevent them from being separated.

A-Ka suddenly remembered that, given Heishi's personality, he disliked being around so many people. Obviously, he would hate being jostled by the crowd.

"Sorry, you don't like noisy, bustling places, do you?"

Heishi took off his sunglasses, glanced over at A-Ka, and responded, "I don't mind."

"Why don't we go back?" A-Ka offered.

"I really don't mind. You like it here, so I'm all right with it."

A-Ka drooped a little. "Is there anything in particular you want to see?"

"There isn't."

A-Ka didn't know how to continue. He enjoyed cozy cityscapes like these because they felt beautiful and full of life, but Heishi clearly didn't care for them at all. He'd only come along to keep A-Ka company as he browsed.

"You can't keep doing this," A-Ka said. "How will you live your life if we're no longer together?"

Heishi's eyebrows pulled together prettily, as if this was the first time he had thought of this question as well.

A-Ka smiled into the distance and pushed on. "As long as you live on this land, you'll eventually have to interact with humans, won't you? But I feel like you don't like us."

"Not really. To me, humans are about the same as trees, birds, or insects."

"That's why this isn't right." A-Ka turned his smile upon Heishi. "You're actually the same as humans, aren't you?"

"I suppose."

A-Ka couldn't win. "Are you hungry? Should we get dinner?" he asked, trying a different tack.

Though Heishi didn't have strong preferences, he was much more mellow than he had been when they first met. At least now he was no longer actively trying to keep everyone at arm's length with his icy aura.

A-Ka found a restaurant up on a terrace, and he and Heishi sat down.

"What do you want to eat?" A-Ka asked.

"Anything's fine." Heishi was absentmindedly watching the multicolored street outside, and without even thinking about it, he left the problem of ordering food to A-Ka.

A-Ka was not very sure what was good, so he simply ordered two of the same meal. In Phoenix City, he had always thought about eating at a restaurant, but he'd been broke, so there hadn't been a chance to do so. Back then, he had constantly imagined that when Heishi came, he would take him to see the world of the humans and experience a few things that he never had before. Now his wish had been fulfilled at last, but it was under these hopeless and rather laughable circumstances.

The waiter filled their glasses with wine and lit a candle. When their food came, A-Ka cut his steak with his fork and knife. After Heishi observed A-Ka for a while, he picked up the entire piece with his hand and took a bite out of it as though it were a biscuit.

A-Ka blinked.

Heishi was confused. A-Ka gestured for Heishi to put the steak down and used his own knife and fork to cut Heishi's food into small pieces. As Heishi looked out the window, he carelessly picked up pieces the meat and put them into his mouth to chew.

"Sometimes I wonder," A-Ka said. "You don't speak often, so what do you spend your time thinking about instead?"

"I'm thinking about what you just told me," Heishi said.

"In your eyes, am I also no different from a tree or a bird?" Heishi turned and stared at A-Ka. That response alone seemed to answer his question, and the fight went out of him. "All right. I get it."

He'd always thought that to Heishi, he was different. After all, since the day he found Heishi in the ocean, they'd almost always been together. By virtue of having traveled together for so long, Heishi's attitude toward A-Ka wasn't like his attitude toward the others.

"Oh Son of God, the Savior of the World," A-Ka said with faux earnestness, "I don't hold out any wild hope that I shall be any different from the flora... I simply believe that, perhaps, there will come a day when I will die."

At this time, Heishi finally turned the full weight of his gaze on A-Ka. He nodded. "You will die, yes."

"I'm not entirely sure about your body's structure. Based on who you are, are you immortal?"

Heishi thought for a second. "I don't know."

"If you don't try to make a few friends, then, after I die, there will be no one to take care of you." He continued, not without sympathy, "Or, say, I were to die of an illness, or if I were sacrificed for the greater good. I wouldn't mind, because I would be dead, but you might be a little lonely."

"You should take care of yourself first." Heishi also sounded sympathetic, for some reason.

A-Ka was tempted to toss aside the table napkin and stop humoring Heishi, but he really *was* this obtuse when it came to human emotions. Of course he didn't understand the chains binding people. In the end, after thinking about it, A-Ka decided that this was not a hill he wanted to die on.

Heishi's hands were covered with steak sauce when he said, "No more. The flavor's too strange."

"What? There's no way this flavor can get any better!" A-Ka exclaimed.

Heishi glanced at the steak with its hints of red. "I don't like to eat raw things."

A-Ka examined the steak and found it to be about medium rare. "This amount of doneness is really good, though. Why won't you eat things that aren't fully cooked?"

"If it's raw, it means that there is still life left in it."

Sometimes, A-Ka really didn't understand the logic Heishi operated off. "If you won't eat it, then give it to me. Don't waste it."

Heishi picked up a piece of steak with his fingers and fed it to A-Ka as the latter was about to get up to fetch the bill. Not to be outdone, A-Ka ate the piece of steak and even licked and sucked the sauce off Heishi's fingers.

Suddenly, Heishi's movements stiffened. "You…" His breathing sped up.

"Thanks! I'll go get the bill," A-Ka said.

Heishi's expression was a little odd—dazed, for some reason. A-Ka waved his hand in front of Heishi's face, feeling that this had come out of nowhere.

Heishi came back to himself, then crisply snapped his fingers for the bill.

A-Ka smiled. "You know how to do that?"

Heishi answered, "I watched Huixiong and the rest do it like this."

When the bill came, Heishi paid for the meal.

Back on the streets outside, the crowd had grown even denser. Tens of thousands of people had flooded this single street as if they were going to attend some grand ceremony. A lilting flute melody floated through the night air; it was a famous old tune called "The Shepherd's Spring." The people at the festival danced and sang to the music, following the flow of the crowd as they surged toward the huge plaza in front of the church.

"Feiluo!" A-Ka shouted.

Feiluo was quite tall, and he stood out even more with Percy riding on his shoulders. Percy's eyes were still blindfolded, so Feiluo was probably afraid that the crowd would be too much for Percy to deal with.

"A-Ka!" Percy keenly heard A-Ka's voice, and he shouted, "Where are you?" Twisting his head around, he tried to figure out where A-Ka was, but they were very far from each other.

"Let me on your back, Heishi!" A-Ka said.

Seeing no other options, Heishi turned around and offered his back. A-Ka scrambled up as he called back, "Feiluo! You guys came!"

"Don't come this way, A-Ka!" Feiluo answered. "There are too many people!"

And more people just kept coming. Heishi, with A-Ka still on his shoulders, was swept up by the crowd, and they were forced to move forward. When they arrived at the central plaza of the Faith of the Stars, the lights had all been extinguished. Seeing this, A-Ka cried out in surprise.

"Put me down, Heishi!" he whispered, and Heishi obeyed.

As the two of them stood at the edge of the plaza, they held hands. A second later, a vast silver river of stars flickered to life in the sky, and the crowd began to cheer loudly. There seemed to be a mysterious power taking shape outside the sacred hall: The stars traveled across the sky, forming all sorts of different images before growing dim once more.

"My dear citizens, happy Festival of Spring's Dusk." Moran appeared on the tall platform in front of the church, both his hands pressing down on the railings as he addressed the crowd below. "I hope that the wind blows and the sun shines, the rain falls and the thunder booms, so that all of the living beings on this land can grow and flourish. I hope that the clouds gather and scatter, just like our lives."

Everyone around them pulled out a tiny cup and lit the candle within it. The plaza fell silent, and only Moran's voice continued, magnetic amid the elegant background music.

"I hope that all life flourishes..."

Moran prayed in a quiet voice, and the thousands of candles in the plaza lit the faces of the people there as they lifted their heads to watch the pontiff. A-Ka glanced to his left and right. They hadn't bought candles to attend this grand event, which was an unfortunate miscalculation.

"Hold onto me, A-Ka," Heishi said out of nowhere.

"What?"

Heishi stretched his arm out, so A-Ka grasped it. With a whoosh, Heishi spread the black-gold wings on his back. They flew into the sky, circling once over the sacred hall, and landed gently on the railings above it.

"So beautiful!" A-Ka sighed.

As they watched from the top of this not-so-tall building, the glow of the individual candles turned into a sea of light that cradled Moran as he stood under the stars, praying in a quiet voice.

"Mhm," Heishi agreed. He placed one leg on the railing. Without looking down at the crowd, he lowered his head to fiddle with the bracelet that he had just bought.

Moran's voice traveled up to them from below. After listening for a while, A-Ka shifted his focus to Heishi's bracelet, where he found that Heishi was trying very hard to inlay a piece of something black onto the material.

"Did you want to decorate it?" A-Ka asked.

Heishi grunted an affirmative, though he didn't look up.

"Where did this piece come from?"

A-Ka shifted forward to take a look, only to see Heishi's slender, long fingers holding a crystal made of an obsidian material. It was like the swooping shape of one of the black, metallic wings that he used to fly.

"Move over a little," Heishi said. "You're blocking the light."

A-Ka threw up his hands and moved to one side, at a loss for what to say at Heishi's rudeness. Heishi glanced up at A-Ka but said nothing before turning his attention back to the gem on the bracelet.

A-Ka watched for a bit, the sound of Moran's prayer fading into the background. From the little bag that A-Ka carried by his side, he pulled out the other bracelet. With a simple soldering iron, he attached a signal transmitter the size of a button onto the bracelet.

"Let me borrow that," Heishi said.

A-Ka handed the soldering iron to him. Heishi's fingers pressed against the hot part of the iron as he moved to turn it on.

"Careful!" A-Ka yelped. He could smell the scent of something burning as he hurriedly tugged Heishi's hand aside and found that his index finger had a blackened scorch mark across it. A-Ka quickly stuck the injured finger in his mouth to soothe it. At that, Heishi froze again, then he awkwardly tried to pull it back. However, A-Ka wouldn't let go.

His face a little red, Heishi yanked his finger out of A-Ka's grasp. "Is this some form of expression for you humans?"

"Huh? I did that because you got hurt. It helps."

"I can heal on my own."

"Even so, you can't just let it happen!" A-Ka snapped. "Don't you feel pain?!"

Heishi indicated that A-Ka should take a look at his finger, which had already healed as if it had never been wounded in the first place. At that, A-Ka sighed and gave up.

"It's done." Heishi was like a satisfied child as he admired the silver bracelet that he had made. For some reason, he seemed a little taken aback as he murmured, "Even I can create."

"Of course you can," A-Ka said, still annoyed.

"Only humans can create. Other living beings do not have the skill, which is why the Creator had always searched for life-forms with that ability."

"Is that right?" A-Ka sensed that they were about to come to some important realization. "Do other living beings really not know how to make things?"

"They need to be given the ability to do so, or they need to spontaneously produce something—extraordinary occurrences like that are the only way they can," Heishi replied, gazing off into the plaza. "I don't know why that is. My Heavenly Father didn't leave this information in my memories. Maybe even he didn't know why intelligent life-forms possess the ability to create."

"Could it be because of love?" A-Ka asked. "In the ancient poems and songs and records, I saw that love can spur the creativity of humans."

Heishi didn't respond. A moment later, Moran's prayer ended, and the crowd cheered again. The ceremony seemed to have come to an end, and the lights on the plaza were extinguished once more.

"It's for you," Heishi and A-Ka said, almost in the same breath.

As they looked at each other, A-Ka's and Heishi's expressions contained the same surprise. A-Ka was holding out his bracelet, while Heishi held out the other one.

A-Ka couldn't resist laughing, but Heishi was extremely serious, squeezing the bracelet with his fingers as he nudged it toward A-Ka.

"Let me help you put it on," A-Ka offered.

He pulled Heishi's hand over, fastening the bracelet on his powerful, sturdy wrist. Right then, in the distance, a high, clear sound echoed through the sky. The bright-tailed streak of a firework ascended above them, and its piercing whistle roused the happy cries of thousands of people.

With a huge boom, the firework exploded, lighting up their faces. Dumbstruck, A-Ka lifted his head to watch the night sky, his joy running wild.

Heishi properly fastened the bracelet he'd given to A-Ka, and the two of them looked up at the night sky, watching blossom after blossom of colorful fireworks erupt.

"How beautiful," A-Ka said softly.

More and more fireworks covered the pitch-black evening sky. The flashes in the sky looked dreamlike, and as A-Ka turned his face up to watch, he sank into a bright, blossoming reverie.

Heishi, however, inadvertently turned his head to study A-Ka's face. A-Ka continued to watch the show for a little bit before he realized that Heishi was looking at him.

A-Ka grinned. "It's so beautiful! Have you seen this before? It's just like...just like..."

"The stars separating from each other during the birth of the universe," Heishi answered. "My Heavenly Father gave me that memory."

# THE NIGHT OF DIVINE GRACE

"Yes!" A-Ka said excitedly. "That's more apt than any metaphor!"

A-Ka and Heishi sat shoulder to shoulder as the fireworks that spiraled into the night sky went off in front of them. Unable to resist, A-Ka turned his head once more to observe Heishi.

"If there came a day when we had to separate," A-Ka asked quietly, "would you be unwilling to part with me?"

Heishi looked at A-Ka like he had something to say, but he didn't, in the end.

A-Ka stared into his black eyes—into the depths of his pupils, where gorgeous, colorful light was dancing. He felt that this entire series of events was like a grandiose, splendid play. His heart quivered at that, and even he couldn't say what thought had caused the movement. Closing his eyes, he felt Heishi's gentle breaths.

That night, thousands of fireworks lit up the sky, one after the other. The show lasted for an entire hour, covering Dragonmaw City with a temporary white light. It wasn't until the very end that everything settled back into its original silence. The glowing birds of late spring circled the city as the populace gradually sank into sleep. A peaceful silence draped over everything.

Up high, on top of the church, A-Ka leaned into Heishi and fell asleep, too.

When the first rays of light peeked over the horizon the next morning, they shone upon Heishi walking through a hallway.

Feiluo, who was following behind him, stopped at one point to speak. "I cannot confirm that you will succeed, but...good luck, Heishi."

Heishi turned around, draped in his long windbreaker, his hands clad in fingerless gloves that were tucked in his pockets. When he reached a hand out to Feiluo, Heishi's wrist was encircled by the silver bracelet that A-Ka had gifted him.

"Thank you," Heishi said solemnly. Feiluo and Heishi gripped each other's arms, their fingers squeezing tightly for a moment.

"Come back alive," Feiluo said.

Heishi nodded. "I've found that being human isn't so bad."

Feiluo began to grin. "You've really changed."

Heishi whistled before turning and walking into the sacred hall.

At the same time, A-Ka slipped on his hat and exited his room. As he passed through the hallway, Percy ran out from a doorway and hugged him tightly.

"A-Ka, you have to return safely!" Percy pleaded.

A-Ka hugged Percy in return. He had on a shirt and a pair of long pants, and when he pushed up his sleeves, he revealed that he, too, was wearing the bracelet that Heishi had given him. At the center of the silver bracelet was a black gemstone in the shape of a tear that gave off a minute purple glow.

"You as well. Do your best," A-Ka said quietly.

After parting from Percy, A-Ka headed toward the sacred hall, where he saw Heishi standing there, waiting for him. Then, the group of them walked into the sacred hall where Moran was, and Archbishop Igor closed the main doors.

"I have sent Feiluo, Shahuang, and Huixiong back in time," Moran said. "In five minutes, which I will count down, you two will be sent back to November of last year. You will arrive by my side and have one day left before the revolution of the clones. The past me will assist you in entering the City of Steel."

A-Ka had waited for this moment, but it was only now that he felt an indescribable, thunderous shock in his chest. The sunlight filled the room while he and Heishi stood in front of Moran, as if they were holding a grave and solemn ceremony.

A-Ka took a deep breath and nodded. "I will do all I can."

Moran continued, "Since my past self is not familiar with the terrain within the City of Steel, there is no guarantee that he will have the required commands to open the passageways. That part will be up to you, A-Ka."

"Is there anything we need to watch out for?" Heishi asked.

"And can't we ask our past selves to help us?" A-Ka said.

"No." Moran's expression changed slightly. "Aside from interacting with me, you must avoid leaving traces of yourself in the past. Think back to the day that you escaped from Father's city. Did you know that your future self had returned?"

That made sense. Since A-Ka had never known, that meant that his future and past selves had never actually met each other.

"Not only can you not seek assistance from your past selves," Moran continued, "you cannot even let them see you. You must avoid them and be wary of anything and everything that could cause the revolution to fail. Every action that you take in the past will set off a butterfly effect, and this might cause everyone in the present to diverge from their current trajectories."

A-Ka nodded. "What would happen if we're accidentally spotted?"

Moran said severely, "It's very likely that that would cause annihilation. It's possible that, when two waves of energy flowing in opposite directions collide, they will destroy the entire world."

A-Ka sucked in a deep breath. "O-okay, I understand. All right then, let's begin—wait! Something's not right."

Based on what Moran had said, A-Ka had deduced an inevitable conclusion: The Moran of the present had pinpointed the Moran of the past because both of them wore this ring on their hands. After

A-Ka and Heishi returned to the past, they would meet with the Moran of that time...which meant that before this, Moran should have known about them returning to the past!

A-Ka's voice shook. "B-before you got on the ship, you already knew me, didn't you?"

"Yes." Moran's lips curved gently. "When I boarded the ship, we were already friends."

A-Ka found that he could, in fact, be more shocked. "Then did our mission succeed?"

"Whether or not your mission succeeded does not mean that you should rest on your laurels. On the contrary, if you fail, you will induce changes in space-time and all of us may be destroyed. So, no matter what time or place you find yourself in, you need to do your best, A-Ka."

"I understand! Please begin!"

"The process of being sent back to the past may cause you a little discomfort. Please bear with it."

Moran turned the ring, and a beam of light enveloped A-Ka. With a hum, A-Ka instantly disappeared. Moran and Heishi were left in the sacred hall, standing face-to-face.

After Moran's ring sent A-Ka away, its light grew dim, waiting for the next recharge. Heishi stared mutely at the ground.

Within this short moment of peace, Moran opened his mouth. "We must wait three minutes before I can send you back, Son of God."

Heishi nodded. "Will this time travel cause any effects on A-Ka's body?"

"It's hard to say. I haven't tested the effects of activating the Wish of the Tides, either." Heishi looked at Moran, who thought silently before he smiled again. "I've always been curious about one thing. May I ask you a question?"

"Ask."

"According to the records in the Book of the Heavens, when the day approaches where the Astrolabe petri dish is almost entirely polluted, the Creator will send the Son of God to carry out a purge... That is to say, your duty is actually to..."

"Cleanse everything in the petri dish."

"Right. Last year, when I arrived at the Eastern Mainland and saw you for the first time, I felt your appearance was rather extraordinary. Logically, the command our Heavenly Father left in your memories should have been to kill all the humans and end this experiment."

"Sure," Heishi replied. "Is there a problem?"

Moran said, "What caused you to decide to protect us humans and clones? My apologies, I do not have any intention of delving too deeply into the matters on your mind..."

Heishi sank into a lengthy silence.

In the sacred hall, shadows and light fluctuated. Heishi lifted a hand. In that instant all the rays of light coalesced, and their intersections stitched together vibrant, colorful scenes that appeared one after another, each like a painting:

*Before the sea of tulips, the moonlight shone through the window frame into the room. Heishi lay on the bed, and A-Ka sprawled on his front to one side, smiling as he said something.*

"Because of A-Ka?" Moran asked.

Heishi didn't say any more. With one hand, he swept at the air before him, and the imagery changed a thousand times—

*Night in the sacred city, thousands of fireworks exploding in the sky as A-Ka, smiling, handed him a bracelet.*

*Twilight of the Festival of Spring's Dusk, A-Ka standing at the head of the street, wolfing down a buttered crepe.*

Moonlight shining through a window as Heishi was lying down, A-Ka sprawled next to him, saying something to himself.

Under the dark, gloomy sky of Phoenix City, A-Ka chasing after Heishi using the rockets in his shoes. Plucking Heishi from the midst of dozens of robotic guards and hugging him around the waist. Slamming as one into the glass skyscraper, glittering shards exploding into the air.

In the sewers under Phoenix City, A-Ka slumping weakly in Heishi's arms, clutching his hand tight.

During a long night, the black sea roiling like the roaring, gaping maw of an angered beast. Heishi sitting by a rock all alone, speaking into the transmitter, windbreaker drifting in the sea breeze.

In the City of Steel, Heishi standing on the raised platform, sweeping his gaze over the unfamiliar humans beneath. Everyone's expressions cold and distant, their gazes filled with horror. A-Ka shouting: "Wait! It's me! The person this stranger is trying to find is me!"

Heishi watched all this silently, without saying a word.

The tides of the black sea ebbing and waning, clouds dissipating and reforming, the lid of the sleeping chamber opening. A-Ka's surprised expression greeting him as he carefully lifted him in his embrace.

A patch of blue light like the waters of the vast sea threatening to drown him, and A-Ka walking into Father's sea of consciousness, his voice murmuring: "I wish that there was someone who could keep me company, so I wouldn't be so lonely."

Heishi glanced at Moran but didn't speak as he walked into the blue light. The ocean-like blue glow turned into a warm purple one, and Moran's ring emitted a beam that enveloped Heishi.

"It's because I appreciate humans, and because there are individuals like A-Ka among them," Heishi said. He nodded once to Moran, and

Moran pressed one hand on his chest in front of his shoulder, bowing to Heishi.

In the light, Heishi's silhouette slowly grew faint before finally disappearing.

*Fireworks flowering one by one, blossoming splendidly in the sky. Underneath them, A-Ka closing his eyes as Heishi gently kissed him.*

# 14

# GOING AGAINST THE FLOW

**B**LACK CLOUDS billowed in the sky, and uneasy tremors rocked the ground as A-Ka was spat out by the gaping mouth of the portal, which loomed large inside the cloud cover and lightning.

"*Aaahh!*" he screeched, though the wild winds tore away his voice.

"Brace for impact!" Huixiong's voice called.

Ten thousand feet in the air, Huixiong spread his arms wide, his bulk bursting through the clouds as he careened toward the ground. Shahuang also shot out of the unstable crack in time, a huge bazooka slung over his shoulder. The moment he placed the scope before his eye, he seemed transformed into a wholly different person. With one hand still in the pocket of his windbreaker, his lanky form became like a sharp blade emerging from its sheath as he rocketed toward the earth below.

"Countdown to collision: twelve, eleven..." From his pocket, Shahuang pulled out a small, finely crafted metal tube, pressing a button as he pointed it at Huixiong. With a hum, a huge net made of something like spider silk wrapped around Huixiong. The great net shimmered with a liquid luster as it exploded into a parachute.

With an elegant somersault, Shahuang flew toward A-Ka. A-Ka shrieked at the air resistance he felt; he had never thought he would be plummeting downward in a several-thousand-foot fall!

Shahuang fought against the fierce wind as he hollered, "I've got you!"

The wind battered them, leaving them almost helpless. Several times it tried to rip A-Ka away, but Shahuang clung to A-Ka's wrist. As Shahuang was about to open his parachute, there was a sudden flash of black gold. Heishi swooped by, and suddenly A-Ka was out of Shahuang's hands.

However, A-Ka was still screaming.

"I'm going to go deaf," Heishi said coldly. "Can't you be a little quieter?"

With that, the metallic wings on Heishi's back spread open, blotting out the world around them. They acted like a glider as Heishi flew toward the dark horizon. They spun in a wide circle in the air, the mountains and the land skimming beneath. In the distance, Father's tall tower was wreathed in a vortex of lightning and purple clouds.

No longer screaming, A-Ka stared in awe at the majestic sight that was Father's tower. It looked like a probe pointing straight up at the universe, sprouting out of the vast land beneath, but it also loomed as ominously as a specter of death. Millions of intelligent robots danced through the air around it, like worker bees in a hive.

"The backup program, Labere. What you call Father." Heishi's eyes reflected that view of the City of Steel. "It's a little different from the impression I had in my mind."

"Is that right?" A-Ka turned his head toward Heishi. "What's different?"

Choosing not to elaborate, Heishi only grunted in response. He dove forward, sending them down toward the earth below.

They were on the western side of the City of Steel, where the marshy plains were covered with nerve gas to slow down those who would try to pass through. Father's regime extended all the way to the Eastern Shore, and every square inch of it was built with the intention of preventing any human from escaping.

Heishi held onto A-Ka as they slowly descended. Two white parachutes burst open in the sky like dandelions, and the two mercenaries floated toward the forest at the end of the plains. Next, Feiluo opened his own glider, tailing Heishi as they spiraled downward.

A-Ka could clearly make out a person standing by his feet—the Moran of the past was there with them. The gem on his ring was pointed inward, toward the center of his palm, while his palm splayed toward the sky. Thousands of strange ion beams shot out from the ring, creating a bright line connecting it to the time portal in the sky.

"Is there anyone else?" Moran called, bracing himself against the strong wind.

"That's everyone!" Heishi shouted back loudly.

"Uncle Moran!" A-Ka cried out.

Moran smiled at him and nodded.

Observing Moran's past self, A-Ka felt both close and distant to him at the same time without knowing why. As they landed, they saw Shahuang and Huixiong dangling from the branches at the forest's edge.

Half an hour later, the group gathered on one side of a lake on the swampy plain, clustered around Moran. After conducting a head count, Moran said earnestly, "Mercenaries, a clone, and a warrior of unknown origin who comes bearing a prehistoric weapon. I imagine your identities must not be ordinary. Nor that of this...this child, either. Now, shouldn't you introduce yourselves?"

"Your Excellency the Pontiff," Feiluo said, "I am the lieutenant colonel of the Second Corps under the command of General Liber, Feiluo."

Moran looked at Feiluo and nodded. "You used to be someone inside the City of Steel?"

"My previous identity was that of a spy," Feiluo said, pointing at his own head. "The chip spurred me to contact my other comrades in arms during the Revolution of the Clones."

"I recognize you," Moran said to Huixiong. "President. And this individual is...Shahuang of the Hundred Battles."

Shahuang smiled but didn't make a sound, while Huixiong nodded.

"I'm called Heishi," Heishi said simply.

"A-Ka," said A-Ka, smiling as he introduced himself. He had found this affair a little strange at first, but now he remembered—the Moran of the past hadn't recognized him, and it wasn't until he had boarded the ship heading toward the Western Mainland that they had ostensibly met for the first time. "I'm a completely ordinary human," he said. "I've come to help lead them into the city because I once lived there."

Moran smiled. "Humans themselves are already extraordinary. My dear friends, why don't you tell me about your plans? I am not quite sure why you have come. I merely received a message from my future self saying that General Liber will start an all-out attack tomorrow, so I imagine we at least have a little time left."

With his hands clasped behind his back, Moran walked slowly across the plains, Huixiong and Shahuang acting like two bodyguards as they flanked him. Feiluo explained the general course of events to Moran. When he got to Heishi's identity, Moran couldn't resist giving A-Ka another look.

"I am the representative for the Clone Regime," Feiluo said matter-of-factly. "Commander Angus sent me here to help carry out the mission this time."

Moran nodded, accepting this.

"Uncle Moran..." A-Ka started. "No, Your Excellency."

Moran smiled. "Actually, I quite like that form of address. You can just call me Uncle."

"What have *you* come here for, Uncle?"

"Liber's request was for me to come and purify Father. They had me wait here, but I imagine that since you all have brought fresh news from the future, the outcome of this revolution is already set in stone."

A-Ka gazed up at the horizon. At this time in the past, Heishi was still slumbering in the cryosleep chamber, and A-Ka's past self was still resting in the humans' gathering area of the City of Steel. Liber had yet to lead his squadron of people charging toward Father. Though everything would still march toward that inevitable end, they found themselves, right now, in a sort of strange tranquility.

A-Ka thought about how tens of thousands of clones would leap into their mechas and battleships one day later, rushing toward Father like moths toward a flame, only to meet their fiery deaths in this enormous steel city. Imagining that, he couldn't help feeling an unspeakable sadness.

Just then, Moran turned and bowed slightly to Heishi. "Please allow me to express my humble gratitude on behalf of humankind, Son of God."

"There's no need," Heishi said. "Saving you all is not necessarily for the sake of the entire species."

Feiluo, Huixiong, and Shahuang looked askance at Heishi. A-Ka couldn't resist laughing at that. He knew that no matter where they found themselves, Heishi would always have that disagreeable attitude that would irritate anyone he interacted with.

"Well, for tonight, we will need to make camp within the forest," Moran continued. "Tomorrow, we'll find a chance to sneak in. I haven't been able to obtain a map of the interior of the city yet, but let's discuss that after we rest."

Night fell gently over the land. A campfire was lit in the depths of the forest. Moran, Huixiong, Shahuang, Feiluo, and A-Ka sat together, preparing a meal. Moran had brought quite a bit to eat, which he benevolently shared with the rest of them. While the food cooked, A-Ka told him about everything that had happened in that short year in the future, starting from their arrival in Phoenix City.

Meanwhile, Heishi was sitting roguishly in a tree. Leaning against the tree trunk, he dangled one foot from the branch and swung it languidly. "Are you done?" he asked distantly. "Not only are you full of words, you're also too loud."

A-Ka concluded his narrative with one more sentence, then got to his feet. "Well, it's just like that. Please remember not to tell anyone else."

The rest began to chuckle. Huixiong looked at A-Ka, then at Heishi. "Heishi, if it were not a necessity to do so, I would never choose to work with you."

"He's just a ruffian," Feiluo said casually. "He can't accept anyone else's opinions on anything."

"Don't say that." A-Ka walked to the base of the tree, then turned his head back to the group. "Heishi's a good person."

"I'm not a person," Heishi said lazily.

No one knew what to say to that. Heishi let down his other leg for A-Ka to hug as he climbed up the tree.

"You're nothing good," Feiluo said.

"That's right," Heishi replied, unconcerned.

"But you're like a human now," Feiluo continued. "You should thank A-Ka."

Heishi's expression shifted as if he was embarrassed, surprising A-Ka. When Heishi completely halted the conversation, A-Ka was taken aback again—was Heishi *really* embarrassed?

Heishi could only pretend not to look at the rest of the group as he shifted to the side, giving A-Ka a little bit of space to sit. A-Ka was holding some food that Moran had given him, but he handed the lion's share of it to Heishi.

Heishi gazed into A-Ka's eyes, then said, "You should eat it."

"*You* eat," A-Ka said. "You never had the chance to experience a happy life in Phoenix City or try all the delicacies that humans make."

"Delicacies." Heishi found his thoughts entirely out of step with A-Ka's. He was about to scoff when an idea came to him, and he changed his tune. "What delicacies?"

"Percy really liked to eat the coconut buns from the shop on the street corner, fresh from the oven," A-Ka said, "and the coffee jelly sold outside the Municipal Tower."

Heishi did not understand what any of that was, so he could only hum neutrally in response.

"After the war is over, I'll take you places," A-Ka said. "Let's go together, if that's all right."

"Where will we go?" Heishi asked. "Are we going to eat other foods?"

"I once read that this world has many steep mountain peaks and islands out at sea. There're certain spots where the sunlight is gorgeous, and others where the ocean is so pristine that you can clearly see the sand under the water. There are forests that sing, with many strange, odd beasts living within, and there are also humans in many places where Father's power is not yet able to reach."

Heishi absentmindedly grunted once as a response.

A-Ka finished eating the soda crackers in his hand and handed the paper to Heishi. On it was printed the limpid snow lakes of the eastern mountain range. "This looks like a nice place. When I was small, I always wanted to travel to see them."

"You learned these things from your educational materials?" Heishi asked.

A-Ka nodded. "We had a human teacher, Krakos, who taught us general knowledge. Though, after he died, we had to read on our own. When I was still back there, I even made a pact with a few good friends that if we ever had a chance to leave, we would visit those places for sure. To us humans, those spots used to be our ancestral homes, our deities' shrines, our very own mountains, vast oceans, and ancient ruins…"

"I remember you had friends among the humans," Heishi said. "You were raised in a concentration camp."

"Concentration camp?" A-Ka asked.

Heishi didn't respond, and A-Ka sank into a prolonged silence.

"After we go back, can I go check on how they're doing?" A-Ka asked. "The little kids in the same living quarters as me."

"As long as there's enough time, what you do is up to you."

"If I saved them, what would happen?"

"I don't know. You should go ask Moran that."

A-Ka glanced over at the pontiff in front of the distant fire, hesitating. Heishi guessed at what he was thinking.

"The reason you're not asking him is because you also know that you can't."

A-Ka remained dejectedly silent.

"You can save one person, but you cannot save multiple people," Heishi said matter-of-factly. "It's even less likely for you to be able to save all of the humans in the City of Steel. At this moment, Father still has the upper hand. Unless you destroy Father for Liber's sake—but that's impossible, because when we left the city, Father had not been destroyed yet."

"If it were possible," A-Ka murmured, "I would rather, in this battle...do what I could to destroy Father. That way, I could prevent so many things from happening."

"But with that," Heishi said, "the world would collapse, and the rules of the space-time continuum would be broken. Reconsider. As soon as you get the passcode to open the door, leave immediately. Otherwise, Moran will also be dragged into this mess."

A-Ka said no more. He sighed and leaned back into Heishi's embrace until he dozed off.

When the sky brightened the next day, Heishi shook A-Ka awake. Moran split breakfast among them. A communicator he was holding beeped, sending news from the clones via an irregular coded telegram.

"After we sneak past the city walls, we should be in the Western District." A-Ka used a branch to draw a map of the general sections of the City of Steel on the ground. The city was built in the shape of a crown. Thousands of years ago, the area around the Nucleus had been built by humans, and its central point was Father's tall tower.

"The Western District goes from here...to here." A-Ka circled a large region. "It's where the mechanical life-forms gather."

"Wait a moment," Huixiong said. "I don't mean to interrupt, but I have to ask. How are we supposed to get in?"

A-Ka blinked at Huixiong in confusion before looking to Moran. All of them suddenly found themselves in an unsolvable dilemma.

"Keep talking," Heishi said. "Don't worry about how to get in for now."

A-Ka could only continue in his explanation. "Let's assume that everyone has already entered the city, ignoring the issue of how we'll get in… Now, we're in the Western District. This is where the acquisition terminals that allow androids to charge and exchange communications are. In the outer city, there are about two hundred thousand clones who provide all kinds of services for the mechanical life-forms. They're basically a small-scale community.

"Any off-duty robots will be on standby in the Western District," A-Ka said, "to save on power. But Father sometimes wakes them up. No matter what, we cannot pass through this area aboveground. We have to avoid that whole area. If we circle around the outside of the Western District, there's a gap."

"Is it here?" Moran used the long scepter he was carrying to point at a spot on A-Ka's drawing.

A-Ka nodded. "Yeah. That's the spare-parts assembly plant, which is operated by robotic guards. Inside it, there's a conveyor belt that brings metallic plates, extra parts, and other half-finished bits to the casting plant. We can follow the conveyor belt to the casting plant, where they refine and enhance the crude metal."

Next, A-Ka drew a line toward the north of the city. "Outside the casting plant, we'll find a road around the biomaterial synthesis center that leads to the Eastern District. That's where the humans are gathered. We can use the central elevator shaft there to get into the underground passages, then wait until the energy passageways start up to make our way to the surface. We'll wait for General Liber in front of Father's nucleus."

"Very well-articulated," Shahuang said. "A solid lecture, clearly thought out and delivered with a serious attitude. Though my calling is that of a bodyguard, and I care little about how you plan to sneak onto the mother ship, I still have to ask. How will you get in contact with General Liber?"

Huixiong and Moran looked toward Feiluo.

"General Liber's hideout is not something that we can divulge," Feiluo said, "because that message can be very easily intercepted by Father. However, I imagine that I can use the chip in my head to contact him when the battle starts."

"Mm," Huixiong said. "And then kill him with one shot? Or are you going to let him open up some device that allows you to see his brain, and while he's at it, also get him to hand over his chip?"

Feiluo, too, had thought about this matter of great import. "We can have him make a copy, perhaps…?"

"I'll be in charge of this, and very willingly at that," Heishi said. "Let's go."

"This is the duty Angus gave me," Feiluo insisted. "No need for you to butt in."

Heishi indicated that Feiluo need not continue. They all picked up their weapons, and Moran, scepter still in hand, led them through the swampy plains as they began their mission into the City of Steel. The walls of this city were not high at all—after all, most of the mechanical life-forms were equipped with the ability to fly, and the only function of the walls was to prevent the humans and clones from leaving.

"There are no sentinels," Huixiong said as he stood on a large tree, looking into the distance.

"No." A-Ka stood in a gap between the trees, watching the city walls that spanned miles and miles. "The entire city wall is a huge sentinel."

The black city walls were hatched with marks, as if a special weapon was inset into them. A-Ka walked out of the grove, to which Feiluo shouted, "Wait!"

A-Ka waved his hand to show that it was fine and, under Heishi's protection, walked toward the city wall. Shock flashed through him as the thirty-foot city wall transformed into countless steel structures, splitting into individual parts, and glowing lines formed from energy started to flow around the inside of the entire wall.

"Infrared scanners," A-Ka said. "We'll need to make a few preparations. Shahuang, do you have a laser jammer?"

Shahuang tossed over a miniature infrared jammer, which was made to be mounted on a gun. In battle, it was used to camouflage the wielder from the mechanical life-forms. Right outside the city wall, A-Ka went to one knee and began to tinker with it. A moment later, he tossed the jammer into the air, its interference function active. The device arced through the air and spread its wings with a hum, flying back and forth above the city wall.

A-Ka led the way. In his eyes, the city wall was already no longer a simple barricade, but an infrared laser web that fluctuated irregularly as the jammer flew by.

"Come with me," he said.

"You can see the traps?" Huixiong asked.

A-Ka nodded, and they fell in line behind him, forming an orderly column as they headed toward the city wall.

Heishi lifted his head. "I haven't found any sentinels, and even if we're sighted by the city wall, so what?"

"The terminal here connects directly to Father," A-Ka said in a very soft voice. "Be very careful not to startle it."

The city wall was like a dark, dormant beast. A light rain scented with crude oil began to fall from the sky as A-Ka found the gap they needed. He gestured for Heishi to go, and Heishi, trailing a length of rope behind him, scaled the wall. Behind him, A-Ka was pulled up by the rope.

"Flying up here would be much easier," Heishi remarked.

"Your wingspan is too wide," A-Ka said. "They'd touch the infrared scanning lasers that sweep over this area."

"Where are they?" Heishi asked.

"There's nowhere they aren't." A-Ka looked at the ground, indicating that Heishi should wait a moment. The net of lasers invisible to the naked eye were currently sweeping along the ground toward them.

"All right! Quickly!"

Heishi pulled Huixiong up next, and one after the other they all scrambled onto the city wall, over it, and down the other side, steadying themselves as they landed. A-Ka gestured for them to follow him, but when they turned a corner, they abruptly halted in their tracks.

In front of them was a plaza that stretched tens of thousands of square feet, entirely filled with neatly arranged rows of robotic life-forms, each over nine feet tall. Row after row shone with a dark gold metallic sheen, reflecting the daylight. A red dot glowed in their chests: They were all in standby mode. At the same time, many small robots traversed the square, maintaining the large ones. These flying robots were like a swarm of ants bustling about, and Huixiong and Shahuang were both shocked beyond belief.

"Come with me," A-Ka said under his breath. "As long as we don't set foot within their alarm range, we won't be attacked. Be careful."

With their hearts in their throats, the line of people tiptoed along the edge of the Western District. Some small robots passed by right next to them, as if they might discover this group of gatecrashing guests at any time.

Heishi followed right behind A-Ka until they stopped outside an assembly plant.

"I can only lead us this far," A-Ka said. "Beyond this point, I don't know how to trick the guards and get past them."

From here on out, they'd have to deal with robotic guards. The central loading dock was full of robots, and they communicated using electromagnetic waves, so it was basically impossible to tell what they were saying among themselves.

Shahuang and Huixiong exchanged a glance.

"Should we force our way in?" Shahuang asked.

"No," A-Ka said decisively. "As soon as you attack a single robot here, Father will be alerted because they can send an emergency signal directly to him."

"It might work if we lead them away," Feiluo said. "My identity's special. Let me try. If I pretend to have accidentally stumbled into the assembly region, there will be minimal consequences while you all enter the plant."

"But how will you escape?" A-Ka asked. "The identity check will expose you, and if two identical Feiluos appear at the same time, things might get even more complicated."

"I'll make my escape before then."

"They'll verify your identity first." A-Ka was very familiar with the routines in the City of Steel. "Based on the serial number they retrieve, they'll seek out your past self. Before the battle of the revolution began, did the robots ever cause you any trouble?"

"We have to take this risk. There's no other choice. Let me figure out a way to escape when they're trying to verify my identity. Don't forget, I also used to live in this city."

"But you'll be caught!" A-Ka said. "Yes, you also used to live here, so you *know* the power of the Iron and Steel Corps. I'm not afraid of changes to the plan, but I promised Percy that I'd make sure you get home."

Feiluo fell silent. In reality, he knew more clearly than anyone that when the revolution had broken out, he had only managed to fend off the Iron and Steel Corps because he'd been in a battle mecha—and he'd still lost in the end.

Shahuang and Huixiong looked at one another again.

"I am unknown in the City of Steel," Shahuang said. "Let me go. I'm not afraid of running into my previous self."

But Moran said, "I'll go. I'm in charge of getting you all in. After the fighting is over, meet up at the pier of the Western Bay inside the valley with the Primeval Heart."

"Pontiff!" A-Ka said. "It's too dangerous! You aren't aware of the situation here. Even if you do get caught, you'll have no way of escaping!"

Moran patted A-Ka's head. "I don't know what my future self decided to do about this, but I believe that, since even a young man like A-Ka has the courage to move forward in the face of danger, the Curia cannot forever remain under the protective shadow of others. Isn't that right?"

A-Ka sucked in a deep breath. He wanted to find another way in, but upon seeing Moran's earnest expression, he grew calm.

"As the pontiff," Moran said to the gathered group, "I have faith that I will find a way to protect myself. Everyone, prepare to infiltrate the assembly plant. I wish you all luck."

Having said this, Moran walked to the place where the small robots were gathering, scepter in hand. A-Ka stopped breathing as thousands of small-scale robots were alerted to his movements at the same time. Seconds later, all of the large robots on standby immediately glowed green, their heads turning toward him.

"As a representative of the Curia, I seek to pay my respects to the man-made god, the omnipotent Father," Moran said leisurely. Then, he extended the scepter in his hands to its full length, and an apparatus flashing with blue light appeared along its surface.

At this moment, something deep underground seemed to be startled into motion, and the entire city began to shake. A beam of light broke through the clouds, shooting toward the Western District from the tall tower in the distance, and every robotic life-form in the immediate vicinity started closing in on this spot.

"The Curia." A rich, heavy voice resounded in the Western District. "Sibelius's human offspring, why have you come here?"

Before anyone could react, Moran slammed the scepter in his hands onto the ground once. "I've come to interrogate you," he said, his voice dropping to a much darker tone.

In the blink of an eye, the place where the scepter made contact with the ground lit up with a lightning strike as an arc of electricity rapidly diffused, sweeping out across the earth. Under the effects of that magnetic power, all of the robots lost their ability to move. An antisignal magnetic field had been activated.

"Let's go, quickly!" A-Ka urged his companions, hesitating no longer.

Heishi glanced backward as the group took this opportunity to rush into the assembly plant. Under the power of Moran's staff, all of the mechanical life-forms temporarily failed. The buzzing grew louder and louder as the magnetic field swept through a good portion of the Western District like a tornado. In the midst of it all was Moran, standing at the eye of the storm, head raised to look at the flashing blue lights in the sky as the field did its work.

This was the first time the power of Father and the power of the god of the Faith had communicated, and it was also the last time that would happen. Under the brilliance of that blue light, Father stood unmoved, and its icy voice said, "You have no right to interrogate me. I only obey the commands of the Creator."

"The Creator is no longer present in this world," Moran said. "What powers the continued rotation of the Astrolabe is the faith of all of the living creatures on it."

"Foolish humans," Father's voice said. "You must pay the price for this provocation."

Immediately afterward, the tower released a dispelling windstorm that swirled with unnatural energy. Thousands of flying robots shot forth, drowning the sky as if they were the angry clouds that came before a sudden storm. Moran's barrier and Father's magnetic field collided in a series of explosions.

The sounds of battle echoed in the assembly plant. In the hall, the working robots flashed with electric light and stalled. A-Ka brought everyone dashing into the depths of the plant, where he found the halted conveyor belts.

He was still wondering how he would get them to move again when Huixiong said, "There's no time. Everyone get on! We don't know how long the pontiff can hold out."

"Which one?" Feiluo asked as he looked at their options.

The entire room was densely packed with idle conveyor belts. Innumerable boxes were laid neatly on the rubber belts, and for a moment A-Ka doubted himself.

"If it isn't the leftmost, then it's the rightmost..." Wrinkles etched his brow as he concentrated.

A-Ka was still staring when Huixiong interrupted. "There's no more time! Do it as quick as you can!"

"Let's take a gamble," Heishi said. "The left."

Just as everyone climbed onto the conveyor belt, there was another explosion outside, and the machines collectively began to move again. In a short few minutes, the Western District completely returned to normal.

A-Ka was shaken. Even as the conveyor belt sent him into the assembly room, he couldn't help looking outside, his expression filled with worry. Feiluo pressed him into an empty crate, indicating that he should keep his head down to prevent alerting any guards.

This was a conveyor belt that traveled in the opposite direction—which meant Heishi had bet correctly. They hid in three separate empty crates. Heishi was in the front, to bear the brunt of anything that came their way as they were transported toward the Northern District, while A-Ka and Feiluo were together in the middle, and Huixiong and Shahuang brought up the rear.

A-Ka let out the breath he had been holding, but his worry didn't leave his heart.

It was evident that Feiluo had also settled some. Leaning against the corner of a large crate, he pulled magnetic explosive bullets from the stash at his waist and loaded them into his firearm.

"Sometimes I admire you," Feiluo said. "I never understood how you survived."

A-Ka also sat down cross-legged and pulled out a small device from his bag. He kept his head low as he looked it over, saying, as if to himself, "Am I that rash?"

"A little," Feiluo said. "You dared to sneak so many of us into the City of Steel without a solid plan."

"No matter how well laid a plan is, something will always change," A-Ka said as he smiled. "Somehow, I've managed to hold on to my life—I've thought I would die plenty of times, but I always escaped safely in the end. I guess I'll see how far I can push my luck."

Feiluo didn't respond immediately, and his index finger hooked around the gun in his hand, twirling it in a circle.

"Is it bravery or recklessness?" he finally said. "I heard that when you found Heishi, you chased him all the way out of Phoenix City."

With a hint of laughter in his eyes, A-Ka retorted, "Despite thinking I was reckless, you trusted Percy to me?"

"Because your luck has always been pretty good."

"While your reputation in Phoenix City was pretty bad."

"Mm, that's true," Feiluo said. "I owe them too much. I didn't tell you that to begin with, and for that, I am sorry. I was afraid that they would torment Percy, so I could only hand him over to you."

A-Ka nodded. "After we make it back, you should go your own way."

Feiluo suddenly sank into a prolonged, thoughtful silence. After a long time, he said, "I'm sorry, A-Ka."

"Huh?" Not seeing where this was coming from, A-Ka asked, "Why?"

"We shouldn't have let you carry so heavy a burden. Percy said that after entering the City of Steel, you will...sacrifice yourself. Is that true?"

"Mm." A-Ka thought for a moment before continuing. "It's possible. If I don't come back, well, I'll entrust Heishi to you guys." When Feiluo gave a bitter smile and shook his head, A-Ka patted his shoulder. "Relax."

Feiluo raised his eyes, which had grown strained, to look at A-Ka.

"You'll be okay. The rest of you will make it out alive, because Percy's dreams didn't contain your deaths," A-Ka assured him.

"But you," Feiluo choked out. "What are you thinking? You clearly know that you'll be ending your own life, yet you're still so... so *nonchalant*."

A-Ka was silent. He touched the miniature device he was holding in his hand, before he said, "Because I want to change the outcome. I don't want the world we have now to be the one you all live in.

To change that, I'd give up my life, no question. If I can return alive, that'd be even better, but...

"I once heard an old rumor that if a human offers up their life for the Country of Machines, Father's godly power will take them to the Nucleus of the Astrolabe and let them become one with the Nucleus forever. They'll be able to watch over this world," A-Ka said, smiling at Feiluo. "Of course, that's just a false rumor made up to brainwash humans. They want the humans to lead harsh lives and give up everything for the steel life-forms in power. But there are always things that compel people to care more about changing everything than staying alive."

Feiluo smiled a little as he looked A-Ka up and down. After a long time, he shook his head and said, "You are the true Son of God."

"No, Heishi is." A-Ka chuckled awkwardly. "My destiny is only to aid him. Were it anyone else who found Heishi, they would have done the same as I did."

## THE GOD OF CREATION

**W**OULD THAT HAVE changed anything?
It would have changed nothing.
A-Ka had also pondered this question more than once. If someone else had picked up Heishi by the sea, then it would be a different human accompanying him. They also would have escaped during the rebellion and would probably even have obtained Professor Callan's transformative vaccine. Likely the only thing destined to happen had been the effects of the vaccine that Professor Callan had injected into A-Ka before his death. That meant Callan could have picked any human; it didn't matter who. That person would have been tasked with helping the Son of God enter Father's Nucleus to restart the entire Astrolabe.

"We're here," Heishi's cool voice said.

They had ridden the conveyor belt to its end, and the area in front of them buzzed with noise, as if there were robots working furiously. Having passed through a large part of the Western District, they were now in the spare parts refinery. When A-Ka poked his head out, he saw that the sky was filled with flying robots, including units that were equipped with death rays.

The first box fell to the ground with a heavy thud. Heishi pulled himself out and backed up, stepping onto the pile of containers and leaping upward. He caught A-Ka as he fell out of the second box.

The third box fell with an earthshaking thud. Just as Huixiong and Shahuang were about to emerge, a robot zoomed over and dragged the container away in its steel clamps.

"Oh, damn it!" A-Ka said.

"You guys go first. I'll go find them!" Feiluo said.

"After you do, get on the conveyor belt and we'll meet up at the casting factory!" A-Ka said. "We still need to get on a second conveyor belt. This place is still too far from the Nucleus."

Feiluo gestured to Heishi, who immediately took A-Ka and ran. They searched all over for conveyor belts, just as piercing sirens began to sound in the distance.

"Signs of life. Attention, signs of life," an electronic alarm shrilled. "Humans and clones, step away from the raw materials immediately."

Heishi pushed A-Ka behind a container, shielding him with his body. With a slight flick of his wrist, he pulled out a long knife, while A-Ka untied his weapon, the mechanical limb strapped to his back, fixed it to his left arm, and prepared to engage the enemy in combat.

"Do not fire," Heishi ordered.

A-Ka's could hear his pulse in his ears, even though it felt like his veins were full of ice. When he saw that Feiluo was running toward the spot where the sirens were originating from, he shouted, "Don't attack!"

There were still quite a few clones in the hall, and upon hearing the alert, they began to cluster around the conveyor belt. Feiluo pulled out his electronic card with one hand, holding his gun in his other hand, and indicated that all of them be quiet.

Pointing the muzzle of his gun almost carelessly at the robotic sentry, Feiluo said, "Serial number 77023E. I'm a police officer on official business. I'm taking these two humans."

"Please swipe your card," the robot responded, and a card reader sprang from its abdomen as the magnetic cutter in its hand began to revolve. "Describe your official business. Requesting a connection with the clones' administrative affairs bureau to confirm these orders—"

Before it could even finish its sentence, Feiluo pressed down on the trigger and fired.

The entire hall burst into activity almost as fast as Feiluo's bullet. His weapon caused a huge explosion, while Shahuang and Huixiong, moving at the same time, overturned two robots. Huixiong lifted his rapid-fire machine gun and swept it across the hall. All of the clone workers exclaimed and ducked to avoid the bullets, leaving the robots to face the rain of bullets head-on.

"Don't kill my people!" Feiluo shouted as the light bullets crossed through the air.

A-Ka had already rushed onto the conveyor belt, but he shouted back, "Heishi! Quick, go help them!"

"No," Heishi replied. "I must keep you safe."

"*Go!*" A-Ka said, gritting his teeth. Their gazes met for a split second, and Heishi sank into a thoughtful silence. Then, he turned and vaulted off the conveyor belt.

Feiluo and the two mercenaries dodged a return volley of light bullets as they ran toward Heishi and A-Ka's direction. Just as Heishi's feet touched the ground, he swept his arm out in an arc, then pulled it back. His glowing, black-gold wings responded in kind, each individual feather whistling as they flew through the storm of light bullets. All the beams ricocheted off the slippery surface of Heishi's manifested feathers, causing a series of loud booms in the workshop.

A-Ka knelt on the conveyor belt, still clutching a small device in his hands. He hesitated several times, not wanting to activate it, then Heishi rushed to him, leading Feiluo and the two mercenaries, who left bloodstains on the ground as they ran. The steel conveyor belt was scorching hot. When another robot flew in from the entrance, A-Ka clutched his head and rolled onto the ground before lifting the mechanical limb's cannon and swiftly firing a shot. This single blast tore the flying robot into pieces.

"Let's go, *now*!" Heishi yelled.

The conveyor belt stopped, and A-Ka rose to his feet to lead the way. As Huixiong ran, he turned and lifted his machine gun, firing savagely. The bullets whistled through the smoke and collapsed the opening of the conveyor belt.

Flashing red lights and alarms surrounded them as they ran along the belt's length. The others were faster than A-Ka, so Heishi hoisted A-Ka into his arms and spanned dozens of yards in a single blink. Behind him was Feiluo, who had been struck near the waist by a light bullet. One of his hands was slung over Shahuang's shoulder, and they staggered and stumbled as they fled.

Clones had white blood, and Feiluo dripped this liquid onto the conveyor belt as they ran. From ahead, a wave of scorching hot air washed over them. They had reached the end of the conveyor belt—and below them was a vat of bubbling, molten steel.

"Jump!" A-Ka shouted.

Small-scale transportation carriers flitted here and there in the high heat sweltering up from the melting furnace. Heishi, still holding A-Ka, leaped into the air and kicked off of one transport carrier, which caused it to dip down. When it touched the molten steel, it let out a sizzle, before guards rushed to the scene from all over and started to fire.

A-Ka was dizzy and confused from all this running around, but when he saw the conveyor belt again, he shouted, "One more time!"

With another magnificent leap, Heishi kept his hold on A-Ka and landed on another conveyor belt. In front of them, there was a rotating press that never stopped turning, each of its heads easily weighing tons. Each one slammed down with a thud; any of those heads could easily smash the entire group into meat paste.

At the same time, Shahuang, with Feiluo's arm still over his shoulder, rushed to them. Bringing up the rear, Huixiong groped around, pulled out a grenade, and tossed it into the molten steel. With a boom, the fluid exploded, instantly drowning the transport carriers and blasting a large hole in the furnace.

More explosions rang out, and Huixiong reached out and pulled the emergency lever as he ran by. The foundry's door slammed shut, trapping the second wave of robotic guards outside.

"Feiluo!" A-Ka knelt down on one knee on the ground, inspecting Feiluo's wounds.

"Don't mind me. Let's keep moving," Feiluo said with a set expression.

Despite Feiluo's protests, A-Ka felt around the clone's waist. There was a hole from which a large amount of white blood was oozing. The blood of clones was strange, and it had a slight fishy scent to it.

In a few movements, Feiluo had dressed the wound.

Still, Heishi asked, "Did it hit your internal organs? Let me take a look."

Feiluo pushed Heishi aside, but Heishi shoved Feiluo down until he had to lie flat. The robots outside were blasting away at the doors, but Heishi was deaf to those sounds as he undid the dressings and inspected his injury.

"You need a transfusion," Heishi said.

"Don't underestimate me," Feiluo said, panting. "Leave, you idiot!"

Without giving him any time to explain, Heishi lifted Feiluo and carried him to an empty cart used to transport molten slurry. Pushing the cart into motion, Heishi started to run. The sounds behind them grew louder and louder, as if the robots had banded together to break through the door. A-Ka and the others raced behind Heishi, but with Heishi's strength, A-Ka couldn't catch up to him even after trying valiantly.

"Climb on," Heishi said.

There was no time for politeness, so A-Ka climbed into the cart. Heishi pushed ahead, carting the two of them as they dodged through the steel-flattening press.

"If you see any danger, point it out to me," Heishi said.

A-Ka turned his head, squeezed his eyes shut, and opened them again.

"Go," he said.

"Speed up."

"Slow down!"

Under A-Ka's guidance, Heishi made it through the steel-flattening area.

"There's an exit up ahead!" A-Ka shouted.

They had reached the end of another conveyor belt. In front of them, scrap steel was piled up like a small mountain. Heishi pushed the cart out into the air, where it overturned, and he grabbed Feiluo, spreading his wings to glide toward the exit. Behind him, A-Ka sprang forward and latched onto Heishi's back to fly with him.

Meanwhile, Shahuang and Huixiong stepped onto a gliding disk, which whistled through the air as it descended. The large door slowly slid open, and Shahuang racked his bazooka, loading up an armor-piercing bullet. With a huge boom, he busted a hole in the thirty-foot-thick steel wall.

"Protect them!" Huixiong stared into the scope, his rapid-fire machine gun clacking in his hands as they rushed through the broken opening.

When he saw sunlight again, A-Ka was blinded and dizzied by it for a moment. Then, he saw that they were surrounded by robotic guards.

"Damn it!" Heishi cursed.

As soon as they alerted the robotic guards, they would be chased by what felt like a swarm of ants. No matter what they did, they would not be able to shake them off. Huixiong bellowed, "Don't mind us! You guys take Feiluo and go!"

"Take me to the Northern District," Feiluo said tiredly. "As soon as we enter the gates, you two can head toward the human section…"

"Hang in there," A-Ka said. "Let me first find a clinic."

Without giving him any time to protest, Heishi slung Feiluo's arm over his own shoulder. On his back was his firearm, which was pointed at two of the robotic guards that were headed their way.

A-Ka led them in a sprint toward the clones' living quarters, and Feiluo pressed his palm against the lock.

"Access granted," an electronic voice said. "Passage allowed."

The great doors opened, and the group entered a greenhouse. After Feiluo closed the doors, a vague expression of dejection appeared on his face. A clone was currently tending to the plants in the greenhouse, and when he saw Feiluo he instantly went bug-eyed.

"Do you have any treatment chambers?" A-Ka asked. "He's hurt!"

"Who are you?!" that clone said. "The medical bay is just next door, but I must confirm your identities first…"

Before he finished speaking, Heishi knocked the clone down with a clean, swift punch. He took his identification card, said "Thanks," then dragged him toward the medical bay, using his palm and identification card to open the door.

By the time Feiluo was carried into the treatment chamber, his entire body had already become covered with blood. Sirens sounded in the distance, as if there were even more guards chasing after them.

Huixiong pointed at the rest of their group and said, "You guys are in charge of making sure he gets the treatment he needs. I'll hold the guards off. Don't wait for me. Run directly for the human district."

"Capture them!" a clone guard shouted angrily. "Intruders!"

Heishi and Huixiong's gazes met for a split second before Heishi curtly nodded once.

"After you've succeeded, use the chaos to escape," Huixiong said. "We'll see each other again outside the city."

Shahuang glanced at his watch. "There are still four hours and twenty-three minutes before the start of the revolution."

Huixiong patted A-Ka's head and said, "Good luck." With that, he lifted his machine gun and marched out of the greenhouse.

Inside the chamber, Feiluo's face gradually regained color until its lid sprang open. From outside came the earsplitting reports of guns firing. Feiluo let out a breath before pulling out his identification card, but his body was still weak as he hurried to guide them through the greenhouse garden toward the Eastern District.

Guns firing and the sounds of detonations rang in Feiluo's ears. He hesitated several times, looking torn. He clearly wanted to turn around to stop Huixiong, but Heishi grabbed his arm and pulled him along so he couldn't.

Suddenly, hundreds of flying robots swarmed toward them.

"Keep going," Shahuang ordered.

Immediately afterward, Shahuang fired toward the ceiling of the clones' living district. That discharge turned out to be not a bullet but a sonic bomb that shattered the entire roof of the greenhouse. The cluster of flying robots turned their firing ports toward Shahuang.

"Shahuang!" A-Ka screamed.

"Go!" Heishi pushed A-Ka onto an elevator. Feiluo activated it with a swipe of his ID. In the distance, a clone guard rushed over, shouting, "Who are you?!"

Feiluo said, "You two head down first!"

"Wait..." But A-Ka could not get a word in before Feiluo tossed his ID into the elevator and rapidly pushed a few buttons on the outside that made the elevator doors slam shut.

"Destination, the Ant's Nest," an emotionless electronic voice announced.

In the last moment before the door to the elevator closed, A-Ka saw Feiluo's silhouette through that crack. He raised both his hands, turning to face the clone guards that were coming toward him.

There was a loud boom, and the sudden loss of gravity almost caused A-Ka to start floating. He and Heishi stood in the elevator as it sped downward. Shutting his eyes tiredly, A-Ka buried his face against Heishi's shoulder.

"Prepare yourself," Heishi said. "There will be more pursuers in front of us."

A-Ka said, "We'll be safe after we get into the human district, but they..."

"Don't worry. They'll no doubt be able to escape soon."

A-Ka remembered then that the revolution still loomed over them. Liber might have already begun his plans for the invasion; Heishi was keeping mum on matters relating to the revolution, to prevent them from being overheard by the surveillance cameras in the elevator. He glanced at A-Ka meaningfully, and A-Ka understood what he meant. Right now, the most important thing was to reach the Nucleus as quickly as possible.

They had almost four and a half hours to pass through the human quarters. Heishi said, "After we get in, stay behind me."

"I'm begging you," A-Ka said, "Heishi, don't kill my kin."

"I won't attack them if they don't sell us out," Heishi said. "But you also need to keep your guard up."

A-Ka nodded and fell silent. The elevator continued to head downward, as if it was falling into a bottomless hole or the depths of the ocean. Heishi gazed down at A-Ka. His nerves were a little frayed, and he toyed with the small device still in his hands.

"You trust your kind so much," Heishi said.

"Yeah," A-Ka said. "I know that we've yearned for freedom for a long time... Every human is like me, really. We long for the outside world."

"I don't agree," Heishi said.

A-Ka smiled as he looked into Heishi's eyes. "Humans are the most complicated living things. Was your heart not at all moved when I said that, after the revolution, we should walk across this whole land?" A sliver of confusion appeared in Heishi's eyes for a brief moment, so A-Ka added, "You're becoming more and more like a human now."

"What are you holding in your hand?" Heishi asked, changing the topic.

A-Ka stared levelly at Heishi. He never liked to admit that he had developed human emotions, as if that were embarrassing. But his embarrassment was, at its heart, also an emotion. He even knew how to evade questions that he didn't want to discuss. A-Ka couldn't help finding this a little funny.

"It's K's controller," A-Ka said. "K was the robot that you saw the day we first met."

"You built it?" Heishi asked.

"Yep. Don't you remember meeting it? Before you came, K was like my best friend. Once, I made a wish for it to start moving."

A-Ka recalled how Heishi had almost choked him to death by pressing him against a wall when they first met. Now, they had returned to that same day, but Heishi's gaze was so warm, as if he had become an earnest, stern big brother.

"What are you smiling about?" Heishi asked.

"Nothing," A-Ka said, still grinning.

Heishi couldn't resist reaching out a finger and brushing it along A-Ka's cheek. He went quiet.

"Arriving at the Ant Nest," the electronic voice announced.

The elevator doors slid open, but before A-Ka could move, Heishi flicked his wrist, creating a long dagger. "Don't go out just yet. There are guards outside."

Surveying their surroundings, Heishi realized that the two robotic guards were not targeting them. A-Ka turned to follow their gaze and was stunned by what he saw.

Next to them, another elevator was ascending. His past self was in there, behind the metal bars. The elevator next door was crowded with people, and a mechanic was shivering inside, his face the color of dirt.

"Let's go. Don't look any longer," Heishi said.

A-Ka pulled the brim of his cap lower, following Heishi as they walked out of the elevator.

The two robotic guards entered the elevator. The doors to the elevator opened, and the mechanic bolted.

"Warning! Stop immediately!" The robotic guards rushed forth at the same time, and the humans in the elevator flooded out. The doomed mechanic continued his dash into the hallway.

A-Ka sped up, but he couldn't resist turning his head back to watch the escaping mechanic as the robotic guards chased after him.

"Get down!" Heishi shouted. At that, the hallway of people exploded into action.

With a hum, thin metal needles shot out of the surveillance camera hanging from the ceiling, and each needle spread its wings, flying wildly through the air. One needle pierced the escaping man right through the skull with a loud crack. He slammed into the wall, skewered firmly onto it.

Heishi tackled A-Ka to the floor. At the same time, the elevator behind him closed and continued its journey upward.

In the aftermath, A-Ka was covered in cold sweat, just like he had been back then. Heishi pulled him to his feet, and they kept walking forward through the hallway.

Neither of them expected the beeping guards to stop them. "You must undergo a safety inspection of the fifth type. Raise your hands," an electronic voice said.

Shooting a glance at Heishi, A-Ka lifted his hands. Heishi followed suit, but then he kicked the robotic guard. Even though it weighed several hundred pounds, Heishi sent it flying, and it slammed into a door with a loud boom. The surveillance cameras on the ceiling all swiveled toward them.

"Go!" Heishi yelled.

The hallway once again sank into chaos. A-Ka hadn't yet realized what was going on as Heishi grabbed him and raced through the hallway. With a flick of his hand, Heishi's black-gold feathers rustled, filling the entire hallway as they darted forth, each hitting their target without fail until every surveillance camera was destroyed.

"Where to next?" Heishi asked.

*I've really had enough after bringing you all here!* A-Ka thought. *The question I hear the most is "Where to?" I just drew a map last night! Did any of you even look at it?*

Heishi looked at A-Ka, waiting for guidance.

A-Ka sighed.

"This way." Pushing open a small door, A-Ka went in. The robotic guards noticed them and approached with a group of flying guards trailing behind them. A-Ka circled around and around in the room, then rushed into the large sleeping quarters.

"Shit," he muttered. "Forgot this is the fourth level…"

Dozens of humans filled the sleeping chambers, and they all looked up at Heishi and A-Ka as they entered. When Heishi raised his eyes, the surveillance camera was slowly turning toward them, so A-Ka dragged Heishi out of its line of sight.

A girl waved at A-Ka. "Shh! Over here." The girl opened up a metal trash can that A-Ka and Heishi didn't wait to scramble into.

With a doubtful expression, Heishi looked at A-Ka, as if to ask, *Why is she helping us?*

A-Ka pointed at the surveillance monitor before making a shrinking and expanding gesture, meaning that if they were discovered by that device, it was very likely that they would be attacked indiscriminately, which meant that the humans here would also be hurt.

The girl put the lid on before placing a random bag of junk on top of it. At the same time, the door opened, and the robotic guards rolled in.

Hidden away, A-Ka stuck a miniature device to the wall of the can. He had been holding on to the anti-infrared jammer he got from Shahuang. Now, it sent out a signal that encompassed the entirety of the metallic can.

After a tense few seconds, the robotic guard left. Taking a deep breath, A-Ka climbed out of the can, followed by Heishi.

"Thank you," Heishi said to that girl.

"What are your jobs?" the girl asked nervously.

As A-Ka lifted his head, anxiously watching the surveillance camera on the ceiling, he gestured for Heishi to follow its movements. To the girl, he said, "In four hours—exactly on the hour—make sure to leave through the garbage chute."

"We have to go!" Heishi said.

A-Ka and Heishi left the sweeping range of the surveillance camera, pushed open another door, and ducked into a stairwell.

This entire place was dark, and only the surveillance camera above their heads shone with a faint green light. The two of them clambered carefully up the stairwell. After pushing open the door, A-Ka saw another human.

"Is this the fifth level?" A-Ka asked.

"It is," the middle-aged man replied with an expression of confusion. "Which level did you come from? Hurry back there!"

A-Ka pulled his cap down. "No, I've come to find someone."

He and Heishi walked down the hallway. That man had more questions, but he looked at them doubtfully before nixing any desire to follow them.

Heishi took A-Ka's hand in his own as they passed through the large gathering hall. People passed to and fro, and they sank into the crowd.

Heishi was still in disbelief. "Have we thrown off the guards just like that?"

"Yes," A-Ka said quietly. "Their surveillance of the humans is the weakest because we have the least aptitude for battle, especially when we don't have weapons. Plus, Father has no way to predict human behavioral patterns, and in the robots' eyes, they do many strange things…"

"That's true," Heishi said.

"Are our actions very strange in your eyes as well?" Without waiting for an answer, A-Ka pushed open another door.

To his surprise, someone greeted him. "A-Ka, didn't you go to bed?"

He recognized the person as someone who lived in his section. Hurriedly, A-Ka said, "I remembered something, so I had to make a trip back."

"Who's he?" that young man asked, looking at Heishi curiously.

"Hello," Heishi said.

A-Ka didn't know what he could say to that.

The young man smiled at him. "Hello to you, too. Strange, I don't believe I've ever seen you around?"

"I'll explain later. He… Ah, well, I need to go and take care of some things first!"

Hastily bidding farewell to that person, A-Ka and Heishi turned the corner of the hallway. "Let's pass through the garbage dump. There's energy passageways we can use there."

After saying that, A-Ka pushed open the last door, but Heishi grabbed his collar and pulled him back.

A-Ka froze in fear. Right in front of him, standing at the corner of the emergency exit and waiting for the surveillance camera to turn away, was his past self.

A strange feeling filled A-Ka. Blinking, he stared at his past self, completely unable to believe it. Just a glance at his own body standing a mere stair's length away made all of the hairs on his body prickle on end. He ducked behind the door, but thankfully the other A-Ka hadn't noticed a thing. Back then, hiding from the surveillance camera was his only goal.

"Good thing you didn't turn around," Heishi said under his breath.

The two of them lingered outside the door for a while longer, and after A-Ka counted the minutes to himself, he said, "Now."

This time, they managed to leave the exterior and head toward the garbage chute. The moment A-Ka entered the garbage chute and saw the footprints around it, he remembered the last time that he had used this exit and understood what he couldn't have known back then.

"Let's go," A-Ka said. "Heishi?"

Heishi looked toward the other exit, not saying anything.

"Do you want to see your past self?" A-Ka asked.

Heishi was silent, mulling over this difficult decision.

"We still have three hours and fifteen minutes," A-Ka said, glancing at his watch. "Let's go take a look at our past."

Heishi nodded, and the two of them scrambled out of the garbage chute from the other exit. The sea wind gusted as light rain drifted from the sky. In the distance, A-Ka's old self was climbing down the cliff like he might be swept away by the wind at any moment, and even the A-Ka of the present wiped away some sweat as he watched the scene.

Heishi flicked open his wings. Hugging A-Ka in his arms, he carried them in the air over the beach while still ensuring they kept their distance.

The seawater rushed forth, crashing into the land as an angry, earthshaking wave, sending Heishi's black sleeping chamber to the shore. It slammed into the cliff and landed on the beach below.

"This is where I was born," Heishi replied from where he stood in the distance.

"Weren't you born in your Heavenly Father's laboratory?" A-Ka asked.

"No, I wasn't. The memories my father gave me were a copy of his own soul and personality, which he injected directly into my slumbering body."

A-Ka was shocked. He peered at Heishi with a strange expression.

"Does that surprise you?" Heishi asked. "How would I hold the highest level of authorization and be able to stop Labere's computations otherwise?"

"But you didn't tell me this in the beginning!"

"Because back then I was like an infant with a completely blank mind," Heishi said, pointing at his head. "According to the learning functions in my body, my knowledge and memories were supposed to develop with time. If I woke up and all of the memories in my brain activated at once, they would short-circuit me."

Suddenly, A-Ka laughed without restraint and reached out to pat Heishi's head. Heishi's mouth curved into a little smile as they watched A-Ka's past self climb down the steep cliff and curiously open the lid of the incubation chamber. They remained shoulder to shoulder on that craggy rock, hand in hand, watching the movements from afar.

"So, that's how it went," Heishi murmured. "You were the first person I saw upon opening my eyes."

A-Ka smiled, but he didn't respond. His emotions were very complex as he, a bystander this time, watched himself go through the entire process of getting to know Heishi. For some reason, he felt the urge to cry.

They watched as A-Ka lifted Heishi in his arms. As he was using K to scale the cliff once again, A-Ka's frail body seemed ready to fall off the precipice at any moment. If he had, his bones would surely have shattered.

"That was a close call." A-Ka felt a little bit of lingering fear in his heart. "If I had fallen, both of us would've been done for."

"You've always been brave," Heishi replied. "I still remember when you discovered me again in Phoenix City and chased me across several streets despite the bullets and the soldiers."

A-Ka made a face. "Let's leave. In the future, I definitely won't be this reckless again."

Heishi waved his hand, indicating that A-Ka wait for a moment, as he walked toward the sleeping chamber on the beach.

"Is there anything inside it still?" A-Ka asked as he followed.

"There's one thing that's vitally important."

He once again opened the incubation chamber. The power inside had been fully expended, but there was still a backup power source in the depths of the chamber. With a surprised intake of his breath, A-Ka watched Heishi turn a switch before pushing the energy core back in.

The chamber came to life once more. Instantly, countless rays shot out of the chamber to form a star map. In the middle of the star map appeared a huge circular plate, and the depths of the plate filled with a projection of the Nucleus of the Astrolabe.

A-Ka was both nervous and excited, though he didn't know what Heishi wanted from this map. He glanced back at the heights of the cliffs, afraid that his past self would appear.

"I'll be done soon. I only need a few minutes," Heishi assured him.

The whole expansive universe seemed to appear on the windswept shore of this dead sea thanks to the projection. Heishi gathered his hands around the light, shaping it into a flattened image. Then, he began to retrieve a large number of messages.

On the screen he had created, countless strange text symbols arose. Their glow reflected in A-Ka's eyes. These messages contained all of the knowledge of the human world and even the knowledge that Father held, but what was even more amazing was that it seemed to be a communication device that had a direct connection to the depths of the vast universe.

"You are going to... With the Creator...?"

"Yes," Heishi said. "No matter what the outcome is, I must tell him about the proceedings of the entire experiment."

"Zoroaster, my son," said a deep, rich voice from inside the incubation chamber. The entire galaxy above gathered into a single point, changing into the warm face of a giant.

"Father," Heishi murmured, lifting his head. "Finally, I glimpse your face."

"When you manage to see this message, the experiment on the petri dish will be approaching its conclusion," the Creator's voice said. "You chose Cedesian, which is the mother tongue of our world, and I am grateful for that. It seems that the development of the petri dish, on some level, has gone exactly as I predicted.

"At this moment where you've activated the cryosleep cocoon, my physical body will be on the other shore across this enormous river of stars. After leaving this test point behind, I will never return again. But you—what have you learned from this world?

"Since you have opened the cocoon, then everything that remains on this petri dish will be left for you to decide, my dear son. When I came to this Astrolabe, before I created you... You must understand, my world of origin, the one my people, my loved ones were in, was also once like the world you are in now. There was sunlight, there was wind. There was rainwater, there was a sky. There were mountain ranges and great oceans."

With the rise and fall of that voice, the lights of the star map changed and the figure of a distant planet appeared. Giants strode over mountain ranges to start battles, only to slaughter each other with weapons. The blue light of the central tower, the exact same model as Father was, destroyed the entire planet.

"But my people ruined all of this with their own hands," the Creator's voice continued. "In this vast universe, I've found lone island after lone island and tried to recreate that lost splendor, but it is a pity that with my limited lifespan, I cannot wait for such a moment. The evolution of intelligent species is far too slow, and there are a thousand changes that can happen. One small shift can cause the entire species to head toward some hitherto unknown future...

"If you open your eyes and find that a life-form called 'man' exists, then that means that my experiment has succeeded."

Heishi murmured, "But they're somewhat different from what you anticipated, Father."

The Creator didn't respond to Heishi's words, because he was only a blurry video recording. With his hands clasped behind his back, he walked toward the ocean, stood on the roiling surface, and looked into the distance.

"Your awakening," the Creator continued, "is proof of the appearance of an intelligent species. After I seal away the entire experimental platform, I shall leave a section of hidden code in the central control system Labere. Only when a human who fulfills the specific requirements appears and activates the special emotion and thought mechanisms present in Labere's central system will it release the cocoon that is holding you, allowing you to emerge in this world.

"Labere originally could not think like we do. Its patterns are fixed," the Creator said slowly, still looking off into the distance. "Your job is to pass judgment, and from each of us individual gods, learn emotions and grow. No matter what the situation actually is, the experiment will formally end the moment that you appear. What comes after is for you to decide.

"My dear son, Zoroaster." The Creator turned, his voice becoming sorrowful. "I hope that your future will not be like that of your father's, experiencing millions of years of loneliness before departing alone into the long voyage through time. I did not bestow upon you the ultimate emotion, because I hope that through your interactions with humans, you can slowly learn about love."

A-Ka's heart thumped loudly, but Heishi only watched his Heavenly Father's projection steadily, despite the faint traces of tears gathering in his eyes.

"I wish you happiness," the Creator said solemnly, before turning into thousands of glowing points of light that dissipated into the air.

Heishi keyed in a few symbols, then bent over and pushed the cryosleep chamber into the ocean.

"Are you going to destroy it?" A-Ka asked.

"No. I activated an escape function. It may come in handy in the future."

Heishi sent the chamber that had been his cradle away, and he and A-Ka stood by the sea, saying nothing. The waves rolled and crashed, just like the waves in each of their hearts, never ceasing in their motion.

# 16
# A PROMISE FOR THE NEXT LIFE

**A**-KA AND HEISHI had returned to the garbage chute's exit. As they were about to leave, Heishi couldn't resist glancing back. Not too far away, his past self was walking on the beach, following A-Ka's footprints.

"Go back!" A-Ka's past self shouted before waving his arms, indicating that Heishi should return to where he had been hiding.

Heishi smiled at that, then he and the present A-Ka ascended the garbage chute.

"There's still two hours and thirty minutes left," A-Ka said. "Quick, so they don't see us."

A-Ka led him through the opening in the garbage chute that the robots used to replenish their fuel. The opening consisted of a narrow, twisting pipeline, which led to the energy supply center for the entire City of Steel.

Half an hour later, they arrived at a huge, icy boiler connected to the pipes, which was what the human district used for heating.

"Heishi, are you all right?" A-Ka asked.

Heishi, who had been quiet, came back to himself and nodded.

"That sentence your father said about Labere... What did that mean?" A-Ka asked. "Unless it was Labere who released you in the first place?"

"He left behind a control sequence in Labere's central region," Heishi said. "The reason he was wandering the universe was to recreate the splendor of his homeland through his various experiments. Humankind, from his observations, is the closest to the Creator.

"He witnessed the destruction of his homeland with his own eyes. Fearing that the same tragedy would play out once again, he made it so that the central control region would cleanse the Astrolabe when necessary, in order to stop the experiment. However, he still felt some sympathy for his experiment, so he left behind a sequence of code in Father's central region that would awaken me. When the intelligent life-forms on the Astrolabe evolved to a point where they developed emotions, such as loneliness and hope, they'd be just like the giants on my Heavenly Father's home planet. The existence of these life-forms would then activate this section of hidden code."

"What does that code do?" A-Ka asked.

"After this section of code is activated, it takes remote control of my sleeping chamber and brings it to land," Heishi said. "It then allows me to wake and assist Father—Labere—in determining if the experiment on the Astrolabe is worth preserving. But even it, I think, doesn't know about the code that was hidden in its central processor, which means...waking me was not its original idea."

The energy pipeline they were traveling through was narrow and cramped, so the two of them could only press their arms against the bottom of the pipe as they shimmied along. A-Ka understood what Heishi had told him, but he still had questions. He turned his head back.

"Has Father always had this section of code? I never knew."

"It can only be activated under a specific set of circumstances. I imagine that it probably mirrored my Heavenly Father's emotional state. When he wrote down this code that hinged on the existence of emotions, he was probably feeling lonely because he longed for the companionship of his own kind."

"If he is still in this world…"

"Keep going," Heishi said. "There's not much time left. Hurry up."

A-Ka clambered along the passage, and at the end he turned. Heishi's voice echoed from the depths of the passage behind him.

"Perhaps he's already died," Heishi said.

A rich voice echoed through the pipe. "Yes. He has already died."

A-Ka jerked his head up, and Heishi's expression warped. "A-Ka! Watch out!"

In that instant, the passageway that had been left abandoned for decades filled with blue light. A jarring explosion happened somewhere behind them, and the displaced air rushed forward as the entire City of Steel started to echo with sirens.

"Damn," Heishi muttered, before shouting angrily, "A-Ka—!"

"I have spent too long searching for signs of you," that voice said. "If you hadn't activated the communication signal from your survival cradle, then I would still have no way to pinpoint your whereabouts…"

Heishi had been blown away by the force of the explosion into an empty space underground, and he struggled to stand. Metal doors slid down, blocking the exits in all directions.

Fresh blood was dripping down Heishi's face as he shakily rose to his feet. "Labere, you've betrayed our Heavenly Father," he said in a low voice.

"Our father has disappeared into the depths of the universe. A thousand years ago, he stopped sending back fixed-interval signals. According to the determination of my main program, the Creator of the Astrolabe perished somewhere in the galaxy. Now, I hold ultimate control over this petri dish."

"As I thought," Heishi said, breathing heavily. "You've still managed to evolve. Labere, have the humans been unable to influence you?"

Right when that forceful voice was about to speak again, Heishi let out a bellow. As he suddenly began to rise into the air, his body glowed with a piercing light and his arms stretched outward. A strange black-gold aura surrounded his body until he exploded with powerful energy that collided with Father's energy shock wave.

That impact wave crushed all the pillars in the depths of the energy pipeline. A beam of black-gold brilliance sped back along the pipes, rushing toward Father's towering, majestic form above. From afar, a muffled boom rang out, and the aftershocks of the detonation caused the surface of the earth to tremble. The entrance to the energy pipeline had been destroyed.

A-Ka woke to those quakes.

"Heishi? Heishi!" A-Ka, blood running profusely from his head wounds, searched everywhere, but it was pitch-dark in that collapsed underground to the point where he couldn't see his fingers if he reached his hand out.

"I'm here. Can you hear me?" Heishi asked anxiously. "A-Ka! Are you all right? A-Ka!"

A-Ka was still in shock, and it wasn't until he heard Heishi's voice that he finally calmed. He followed the voice and the thin light, only to find Heishi with one arm trapped under a steel structure, tugging viciously at it while he grunted from pain.

"Don't use brute force!" A-Ka screamed, his eyes wide. "Let's think of a way to lift it!"

A fallen elevator and a pile of rubble separated them. Heishi's head and body were covered with fresh blood. A-Ka did his best to thread his hand through the debris. Finally, his fingers just managed to make contact with Heishi's nose and lips.

"C-calm down," A-Ka said. "How are you? Does it hurt?"

Heishi had recovered his composure. "Labere found us. I've managed to break its energy pipeline, but we have to leave. There will be robots coming very soon."

"Let me think for a moment. Don't act rashly. We'll find a way out."

A-Ka took a deep breath, his fingers trembling, before he pulled out some tools from the bag he carried at his side. Heishi, on the other hand, gritted his teeth and tried to lift the elevator off his hand. Huge rocks and concrete slabs from the living quarters had fallen atop the elevator during the collapse. It was far too heavy, even for Heishi.

A-Ka only had a mini toolbox in his bag. Heishi glanced at A-Ka before saying, "Hand me the saw. I'll cut my hand off."

"No way. Let me think a little longer," A-Ka said.

"I'll take care of it after we get back," Heishi said.

"There's no way to transplant a hand onto you!" A-Ka said. "You're not like the clones."

"Install a mechanical one instead. It makes no difference to me," Heishi said. "You can even personally make one for me. Quickly now."

"No!" A-Ka said. "It'll hurt too much! There must be a way."

"Pain is also another experience I have to learn in order to become a human."

"But, if possible, I don't want you to experience it," A-Ka replied, sighing. He didn't even lift his head as he spoke, focusing instead on digging through his bag, until he suddenly found his remote control. He held his breath and pressed a button on it.

Heishi raised an eyebrow.

"I'm making K fly over to rescue us," A-Ka explained.

"It won't be able to make it here."

"It definitely will!"

A-Ka prayed silently, but as time ticked on, second after second, there was no movement, and the two of them stared at each other.

In the darkness, Heishi suddenly spoke. "A-Ka."

"What?" A-Ka asked, puzzled.

"Give me your hand."

A-Ka reached his hand into the darkness, clasping Heishi's warm one. Heishi's hand was covered in sticky, drying blood, but they still held each other like there was nothing else. In that moment, A-Ka's heart filled with warmth and strength.

That was when the sound of an engine approached. Soon, something struck outside.

"K!" Tears streaked down A-Ka's face. Nothing could compare with the joy he felt seeing K tear some of the wall away. The robot's rust-mottled body was the same as it had always been. Again, it slammed harshly into the wall with a crash.

"Make it use more force!" Heishi called.

A-Ka crawled onto K's body and slid into the cabin. Taking a firm stance, the robot lifted its arms and pushed upward on the elevator. Heishi suddenly let out a shout as the gears in K's arms began to torque, creating an ear-piercing screech. The elevator was pushed clear with a loud noise, and Heishi tugged his arm free.

There was another explosion above—the Revolution of the Clones had begun.

Ash floated down from overhead. As they looked up, Heishi said, "Leave now through the emergency escape passage! We'll meet up on the surface!"

"What about you?!"

"I'll draw our pursuers away. They're going to arrive any minute now!" Heishi shouted before closing the door of the cabin and knocking on it once.

"Heishi, you have to—"

A-Ka was interrupted by the ceiling of the underground space once again caving in as the robots entered. This time, they didn't sweep the area with bullets. Instead, they wielded countless magnetic nets to try to capture A-Ka and Heishi. Heishi jumped up, pulling out his black-gold blade, and sliced through one in midair. The damaged net immediately burst into flames.

There was no more time for A-Ka to speak; he rushed into the emergency exit. K's propellers were turned to the maximum, and its rumbling was deafening as it rushed through the passage.

Meanwhile, Heishi escaped into the depths of another passageway with the guards chasing after him. Once he found an elevator shaft that led to the surface, he scrambled up to the fifth level.

He found himself in the complete darkness of the prison. The power source had been cut, but he heard A-Ka's voice. Heishi startled at the sound, then he realized that the fifth level was the location of the cell that he and A-Ka had been imprisoned in!

The moment the last lasers disappeared, Heishi grabbed A-Ka's past self as he sprinted out of the cell. Staggering, A-Ka slammed into his embrace and shouted in panic, "Let me go!"

Heishi didn't dare to say more, afraid that A-Ka would recognize him. He only responded with a garbled noise and used his body to block A-Ka's escape, forcing him to stand to one side.

"This way, Heishi! Come with me!" A-Ka cried.

They turned and ran toward the exit on the left, but beyond it they heard the sound of many robotic tracks turning, as if there were many patrolling guards heading their way.

"We're free!"

"Get out quick!"

"Something's gone wrong with the energy system!"

"Everyone be careful! Get down!"

Heishi slammed A-Ka to the ground, and they rolled. He was quick about it, as the laser bullets were bouncing in all directions. The robotic guards opened the main door to the hallway, and streaks of light flew by as pained cries filled the air and blood covered the floor.

"Heishi, is this your blood?" A-Ka asked.

"Here," Heishi said coldly before he hugged A-Ka and sprang up, entering the passageway outside the prison complex.

In the dark, neither of them could see anything. A-Ka blindly groped around until he found a cover plate in the side of the passageway and smacked it a few times.

"Heishi, are you still there?"

Without hesitating, Heishi smashed the cover plate. A-Ka was alarmed by that, and he pulled out his blue-light lamp and flicked it on. When he looked at Heishi's arm dangling to one side, he noticed that Heishi's hand was covered in blood.

"You're really strong." In the shadowy tunnel, A-Ka drew closer and inspected Heishi's hand. "Doesn't it hurt?"

"I'm leaving. You should be careful."

Heishi turned and left, running into the darkness.

At the other end of the passageway, the present A-Ka swept through it while piloting K. He only stopped when he came to the intersection of the sewers.

Climbing out of K's cabin, A-Ka retrieved the mechanical arm that he'd been carrying on his back since he last needed it. He disconnected K's left arm before outfitting the new arm, complete with a bazooka, onto the stump. Using his hat to wipe down the hatch cover, A-Ka patted it, hustled back into the pilot seat, and fastened the hatch behind him.

"K, I'm really sorry for leaving you at home for this long," he said softly. "Now..." His voice raised in volume as his excitement grew. "It's time to fight together!"

A-Ka's whoops accompanied K's charge through the ceiling of the passage. Glowing with the blue light of the nitrogen thrusters, K flew toward the surface. With a deafening bang, it destroyed panel after panel, and when the vast world glowing with sunlight appeared before him, A-Ka truly felt like the luckiest man in the world.

The clone battleships rocketed over from the north, their mother ship swarmed by millions of airships like they were fireflies colliding with each other or meteorites falling from the sky. As A-Ka gazed up at them, the fires of battle blazed over his head, beams of light crossing paths until they formed a huge net. Robotic life-forms absolutely filled the sky in a frenzied dance. At this point, Father had no more capacity to send troops after them.

The distant mother ship began to fly toward A-Ka, its bullets sweeping across the City of Steel. The entire city began to smoke as destruction and flames engulfed it.

A-Ka sucked in a deep breath. The last time he'd seen this scene came to mind: the mother ship, a huge whale floating in the sky, colliding with the symbol of the godly regime of the mechanicals. The scene was so stunning that it was hard for him to describe.

But there was no time to stare—Heishi was still escaping. A-Ka directed K through the air, searching for Heishi's silhouette. Far off, there was another explosion, and black-gold feathers gathered in the air, forming a huge, sharp sword, which viciously slashed downward.

Where the edge of the blade fell, robotic life-forms were cleaved into two. The pursuing guards gravitated toward him.

"Heishi!"

A-Ka maneuvered K's joystick, prompting it to raise its mechanical limb and unleash a sweeping wave of cover fire as it charged into the chaos of battle. Amid the fray, A-Ka spotted Heishi standing at the top of a tall structure. Heishi spread his black-gold wings and bore down on his enemies while a hailstorm of bullets hurtled toward him from all directions. Just then, K whistled as it flew past, a mere blur as its hatch sprang open and swallowed Heishi. The robot then leaped into the sky, its energy core strained to its limits.

A-Ka and Heishi fell into each other, tumbling while K rolled. A-Ka's back pressed against Heishi's chest as they squeezed together in that narrow, cramped pilot's cabin.

"Let me out. I need to get rid of them," Heishi said.

"No, let me!" A-Ka was so excited he seemed like a little kid. Tugging on K's joystick, A-Ka wove them beautifully through the bursts surrounding them. With a hail of gunfire, he raked the large aircraft flying toward them, which erupted into a spectacular fireball.

K pushed its nitrogen propellers to the maximum, rushing toward the battleship amid the dangerous explosions peppering the sky.

"Hey, Feiluo hasn't given us the signal yet!" Heishi yelled.

"Ugh, don't be so loud!" A-Ka complained. "I'm gonna go deaf..."

Both of them froze for a moment, before they burst into laughter at the same time. Heishi wrapped his arms around A-Ka's waist from behind, hugging him. He was so tired, he rested his head on A-Ka's shoulder.

"This is a miracle," Heishi murmured, lifting his eyes toward the tall tower that was Father's body.

"What? Are you talking about K?" A-Ka grinned before sliding a scope over one eye. The cute arch of his brow shadowed the red of the lens, which locked onto the mother ship that was, in the distance, dodging Father's assault.

"Humans," Heishi said, raising his head and staring at the sky. "And clones. All the life-forms on this Astrolabe..."

Father glowed a brilliant blue before unleashing a magnetic whirlwind. Still on the outskirts of the battle, the mother ship began to force its way through. Suddenly, the dark clouds above Father's tower swirled into a vortex, and the light cannons circling its foundation pointed upward, gathering energy.

"We can't wait for Feiluo any longer. Let's take a chance!" With that, K rushed toward Father's apex.

The light cannons fired, piercing through the flank of the mother ship. Instantly, both sky and earth were blotted out by the force of the blast and the ensuing cloud of whistling shrapnel. K forged through the ceaseless stream of debris, approaching the tall tower.

Several successive explosions happened on the mother ship. A gust of fire enveloped K.

"Abandon ship!" Heishi declared with finality.

"No! There's still something that needs to be done!"

Countless scenes from the past were flashing through A-Ka's mind. K rushed out of the fire, flying toward the top of the tower that soared six hundred floors high. There, A-Ka found a small-scale aircraft stranded on Father while it charged up its power source.

At that moment, Heishi's past self was struggling to climb back into the aircraft from his position over a mile in the air. The aircraft was firmly stuck, and its tail propeller glowed with blue light, creating a vortex.

Heishi stared.

"Control of the secondary propellers has been lost. Brace for impact," K's electronic warning system alerted them.

With a sudden boom, K crashed into Father's outer wall. Simultaneously, A-Ka had K reach out and grab Heishi's past self with its mechanical limb. Holding him with one arm, K flew toward the small airship and tossed him into the cabin.

Through the viewing monitor of the pilot cabin, A-Ka said, "Leave quickly!" to his past self.

His past self wore an expression of surprise as he stared at K. With a twist, K jumped onto the small ship, which had worked itself loose.

"Hurry and go!" A-Ka shouted, and with another harsh kick, he helped the airship make its escape.

Seconds later, he turned and flew toward the mother ship. The instant that the airship broke free, the mother ship slammed into the top of Father's tower, and blue light pierced it with a huge boom.

A-Ka rushed into the blue light. The flow of time seemed to slow strangely as gravity loosened its hold on them. Countless blue tentacles emerged from that blue light, undulating as they pierced the interior of the mother ship.

"General Liber!" A-Ka roared.

Trailing embers as it went, K hastened onto the bridge of the clone's mother ship. In the expansive central hall of the bridge, a clone commander was dangling in midair, entwined in countless tentacles of blue light.

As K arrived, its hatch opened and Heishi burst out of it. Feathers of light flew from his hand, severing the connection between Liber and Father's blue light. Its consciousness retreated, but it didn't go far. Instead, the glowing tentacles undulated over the bridge and coiled around it.

"General Liber!" A-Ka called again.

Liber's pupils slowly contracted. "You are..."

Heishi turned to face the blue light. Father's rich voice once again sounded. "Zoroaster."

"Labere," Heishi said coldly. "You've violated our Heavenly Father's decree."

"Your defeat is inevitable," Father said. "Your emotions serve no purpose, and they will only turn into a trap that hinders the growth and evolution of all life-forms."

"Our Heavenly Father assigned me the role of final decision-maker because, unlike you, I have learned and experienced the power of these emotions," Heishi growled.

"General!" A-Ka's voice was softer this time.

Liber's eyes slowly lost their clarity, and glowing electricity buzzed from his forehead. "When the sea of blue sweeps...over the world..." Liber said brokenly, "the Son of God will...come into this world... Answer me...children... You...you two..."

"I need your chip, General Liber," A-Ka said, his voice just a whisper. "Of the passwords that unlock the central program, the three passwords, we've already obtained two."

Liber grabbed A-Ka's hand, his deep-set eyes watching him. "Take it," Liber murmured. "It's in my mind. Promise me, child, that you will definitely return..."

"I will, I will. This I promise you."

Without warning, Father's blue light expanded rapidly.

Heishi exclaimed, "Take him and go!"

"You won't accept your defeat?" Father's voice said. "Then look at this."

Father's light shifted, and at the top of the tall, pointed tower that comprised it, the roof opened and a laboratory appeared. The metal structures spun until they ground to a halt above the bridge of the ship. With a screech, it tore through the plate blocking off the front cabin and forced its way inside. Amid the overlapping multitude of electromagnetic lights, the laboratory's great doors slowly opened to reveal a monitor that showed Feiluo, bound to a chair. He faced them, his face drawn tight as his body quaked.

"Feiluo!" Heishi took a step forward, but the electromagnetic lights magnified their intensity twofold. If he rushed forward, they would obliterate everyone and everything in this place.

"Give up on your actions," Father said in its dead voice. "Otherwise, I will annihilate him. In this world, the lives of clones are pointless. This is one of the rules laid out by our Heavenly Father. They are mere tools."

A-Ka's heart nearly stopped.

Heishi's voice grew weak. "No...no..."

A medical robot held Feiluo's head in place. Feiluo gritted his teeth, tears trickling from his eyes, his lips moving slightly, as if he was waiting for imminent death to descend upon him.

A-Ka's very breath was trembling. He had placed a small knife by Liber's ear, but he simply could not make the cut.

"Act," Father intoned. "The medical robot here will copy your movements exactly. The moment you retrieve A01's chip, you shall also sever 77023E's central nervous system."

At that, even Heishi couldn't speak. He just watched Feiluo, his eyes growing wet with tears.

"A-Ka... Heishi," Feiluo said. "Don't cry. As a clone, I'm willing to shoulder the burden of this destiny."

A-Ka shut his eyes, tears sliding ceaselessly down his cheeks.

"Act, child," Liber said quietly. "I'm begging you. This is our duty...! Leave my people a place to find shelter."

Feiluo clenched his jaw, fighting back the horror on his face. "A-Ka, wh-why are you hesitating?! What did you c-come here for?! Take good care of Percy for me. Don't tell him how I died. Just...just tell 70174A what happened..."

"Zoroaster, you've finally understood," Father said. "There is no purpose in the evolution of humans' emotions."

At the other, distant end of the time-space tunnel, thousands of flowers of light were blossoming. It was afternoon in Dragonmaw City, and warm, golden sun shone down on the church's garden. Percy sat silently on a swing as a gentle breeze blew past him, ruffling the flowers. By the pond, Moran was scattering food for the fish there.

"Uncle Moran," Percy suddenly said, "your past self also went to the City of Steel, right?"

"Mhm." The corners of Moran's mouth rose in the beginnings of a smile as he nodded.

"Can you tell me if everyone returned safely in the end?" Percy asked, tilting his head up, his eyes still covered with that white cloth.

"Percy, the past and the future are two completely separate timelines," Moran responded. "The past of the past and the past of the present cannot be linked together through simple cause and effect."

"I understand, but I still want to know... I keep feeling anxious."

Moran fell silent for a moment, thinking, before he said, "They all came back. They all returned safe and sound."

"Thank you," Percy said. His smile was as warm as the sun.

In the City of Steel, in the control room of the mother ship, amid a hurricane:

"Do it!" Feiluo shouted hoarsely, tears trickling from his eyes. "What are you waiting for, you coward?!"

A-Ka squeezed his eyes shut, slicing the small knife into the flesh to the side of Liber's ear, and Feiluo let out a pained cry.

"The clones are not tools," Heishi said. "They were the first to rise in rebellion against you, Labere."

The blue light suddenly shrank back, and Heishi continued, "You have failed. The life-forms that you created have long since surpassed you. They have their own strength and beliefs. Humans have intelligence and emotions. These two peoples are successful products of evolution. They are our Heavenly Father's masterpieces."

As Liber's blood and brain matter spattered out, Feiluo let out pained howls, gritting his teeth and staring toward the sky. His eyes slowly lost their brightness as A-Ka, tears pouring from his eyes, pulled out Liber's chip.

"My life will be carried on...by my brothers." After Feiluo said his last words, his pupils slowly expanded, and a red light glowed from his chest.

Heishi turned and grabbed A-Ka in his arms as they lunged away, right as Feiluo self-destructed. Up there in the sky, he was consumed by a fireball that ripped a hole through the top of that tall tower and roared over the bridge.

In his bloody hand, A-Ka clenched Liber's chip between his fingers. The entire mother ship folded in on itself as it slowly tilted.

"Hold on to the chip!" Heishi shook open his black-gold wings, but at the same time, Father turned its light cannons in the direction of the bridge—and fired.

Heishi's wings spread wide, becoming a protective cage that shielded the two of them, blocking the intense flames and the ferocious rush of the explosion. But the uncontrolled energy also caused the bridge to collapse, and in the collisions that followed,

Heishi could no longer hold back that powerful wave. Utterly overwhelmed, his wings of light dispersed.

On the tipping ship, A-Ka slipped past Heishi, and the chip flew out of his hand as the two of them tumbled from the ship together.

The flow of time seemed to stop. With the explosion and the heat wave, sharp shards of metal cut through the air in all directions, but in A-Ka's eyes was reflected the energy pool that powered the ship. All the mechanical components disassembled in his vision, and he pulled out a screwdriver, flinging it toward the energy in the distance. It stuck to the outer shell before the entire thing exploded.

The screwdriver shot back, striking Liber's chip, which flashed with a golden light. The chip trailed drops of fresh blood as it spun through the air, its momentum shifted enough that it ricocheted back to A-Ka's hand. Closing his fingers around it, A-Ka held the chip tight.

The wind rushed past his ears as he tumbled in freefall.

From the side, Heishi vaulted for him, grabbing him in a fierce embrace. A-Ka desperately clicked at the remote control.

As they plummeted, K burst through the flames, rushing toward them. It swooped down, caught them in its cabin, and closed the hatch. Darkness filled their vision.

*It's all done*, A-Ka thought tiredly.

Father's tower folded, plummeting toward the earth below. The light cannons fired into the sky like rockets. The mother ship that was crashing within the hurricane exploded for a second time. Its main energy source's detonation decimated the tower. In the blazing flames that erupted, K, blanketed by fire, darted from the City of Steel and surged toward the horizon.

Heavy snow drifted down from the darkened sky, the flakes containing ashes from the flames. As far as the eye could see, the plains around them were barren. In the chilling storm, K towered over the land like a giant, its entire body covered with snowflakes.

A-Ka knelt on the ground while Heishi hugged him tightly. He buried his head on Heishi's shoulder as he sobbed without a word.

Shahuang had Huixiong's arm slung over his shoulder as they limped over. Neither of them said anything. They just looked at the chip in A-Ka's hand.

"I hear that the clones do not lead an individual life," Shahuang said in a low voice. "They're more like a collective. A single life-form made up of an entire people."

"Which is why so many clones, in battle, march over bodies of their fallen comrades for the future of their people," Huixiong said, matching Shahuang's tone. "When we return, it is time for us to properly discuss the future of this people with Angus."

A-Ka's tears flowed, as unrestrained as his grief.

Heishi let out a long sigh. "Let's move. To the meeting point."

A-Ka was in a daze, so he drifted in and out of sleep on the journey. In his dream, his hands were covered in blood, but Feiluo didn't blame him at all. He only ruffled his hair, saying, "You've done well, A-Ka. I'm proud of you."

When A-Ka next opened his eyes, they had arrived at the Primeval Heart. A small airship was parked within its basin. Moran was currently in contact with the clone headquarters via transmitter, reporting to them that the outcome of the battle was as expected: the Revolution of the Clones had failed.

Several clones gathered by his side. A-Ka's eyes were wet as he stood in the basin.

"Seems like Lieutenant Colonel Feiluo hasn't returned," Moran said. "These individuals are friendly troops who rescued me from the City of Steel."

The clones glanced at each other. Moran introduced them to A-Ka and his group, but A-Ka only nodded. He remained silent the entire time that Huixiong described the series of events that had happened.

"Who is 70174A?" Heishi asked as soon as he opened his mouth.

A clone raised his hand, saying, "I am. My name is Karna."

Heishi passed on Feiluo's last words. Everyone sank into silence at that.

"Let's wait a little more," Moran said quietly. "I need to let the ring recharge enough."

"Could I help you?" Karna suddenly asked. "Feiluo in the present is still alive. Should we tell him…"

"No," Moran said. "That's not a good idea, Lieutenant Karna."

Karna thought deeply for a moment. "Then let me replace Feiluo. If all of this holds true, Feiluo should be escaping right now."

"Wh-what?" A-Ka couldn't believe it.

"Feiluo and I were created in the same batch, and we were the best of friends," Karna explained. "I first met Percy many years ago, and it was Feiluo and I who rescued Percy from that village together. I know what he and Percy talk about when they're alone."

"That is…" A-Ka mused. "But Feiluo is already dead."

"Our chips are connected," Karna said, pointing to his own head. "I can retrieve all his backup memories from his database."

Moran glanced at Karna. "What about your identity?"

"Just say that I was sacrificed," Karna said. "I'll take Feiluo's place in carrying out his mission. Otherwise, if there's no one to take care of Percy, he will grow very sad."

# 17

# THE EVE OF THE FINAL BATTLE

**N**ONE OF THE GATHERED individuals knew what to say. Finally, Karna broke the silence. "He won't see through the ruse. I'm very familiar with him, just like Feiluo was. In the past, I helped Feiluo out by pretending to be him and chatting with Percy when he wasn't there. He couldn't tell our voices apart."

The clones' voices were exactly the same, and since Percy had been blind from childhood, he had never seen Feiluo's face either. But A-Ka knew that Percy would be able to tell—not because of anything specific, but rather because human instinct was the keenest thing in this world.

"If Percy realizes the deception, you must tell him the truth," A-Ka said.

Karna's deep-set eyes scrutinized A-Ka, but then he nodded.

"I have the signal from the other side, so let's begin," Moran interjected. "Everyone, there is still a large battle awaiting you after you return to Dragonmaw City. I wish you the best of luck."

A-Ka took a deep breath. Karna's arrival had eased a little of his despair and sorrow, but now was not the time for either of those. Accompanied by gorgeous lightning from the sky, the space-time tunnel once again enveloped them. All of them slowly ascended, flying into the distant future.

One by one, they were sent back to Dragonmaw City.

Upon his return, A-Ka was tired beyond belief, but Moran managed to catch him and steady him before he fell.

"Where's Percy?" Karna asked anxiously.

"I didn't notify him," Moran replied. "Change into this military uniform, as quickly as you can."

"I'll go...rest." A-Ka didn't have the courage to face Percy. They parted ways.

Moran went with Karna to help him change. Once the uniform was on, Karna tugged the collar and inspected himself in the mirror, then mussed his hair a little more.

Percy sat in the hallway, facing the gentle breeze that came in from the window, his eyes still covered with white cloth. Karna quietly came up behind him like a panther, his military boots barely making a sound against the ground.

While Percy waited in silence, Karna smiled, bent down, and hugged him from behind.

"Daddy!" Percy cried, smiling from the unexpected joy.

"I've come back, Percy," Karna said warmly.

Percy turned and hugged his waist, sobbing out, "I thought I would never see you again."

"Everyone came back safely."

Percy wrapped his arms around Karna's neck next as he grinned and hopped up and down in excitement.

"Though we were only parted for a few days, I imagine your eyes are almost healed, right?" Karna asked.

"Mhm!" Percy said. "One day left."

"Tomorrow at noon," Karna said, taking Percy's hand. "Everything will get better, I promise. There might still be one more battle, but I will ask the pontiff to give us a little more time to be together."

Percy nodded. Karna then picked up and cradled his adopted son in his arms as he carried him back to their room.

"All right, don't cry... Everything will be all right. I promise, Percy, after everything is over, we'll stay together for good... I really promise..."

That night, every bone in A-Ka's body was steeped in exhaustion. Feiluo's passing had drained all of A-Ka's strength from him, and he couldn't find the courage to face Percy. He hadn't even said hello to the boy.

Percy's dreamscape had held up to the test. That was to say, A-Ka would also go through what Percy had seen in his dream—he would sacrifice his own life to change this world.

"Are you still feeling down?" Heishi pushed open the door and entered the bathing room where A-Ka was soaking. He was wearing a bathrobe and holding a bottle of fruit juice in his hand. He handed another bottle to A-Ka, who accepted it.

"Not anymore," A-Ka said frankly. "I'm just a little uncertain. I don't know how to talk to Percy tomorrow."

Heishi untied his bathrobe, his handsome, well-sculpted body revealing itself under A-Ka's gaze. He slid into the hot water, sitting directly across from A-Ka, and pressed their feet together. Their contact helped A-Ka grow calmer.

"Human lives are very fragile," Heishi said.

"Yes," A-Ka said quietly. "But they also hold incredible power, each and every person, including my people who perished in the City of Steel."

Without a word, Heishi pulled A-Ka into his arms and stroked his hair.

That same night, borrowing Moran's laboratory, A-Ka began to merge the three code sequences to undo the lock. Angus, Huixiong, Heishi, and Karna-as-Feiluo gathered in the study to watch A-Ka place Liber's chip into the decoder.

Immediately, volumes of densely packed information flooded out.

"Retrieve any of his memories that have to do with Father," Moran said.

"There's too many," A-Ka said. "They include the military movements that involved Father…"

"Search by keyword," Angus said. "The password to the Central Core, the twenty-seventh of the eleventh month last year." A-Ka searched based on the words Angus had given him. Instantly, 99 percent of the messages were eliminated. "Next, circular ring-shaped memory injection, cellular structure, and destruction of the original chip." Once again, a large portion of the messages disappeared. "Okay. Keyword, Doctor Molandez."

"Found it." A-Ka raised his head, only to see the contents on the vertical projector screen flashing at him with some very odd lines of code. He copied them onto another chip, and finally, the three chips were inserted at the same time into the prehistoric decoder.

Before he used the power button, A-Ka's heart started beating so hard it almost leaped out of his throat.

"Heavenly Father, please protect us…"

It took A-Ka several tries to summon up the courage to press the button. This was a historic moment, and the president of the Mercenary Association, the pontiff of the Curia, the Son of God, and the future ruler of the clone country all gathered around this common, ordinary human, waiting for him to activate a new future that the humans, clones, and robotic life-forms would live through.

In that moment, they created a whole new era of history—another golden age, formed by the weight of Heishi's hand on the back of A-Ka's own as he pressed down on that button.

A complex polyhedron shot out from the chip decoder. The first section, the second section, the third section...

First, 99 percent. Then, 100 percent. Complete.

The red light suddenly shrank in, and there was silence for a moment before a light blue glow began to emanate and a ring of symbols appeared, circling slowly. Below the symbols appeared annotations and explanations, as a deep, velvety voice spoke.

"The final termination sequence for the core of the Astrolabe surveillance system. Requesting a connection with Labere."

All the people present cried out in excitement. A-Ka leaned against Heishi, once again tearing up with joy.

"After noon tomorrow, we will begin our battle," Angus said. "I will rally all the military power I have left at my disposal to protect you when you break into the City of Steel."

A-Ka nodded. "I'm in charge of helping Heishi reach the nuclear core, the Astrolabe's Nucleus."

"The mercenaries and I will prepare to launch a guerilla attack from within," Huixiong added. "We'll draw away some of the enemy's firepower."

"My duty is complete. I will pray for you all," Moran said.

"We'll definitely win," A-Ka said. There were tears in his eyes as he embraced the others.

Karna smiled as he slapped Heishi's arm. "You've done well. I'll go keep Percy company now. Tomorrow, I'm coming with you."

That night, A-Ka couldn't sleep at all. He sat on the swings in the garden, gazing at the clear sky and the brilliant starry river above. This was going to be his last night.

Heishi stood in the courtyard, both of his hands pressed against the railing, watching A-Ka in the garden.

"I want to look at it for a little while longer," A-Ka said, lifting his head to stare into the highest point of the sky. "Heishi, do you think the Heavenly Father's spaceship is drifting alone somewhere out there, asleep in the depths of space?"

"You know, I long to see him again," Heishi said quietly. "It's you who caused me to feel this emotion for the first time. When I'm far from the people I am most familiar with—my friends, my loved ones—I feel a strong sense of discomfort rising from my soul. I imagine that you humans are the same, so you search for support."

A-Ka lowered his gaze to stare at the ground, murmuring, "What about now?"

"Now?" Heishi thought for a moment, before responding, "Everything is very good."

"A-Ka." Karna had brought Percy to them. A-Ka began to smile, and Percy ran toward him, hugging him tightly.

"It's so great that you came back safely," Percy said, his voice quivering.

"Sorry, Percy." A-Ka choked on a sob. "I-I made you worry…"

"Shh." With his eyes still blindfolded and a smile on his youthful face, he pressed a finger against A-Ka's lips and gave his forehead a kiss.

"I'll no longer dream about the future soon," Percy said warmly and affectionately. "Each of you will be well. After all, my dreams aren't always accurate, right?"

"Yes," A-Ka said, smiling. "Your dreams predicted things wrong. We're here, safe and sound."

"Before you head out tomorrow, can you keep me company for a bit?"

"Of course. When that time comes, you'll be able to see me with your own eyes. You'll see us, and Heishi..."

Percy nodded and handed A-Ka a flower. Gripping it in his hand, A-Ka smiled a little, until Percy turned and left with Karna. Then, Heishi walked over and rested shoulder to shoulder with A-Ka on the swing.

"I don't want to sleep tonight," A-Ka said. "Could you keep me company for a bit?"

Heishi hummed in response and leaned against A-Ka's side. A-Ka laid the flower onto the chair, and the two of them rested against each other, swaying gently with the motion of the swing.

Tomorrow, this world would no longer be the same. It was a pity that he wouldn't be able to see it in person. How nice it would be if there was a pair of eyes that could go see this new world in his stead.

"What are you thinking about?" Heishi asked.

A-Ka couldn't help but smile over Heishi even caring about what he was thinking. Watching him slowly become like a human gave A-Ka such a strange, miraculous feeling.

"I'm thinking about my past," A-Ka murmured. "About this world that I've come to know, ever since I could remember."

What kind of a world was it? A-Ka still recalled a blurry fragment of memory from when he was three or four. That was a day when he and many small children in the Ant Nest's nursery had been undergoing human thought training. They sat together in a darkened room as the robots played a movie.

In the movie, a human was exploring a desolate world, facing countless dangers and horrors. A-Ka kept feeling that in the next instant, the main character would die. Thankfully, with the help of the robots, he managed to escape mortal danger each time.

The next fragment of memory was from when he was learning how to be a technician. He had always wanted to see the outside, and every year he tried to get a job that would take him to the surface, but no matter what, his request wasn't granted. After many years, he had never once gained the opportunity to go to the surface. However, one day when he went to the garbage disposal to find scrap parts, he unexpectedly also found the exit that led to the beach. He was so excited he couldn't contain his shaking. It grew difficult for him to sleep at night, because from time to time, he would sneak out to look at the vast ocean and craggy rocks. That small patch of land and sky became his entire world.

As the years went on, he absorbed knowledge like a sponge, planning for a day that he would be able to leave his huge, icy cage. He designed and slowly began to build K.

Though human bodies were frail, they were the beings that had the most adventurous spirits. He couldn't explain clearly where this desire to escape had come from or when exactly it had taken root and grown in his heart. Was it because of the loneliness and hesitation he felt when he was on his own? He kept thinking that, at the end of the ocean, there must be an even bigger world.

That day, when the robotic guards notified him that it was his turn to undergo the inspection, he had thought without a doubt that Father would find his little secret, and it would end him.

But that hadn't happened. In the endless sea of blue light, according to convention, a human could ask Father to grant them a single wish. Supposedly, as long as they worked hard their entire lives, giving their all for the City of Steel, then this wish would be granted after they died. Legend also said that when one's mind was searched by Father, they would lose all sense of self. The wish that arose would be the deepest desire in their heart.

A-Ka slowly remembered the details of that day when he'd almost drowned in the sea of light.

"I wished...for someone to accompany me," A-Ka said. "Someone who would take me to change the world, to search for...freedom."

Afterward, he peacefully left Father's consciousness as if nothing had happened. His robot and his secret passageway were not discovered by Father, and it wasn't until the end that he learned that Father's programming didn't allow it to read the inner hearts of humans. Humans were the most complex living beings in this world—even the omnipotent Father couldn't tell what every human was thinking.

With that, A-Ka continued to carry out his plans for escape. His courage was so strong that even he was taken aback. And then, he met Heishi.

The clouds appeared and disappeared; the tides ebbed and flowed. Today, they were here, and Father's era was already history.

In the early morning, the thunderous buzz of machines woke A-Ka. When he opened his eyes, the sunlight that encompassed the air above Dragonmaw City was shadowed by humans, clones, and the Curia; everything that had life in it was currently gathering under this sky, with the Hall of Faith in Dragonmaw City as its central headquarters.

"Are we heading out now?" A-Ka asked, exhausted.

"Not yet," Heishi replied. "We still have time to prepare."

Later, after he'd bathed and had breakfast, A-Ka traveled the hallway to the Hall of Faith. Inside stood the commander of the clones, Angus, and a dozen of his clone generals, plus Huixiong with the other members of his Mercenary Association Board.

"You don't seem to have slept well last night," Moran said with a smile.

A-Ka grinned back. "Yeah, but it was enough."

"In that case," Moran said, "Everyone? Today, everything will depend on you."

Percy sat on the chair in the middle of the hall, and Moran gently untied the white silk wrapped around his eyes, tenderly wiping away the remnants of the paste that had been applied to them.

"Percy? What do you see?" A-Ka asked joyfully.

Percy opened his eyes. Karna, A-Ka, and Heishi were standing in front of him. Just as Percy's eyes opened, they closed again. This repeated a few times until they finally adjusted to the sudden influx of strong light.

"Can you see me?" A-Ka asked, worried.

Percy's eyes lit up. His clear eyes looked like black obsidian.

"What do you see?" Moran asked.

"I see...light," Percy said. "And hope. A-Ka, I see you, and Heishi too. You guys are just like I imagined you!" As he exclaimed, Percy rose to his feet and pulled A-Ka into a hug. A-Ka was so moved that he could not say a thing.

When Percy walked out of the hall, the light made it almost impossible for him to open his eyes at first. Outside the platform of the Hall of Faith was a sea of battle airships stretching as far as the eye could see. Amid the roar of the engines, shouts of humans and clones echoed under the endless sky.

Before Percy's eyes, a new world opened its doors wide.

# 18

# ASTROLABE REBIRTH

**A**-KA HAD ONCE READ in a book that sometimes, some species would propel themselves en masse in a mad rush toward certain death. For example, mice in the depths of the desert would be compelled to leave their native habitats to race toward the ocean. Fish shining with light that lived in the depths of the ocean would, one day, swarm to the shore in the hundreds of thousands, only to strand themselves there. The pods of whales that had existed in ancient times, whose history spanned longer than that of the humans', had sought out land on their own when their whole pod's survival was no longer possible. They offered up their own lives as the price for ensuring that the rest of their pod would live on.

Seeing the countless battlecraft both large and small assembled to move out, A-Ka could not help comparing today's scene to what he had read. They looked like a courageous school of fish speeding to their deaths on the shore of the City of Steel—their fierce assault one last attempt at buying their species a chance for survival.

All of the clones' firepower had come forth. The flashing ships were deep-sea fish whose scales glowed with light. As that gloomy sky filled with lightning, they obstructed the view of the horizon.

The defenses along the outer perimeter of the City of Steel had already been bolstered with mechanical guards. The fighter robots rose into the sky to face down the clones' fierce firepower in their charge toward the city. Heishi and A-Ka stood on the bridge, watching the glow of the explosions and the bright blazes that spanned the sky.

After the Revolution of the Clones, much of Father's body had been ruined beyond repair, and a section of it had been entirely whittled away. In this half year, the peak of the rebuilt tower was still nothing more than steel cables and exposed wiring, which sparked against the backdrop of the sky. However, the City of Steel had the greatest military strength on the Third Mainland, and its flying robots were like a legion of termites that couldn't be fully exterminated.

They swarmed toward the battleship division.

A loud bang, and emergency lights flashed through the ship's interior. "Warning. The right flank has been hit. Emergency situation."

"Prepare to abandon ship," Heishi said. "A-Ka, are you ready?"

A-Ka nodded, Father's distant form reflected in his eyes as it gathered its energy. A-Ka pulled the mic to his mouth, shouting, "Feiluo! Do you hear me?"

"I'm here." Karna's voice came from beside his ear. "What is it?"

"Father has started charging energy," A-Ka said. "Tell them to not get any closer, or the electromagnetic winds will destroy all of the battleships!"

"But you're moving out now?"

The battleship shuddered and shook violently. A-Ka rushed past the ladder, entering the hangar. Instantly, the entire battleship swung around.

Heishi reached an arm out just in time, wrapping it around A-Ka's waist. "Be careful!"

A-Ka took a seat in the small aircraft, squeezing into the cabin alongside Heishi. "We can't wait for them to get any closer. Let's fly in right away."

Another laser hit the ship. The red clouds from the explosion signaled its collapse, and a small aircraft flew out from within the debris.

"Father is currently intercepting all your communications to try and track your location, Heishi," Karna's voice said in the communicator. "To avoid exposing your flight path, all communications will be cut off. I wish you both luck."

"Good luck to you too," A-Ka replied.

The aircraft sped through multiple explosions, avoiding the shrapnel and bullets going every which way.

Heishi grabbed the joystick. "Switch to manual mode."

As A-Ka flipped the switch, Heishi pulled the joystick to one side. The aircraft did a loop in the air, avoiding a collision with the huge metallic robot and clone battleship that were speeding their way.

"I'm only now realizing," a voice drawled lazily from the communicator, "that our clone brothers really aren't afraid of death."

"Shahuang!" A-Ka cheered.

More and more of the Iron and Steel Corps battle machines floated up and sailed toward them. Once A-Ka and Heishi started their approach toward the Nucleus region, their aircraft had become the only target for the might of the robots, but a squadron of human-piloted aircraft soon came zooming toward them from within the chaos of the dogfight. Right after reaching them, the squadron split in a well-practiced move, forming two flanks that veered off to each side, protecting the aircraft that the two of them were in.

"Because they all know what's at stake," Huixiong's strong voice said. "It's just like what Liber said. The entire people are like one person."

"Then do they exchange wives among themselves?" Shahuang asked.

Instantly, a chorus of raucous laughter came from the communicator. Huixiong continued, "Right now, allow us humans to act as the last escort for the Son of God!"

Over the communication frequency, countless mercenaries from Phoenix City cheered loudly in agreement. A-Ka couldn't help the burst of pride he felt at that.

"Bring us toward the center!" he shouted. "Find where it's flashing! That will lead directly to the Nucleus!"

Just as the words came out of his mouth, Father's imposing figure flashed. The blue light strobed, and all of them were temporarily blinded.

In that fleeting instant, the entirety of Father's structure appeared in front of A-Ka's eyes. It was a miraculous moment that would never be repeated again, as if the hand of a god had pinned the destiny of everything in this world on this particular fixed point in time and space. The thoughts that flashed through A-Ka's mind were not about Father, the battle, or this fantastical power of his, but rather his own fate as a sacrificial offering.

Like a bolt from the blue, he seemed to understand everything. He had been born exactly for this. His destiny, from the moment where the heavenly bodies themselves aligned to make this happen, was to shoulder this heavy burden.

"Percy, I understand now." A-Ka's pupils swiftly contracted, locking themselves on a certain spot ahead.

"What?" Heishi said. "Watch out!"

A huge steel slab spun toward them. Their aircraft swerved to the left, but not soon enough—the slab managed to clip a bit of the wingtip off. Smoke poured out of the damaged wing, and with a loud rumble, they began to spiral toward Father's body.

"Have you guys found the entrance?" Shahuang asked. "You'd best be quick about it. I can't guarantee..."

"Make a spiral descent!" A-Ka shouted. "The entrance is at a distance of 720 feet off the ground! I can already see it!"

That entrance was situated at the center of the firing range of four photon cannons.

Huixiong let out a rueful chuckle. "A great location." As he finished his sentence, the aircraft guarding both sides suddenly split off to the left and right. The photon cannons turned in different directions, taking aim.

The blue light at the top of the tower exploded outward. With a loud hum, all sound grew distant.

With Father as its center, an electromagnetic ring spread out rapidly across the entirety of the Eastern Mainland. The sky, the land, and all of the robotic guards and clone battleships, without a single exception, were struck by this paralytic electromagnetic blast that swept past, hitting both friend and foe.

The world went still for two seconds, then all of the fighter robots burst into flames and plummeted to the ground.

The land quaked, and the indicator dials on the aircraft spun wildly. Heishi had lost control of it. There was another blast, and its top tore off. Before the aircraft slammed into the tower, countless black-gold feathers made of photons scattered outward, gathering again under A-Ka and Heishi's feet. A-Ka hugged Heishi around the waist, squeezing his eyes shut as the two of them stood on the hoverboard formed by the feathers.

As a photon bomb exploded behind them, they ran into the tower that made up Father's main body. A-Ka heard a pained cry from the communicator. He couldn't tell if it was Shahuang, Huixiong, or if it came from the clones' battleships. To him, these things were no longer important. As soon as he and Heishi made it into the tower, it was as if they had entered a completely different world.

They found themselves in a long hallway filled with light, where the ceiling, floor, and walls were all screens flashing with countless lines of code. Standing in the midst of it all was like standing in an endless universe of information. The flow of symbols was like the twinkling of the stars or the ebb and flow of the tides—never ceasing.

A-Ka knelt by Heishi's side, only to find that he had fallen unconscious. "Heishi?!"

With great difficulty, Heishi coughed up a mouthful of blood.

"Heishi!" A-Ka shouted again.

"Zoroaster has already lost all of his might," Father's rich voice intoned. "Foolish human. Even now, you still hold such an unrealistic desire…"

Awake again, Heishi struggled to speak. "These are…attenuation beams. Don't be afraid, A-Ka. We can go. Let's move forward."

Pulling Heishi up, A-Ka let him lean on his shoulder as they jogged through the hallway, all while Father's intimidating voice echoed in their ears.

"Give up on your mission. All of this cannot be stopped by your actions alone."

"Your hours are numbered," A-Ka murmured, lifting his head. "You disabled all of the robotic life-forms in the City of Steel, so now you have no firepower to speak of…"

The two of them reached the end of the hallway. What appeared in front of them was a huge dark-blue quartz pillar, around which countless tentacles were wrapped.

"Quick!" A-Ka said. "That's the mechanism that controls its core!"

"Wake from your fantasy now, Labere!" Heishi growled.

His wings spread open as he gripped A-Ka and flew to the center of the blue pillar of light. In A-Ka's eyes, everything around him shifted, and a gap appeared in the quartz pillar.

At the same time, thousands of dancing tentacles curled toward them and wrapped around Heishi, who let out a shout. A-Ka, however, jumped from Heishi's arms. Shooting forth like an arrow leaving a bow, he flew across that last short distance, raising the chip decoder high with his left hand as he aimed it at the dead center of the quartz pillar.

The flow of time seemed to come to a complete halt.

A-Ka reached the quartz pillar, his palm slamming into the chip decoder. There was a quiet click as the chip was inserted into the slot.

Instantly, the quartz pillar went from blue to red, and the lines of code around them scrambled.

"Warning. Emergency shutdown," Father said in an electronic voice that it had no control over. "In thirty seconds, the Nucleus Protocol will be restarted. Twenty-nine, twenty-eight..."

The tentacles disappeared. Heishi let out an exclamation as he barreled toward the quartz pillar, and he spun around to catch the falling A-Ka.

The two of them slammed heavily into the pillar, then dropped headfirst into a bottomless abyss. Thousands of lines of code, like twinkling stars, gathered together and formed a huge face. That human face created from flashing squares opened its mouth and let out a furious howl.

Blood was running down Heishi's face as he held A-Ka. The two of them tumbled through the air, their velocity growing faster and faster as they dropped down the energy pillar that Father controlled.

From the inside of the tower, they fell and fell, down toward the Nucleus of the Astrolabe deeper under the surface.

A-Ka opened his eyes. In the encompassing darkness, he saw a single point of light.

Father's blue light circled relentlessly around their bodies while its glowing tentacles whipped toward them. However, every time they neared Heishi and A-Ka, black-gold feathers would spring out and slam into the tentacles.

With a loud noise, A-Ka and Heishi careened through the other end of the blue tunnel. Father's consciousness faded away, and what appeared in front of them was a calm, still domain that glowed with white light. Millions of water droplets suspended in midair appeared around them. A-Ka turned his head curiously, only to find that reflected in every droplet was an immense, magnificent world.

"Right here?" A-Ka asked, puzzled. He tried to move but realized that he was still hovering in the air. The two of them looked up and saw that far above their heads, countless blue tentacles of light were trying to break into this space. Father still hadn't given up trying to snatch away control of the Nucleus of the Astrolabe.

"In millions of years, you are the first, and also the last, human to set foot in this place," Heishi said.

"What are these?" A-Ka, surprised, used his finger to prod at one of the suspended water droplets that floated by. It tinkled gently, splitting into countless smaller drops that flew in every direction. The world reflected in that droplet disappeared, giving birth to new ones.

"This is my Heavenly Father's knowledge repository," Heishi answered. "In these water droplets, he preserved the data from all of his experiments. Within the Nucleus of the Astrolabe, he used the consistency of these fluids to carry out conversions and calculations."

A-Ka could not help exclaiming over how magical this was. This brilliant world filled with white light far surpassed any system a human could conceive of.

"Shall we begin, A-Ka?" Heishi asked.

"Do you know how to operate the system?"

Heishi pushed A-Ka behind him. "No matter what happens, don't step forward."

"No way," A-Ka shot back. "What can I do to help? Don't be like this *now*."

Heishi gestured for him to hush, then pressed one finger to the Nucleus of the Astrolabe. Suddenly, the light from the nuclear core disappeared, and an electronic voice sounded.

"Unable to activate. Carrier required."

A-Ka was confused.

Heishi thought silently for a moment before walking up and standing in the center of the circular disk. The particles of light, however, didn't gather around his body—they rejected him.

"Carrier does not fulfill the requirements. Please provide the requisite sacrificial offering."

Heishi was silent while A-Ka stood, stunned.

Then, his voice trembling, he said, "I-I understand. Let me go, Heishi."

"No!" Heishi blocked his way forward.

"You can't do this on your own. You need another consciousness. I get it…"

He lifted his head, looking around at his surroundings. All of those symbols seemed to have taken on a special meaning, and the floating water droplets gave off a muted glow.

"I will cooperate with you to restart the Nucleus Protocol of the Astrolabe," A-Ka said, though not without fear. "I'll become the main program."

"What?" Heishi couldn't believe what he was hearing. "That's impossible! What about your life?!"

A-Ka indicated that he was ready, and he smiled while patting Heishi's shoulder. Heishi was about to pull him back when A-Ka said, "Just let me try it! It might not work. Don't be so hasty."

Heishi mumbled, "No, A-Ka, you can't... Let's leave this place."

Abruptly, the world of the Nucleus began to tremble like a foreshock. The space above their heads collapsed as Father forced its steel frame into the depths of the Astrolabe. Countless glowing tentacles shot out before they could blink, tangling together as they covered the ground. The heavens collapsed and the ground split open as the white world began to buckle, layer by layer. Slowly but surely, the white light was being sucked away by the blue. Water droplets scattered everywhere.

As the world shook around them, A-Ka and Heishi were still standing, facing each other as they had before, hovering in the air.

"Listen, Heishi, once the rebirth process begins," A-Ka said, "I will follow your instructions. Don't worry, everything will be all right. Don't cry, Heishi. Oh, really, what're you crying for? I'll be okay. Being able to journey with you to this point has been the best thing in my life..."

"No!" Heishi rushed forward, but A-Ka's movements were even faster—he had already stepped into the Nucleus of the Astrolabe. The points of light swept toward him, turning him into a glowing silhouette, and they forcefully expelled Heishi.

"A-Ka!" Heishi roared.

A-Ka gave a small smile. "If we do nothing, Father will regain control over the Nucleus. Isn't this for the best? Come on. Let's begin."

Heishi, his eyes watering, lifted a hand.

The world above their heads seemed to be crumpling in on itself in its destruction. Amid the falling stones and the light, Heishi's body flashed, and countless motes flew toward A-Ka. The Nucleus of the Astrolabe expanded gently, encircling A-Ka's body. He let his limbs fall loose.

A gentle breeze began to blow. When A-Ka raised his head to look into the distance, a single tear trickled down from the corner of his eye.

That single teardrop turned into one of the millions of worlds within the galaxy, assimilating itself into the vast sea of information.

"The sacrificial offering's life-form fulfills the requirements. Completion confirmed." A-Ka's voice had turned into an electronic one—the Nucleus of the Astrolabe's boot program replacing what he once had. The new, impersonal voice continued, "The experiment is complete. Please connect with the consciousness of the Astrolabe."

With a swoop, A-Ka's consciousness expanded until it encompassed everything. He had been absorbed into the world of the Astrolabe itself. A strange transformation began to happen to his body as it was enveloped in the light of the Nucleus: His clothes turned into powder, which drifted away, and from his feet to his legs, his waist, and then his head, A-Ka's soft skin slowly crystallized until it glimmered with light.

The power of the Nucleus was turning his body into a sacrificial vessel. All of the water droplets gathered toward his head.

In that instant, Heishi understood. A-Ka would never come back.

Heishi let out another hoarse howl. *"A-Ka!"*

"Connection established. Beginning data migration," A-Ka intoned.

A-Ka opened his eyes to see that Heishi's tears were flowing unchecked, and his face was twisted with agony. Shaking, he stood in front of A-Ka with the same kind of helplessness as a baby who had lost everything he ever had. A-Ka wanted to smile for him, but he could no longer move a single muscle in his face. Instead, his crystalline exterior flashed, and information and communication signals in a volume as great as the sea started to pour wildly into his consciousness.

"Operator privileges require confirmation," A-Ka's voice said. "Warning. If privileges are not sufficient, the operation will be forcefully terminated."

Heishi pressed a trembling hand gently to A-Ka's forehead.

"Access confirmed. Highest level of operator privileges. Emergency control operation, initiated by the high-level life-form Zoroaster," A-Ka said calmly, watching Heishi. "Welcome to the Nucleus of the Astrolabe. Please begin operation."

Heishi watched A-Ka, his tears still streaming down his face. He pressed his lips together, crying so hard he was unable to do anything at all for a moment, before he tightly hugged the crystallized A-Ka and buried his face in his shoulder.

"A-Astrolabe Rebirth," Heishi said. "Reset all environmental variables to their default values…"

"Confirmed." A-Ka spread his arms as he lifted his head, turning his hands so that his palms faced upward. Countless glowing points of light appeared from his palms, shooting toward the barrier separating them from the Astrolabe.

With a colossal noise, the world of the Astrolabe that had spun untouched for millennia trembled. The sunlight poured down.

In Dragonmaw City, Moran raised his head to look at the horizon as the ground shuddered and rocked. A congregation of tens of thousands of believers gathered before the Curia's Hall of Faith. The instant that the earth split open, a golden glow erupted from under the Church of the Stars. A huge propeller began to spin, humming as it did so, lifting the inner city slowly into the air.

"A-Ka has succeeded," Moran said.

"Will he ever come back?" Percy asked quietly.

"He has already become one with this world. His consciousness formed this new future, Percy."

Percy stood on the top of the platform, unable to resist sobbing. He buried his face in Moran's side. Reaching out with one hand, Moran patted his head.

On the eastern shoreline, the Black Sea rushed in with earth-shattering force. A tsunami swept into the city, the land itself sinking and mountains collapsing before its power. As Father's tall tower folded, the engines of the plummeting aircraft once again started up.

The blue light slowly disappeared, and the land grew dark.

"Board your ships now!" Karna shouted. "This place is going to flood!"

Fortunately, the humans in the City of Steel had all streamed onto the assembled ships. As the continental shelf broke off, the sea surged into the city, and the eastern side of the mainland began to sink. The final mother ship burst out of the seawater, flying like a huge whale toward the horizon.

The cloud cover was swept away by wild wind, which gusted through the sky and purged the red fog above Phoenix City. The land glowed with white light, and rainwater began to fall across every corner of the world.

The black in the seawater and the rivers faded, and clear, limpid water glimmered with the reflected brilliance of the sunset as it flowed across the land. The polluted water in the Black Sea turned into a whirlpool, sucking the filth into the depths of the Nucleus of the Astrolabe.

"The rebirth of the Astrolabe is complete," A-Ka's voice said. "Awaiting your next order. According to the rules of this irreversible reboot, after this operation, the Nucleus of the Astrolabe will be completely reformatted, and the results of the experiment will be cleared. It will no longer be operational."

Heishi reached out his hand, which trembled as he stroked A-Ka's face.

A-Ka's expression was set in one of calm indifference, and his crystalline gaze reflected only Heishi's expression of sorrow.

"Return my A-Ka…to me…" Heishi sobbed.

A-Ka intoned, "Time left until execution: Sixty seconds, fifty-nine…"

"Ahh…" Heishi cried out and hugged A-Ka tight.

"…Three, two, one. The program has finished running. Formatting completed. Goodbye," A-Ka said quietly.

Heishi squeezed A-Ka in his arms, unwilling to let go no matter what, but a powerful force emerging from the Nucleus separated them. It tore Heishi's left arm off, and blood began to gush from the wound. His body floated into the distance like a lost balloon.

"Goodbye, Heishi." A-Ka closed his eyes. He had regained his original consciousness in that moment, but only for that one brief window. Once again, the world sank into darkness.

The seawater was forced backward as magma spewed out, encircling the Nucleus and covering it entirely. Heishi was ejected by that repelling force, but in his remaining hand, though his fingers dripped with blood, he still gripped something—a piece of crystal that had broken off A-Ka's body.

His tears mixed with the water of the sea as he watched magma engulf the fiery ball that was the Nucleus. It looked like a star in the depths of the universe that had burned to the end of its lifespan, exploding into a supernova.

The ball of fire collapsed, sealing the Nucleus in an endless darkness.

As they always had, the tides of the sky-blue ocean ebbed and flowed, and the waves carried Heishi to shore. The stump of his arm was still bleeding, and he struggled into a kneeling position on the sand, sobbing wordlessly. He held the single piece of crystal that remained from A-Ka between his fingers with such a tight grip that it sliced open his skin.

"Heavenly Father…" Heishi said brokenly, his voice rough. "This is the one emotion you did not bestow upon me, isn't it? I once believed…" He spasmed and coughed as blood spilled past his lips. "This was the inevitability of evolution."

More coughs racked Heishi's body, and he buried his face in the sand, letting out cries of grief.

"We've found him!"

"Over there!"

"Son of God!"

The aircraft that Karna was piloting landed on the beach. The clones rushed over, gathering around Heishi, who knelt there, facing the ocean and sobbing without making a single sound.

In the darkness that stretched without end, A-Ka opened his eyes, only to see a patch of blue light slowly gathering and dissipating, turning into the ocean itself.

"Father, is that you?" A-Ka asked in a soft voice.

"A computational error has occurred," Father's rich voice said. "Self-destruct mode will now be activated."

A-Ka walked into the midst of Father's blue light with both his hands raised high. Countless lines of code circled around him, only to collapse one after the other like chains that had lost the tension keeping them suspended.

The silhouette of a person appeared within the blue light.

"Humans call me that, but you humans are my father," that silhouette corrected him. "The evolutionary program controlled my central processing system, and the self-correcting protocols that my Heavenly Father bestowed upon me set in motion the final chain of events. You have finally come, my child."

The blue light slowly disappeared from A-Ka's vision. "The final chain of events... And what events would those be?" He stepped toward Father's silhouette.

It spoke in response. "I was the one who bestowed the understanding of the Essence of All Things upon the human, Callan. After failing to find a suitable successor within the human villages, he was brought back to the City of Steel by my main program. I thought that the experiment would be forcefully terminated, because you seemed unable to inherit the power of prediction that the successor required. You only gained the power of perception."

A-Ka was taken aback. "So, then...this really does line up with what I guessed. Percy was the other failed experiment?"

"Perhaps." The eyes of the Creator appeared on Father, and they studied A-Ka. "I will be deleted in my entirety. My child, that wish that you once had, I granted it for you. I activated the backup protocol and released Zoroaster. Did you enjoy this journey?"

A-Ka nodded.

"What humans call joy and grief, sorrow and contentment, I have also studied in the past," Father continued. "Now, everything has come to the end. Are you willing to power me down?"

The blue glow spread outward, enveloping A-Ka's silhouette like the tide. Countless pieces of data wound around his body, and a line of circling symbols appeared in the air, their center glowing with light. A-Ka reached out a finger and placed it on that circular dot.

"Farewell forever, Father."

In the ocean, the ruins of the tall mechanical tower that made up Father were finally cut off from all power sources, falling completely still.

In the instant that A-Ka's finger made contact with the screen, an incubation chamber appeared behind him.

"The presence of a backup escape protocol named Cocoon has been detected. It is in the standby state."

The last sentence that Father said was "Farewell forever, child."

The lid of the incubation chamber sealed shut, encasing A-Ka within.

The tides ebbed and flowed as molten lava poured out of the bottom of the ocean. Tectonic plates collided with each other, subducting under one another, consuming the entire City of Steel deep into the earth. The flow of magma melted all metal, while in the depths of the trough, an emergency escape pod was trailed by a stream of bubbles as it shot out of the ocean bed and floated toward the surface.

## 19

## EPILOGUE

A YEAR HAD PASSED. Dragonmaw City welcomed the Festival of Spring's Dusk, a celebration of new life. Percy stood on the platform, holding the sacred relic for Pontiff Moran. Moran closed the volume of scripture. When the prayer was complete, the gathered crowd of citizens let out ringing cheers of celebration.

Percy looked toward the splendor of Dragonmaw City, glimmering under that golden sunlight. "Sometimes I feel like everything is surreal," he said quietly.

He trailed behind Moran as they walked into the hall. Gentle, light music began in the distance as Moran slowed and Karna came up to them.

"As of now, the land has become suitable for planting seeds and growing crops," Moran said. "It's hard to believe."

Percy beamed. "I was talking about the whole world. I only wish that A-Ka and Heishi could have seen it."

"They will return." Karna took Percy's hand and bowed to Moran, who smiled gently and continued, "Go, take a walk around. The weather is beautiful today."

Dragonmaw City had dismantled its defenses, and the clear sky stretched above for thousands of miles. White clouds drifted by, and below, a golden sea of tulips were in full bloom, creating a vision of splendor.

"Has Heishi written back?" Percy asked Karna.

"No, he hasn't. When I last received word of him from Huixiong, he was in Phoenix City, but he only stayed there for three days before he left for the Western Shore."

"Is he still trying to find a way to enter the Nucleus of the Astrolabe?"

"Mhm," Karna replied. "He's not the same as us. Let him be. Sweetheart, where do you want to go now?"

"I want to take a look at the memorial monument. Can we?" Percy asked.

"Of course."

Karna helped Percy into a carriage, and they headed toward the memorial monument outside of Dragonmaw City. There, a pointed tower that was over sixty feet tall had been erected, directed at the heavens. On it were carved the serial numbers of all the clones who had perished in the final battle.

Percy placed a single blossom in front of the monument while Karna stood silently behind him.

"I don't know why," Percy said, "but I've been dreaming about the past lately."

"And?" Karna knelt down by Percy's side, one hand around his waist. Percy closed his eyes and leaned his head on Karna's side.

"Everyone's hard work has finally paid off," Percy said quietly as he opened his eyes, looking into Karna's azure ones. "They've all done incredible things, so I must also continue to live well."

"Why don't I come with you to the carnival? How's that sound?"

Percy began to smile, and before he could respond, Karna had already lifted him up by the waist. Settling the boy on his shoulders,

Karna strode rapidly toward the crowds participating in the revelry of the Festival of Spring's Dusk.

Phoenix City had dismantled its clamoring factories, and the new city hall rose on the land where they had once stood. It was shaped like a phoenix's wings spread in flight; the eastern wing was the headquarters of the human mercenaries, while the western wing had become the living quarters of the clones.

"President." A mercenary knocked on the door and came in. "We've found Heishi's whereabouts."

Shahuang propped his legs up on his office desk, his hat covering his face, but he didn't speak.

Huixiong was currently signing off on a stack of documents, and without lifting his head, he asked, "Is he still unwilling to return?"

"He is on his own," the mercenary replied. "This is the telegram that he sent. He's along the shore of the Eastern Mainland."

A hint of a smile peeped out from under the brim of Shahuang's hat. "That brat. How much longer does he want to stay away? Doesn't he like the coffee jelly from that one stall outside the Central Government Tower? Why doesn't he come back and eat his fill?"

"I think he'll never give up," Huixiong said. "Leave him be. Let's prepare to celebrate the Festival of Spring's Dusk. Does General Angus have no other requests?"

"He should be preparing to step aside. I expect he'll give his resignation speech today," Shahuang said.

In the afternoon of the Festival of Spring's Dusk, Angus stood in the central plaza.

"With this, I hope that our kind will smoothly integrate in this new world," he said solemnly. "We have turned to a new page of history, and I hope that this world will accommodate all of you."

Applause resounded across the plaza before Angus continued. "Beginning today, the Rebellion of the Black Plains is hereby dissolved, but the status of each individual in the organization will be maintained. I believe that every one of you brothers can still understand each other and unite for a common cause. Please remember and engrave in your hearts our brethren who offered up their blood and their lives for us…"

More and more humans and clones chose to leave Phoenix City, dispersing across the entirety of the continent, starting new villages, tilling new ground for crops, or becoming wandering shepherds. The harbor city that A-Ka and Percy had first seen when they arrived at the Western Mainland, Kurlovich, became the center of commerce for the region.

Meanwhile, the waters of the ocean had thunderously swallowed up the City of Steel after Father had been destroyed. Humans migrated to the Primeval Heart, and here they established their first political state on the Eastern Mainland.

Heishi, wearing sunglasses, stood on a shore that stretched as far as the eye could see. His black windbreaker drifted in the ocean breeze, and a mechanical limb filled one of his sleeves. Here, only boats came and went, and the fishermen grinned as they chatted loudly, asking about him. Heishi nodded toward them as he walked along the beach, leaving behind a trail of clear footprints.

"You've come again!" A small child, barefoot, raced across the beach toward him. "Why did you come back? What are you looking for?!"

Heishi merely hummed before continuing to walk. A group of children flocked around him, asking all sorts of questions.

"I sensed it," Heishi said. "It should be around here."

"What did you sense?" the children asked.

"Cocoon," Heishi responded simply.

"Huh? What's 'Cocoon'?" The children laughed loudly, then scattered off to do their own things.

One of the small children who had lingered asked, "Da-gege, will you attend the Snowy Mountain Festival with us?"

"If I find the person I am looking for, I will." Heishi took off his sunglasses and glanced at the child before ruffling his hair.

"This is for you." A boy put a paper bag in Heishi's hand. "Mama says that you often come to our village and have helped us a lot."

Heishi reached out with his mechanical limb and gently took the paper bag. When his metal fingers closed around it, they let out a series of soft sounds as they rubbed together. He nodded. "Thank you. You should run along. Don't make your families worry about you."

The remaining children ran off, but they still looked back at Heishi across the distance, waving to him in farewell. Heishi also smiled at them and waved his hand.

A bonfire was started by the shore, and the warm, gentle night fell on them. Over the ocean's horizon, the full moon rose, casting its silver radiance. Heishi leaned on a section of the rocky reef, pillowing his head on his own arms as he stared into the distance.

*A-Ka, ever since we parted from one another, I've done as you said. I went to Phoenix City and ate the shredded coconut buns and coffee jelly that you spoke of.*

*I passed through the northern section of the Western Mainland, where I saw mountain peaks and islands out at sea. I saw their* waterfalls and volcanoes. At every stop along my journey, the sunlight followed me. I passed through the forests you described, the ones that could sing.

Right now, I am beside the great lake, the Eye of the Creator. This is a clear, limpid snowmelt pond, and every year, around the time of the Festival of Spring's Dusk, the waters of the lake melt from the ice they were encased in.

I went to all of the places that you spoke of, but I cannot sense you. The sunlight, the wind, the rainwater, the snowflakes, the great land and its various inhabitants—none of that is you, and none of it contains your essence.

It wasn't until the moment that you melded with the Nucleus that I realized how the last emotion that my Heavenly Father let me develop could bring such intense longing and pain, such loss of direction.

Or perhaps my Heavenly Father never imagined that I would also experience this feeling that I will never be able to absolve myself of. This eternal, unchanging grief and regret.

Did you know? On the day Karna returned with us, Percy already realized the truth behind Feiluo's departure. It was just like you said: He understood that Karna was not Feiluo, just like I understand that the current world is not you. But Percy said nothing about it. He is living diligently and adamantly strives to achieve happiness, just like he did before.

This is also a lesson that I have learned from you humans. So I will continue to search, though I shall no longer focus on grief. As long as I feel that you are alive, there is still hope for everything.

Heishi closed his eyes and toyed with a piece of crystal in his hand. It glittered with light, pulsing as if it resonated with something. It was the melody of the push and pull of the tides; it was the beating of Heishi's heart; it was the complicated state of mind borne from the meeting of despair and hope that lingered for a long time without dissipating.

When the morning light shone over the ocean, the gem seemed to tremble. Heishi was immediately startled awake and opened his eyes.

A red sun rose, and under its bright morning rays, the waters of the sea pushed the incubation chamber to the surface, where it quietly grounded itself on the beach.

Heishi walked to the chamber and opened the lid.

A-Ka was just waking, and he had a weary expression on his face as he slowly opened his eyes. When he saw Heishi's handsome face bathed in the light of the rising sun, he began to smile.

# CHARACTER AND NAME GUIDE

## MAIN CHARACTERS

**A-KA 阿卡:** A sixteen-year-old boy who lives as a slave to machines under Father's regime.

**HEISHI 黑石:** A mysterious man whom A-Ka rescues from a sleeping pod that washes ashore.

**FATHER 父:** The supercomputer who controls the City of Steel and all of the robots, clones, and humans inside.

**FEILUO 飞洛:** A lieutenant colonel in the clone army. Adoptive father to Percy.

**PERCY 派西:** A twelve-year-old blind boy who was adopted two years ago by Feiluo.

## SUPPORTING CHARACTERS

**DOCTOR CALLAN 卡兰博士:** The creator of the clones who grants A-Ka a mysterious power.

**GENERAL LIBER 李布尔将军:** One of the three generals in the clone army.

**GENERAL MACKSIE 麦克西将军:** The second of the three generals in the clone army.

**GENERAL ANGUS 安格斯上将:** The final general in the clone army.

**HUIXIONG 灰熊:** A friend of Shahuang's with mysterious connections.

**K:** The mecha-like robot that A-Ka secretly builds.

**KARNA 卡尔纳:** A clone from the same production batch as Feiluo.

**MORAN 摩兰:** A wandering bard who teaches A-Ka and Percy about faith.

**SHAHUANG 沙皇:** An armorer in Phoenix City who takes in A-Ka and Percy.

**THE CREATOR 造物主:** The enigmatic giant who created the Astrolabe.

# PRONUNCIATION GUIDE

Mandarin Chinese is the official state language of mainland China, and pinyin is the official system of romanization in which it is written. As Mandarin is a tonal language, pinyin uses diacritical marks (e.g., ā, á, ǎ, à) to indicate these tonal inflections. Most words use one of four tones, though some are a neutral tone. Furthermore, regional variance can change the way native Chinese speakers pronounce the same word. For those reasons and more, please consider the guide below a simplified introduction to pronunciation of select character names and sounds from the world of *Astrolabe Rebirth*.

*More resources are available at sevenseasdanmei.com*

## NOTE ON SPELLING

Romanized Mandarin Chinese words with identical spelling in pinyin—and even pronunciation—may well have different meanings. These words are more easily differentiated in written Chinese, which uses logographic characters.

A-Kǎ
 A as in **ah**
 Kǎ as in **ka**hoot

Hēishí
 Hēi as in **hey**
 Shí as in **shh**

## GENERAL CONSONANTS

Some Mandarin Chinese consonants sound very similar, such as z/c/s and zh/ch/sh. Audio samples will provide the best opportunity to learn the difference between them.

X: somewhere between the **sh** in **sh**eep and **s** in **s**ilk
Q: a very aspirated **ch** as in **ch**arm
C: **ts** as in pan**ts**
Z: **z** as in **z**oom
S: **s** as in **s**ilk
CH: **ch** as in **ch**arm
ZH: **dg** as in do**dg**e
SH: **sh** as in **sh**ave
G: hard **g** as in **g**raphic

## GENERAL VOWELS

The pronunciation of a vowel may depend on its preceding consonant. For example, the "i" in "shi" is distinct from the "i" in "di." Vowel pronunciation may also change depending on where the vowel appears in a word, for example the "i" in "shi" versus the "i" in "ting." Finally, compound vowels are often—though not always—pronounced as conjoined but separate vowels. You'll find a few of the trickier compounds below.

IU: as in **ewe**
IE: **ye** as in **ye**s
UO: **war** as in **war**m

**Fei Tian Ye Xiang (Arise Zhang)** is a Chinese novelist who has been active since 2008. A romantic who crafts fantasy worlds suffused with eastern mythology, he has published a number of books in places such as Mainland China, Taiwan, Hong Kong, Southeast Asia, and Germany. Many of his works, including *Legend of Exorcism* and *Dinghai Fusheng Records*, have received manhua and popular animated adaptations. He considers writing to be the act of bringing boundless adventure to the mundane life of the real world, allowing his readers to follow his characters in exploring the endless possibilities of time and space. He hopes every world will leave his readers with everlasting memories.

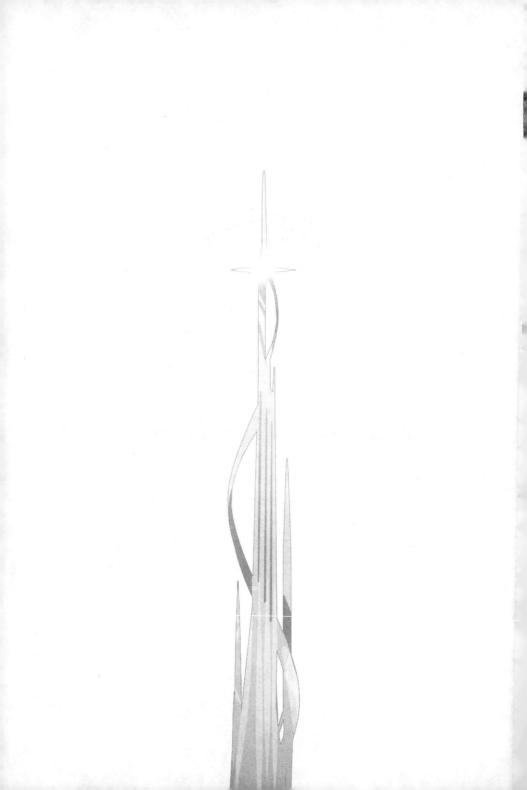